Chosen by the Greek Tycoon

Men who have everything – except brides...

Three glittering, passionate romances from
three favourite Mills & Boon authors!

In October 2009 Mills & Boon bring
you two classic collections, each
featuring three favourite romances
by our bestselling authors

CHOSEN BY THE
GREEK TYCOON

The Antonakos Marriage by Kate Walker
At the Greek Tycoon's Bidding
by Cathy Williams
The Greek's Bridal Purchase
by Susan Stephens

THE PRINCE BROTHERS:
SATISFACTION GUARANTEED!

by Carole Mortimer
Prince's Passion
Prince's Pleasure
Prince's Love-Child

Chosen by the Greek Tycoon

KATE WALKER
CATHY WILLIAMS
SUSAN STEPHENS

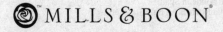

MILLS & BOON

First published in Great Britain 2009
Harlequin Mills & Boon Limited,
Eton House, 18-24 Paradise Road, Richmond, Surrey TW9 1SR

CHOSEN BY THE GREEK TYCOON
© by Harlequin Enterprises II B.V./S.à.r.l 2009

The Antonakos Marriage, At the Greek Tycoon's Bidding and *The Greek's Bridal Purchase* were first published in Great Britain by Harlequin Mills & Boon Limited in separate, single volumes.

The Antonakos Marriage © Kate Walker 2005
At the Greek Tycoon's Bidding © Cathy Williams 2006
The Greek's Bridal Purchase © Susan Stephens 2006

ISBN: 978 0 263 87140 1

05-1009

Printed and bound in Spain
by Litografia Rosés S.A., Barcelona

THE ANTONAKOS
MARRIAGE

BY
KATE WALKER

Kate Walker was born in Nottinghamshire, but as she grew up in Yorkshire she has always felt that her roots are there. She met her husband at university, and originally worked as a children's librarian, but after the birth of her son she returned to her old childhood love of writing. When she's not working, she divides her time between her family, their three cats, and her interests of embroidery, antiques, film and theatre, and, of course, reading.

You can visit Kate at www.kate-walker.com

CHAPTER ONE

THEO ANTONAKOS was not in the least impressed to learn that he was about to get a new stepmother.

He had never come to terms with his father's reputation with women. He'd lost count of the number of lovers who had drifted through the older man's life since his own mother's death and become, for a time, surrogate *materas* to him while he was growing up. Not one of them had stayed, though three of them had become Cyril's wife for a while, usually a very brief time.

Now it seemed that the fifth Mrs Antonakos was about to make her appearance. Quite frankly, Theo didn't hold out much expectation that she would last any longer than any of her predecessors, but she was indirectly responsible for the restlessness and the unsettled mood that were eating at him tonight.

He reached for his glass of wine and drained the rich red liquid from the bottom of it, slamming the glass back down on the table top with a crash that revealed the turmoil of his inner feelings.

He usually loved London's bustling vibrancy, the sense of people going places, living busy lives. The crowded streets, the lights, the hum of cars, reminded him of his home in Athens, the city life he had there, the cut and thrust of the business world that made every day a challenge he enjoyed.

But when it was dark and damp and *cold* as it was now on this October evening, then he wished he were anywhere but here. He missed the heat of the Greek sun on his back, the lazy lap of the ocean against the rocks of the island his family owned. He missed the sound of his native language. He missed his family. Hell, he missed *home*.

It had started with the letter that had arrived that morning.

One look at the stamp with the familiar Greek script had jarred him awake with a speed and roughness that had made his head spin. He hadn't even needed to check the postmark, or the rough, almost illegible scrawl of the address. He had known immediately just who it was from.

His father had broken his long silence and had written at last.

'Oh, come on, Red, lighten up. Sit down and have a drink with us!'

The rough-edged, slightly slurred comment followed by a chorus of laughter drifted over to him from across the other side of the bar, making him glance in that direction. A couple of youths were lounging around a table, beer bottles littering the polished surface.

But it was the woman with them who caught his attention. Caught and held it.

He couldn't see her face because she had her back to him. But what he could see was stunning. Physically, sexually stunning in a way that made desire twist, sharp and hot, in his gut in immediate reaction.

Long hair in a glorious, burnished red gold cascaded down the slender length of her back, gleaming with coppery highlights even under the shaded lamps of the bar. She was tall and shapely: narrow shoulders, neat hips, a pert, tight bottom under the clinging skirt of her black dress.

Skirt? His faint laugh denied the description. That wasn't a skirt, it was a pelmet—little more than an extended belt, leaving exposed the slim, elegant length of her legs in sheerest black nylon, right down to the point where her feet were pushed into the polished, ridiculously high-heeled shoes.

'Anything you like, sweetheart...'

There was something about her that compelled him to watch her.

And he had been without a woman too long. That was the real reason he was interested. Ever since Eva had walked out three months ago, there had been no female company in his life.

He could have had plenty—he knew without false modesty that his dark looks attracted female attention and interest. Add to that the appeal of the wealth that came from both his family background and the results of his own efforts, and he rarely had to spend a night alone unless he wanted to.

But lately that knowledge hadn't satisfied him. He was edgy, wanted more.

Not with Eva, though. That was why they'd argued and why she'd walked. Eva had thought that she was onto a good thing. She had had wedding bells and gold rings in her dreams, and he had had to disillusion her about that pretty forcefully. As a result, she'd left. Eva wasn't the kind of girl to stay around when she knew she wasn't going to get what she wanted.

And if he was honest with himself, he really hadn't missed her.

'No, really, no thanks.'

Her voice fell into one of those sudden lapses into silence in which even the quietest voice sounded clear and audible in the stillness of the room.

And what a voice! It was low and sensual, surprisingly husky for a woman. It made him imagine hearing that voice whispering to him in the deep, warm darkness of a king-size bed. His mouth dried, his body tightened just to think of it. But the next moment, the sexy mood vanished, the erotic thoughts driven away by a dramatic change in her tone.

'I said *no, thank you.*'

Theo was on his feet before he was even aware of having reacted. There had been an edge to her words, a note of unease, of total rejection of the position in which she found herself. She wasn't happy, it was obvious.

Half a dozen long, forceful strides took him across the room to come up close behind her. Neither she nor the men she was talking to had even noticed him.

Skye Marston knew that she was in trouble.

In fact, she had known it from three heartbeats into the conversation she had foolishly started with these two. She should never have stopped, never responded to their casually friendly greeting on her way into the room.

Their *apparently* casually friendly greeting.

She had come into the bar on a whim. It had looked crowded, brightly lit and warm, in contrast to the cold wind and driving rain of the street outside. And she had wanted desperately to be with people. She had spent too much time on her own, and being on her own left her vulnerable to her unhappy thoughts.

Was it really less than a month since her father had broken down and admitted that his money problems were far worse than he had let on? That in an attempt to deal with them, he had made a real mess of things by 'borrowing' from his boss, Greek millionaire Cyril Antonakos, the owner of the hotels he managed—and, even worse, he had now been found out. He faced a lengthy prison sentence if charges were pressed.

'I can't go to jail, Skye!' he had wept. 'Not now, not with your mother so ill! It would kill her. She just can't manage without me. You have to help me!'

'I'll do anything I can, Dad.' Skye had reacted instinctively, knowing there was nothing else she could say.

Her mother's heart condition had been a cause of great

concern for some time, but lately her condition had deteriorated. Now it seemed that if the next operation she had didn't succeed, her only hope was a transplant. 'Anything at all—though I don't know what help I can be!'

But her father had known. Cyril Antonakos had already proposed a way out of the terrible trap in which Andrew Marston found himself. And Skye had listened in horror as he had revealed just how vital she was to their scheme. Cyril wanted an heir. To achieve that end, obviously he needed a wife and, as his last marriage had ended in an acrimonious divorce, he had selected Skye as the potential mother of his child. If she married him, gave him the heir he craved, he wouldn't prosecute.

In order to save Andrew Marston from imprisonment, she was being asked to marry a man older than her father.

And tomorrow she had to give him her answer.

That was why she was here tonight. That was why she was out on her own, spending her one last night of freedom in the impersonal bright lights and busy streets of London. She could only pray that those bright lights—and the crowded bars—were enough to distract her from what tomorrow would bring.

Not giving herself time to reconsider, she had swung into the wide doorway, struggling with the big glass doors, pushing her way through the crowd, trying to reach the bar.

And immediately she had felt that she had made a mistake.

The bar was warm and bright, true. It was also very busy. And everyone there seemed to know someone else. No one was on their own, without anyone else to talk to, to smile at.

And even if they had been alone, she told herself, no one else could ever be quite so lonely, quite so isolated as she felt right now.

She had been about to turn round and go back out when

she had spotted the one other person who, like her, was on his own.

Should she—*could* she—make herself go up and talk to him? That had been her plan from the start. To meet someone and talk to them, so, hopefully, driving away this appalling sense of isolation and loss, melting the cruel block of ice that seemed to surround her world, and giving her some moments of freedom and relaxation before the world closed in on her again.

But this man didn't look the type who could fulfil that hope for her. He was too big, too dark, too dangerous-looking. His long body lounged in the chair, apparently at ease, but there was an air of menace, of carefully leashed power, about him that made her heart kick inside her chest, so that she caught her breath in shock. His black-haired head was turned away from her, and hooded eyes stared down into a glass half-filled with red wine.

It was almost as if she had come across a sleek, honed hunting cat crouching in wait in some small, shaded jungle clearing. Just seeing him slowed her steps to a halt, making her hesitate and rethink.

And that was when the call from the nearest table had distracted her.

'Hello, darling. Looking for someone?'

If she hadn't been so diverted by the appearance of the dark-haired man in the corner, so desperate for company and distraction, Skye would have simply switched on an automatic smile, murmured something about having 'just spotted them, thank you,' and moved on. But her steps had already slowed, she had stopped beside the table, and somehow she couldn't find the words to extricate herself.

And they clearly thought that she was with them for the evening—and more. Their smiles, the hot, lascivious way their eyes travelled over her, made her feel uneasy. She might have been looking for a last chance to spend her time as a free, single twenty-two-year-old, but this was not what she'd had in mind.

She tried to turn down the offers of a drink with what she hoped was an apologetic smile, an expression of regret, but she could see that they weren't appeased. The blond was growing noticeably aggressive, and when she tried to step back and move away she found that his black-haired friend had grabbed her arm and was gripping it in a bruisingly tight hold.

'So what's wrong—aren't we good enough for you?'

'No—really—I—I'm waiting for someone.'

'Like who?' Frank disbelief sounded roughly in his voice.

'My—my boyfriend. He said—he'd meet me here.'

The blond made an elaborate play of looking around the room, searching for the imaginary boyfriend.

'Then I think you've been stood up, Red. He's clearly not coming for you.'

The grip on her arm tightened cruelly, pulling her closer so that she had to bend slightly to adjust to the tug on her wrist.

'He—he's just late.'

'Do you know what I think, Red?'

It was a mocking whisper, a malicious gleam lighting in his eyes.

'I think he's not coming. In fact, I have this suspicion that you're telling me lies—that this lover of yours just doesn't exist.'

'Oh, but he does.'

Skye jumped like a startled cat as the words came from behind her. The deep, gorgeously accented, sexy *male* voice was the last thing she had ever anticipated. It was the fantasy she might have wished for—the dream lover turning up to rescue her from the awkward, uncomfortable situation in which she found herself.

But this was no fantasy. The startled gaze of her tormentors had gone from her face to somewhere behind the back of her head, shock and consternation showing in their eyes. The controlling grip on her wrist had loosened, letting her pull free.

'Oh!'

The soft cry of shock was pushed from her as a pair of tightly muscled arms slid round her waist from behind. A hard, powerful frame was pressed up against her back, its heat and strength reaching right through the material of her jacket, to her skin, her bones—seeming to scorch her soul.

She felt safe, protected, *surrounded* by this unknown man. His warmth and strength enclosed her, the sound of his breathing tantalised her ears, and the scent of his skin filled her nostrils.

'Sorry I'm late, darling,' the husky voice murmured against her neck. 'You know how these meetings drag on. But I'm here now.'

'Mmm.'

It was all she could manage and she didn't care if it sounded more like a sigh of sensual response than any coherent answer.

Her body was tingling all over, burning in instant response to just this unknown man's touch. She couldn't see his face—the only parts of his body that were visible to her were the hands that were clasped around her waist.

And they were intensely *masculine* hands. Big and square and capable-looking. They dwarfed her own smaller, slimmer fingers as they closed warmly over them. No rings. The only adornment was a sleek platinum watch on one wrist, just above an immaculate white shirt cuff, the steel-grey of an elegant and expensive jacket.

'Forgive me?'

'Oh, yes!'

How could she say anything else? She would have

agreed to anything, accepted anything from him. It was impossible to think straight, and what tiny fragments of thoughts still lingered inside her head were totally shattered, blasted into oblivion by what he did next.

She sensed movement behind her, just out of sight. Felt the brush of silky hair against her cheek, then suddenly there was the press of warm lips against the back of her neck. Her breath caught in her throat; her heart thudded hard against her ribcage, and her head went back against a strong, supportive shoulder, her eyes half closing in sensual response.

'Hey!'

The stranger's voice was soft, faintly reproving, edged with a disturbing laughter.

'Not here, darling,' he went on wickedly. 'Better wait until we get home!'

Home! She wasn't going home with this man...

That brought her back to the present in the blink of an eyelid, her head coming up again sharply, her mouth opening on a gasp of protest. But the protest never had a chance to form because the man behind her spoke again before she had a chance to say a word.

'Time to go, sweetheart. Say goodbye to your friends.'

It was the way he said *friends* that alerted her. She had been in danger of giving away their pretence. If she had voiced her protest, she would have made it clear to the men at the table that her rescuer was not the lover she had claimed him as.

'Goodbye, guys! Th-thanks for keeping me company.'

Just who was this man who had come to her rescue so unexpectedly? The question raged in her mind as she made herself turn, ready to walk off with him, struggling to look as if this were something she did every day.

He slid his hand into hers, lacing his strong fingers with hers, holding her in a way that felt light and gentle, but which she was sure would be even harder to break away from than the dark-haired man's hold had been.

'Come on, let's get out of here.'

He was tall, and strongly built, that much she could tell from the swift, sidelong glances she slanted in his direction, not daring to actually turn and stare. In the shadowy light of the bar, his face was turned from her, eyes fixed on the doorway towards which his determined strides were taking them. She could only let herself be pulled along in his wake, wanting to be well away from her earlier tormentors before she did what she knew she was going to have to do and put the brakes on sharply, saying, 'This far and no further.'

'Hang on a minute…' she tried, but he either didn't hear or pretended not to. His ruthless path through the bar didn't falter, and where she had struggled through the crowds on her way in, now they just seemed to part smoothly to let him through.

The next moment they were at the door and moving down the steps into the street.

'Now hang on!'

She dug her heels in as she spoke, mentally slamming on the brakes and praying that his strength and power wouldn't just drag her over, tumbling ignominiously down the stone stairs after him.

'That's far enough!'

This time her voice reached him. Either that, or the pull on his hand was enough to drag him to a halt. He stopped abruptly, then whirled round, coming to face her, and she saw his features for the first time in the full glow of the light of the street lamps.

She'd seen them before. Seen that strong-boned, forcefully arrogant face. The jet-black, deep-set eyes above slashing cheekbones, the long, straight sweep of a nose, and the fall of rich, thick hair, darker than the night's shadows around him.

'You!'

The word escaped on a cry of shock as she recognised the man she had seen at the other side of the bar. The only other person who had been on his own in the busy, noisy room.

The man she had not dared to risk approaching because some intuitive sense of fear had held her back. Her instincts had sprung straight to red alert, flashing warning signs before her eyes and shrieking, 'Danger—keep away! Don't touch!' even before she had had a chance to think why. She just knew that something deep and primitive inside her had made her feel that he was someone to be treated with the intense caution with which she might approach a prowling jungle cat if she came face to face with it out hunting.

And seen up close he looked even more so. More dangerous; more devastating. More blatantly masculine. More shockingly attractive—and yet even his undeniable sexual appeal had a worrying core of threat at the bottom of it.

This wasn't the sort of man she usually encountered. He was nothing like the men she had known at home and in the office, the few, friendly dates she had ever been out on. He was beyond her experience, beyond her knowledge—and very definitely beyond her control.

Those instincts were working overtime again—and this time they were yelling at her that she was completely out of her depth with this man.

And if she wasn't very much mistaken, she had just jumped right out of the frying-pan and straight into the very heart of the fire.

CHAPTER TWO

'ME?'

THEO's response to Skye's shocked exclamation was as calm and relaxed as he could make it, though any real control was the last thing he felt capable of.

He should never have touched her.

His body still burned at the thought of it; his brain had almost melted in the burn of the fierce, erotic heat that had flooded every inch of his body, making him hard and hungry in a second. He still ached from the sudden ebbing of the blazing tide, the effect of the cold night air that had hit him as soon as they had left the bar.

He should never have touched her, but what he hadn't anticipated was the way that she had responded to him.

He'd thought she felt it too.

If she hadn't, then what the hell had she meant by the way she'd reacted—resting her head against his shoulder, leaning back into him?

But now she was behaving as if she thought he was a demon from hell and not at all the person she'd been hoping for

'You were expecting someone else?'

'N-no—not exactly,' she stammered. 'I—it's just—I never thought that you'd be the one to come to my rescue. I should thank you,' she added, too belatedly to smooth his very ruffled feelings.

'Think nothing of it.'

A wave of his hand dismissed her stumbling thanks. Theo was well aware of the way that the frustrated demands of his aroused body were distorting his mood, making him feel bad-tempered and edgy. And what made a bad mood infinitely worse was the way that, seeing her face full on now, in the light from the doorway, he found that the promise suggested by her back, her profile, indoors, was more than fulfilled by the reality.

She was *gorgeous*. A pale, oval face. Stunning light coloured eyes, with incredibly thick, lush lashes. A full, soft mouth seemed just made for kisses, and the thoughts that imagining that mouth on his own skin triggered off were so X-rated that he was glad of the shadows in the street, the darkness of the evening, that hid his response from her.

'And I should introduce myself.'

Her hand came out, stiffly formal.

'I'm—Skye...'

The hesitation before her name and the way that she didn't add a surname told him she didn't want to trust him with the full details of her identity. Fair enough, that was fine with him.

'Anton,' he growled, knowing he was forced to take her hand, but making the contact as brief and brusque as possible before letting it drop.

He didn't want a repeat of the cruelly demanding sensations he'd experienced before, especially when it seemed that this Skye was determined to be on her way as soon as possible and there was no chance of taking things any further.

'Anton.'

The way that she echoed the name he had given her made him wonder if she really knew, or suspected, it was not genuine.

He didn't give a damn one way or another. Even here, in England, the Antonakos name—and, more importantly, the Antonakos fortune—was so well known that the realisation he was a member of that family was enough to

create an interest where there wasn't one, to put a specu-
lative light in the eye of anyone he met.

And, in his experience, women were the worst offenders.
Along with the name Antonakos, they saw the prospect of
a meal ticket for life; a future of luxury and ease, if they
could just play their cards right.

As he was not at all sure what sort of cards this Skye,
whoever she was, was about to play; he preferred to keep
his own—and the truth of his identity—very close to his
chest.

Not that she seemed in the least interested right now.
Those pale eyes were scanning the street, looking up and
down the road.

'Are you looking for someone?'

Suspicion made him voice it. Damn it, had he got this
all wrong from the start? He cursed under his breath at the
way that thought made him feel. He didn't want her to have
been really waiting for anyone. He had assumed that the
lover she had claimed was imaginary—had *wanted* him not
to exist.

The truth was that he wanted this woman for himself,
and right now he was prepared to do whatever it took to
get her.

'Was that boyfriend you mentioned real after all?'

'Oh, no.'

The shake of her head sent the red-gold fall of her hair
flying around her face, tiny drops of rain shimmering in its
depths from the drizzle that was falling.

'No, I made him up in the hope they would let me go.
I wasn't looking for anyone—just a taxi.'

'I can give you a lift anywhere you want to go.'

'A taxi will be fine.' It was the vocal equivalent of several steps backwards and away from him. No physical action could have put more of a distance between them.

A black cab was approaching and she lifted a hand to

hail it, but too late. It swept past in a spray of water from the puddles filling the gutter, spattering her skirt and legs with mud.

'I can give you a lift anywhere you want to go.'

The way he repeated his exact words of just moments before brought Skye's eyes to his face in a rush. Meeting the glittering darkness of his gaze, seeing the way that the muscles of his jaw were drawn tight, she knew a sinking sense of realisation.

She'd insulted him with her refusal. He was angry too, something that told her how much her rejection had meant to him.

'I—was trying to be sensible,' she managed.

'Isn't it a little late for that now?'

'What do you mean by that?'

'Well, the situation you got yourself into back there—' His dark head nodded towards the noisy, smoky bar. 'That was hardly the action of a *sensible* person.'

The deliberate emphasis on the repeated word goaded her, as she was sure it was meant to do, sparking her temper and bringing her chin up, eyes flashing angry fire.

'I didn't exactly *ask* for that!' she snapped. 'It just happened!'

'I only offered you a lift in my car.'

The resignation in his tone had a hard edge to it, one that warned her of the way his temper was fraying at the edges.

'I'm sor—' she began, but he ignored her and rushed on angrily.

'I was brought up never to let a woman risk being on her own, if I could do anything to help her.'

'Then get me a taxi—please.'

She prayed he wouldn't argue further. She was rapidly losing her grip on her self-control as it was.

'No.'

It was cold and hard and unyielding, and it chilled her blood just to hear it.

Out of the frying-pan and into the fire. The ominous phrase that had slipped into her head in the first moments they had been outside now pounded round and round inside her skull until she felt as if her mind would explode.

'You don't need a taxi. I will take you wherever you want to go.'

Skye's eyes closed on a shudder of horror as she tried to imagine just how that scenario would play out. She didn't even want to think of her father's reaction if she was to arrive home in a strange car—with an unknown man. Even less did she want to imagine the way her prospective fiancé would view that situation.

Oh, why had she ever thought she could do this? Why had she let herself believe that she could fling herself into one night of liberty just to try and put a temporary barrier between herself and the future that lay ahead of her?

Why had she ever imagined that she could have one night in which she lived the same sort of life as her friends, as other young women her age? One night of total freedom, of irresponsibility, of reckless abandon before the walls of restraint and restriction closed round her once and for all?

She had never been able to live that way even when she had had her freedom—the freedom of youth. So why had she ever thought she could do it now, just for tonight? She had been out of her depth from the start—and she was sinking in deeper with every second that passed.

'I'll get one myself, then.'

She swung away from him violently, knowing in her heart that she was really running from herself, not from him. But she was closer to the edge of the pavement than she thought. Her heel caught on the kerb, twisted awkwardly and went from beneath her. She would have gone flying off the footpath, falling headlong onto the wet tarmac, into the middle of the road and the path of the on-coming cars, if the man beside her hadn't reacted with in-stinctive speed.

'Skye—look out!'

In the blink of an eye he was beside her, reaching out and catching her before her stumble became a fall. She was held tight, hauled up into arms that felt like tempered steel as they tensed, took her weight and then pulled her back to safety.

Safety? Or right back into the heart of danger?

Skye had no way of knowing and her head was whirling too much in the aftermath of the shock of her near fall to be able to think clearly.

The position she was in didn't help either. Anton had spun her round as he caught her up so that now she was clamped tight against him, enfolded in his arms, with her body crushed against the hard length of his, her head on his chest, her cheek above the heavy, heated thud of his heart, the sound of his pulse in her ears.

And it was all happening again.

Just as it had when he had come up behind her in the bar, so now her blood was heating in urgent response to his closeness, her heart racing in time with the fierce beat of his. She was surrounded by him, held in the heat and hardness of his grip, the clean, male scent of his body sur-rounding her, melting her thoughts inside her head.

It felt like coming home.

It felt as if she had always been there. As if this was truly where she belonged. Where she most wanted to be in all the world. And with the instinctive cuddling movement of a small creature seeking comfort from the cold, hard world outside, she snuggled closer, burying her face in his shirt front, her hands sliding under his jacket, her arms going round the narrow waist.

She felt his grip tighten even more, and his dark head

bent, his face coming so close to hers that the faint roughness of the beginnings of evening growth of beard rubbed
lightly against the delicate skin of her cheek. She sensed—
unbelievingly—the warm caress of his mouth on her neck,
at the base of her ear, and heard his deep sigh as he whispered harshly against the delicate lobe.

'Skye, don't go—stay! I want you to stay.'

'What?'

Had he really said what she thought she had heard? She
couldn't believe it. It couldn't be true. It had to be her ears
deceiving her or the voice of her own hungry longings
sounding inside her head, telling her what she most wanted
to hear.

But she couldn't have heard it. Men like this Anton
didn't suddenly beg girls like her to stay with them, not on
such brief acquaintance.

Had he really said…?

Tilting her head, she tried to look up into his face, to
read the answer there, but even as she moved his dark head
came down towards hers. His mouth closed over hers and
captured it in a searing, blazing kiss that sent a sensation
like a lightning bolt fizzing through her body, right down
to the tips of her toes.

This couldn't be happening, was the one brief thought
that Skye managed before her brain short-circuited and
thinking became impossible. Before it was replaced only
by feeling.

His mouth was pure enticement, pure sinful seduction.
His kiss worked a spell on her that had her melting against
him, into him, losing herself in the feeling of becoming
part of him. Her lips parted, encouraging the heated invasion of his tongue, her sighing moan a sound of pure surrender, all that was female in her responding to the darkly
elemental male in him. Something rich and dark and deeply

sensual uncoiled way down low in her body and set up a heavy, honeyed pounding between her thighs.

The sounds and the lights of the street became nothing but a blur in the back of her mind as the strength of his hold lifted her up onto her toes, almost off her feet. Powerful hands thrust into the fall of hair, sweeping it back from around her face as hard fingers dug into her skull. The rain came down harder, colder, but she was lost and oblivious to it, adrift in a heated world where nothing else could reach her.

In the distance someone wolf-whistled, and slowly, reluctantly, they drew apart, breath coming heavily, eyes wide, expressions slightly dazed as they met each other's gaze and acknowledged the primitive fires they had lit between them.

'I...' Skye began, but her voice broke in the middle, failing her completely as the reality of what had happened to her hit home like a savage blow to her head.

This was what it was all about. This was what male-female relationships really meant. What those words like *desire* and *passion* and *hunger* had had hidden behind them, unrecognised by her until now.

Now.

The single word sounded like a knell inside her head, deadening her thoughts and bringing the cruel sting of tears to her eyes.

Now, when it was too late. When a malevolent fate had stepped in and decided her future for her.

When she knew that these delights, this sort of happiness, were to be denied to her for ever. She had learned the truth too late, only to have it snatched away from her in the same moment that she discovered it. And with no chance of anything more.

Except for tonight, a tiny voice whispered in her mind, bringing with it dreams and hopes of the sort that she had never allowed into her thoughts before. Dreams that made her shiver just to contemplate them.

Dreams that were here, now, within her reach, and all she had to do was to stretch out a hand and grasp them, make them hers, for tonight; for one night only.

'Skye?' the man called Anton questioned softly, making her realise how long she had been standing there, silent, distant, locked in the shadowed, ominous darkness of her thoughts.

The heat of his body still enclosed her, His hold had loosened, but she still pressed up against the powerful length of his body, feeling the hard ridge against her stomach that spoke of the desire that had been in his kiss. The same desire that had been in hers. That still throbbed along every nerve pathway, pulsed in her blood.

He had wanted her every bit as she had wanted him— he still did.

But she had only met him tonight.

'I won't hurt you.' His voice was low and husky with need. So low and husky that it shocked her to think that she could ever have such an effect on any man—least of all *this* man. This tall, darkly imposing, devastating man.

'I promise you, you'll be safe with me. I swear...'

Her heart slammed against the wall of her ribcage, jerky and uneven, coming close to panic at just the thought of what she was considering. But the ache of need still suffused her own body and wouldn't let her go.

If only this had happened sooner. If only she had met this Anton before...

But no. That was to wish for the impossible. Her fate had been sealed and she had no alternative but to go down the path that had been chosen for her. The path she had agreed to.

The path she had had no choice but to agree to.

From tomorrow, everything would change. From tomorrow her life would no longer be her own.

Skye's teeth dug down hard into the softness of her bottom lip, scoring sharp little crescents into the delicate pink flesh.

Tomorrow.

Last week she had prayed that she could run away. She had dreamed of it, longed for it, hoped for a chance. But there was no chance. Too many people depended on her. If she had had any doubts about that, then the latest news only this week of how dangerous her mother's heart condition really was had destroyed them for ever. She couldn't run away and leave them all in the lurch.

But there was tonight.

Tonight she could run away—at least temporarily—from everything that was weighing her down. She could escape into a world of fantasy and sensual delight. A world that was so unreal she couldn't really believe it was happening to her. A world in which, for once in her life—for the one and only time—just for a few short hours, she could experience the full heights of passion and the fierce sensuality that she had tasted so briefly just a few moments before.

One of the hardest things to accept about this marriage to Cyril Antonakos was the fact that her unwanted wedding night would be her first experience of sex. She was still a virgin and had never known any man who could make her feel enough to want to change that situation.

Until now.

Now she couldn't bear the thought that a man nearing sixty would be her first, her only lover—when there was this man who only had to touch her and she felt as if she were going up in flames.

She could have tonight.

I promise you, you'll be safe with me. I swear...

He didn't even have to know her name. And tomorrow,

as in some modern-day Cinderella story, reality would close in around her once again.

But she would have had tonight.

If only she could bring herself to answer him. If only she could find the courage to say...

'Skye?'

Her name was rough on his tongue now, raw impatience and that devastating accent turning it into something new and strange. A sound she didn't recognise as the name she heard every day.

'Are you ever going to answer me?'

Skye tried. Swallowing hard to ease the dryness of her throat, she fought for the control, the strength she needed.

But then his long-fingered hand came under her chin, lifting it so that her face came up to meet his, her grey eyes meeting and locking with the deep, deep blackness of his. Drowning in their darkness.

He bent his head slowly and his mouth took hers. This time his kiss had none of the fierce, wild passion of moments before; instead it was soft and slow and heartbreakingly tender. It seemed to draw her soul out of her body, melt her bones, so that she was trembling against him, needing the potent strength of his body to support her so that she didn't fall to the ground.

'So tell me, my beauty,' he whispered in a voice that was as dark and rich as the black velvet night sky above them. 'Will you go or will you stay?'

My beauty, Skye thought hazily.

No one, not even her mother, had ever called her beautiful. Or made her feel it the way his kiss made her feel right now, here in this cold, rain-spattered street.

And suddenly there was only one answer to give him. Only one answer she *could* give him.

She had to have tonight. She might regret it in the morning, when reality hit her in the face. But the one thing she was sure of was that she could never regret it as much as she would bitterly regret saying no.

And so she lifted her head and kissed him back, putting her answer into the caress, but knowing she had to speak it too.

'Oh, yes,' she breathed softly, confidently. 'Yes, of course I'll stay. But on one condition…'

CHAPTER THREE

THEO flicked on the light and surveyed the room before him with a critical eye, frowning as he did so.

'Are you sure that this is what you want?'

He supposed that the room was all right, as hotel rooms went. It was at least clean and reasonably sized, with a comfortable-looking bed, and the usual furniture and fittings. Through a door off to one side was the tiny *en suite* bathroom, severely tiled in plain, cold white, with toiletries, towels and bath robes all in the same non-colour.

It was all totally soulless, functional but impersonal, and therefore unwelcoming. And not at all the sort of place he would have thought that he would end up in tonight.

But then, nothing tonight had gone the way he had expected it.

He had certainly never anticipated ending up in an anonymous hotel room with a woman who stirred every single one of his most primitive senses, but whose first name was the only thing he knew about her.

'We're strangers,' she had said, 'and I want to keep it that way. You don't know me and I don't know you—that's the way it has to be.'

No way! That was his first response. He actually stiffened, half turned to walk away, but she was still so close to him, he still had his arms around her, and the hot blood racing through his veins, the hungry need that clamoured at his senses, blurred his thoughts.

He couldn't let her go.

He had known that in the moment that he had seen her turn to hail a taxi to take her away and out of his life. And if she went now, then she would be gone for ever. He would have no way of tracking her down. She would disappear into the night and he would never see her again; never know anything more about her.

'You ask a lot, lady,' he managed, his voice husky and rough.

She didn't show any sign of reconsidering. Her light-coloured gaze held his unwaveringly, and her soft mouth firmed to a determined line.

'It's that or nothing,' she said, reaching up a slim hand to smooth it across the front of his shirt, and the small movement brought a waft of her scent up to his nostrils, tantalising his senses and drying his mouth.

Beneath the caress of her fingers, his skin burned and his heart kicked savagely, making his pulse throb, his senses swim.

'That or nothing,' she repeated and he knew that he could never live with 'nothing'. He would always curse himself if he let this woman get away from him now.

'Whatever you want, lady,' he said, knowing it was nothing less than the truth. 'Whatever you want.'

And what she wanted was this.

For tonight at least.

Well, he would let her get away with it for tonight—after all, she wasn't the only one who had been a little...economical with the truth. But tomorrow always came.

Tomorrow he would be asking a lot of questions. And he'd want some very definite answers to all of them.

Meanwhile, he'd spend tonight convincing her that it wasn't 'that or nothing' at all.

'Skye?' he questioned now when the woman who had come into the room just behind him didn't answer. 'What is it? Have you changed your mind about tonight? Do you want to go back on this—renege on what we agreed?'

Did she?

Did she want to back out of the deal? Was that what she wanted?

They were the questions Skye had been asking herself ever since they'd come upstairs. No—before that. The truth was that her courage and conviction had been seeping away from the moment that she had agreed to stay with him.

It was obvious that she'd shocked him to the core with her blunt announcement that if she stayed then he must never ask her her full name, and never give her his.

She'd thought that he was going to walk away when she'd said that. Certainly his expression had seemed to promise that he was going to reject her outrageous proposition out of hand. His whole face had closed off, shutters seeming to come down behind the brilliant black eyes, until every one of his features had appeared to be carved in cold, unyielding marble.

But then he had blinked once, very slowly, and nodded his dark head.

'No,' she said now, miserably aware of the way that her own inner tension made her voice sound tight and hard, coldly distant. 'No, I'm not reneging on anything. It's just…'

Just that I'm no good at this.

The words were burning on her tongue, but she swallowed them back hastily, closing her eyes against the terrible anxiety she was feeling. She couldn't say them, not here, not now, not in this situation. Her stomach muscles were tying themselves into tight, painful knots, twisting each nerve harder and harder with every heartbeat.

'Just what?'

His voice sounded disturbingly close and when her eyes flew open again it was to find that he had taken several long strides forward. He was standing right in front of her, so near that if she just lifted her hand she could touch him without even stretching out her fingers.

And she wanted to touch him. The tips of her fingers tingled with the remembrance of the way his skin, his hair had felt to their touch. Her palms felt again the heat of the muscles beneath his shirt, sensed the thudding of his heart under the strong bones of his chest.

If she slicked her tongue along her lips, she could still taste him, clean, musky, intensely masculine, making her heart skip a beat. And she wanted that taste, those sensations all over again. She wanted to lose herself in that wonderful, sizzling feeling that flooded her senses, swamping her mind and leaving her incapable of thought, knowing only need.

She *wanted* this man.

'Just what?' he prompted again, more roughly this time.

I want you to hold me—to make me forget…

'Just that I wish you would kiss me again.'

'Oh, that!'

It was edged with laughter, threaded through with a knowing triumph.

'You only had to ask.'

He was already moving forward, taking her in his arms, drawing her close to him with the confidence of a man who was sure of his appeal; who had no doubt that he was wanted.

'So tell me, sweetheart…'

A caressing hand slid under her chin, lifting her face to his, and his glittering black eyes locked with her cloudy grey ones, holding her gaze, keeping her so still that even her heartbeat seemed to freeze.

'Where shall I kiss you? Here?'

The warm pressure of his mouth on her forehead was like a butterfly landing, light, delicate, there and gone again so swiftly that she barely even noticed it was there until she felt its loss. And when she did, her lips parted on a sigh of melancholy delight.

'Or here…?'

This time he caressed her cheek, dropping a kiss just below her temple, on the left and then again on the right, making her breathing deepen, her senses start to stir.

'Or perhaps here…?'

Softly, deliberately, he kissed her eyes shut, his lips lingering on the lids just long enough to seal them closed. At least, that was the way it felt to Skye, who found herself locked into a world of sensual darkness where every other sense seemed heightened and sharply sensitised to everything about him.

She could hear each breath he took, low and steady, matching the beat of his heart. His scent was on the air around her, that warm, clean, male essence, subtly blended with the tang of lime and spice in his cologne. When he took her hands in his, the heat seared across her skin like an electric current making her fingers curl in instant response, her breath catch sharply in her throat.

And it was all happening again.

She was melting inside, all the tension seeping out of her body so that she almost expected to see it pool on the floor at her feet. The honeyed pulse of desire was starting through her veins once more, sending the waves of yearning along the path of every nerve and setting them alight with need.

'That will do for a start,' she managed, amazed at her own boldness. A daring that was bolstered by the darkness behind her closed lids.

She couldn't see the man who held her, couldn't look into the darkness of his eyes and read anything—or nothing—from them. She could only *feel*, enclosed in her own private, secret world of sensations she had never known before, but now wanted to experience so much more.

She wanted to plunge into them like a swimmer diving straight into the deepest pool, letting the waters crash over her head and submerge her completely. Wanted to know it all. Wanted to snatch at things greedily and hungrily, grabbing them to her and swallowing them whole.

But Anton seemed determined to take things slowly. When she made a tiny movement of impatience he hushed her softly, smoothing the sound from her lips with a gentle finger.

'Not so fast, my lovely. We have all night.'

All night…

It had a wonderful sound. A sound that seemed to promise hours that would stretch out and out in a never-ending way, delivering pleasure for as long as she could stand it. But at the same time, Skye knew just how quickly those hours would fly by. How soon they would be over.

She had this one chance to know the sensuous delights that instinct told her were ahead of her. She couldn't waste them.

She *wouldn't* waste them. Already her body was on fire with anticipation and longing and she was trembling in his arms, grateful for the security of his hold that was all that kept her upright.

'Anton…'

His name was a moan of need on her lips and she felt as well as heard the soft laughter that shook his powerful frame.

'I know, sweetheart,' he told her and the new thickness in his voice revealed only too clearly just how much he did know. 'I know the way you're feeling—but, believe me, this will be worth taking slowly. It will be worth waiting for. Just go with me on this—let me show you…'

He was kissing her again now, his mouth taking a burning trail from her temple, down to her jaw before it captured her lips again. The touch of his mouth on her skin, the magic it could work, was threatening her ability to think. But there was one vital, practical matter she *had* to think of because the possible consequences if she didn't were too horrific even to consider.

She had just this one night; she couldn't risk the nightmare of any physical legacy that might result from it. That would destroy her and her family at a single stroke.

'Do you...?'

It was a struggle to get the words out and not succumb to the erotic enticement that his lips were promising. But she had to say it. The woman he thought she was would never let it go unmentioned.

'Have you any—protection?'

'Of course.'

He didn't even miss a beat. The response came as his caressing lips moved lower, found another pleasure spot Skye hadn't even known existed.

'The hotel shop stocks everything.'

'Oh, yes.'

She hoped she sounded more assured than she felt. She had had a desperate attack of nerves when he had approached Reception to register and with a muttered excuse had disappeared into the nearest Ladies to hide for a moment. By the time she had emerged, cheeks flushed brightly, he had been waiting for her by the bank of lifts, the room key in his hand.

'So now you can relax and know I'll take care of you.'

There was such a darkly sensuous undertone in that remark that it made her toes curl inside her shiny patent leather shoes. Suddenly wanting to be rid of even such minor restrictions, she kicked off the high-heeled pumps and relaxed into Anton's hold, abandoning herself to the moment. His arms almost lifted her off her feet, taking her up and hard against him so that she shivered at the feel of the hard ridge that marked the arousal he had no intention of hiding.

She flung her arms up around his neck, linking her fin-

gers in the silky strands of the black hair as she gave herself
up to the kiss. It was hard and hot and hungry and it fuelled
an answering need inside her until she was burning up with
it, swimming on a heated flood tide of passion.

Skye had never known her body to feel so alive before.
Her heart was thudding, her head spinning. Her breasts felt
swollen and, oh, so sensitive, the tight buds of her nipples
stinging sharply.

She was swung off her feet, lifted from the floor and
carried the short distance to the bed. Laying her down
gently on the blue and green quilted covering, he kept his
mouth on hers while his wickedly enticing hands found the
fastenings of her dress, dispensing with the buttons in moments, the delicate lace of her bra no protection at all from
his burning gaze.

Or the touch of those knowing hands.

At the sensation of the heat of his palms on her breasts,
stroking delicately over the peach-coloured lace, catching
and rolling the hardened nipples between strong fingers,
Skye's eyes flew open, meeting the glittering black gaze of
the man above her.

'An—' she began, but he silenced her once more, kissing
the exclamation from her trembling mouth.

'Close your eyes,' he commanded against her lips. 'Close
them and keep them shut.'

He caught her uncertain, anxious gaze and lifted his head
to kiss her eyelids closed again, returning her to the warm
velvet darkness once more.

'Don't look, just feel.'

How could she do anything else when already those tormenting hands were easing her bra from her, tracing hot,
erotic patterns across her breasts, circling the peaks, making
the nipples strain against their touch?

'Feel this…' he muttered with another tormenting caress

across the sensitised skin, trailing fiery paths that sent shock waves of sensation pulsing through her.

The gentleness was not enough. She wanted—needed—more! Blindly reaching for him, she closed her hands over his powerful shoulders, pulling him down towards her, crushing her lips to his.

'Help me—show me…' she began against his mouth, only realising just in time what she had almost given away, revealing herself to him more than she truly wanted to.

She didn't want him to realise—or even to suspect—her innocence. What would a man as sophisticated and worldly as this Anton seemed want with an innocent fresh up from the country—a real country bumpkin who had never known how it felt to make love with a man? An innocent whose lack of experience would no doubt make him laugh or shake his head in disbelief.

This man didn't want an untutored lover. He must be used to women as knowing and as experienced as he clearly was. She would die of embarrassment if he realised how far from experienced she was.

'Show me how to please you,' she amended hastily, hoping she had caught the betraying words soon enough.

'You're doing okay all by yourself,' was the muttered response and the raw edge to his voice made her heart jerk in unexpected sensual triumph.

Perhaps with her eyes closed she could be the woman he would want. With her eyes closed she felt less inhibited, less self-conscious. With her eyes closed she could indulge her need to reach out and touch, to let her hands close over the tight muscles of his shoulders and arms under the fine linen of his shirt.

When had he shrugged off his jacket?

Even working blind, her fingers had no problem dealing with the buttons down the front of his shirt, and within moments her searching hands had found the hot, hair-roughened skin of his chest. It felt so warm to her touch, the tingling excitement tantalising her, driving her to explore further—much to Anton's delight, to judge by his groan of response.

'Quite okay...'

'You're not doing badly either.'

Somehow she managed to find just the right, casual tone. She was stunned to realise that he had slipped her clothing from her without any of the awkward tugging and pulling she had anticipated. The air of the overheated hotel room was warm on her exposed flesh, and, keeping her eyes closed, she managed not to blush hotly at the realisation that those dark, deep-set eyes were now fixed on her near naked body.

But she couldn't ignore the fact of his touch. Her heart leapt at the first brush of hard fingers on delicate skin and it was all she could do not to curl up into a defensive ball and, muttering, 'Oh, don't,' try to hide away from him.

The sensation only lasted a moment. A couple of heart-shuddering seconds later she was relaxing into the wonderful sensations his caresses woke in her. Her hungry senses stirred, thrilled, cried out for more. And the whimpering cries that were all she could manage spoke to him only too clearly of her need.

The stroking hands grew harder, urgent, more demanding. And as she writhed beneath his touch his mouth moved over her too, kissing his way along her shoulder, down to the slope of her breast, catching the already aching nipple between his lips and tugging hard.

Skye's only response was a high, wordless sound of wonder as her breath stilled in her throat and her body arched against his in urgent invitation.

'Please...'

It was all she could manage, though she had no idea whether she was begging for more of the sharply sensual caress—or for him to stop before she fainted away completely from a pleasure that was so intense it was almost a pain. Burning sensations of delight sizzled through her, making her head spin, and the spiralling delight took all her ability to think from her.

Those wickedly tormenting hands were heading lower, stroking up the soft inner flesh of her thighs, slipping under the waist of the peach silk knickers that were somehow her only item of clothing, easing the flimsy garment away from her body.

All the embarrassment she had thought that she would feel at being exposed in this way was swept away on a molten tide of hunger. This was what she wanted; what she needed. This was...

Her mind splintered in an explosion of erotic delight as that tormenting touch reached the most sensitive spot of her femininity. The tantalising caress had her gasping in uncontrolled response, moving convulsively, stretching to press herself against that arousing fingertip. Wave after wave of heated pleasure throbbed through her, leaving her weak and abandoned, adrift on the aftershocks of a pleasure she had never known existed.

And in that moment Anton covered her body with his own, fitting his heavy, muscled legs between the splayed whiteness of her thighs, pushing them wide. The hot power of his erection sought the warm, slick darkness of her innermost core, and there was no time for hesitation or for fear. No time to suffer second thoughts or worry about her inexperience.

The actual moment of possession was so swift, so sure, thrusting deep into her already yearning body that only the faintest sting of pain, of protest from the stretching of tender tissues, gave any indication that this was the first experience of an unknown sensation. For just a brief heartbeat her eyes flew open wide, staring up into the dark, intent face above her in stunned bewilderment, blurring into a wild kaleidoscope of misty colour. Dazed grey gaze locked with passion-glazed black and the rest of the world went completely out of focus.

But then he began to move, deep and strong within her; each thrust piling sensation upon sensation, fire upon fire, until she thought her mind would surely melt in the inferno of pleasure that assailed her.

Her eyes fell closed again, the better to enjoy the stunning sensations rippling through her body. Her head went back against the pillows, her mouth slightly open to enable her to catch the breaths that seemed to have abandoned her needy lungs, her whole system going into shutdown, into primitive total concentration on the one vital core of her being.

She was being taken up and up again, lifted higher, higher, higher—climbing towards the peak she hadn't known existed, but had somehow, intuitively, instinctively, been reaching for. And in the instant that at last she reached it she toppled over the edge, no longer inside her body but floating high and free on a wild explosion of starlight, tumbling into complete oblivion, into the blank unconsciousness of total ecstasy.

A heartbeat later, Theo joined her, his harsh cry of fulfilment the last sound before he too lost all consciousness of the world apart from this woman whose body enclosed his so hotly, and the ragged, thudding beat of his own heart.

It was an unconsciousness from which he barely surfaced long into the night. There were times when his senses struggled to the surface of the erotic stupor into which he had fallen, and almost regained the knowledge of reality and where he was.

Almost.

Because each time he came close to waking, each time he stirred and reached out a hand or moved a sensually aching limb, he encountered the soft, warm shape of the woman beside him. And each time he touched her it was like connecting with a live electric current. The wildfire magic flared again, rousing them both from the depths of sleep, making them hungry again, setting their pulses pounding, their breath rasping. Bringing them together in a wild, fierce coupling that once again obliterated thought or any sense beyond the primitive demands of their bodies and the appetites that only each other could appease.

Until in the end a total exhaustion claimed them, dropping him down into a sleep so deep, so all-enclosing, that he didn't even stir when, just as dawn was breaking, Skye managed to drag herself from the depths of oblivion and forced her reluctant body to slip from the bed.

She couldn't even look at the sleeping man as she pulled on her clothes with more haste than finesse though she was painfully, agonisingly aware of his dark head, the powerfully carved features still resting on the softness of the pillows. She didn't want to leave. Tears stung her eyes at the thought of the moment that she would step outside the door of this small room—this small, uninteresting, anonymous room that had come to seem like a tiny piece of heaven to her. She would have to walk out that door, out of the glorious dream she had known for one night, and back into the cold, cruel world of life.

Reality would close around her once again and this very special time would just be a memory.

She didn't even dare press the kiss she hungered for on his sleeping face for fear that even the lightest touch would wake him. That those deep, dark eyes—the eyes she had lost herself in last night—would fly open and look straight into hers. She could almost see the frown that would crease the space between the black, arched brows, hear his softly accented voice demanding to know where she was going.

She couldn't face that. It would destroy her even to try.

Another day; another time. The words echoed like a lament inside her head.

If they had met another day, another time, then perhaps they might have had a future. She might have been able to—

No!

Fiercely she caught back her wayward thoughts, knowing they would weaken her resolve, tie her already leaden feet to the ground if she let them into her head.

She had to go—now—as fast as she could. Not even troubling to pull on tights over her bare legs, she forced her feet into her shoes, snatched up her jacket and bag, and fled towards the door.

There was a long desperate moment of panic as the handle squeaked, the hinges creaked, but then she was out and easing the door shut, allowing herself only a moment for a gasping sigh of relief before she fled down the carpeted corridor, heading for the lift.

Had she forgotten anything? Left a betraying clue behind?

A desperate check of her belongings confirmed she had everything with her—a fact that should have reassured her, but it didn't.

Because the truth was that what she had left behind was a vital part of her soul.

CHAPTER FOUR

'WE'LL be landing in five minutes, sir.'

'Thank you.'

Theo acknowledged his pilot's words with a nod. He hadn't even needed them, really. His own eyes had told him just how close they were getting to Helikos, the small dot in the ocean that was his father's private island.

The island that had been home to Theo himself, all the time he had been growing up.

Then, when he had been just a boy, and had returned home from the long weeks away at the exclusive English boarding-school he had detested but which his father had been determined would turn him into a gentleman, he had recognised every tiny landmark on the flight from Athens airport. He had almost hung out of the helicopter cockpit to spot each change in the scene beneath them, the dozens of other, tiny, uninhabited islands that marked the familiar route to his beloved family home.

And when Helikos had finally come into view, at first as just a small dot on the horizon, he had always let out a great cheer to celebrate that, at last, for him, the holidays had begun.

But this time there was no excited thudding of his heart, no resounding cheer on his lips. Instead he viewed the approaching coastline with a dour, cynical expression, watching it come nearer with a complicated mix of emotions in his soul. He was heading back to Helikos after an absence of five long years, but the island was no longer truly home to him. The split with his father had seen to that. And now there was the new wife to consider, too.

Theo scowled as the sound of the engine changed subtly, indicating that the pilot was beginning their descent. Another complication he could well do without. Though, from the little information he had had about her, this marriage was clearly not a love match. More like a business deal.

'I don't think you'll find the island much changed.'

It was the pilot again, interrupting his thoughts as his voice came through the earphones both men wore.

'I doubt if it's changed in the least.'

Theo kept his eyes on the dark mass of land set in the brilliant sea. He was not in the mood for conversation; in fact he was not in the mood to be here at all. He most definitely was not in the mood for meeting his father's latest floozy and trying to be polite to her. Cyril Antonakos was not known for choosing the most intelligent of female companions, and unless his father had changed dramatically in the past five years, then tonight's dinner when he was to meet the brand-new Antonakos bride-to-be was going to be a long endurance test.

All the more so because his mind would be anywhere but here on Helikos.

From the moment that he had woken to find the space in the bed beside him cold, the room empty, he hadn't been able to get the mysterious Skye out of his thoughts. He had spent the last week hunting for traces of the woman who had shared that one amazing night with him, but, with so little to go on, he had had a frustrating lack of success. He would do better, he knew, to forget the whole thing and put her out of his mind.

But in one brief night she had got completely under his skin and he couldn't forget about her. Even when he slept, his dreams were filled with hot, erotic images of the night they had spent together. He would dream that he held her close, her slender, smooth-skinned limbs entangled with his, her Titian hair spread across the pillows, over his face, her perfume driving him wild.

And then he'd wake with his heart racing, his breath coming in raw, uneven gasps, his body slicked with sweat as if he had actually been making love to her in reality and not just in his mind. But of course none of it was real—none of it except the burning ache in his groin, the throb of unappeased hunger through every nerve.

If he could, he would have made some excuse and not come here. But the division between him and his father had gone on quite long enough. If Cyril was prepared to offer an olive branch, however half-hearted, then he, Theo, would meet him more than part way.

The house was just as he remembered it. High on a cliff above the sea, the huge white building sprawled over a large plot of land on two levels, each with its own vast veranda giving an amazing view of the ocean. A wide arched gateway to one side led to a stone-flagged patio, the oval swimming pool, and a small pool house that doubled as a guest house.

As Theo approached the door was pulled open and a small, plump, dark-haired figure hurried towards him.

'Master Theo! Welcome! It's wonderful to have you back!'

'Amalthea…'

Theo submitted to the exuberant embrace of the tiny woman who had been his nurse as he grew up, and, because his mother had died when he was small, the closest person to a mother he had ever known.

'Where am I staying? Have you put me in my old room?'

Amalthea's dark eyes clouded as she shook her greying head.

'Your father told me to put you in the pool house.'

So the olive branch was not quite as definite as he had thought, Theo told himself with a twist of sardonic resignation. His father was a hard man to like—a difficult man to love. He took offence easily and held onto grudges for a long, long time. It seemed that being invited here for the old man's wedding was only the start of things. There wasn't any sign of the fatted calf being prepared for the return of the prodigal son.

'Who's in my room?'

Surely the guests hadn't started to arrive just yet? The wedding wasn't taking place until the end of the month.

'The new *Kyria* Antonakos.'

'My father's fiancée?'

So his father and the bride-to-be didn't share a room already. That was a surprise.

'What's she like?'

Amalthea rolled her eyes in an expression of disapproval that she could only get away with in front of Theo.

'Not at all his usual sort. But she is very beautiful.'

'They're always beautiful,' Theo commented cynically. 'That's why he chooses them. Is my father at home now?'

'He had to go to the village,' Amalthea told him. 'But he'll be back this evening in time for dinner. His fiancée is at home. Would you want to—'

'Oh, no,' Theo put in swiftly, before she could even form the suggestion. 'Dinner time will be soon enough.'

That way he could get both awkward encounters over and done with in the same time. Perhaps making polite small talk with The Fiancée would be easier than trying to carry on any sort of a conversation with his parent.

'My bags will have been taken to the pool house. I'll unpack and settle in—maybe have a swim.'

He stretched slowly, easing muscles cramped tight after the journey from London.

'It's good to be home.'

So this was to be home.

Skye turned away from the window with its panoramic

view of the sea and sank back down onto the bed with a sigh, digging her teeth into her lower lip in an attempt to force back the tears that were threatening.

She was always on the edge of tears these days. Always only just managing to subdue the panic that gripped her when she contemplated what lay ahead of her. She still couldn't quite take it all in. Still couldn't believe that this was to be her future.

But sitting here brooding wasn't going to change that. She really ought to come out of the bedroom at some point soon, and get to know the rest of the house better. She was going to live here, after all.

That thought only added to her sense of desolate unreality. This house, beautiful as it was, just didn't seem anything like the home she had left in the damp and green countryside of Suffolk, the small village where she had grown up.

She supposed she would get used to it in time. She *had* to get used to it; she had no choice.

Skye rubbed the back of her hand across her eyes, brushing away the tears. When she'd phoned home earlier, her father had told her that her mother had been taken into hospital again. Claire Marston needed yet another operation, and soon. And her doctors had said that it was vital she was kept quiet. Any stress at all could be fatal.

It was a terrible, bitter irony, one that brought a taste like the burn of acid into her mouth, to think that she had always dreamed of visiting Greece, of seeing the cluster of the Sporades Islands, perhaps holidaying there. She had dreamed of the sunshine, the sea, the white houses she had seen in photographs. And now she had achieved her dream, but it had turned into a terrible nightmare; one from which even waking wouldn't mean that she could escape.

Now she had the sun. It had been shining all day. And,

there, beyond her window, was the sea, an almost unbelievable bright and sparkling turquoise in colour. She lived in one of the white houses—a *huge* white house. And she hated it.

She was lonely and lost and terrified of the future.

And she had no way out.

'Oh, Dad! Why did you have to be so stupid? How could you have made such a mess of things?'

If only…

But no! Skye caught herself up sharply, giving herself a brusque, reproving shake.

She couldn't let herself dwell on *if only*. Couldn't even let herself dream of *if only*.

But, oh, *if only* she had never made that mad, foolish mistake last week. If only she hadn't given into the crazy, wild impulse to have one last night of freedom while she could.

And *if only* she had never met the most devastating man called Anton. A man who had taken her to bed for the most amazing, most stunning, most memorable night of passion. The only night of such passion she was ever likely to know. A night of passion she would never forget.

And she could never, *ever* forget the man who had shared it with her.

But because she would never forget, then the situation in which she now found herself became so very much worse. Appallingly so. Perhaps before last week she might have been able to bear the prospect of the future with some degree of equanimity. Now she had been shown, oh, so briefly, the image of another, very different future, only to have it snatched away from her for ever, and she had no idea at all how she was ever going to cope.

But she had to. Even though she felt that her heart would break just with trying.

'Come on, Marston!' she told herself fiercely. 'Pull yourself together. You're going to have to make the best of this!'

She could at least keep herself busy. Keep her mind occupied and not let herself brood.

What was it Cyril had said before he left—to go into the village on business?

'Make yourself at home. The house is yours—anything you want, just ask for it. Use the cinema, or the pool.'

The pool! There was her answer. Some exercise would distract her; it would fill the long, empty afternoon that stretched ahead. And if she was lucky, it would tire her out so that she would finally manage to sleep tonight.

And she needed to sleep, she told herself as she pulled open a drawer, hunting through it for the sleek white costume that Cyril had insisted on buying for her when he had realised that she didn't have anything to wear to swim in, apart from the regulation navy blue one piece that had seen her through school and was now definitely on its last legs.

She would exercise until she was exhausted and then tonight she might crash out, almost unconscious. With luck she would not have to lie there, in the strange bed, staring at the white-painted ceiling, remembering…

Or would falling asleep be worse? Every night she had slept so badly, locked in feverish dreams of a night in a hotel, a long, sleekly muscled body next to hers, powerful arms holding her, jet-black eyes looking down at her. And every morning she had woken with the bedclothes in a twisted tangle, knotted around her body, evidence of the disturbed night she had passed.

She was shivering with reaction to her memories as she pulled on the white swimsuit, grabbed a towel, and headed for the pool.

Theo's unpacking only took a very short time. There was little enough to put away in the cupboards of the pool house where his father had left instructions he was to stay, his old room apparently being occupied by The Fiancée, and now he was at a loss. The afternoon was warm and the thought of the cool, clear water of the pool was appealing. It was the work of seconds to change into black swimming shorts and head outside, padding silently in bare feet over the white-tiled surround.

What he didn't expect was to see someone already in the water. Shock brought him to a halt, eyes narrowing against the glint of the sun on the water as he studied the scene before him.

A sleek form sped through the water, powering from one end of the pool to another. A sleek *female* form in a clinging white costume. The Fiancée, if he wasn't very much mistaken. He couldn't see much of her from here, she was swimming away from him and the water hid most of her body. He had a brief, blurred impression of dark hair, long, slender arms slicing through the water, slim, toned legs kicking out behind the shapely body, high, tight buttocks…

What the *hell* was he doing? He couldn't have thoughts like that about his father's fiancée—the woman who was going to be his stepmother by the end of the month.

Or was this in fact the brand-new fiancée? Because she was much younger than he had ever anticipated…

Perhaps The Fiancée had been married before and this girl was a daughter? Whoever she was, she made him think disturbingly of the mysterious Skye.

He'd better make himself known to her. He didn't want to give the impression of behaving like a peeping Tom, standing here staring at her.

'*Kalimera.*'

She hadn't heard him—the water must still be in her ears. Or perhaps she didn't even understand Greek. A cynical smile twisted his mouth. It was an indication of just how bad things had become between him and his father that he

had no idea whether the new woman in Cyril's life was
Greek or some other nationality entirely. The last time he
had known anything about any of Cyril's mistresses, his
father had been deeply involved with a woman from the
village.

'Good afternoon.' He spoke again, more firmly and
clearly this time, just as she reached the far end of the pool
and held onto the side, wiping the water from her face. 'I
think I ought to introduce myself to you, Stepmama.'

It was her stillness that told him something was wrong.
The sudden total freezing into immobility that caught on a
raw edge in his mind and made him frown, studying her
more closely.

Just what had he said that had startled her so much?

Even from this distance he could see the way that she
clutched at the side of the pool, the pressure that turned the
knuckles white on each delicate hand.

That hand…

Suddenly, shockingly, it was as if he had been kicked in
the stomach hard.

A cold, damp night in London. A smoky bar. The laughter of two men.

A hand held prisoner on the table top.

'*Theos*, no!'

He had to be imagining things. Fooling himself.

But in the warmth of the Greek sun the hair that tumbled
down her back—the hair that he had thought was dark, but
now he could see was only soaked with water from the
pool—was already starting to dry. And as it dried its colour
changed, lightening…revealing a red-gold tint.

'*Ochi*…'

Feeling as if he had been slapped on the side of the head,
Theo reverted to his native Greek, shaking his head in denial of what he was seeing, what he suspected.

'No!'

It couldn't be true.

But if it wasn't, then why was she still standing as if frozen, with her head turned away from him—that long, straight back held tight with tension, the delicate hands clenched over the edge of the pool?

Why didn't she turn and face him—revealing the features of a total stranger, shattering the foolish, damn stupid, appalling delusion that had taken a grip on his mind and wouldn't let go?

She wasn't…she *couldn't* be…

'Skye?'

From the moment that she had first heard that voice, Skye had been fixed to the spot, unable to move, unable to think, unable to breathe.

'Good afternoon,' he had said, and it was as if a cruel hand had reached out through time and yanked her backwards, dragging her away from the present, and back into the past, into a whirlwind of memories that paralysed her mind, slashed at her soul.

'Good afternoon.'

Those were the words she had heard in the clear light of today. But in her mind what she had heard was: *Oh, but he does.*

The first words that Anton had spoken on the night in London. The night that ever since had simply become *that night* in her thoughts, with no further title needed.

That night.

That was when she had first heard that rich, slightly husky voice with the touch of the beautiful accent that made her toes curl in response.

But how could she have heard it here and now?

She had to be imagining things! She couldn't have heard it. He couldn't be here. Fate couldn't be so cruel.

But then he had said, 'I think I ought to introduce myself

to you,' and the world had tilted violently, swinging right off balance, making her head spin crazily.

Her vision had blurred, her stomach had clenched tight in panic. She couldn't see, couldn't think. She *had* to know—and yet she didn't dare to look round, terrified in case she was right. In case it *was* him.

And then the worst horror of all.

'Skye?'

He used her name. In the voice that she had heard him use dozens of times—a hundred times—on *that night*. She had heard it said calmly, heard it said softly, heard it said huskily, seductively, passionately, demandingly. And finally, she had heard her own name used as a cry of fulfilment, as he had lost himself in her. But always, always, in that voice.

Anton?

She didn't dare to speak his name aloud, fearing that she might be tempting fate by doing so. That she might turn into reality what she still fervently hoped was just a delusion, a trick of sound combining with her overactive imagination.

'What the hell?'

The harsh, angry question brought her swinging round, unable to bear the suspense any longer. She *had* to know.

He was standing on the edge of the pool, hands on hips. The sun was behind him so that she had to squint against it to see his face. But she already knew, and her heart was racing so fast that she was sure it would escape the confines of her chest. Already she couldn't breathe and her mind was frozen in stunned horror.

Perhaps it was because of that, or perhaps it was the sun dazzling her eyes, but something made her lose her grip, slip and fall. She reached for the rim of the pool, missed, and went under, still gasping for breath.

Water in her ears and eyes, she didn't hear anything, couldn't see anything. She went down…down…

There was a flurry nearby. A long body slashed into the water at her side. Strong hands seized her; powerful arms hauled her up to the surface. Before she had time to think, she was dragged to the shallow end of the pool, and supported gently as she gasped and wheezed, struggling to get her breath back.

'Steady,' that voice advised her. 'Breathe deeply.'

She would if she could, Skye told herself, but if anything was guaranteed *not* to calm her down, it was this.

Now she didn't have to look into his face to know he was Anton. Even after only one night—*that night*—she knew this male body so intimately that she could never mistake it. There were the hard, strong bones of the ribcage, the black curling hair that marked a path down the centre of his chest, disappearing under the waistband of the swimming trunks. There was the tiny, crescent shaped scar high up on his collar-bone, almost at the base of his throat. And if there had been any room for doubt, then her nostrils were filled with the scent of his body, musky, intensely male, warmed by the sun and blending with the ozone tang of the pool water.

She didn't know if it was her intense physical reaction to him or simply the shock of his sudden appearance that made her tremble all over, her legs feeling too weak to support her.

'Thank you,' she managed, her voice sounding as if she had been running a marathon.

'No problem,' he returned smoothly, though there was a dark thread to his voice that brought her head up sharply, frowning grey eyes meeting the fixed black gaze of his.

He didn't enlighten her further, but instead half dragged, half carried her to the low stone steps into the pool, swing-

ing her up into his arms and carrying her out onto the tiled
edge where he set her down again beside a wooden lounger.

Skye had to bite down hard on her lower lip to keep her
mouth closed against the cry of protest as he let her go. In
his arms, she had been struggling with a terrible longing,
with a weak, dangerous impulse to turn her head into his
chest and let it rest there. The need to nestle close into his
arms, to put her own hands up around his neck and cling
on tight, had almost overwhelmed her. But she had known
that such a response was forbidden her. She had forfeited
the right to it in the moment that she had closed the door
on that hotel room and walked away.

He would never know just how hard she had found it to
do that. How much she had longed to stay, but known that
it was impossible. She had left a piece of her heart with
him, though he would never know it. And as soon as he
worked out just why she was here then he wouldn't even
want her near him, let alone keep her in his arms where
she longed to be.

Still supporting her with one hand, he snatched up a
towel with the other and began to rub her dry. His movements were brisk and impersonal and the one, nervous look
she shot at his face made her stomach tie itself into tight,
painful knots of apprehension.

The stunning face was tight with control, skin drawn so
taut over the forceful bone structure that it was actually
white at the corners of his mouth with the effort of not
speaking. He was only keeping quiet until she had recovered.

And then?

Just the thought made her shiver again, more violently
this time, yelping in discomfort as he increased the pressure
of the towel on her sensitised skin.

'*Sighnomi…*'

The apology was abstracted and he tossed the towel

away, coal-black eyes raking over her from the top of her head, where her wet hair hung in tangled rats' tails around her face, to the bare pink toes on the white-tiled surface.

But it was when they swung back up to her face that her courage almost failed her completely.

Now it was going to begin, she told herself, swallowing hard.

He'd waited long enough, that cold, set expression said. Now he wanted explanations.

CHAPTER FIVE

'WE HAVE some talking to do.'

Theo had no idea how he kept control over his voice. The coldly burning rage inside him would keep fighting to get away from his determination to rein it in, and the resulting conflict made his tone brutal and cold as a sword of ice.

He wanted to know just what the hell was going on. How the woman he had last seen in a London hotel room—the woman who had wanted only a one-night stand, no names, no information—had turned up on Helikos, at his father's house, in his father's pool.

Though he would be able to think much more clearly if she would just cover up.

'Don't you have a wrap or something? Something to put on.'

'I—I'm not cold.'

'It's not your temperature I was thinking of!'

He knew he was glaring ferociously. The look in her eyes and the way that she took an instinctive step backwards, away from him, told him that. But he had been knocked off balance by the discovery of her in the pool and being close to her, like this, only made matters so much worse.

He had thought that his memories of her soft-skinned, naked body were arousing enough—in fact, he had tried to convince himself that he had exaggerated her appeal. No woman, no real, living, breathing woman, could have been as physically appealing as his recollections told him she had been. But those recollections had been nothing but the truth.

Less than the truth, in fact. Because the memories had none of the warm, physical presence of this woman. And though the white swimming costume might be modest when compared with the skimpy bikinis worn by so many on the Greek beaches, its subtle sexuality was doing devastating things to his heart rate and his ability to think. The stretchy material clung to the swell of her breasts and hips, the thin straps revealing the peachy skin and soft curves of her shoulders, while the cutaway shape made her legs seem endlessly elegant. Just to think of those long legs curled around his waist, squeezing tight as she gave herself up to the throes of her orgasm, threatened to blow his mind into tiny, spinning splinters that were impossible to form into any coherent thoughts.

'We might both be able to talk more rationally if you were more—respectably dressed.'

That softly curved mouth took on a mutinous set that wasn't quite matched by the flare of something in her eyes. Not anger, but something wild and defiant, clashing with his dark glare until he almost felt he could see sparks in the air between them.

'And you think that your clothing is so much more decorous?' she flashed back, lacing the words with an unexpected sting.

'Is that a way of saying that you don't trust yourself to keep your hands off me?' Theo said scornfully. 'Because you'll have to forgive me if I don't believe you. You had no trouble tearing yourself away from my bed that night...'

'*That night* was a mistake and one I've regretted ever since.'

'Not as much as I have, lady. I don't happen to go in for one-night stands and if I'd known you were going to disappear like that, I'd have had more than second thoughts about the whole situation. And then when I find you swimming in my father's pool—'

'I never tried to deceive you in any way. I told you exactly what...'

Her voice died abruptly as she realised just what he had said. All colour fled from her cheeks, leaving her looking white as a ghost.

'Your *father's*—!'

She actually glanced back at the pool and then back to his face, her grey eyes wide with shock and disbelief.

'Did you say...?'

This couldn't be real! It couldn't be happening, Skye thought in desperation. Please let it not be happening. Please let it be a dream—a nightmare from which she could wake.

He couldn't have said *my father's pool*. Because that would make him Cyril's son. The son of the man she had to marry. The son of the man who held the fate of her whole family in his hands and who could destroy their hope of a future if he chose.

She actually caught a tiny part of her arm in her fingers and pinched hard, praying it might bring her out of the horror. But, of course, nothing happened. She was still standing there, bathed in the Greek sunlight, with the only sound that of a faint ripple of the water in the pool where a breeze hit it.

And Anton was standing beside her, big and dark and dangerous-looking.

'But you said your name was Anton.'

She flung the accusation into his cold, set face, but his expression didn't change and he continued to regard her with a stony lack of expression.

Anton...*Antonakos*. Suddenly the truth fell into place with a shock that made her head spin.

'You lied to me!'

His shrug was a swift, careless dismissal of the charge.

'I was economical with the truth. I find it's often the best policy until I get to know someone's real motives.'

The cold, slashing look he flung at her left her in no doubt that she had been included in the group of people whose motives he considered suspect. The ice in it seemed to take away all the heat of the sun so that her skin crawled with goose-bumps and it was all she could do to suppress an instinctive shiver. Reaching for the towel she had left on the wooden lounger earlier, she pulled it round her, knotting it securely over her breasts, under her armpits.

Covered, she felt a little more confident until he spoke again.

'And, as I recall, you were the one who insisted we kept to one name only.'

He was right, of course, and the knowledge of it didn't make her feel any better. Dear God, what sort of malign fate had brought her together with this man on that night? How had she had the appalling bad luck to walk into the one bar where Cyril's son had been sitting on his own?

And what had he been doing in London? All she knew about Cyril and his son was that they had not been on the best of terms for some time. So did this man know...?

The terrible reality of the whole truth she had been keeping from him made her stomach heave nauseously.

'Mine was at least my real one,' she said, taking the risk of stepping a little further into the danger zone. 'I'm Skye Marston.'

There was no flicker of anything in the opaque-eyed stare that he turned on her. So was it possible that his father hadn't told him?

'Theodore Antonakos,' he returned, totally deadpan. 'Usually known as Theo.'

The look that scoured over her made her feel as if it had scraped away a much-needed layer of skin, so that in spite of the bulky protection of the towel wrapped around her she felt exposed and naked to his cold scrutiny.

'So now what?' the man she now had to call Theo drawled with lazy mockery. 'Do we shake hands formally and really do everything totally back to front?'

'I think we'll take the handshake as read,' Skye returned stiffly. The idea of even touching him frankly terrified her. She just could not forget the burn of his skin on hers, the caressing touch of those long, powerful hands that could turn as gentle as the patting paws of a kitten when he chose or be as demanding as blazing fire. 'We've already done that bit.'

'And more,' he returned dryly, and the wicked gleam deep in those brilliant black eyes told her that he remembered every moment of it.

As did she.

That night was etched onto her brain in images of fire. It had been bad enough when it was just a memory. But now, with the man himself an actual physical force before her, not just an image in her mind, she felt as if her thoughts might go up in flames as a result.

'I'd rather forget about that.'

The tension in every inch of her body had affected her mouth too, and the words came out so tight and clipped they could hardly have been more stilted. Her voice sounded like some second-rate actress trying to speak like an upper-class Englishwoman, and strangling the sounds as she did so.

Evidently Theo thought so too, as his wide, mobile mouth twitched uncontrollably at her words. But every last trace of humour was erased from it when he spoke, and his eyes had turned to black ice under heavy, hooded lids.

'I'm sure you would, but I have to tell you that I don't feel the same.'

Provocatively he reached out a lazy hand and trailed his

fingers along her throat and across the top of the white towel, coming to a deliberate halt by the knot that held it closed.

'The truth is that the experience is one I would very much like to repeat.'

The bronzed fingertips moved to the edge of her shoulder, then back again, and it was all Skye could do to control the instinctive squirm of response that would have betrayed her feelings.

The instant peaking and hardening of her breasts was something she could do nothing about. A heat that had nothing to do with the sun, licked along her veins, making the towel seem too heavy, the clinging white swimming costume too restricting to wear underneath it. But she could only be thankful that the thick padding hid her intimate reaction from those probing black eyes.

'Then I'm afraid you'll have a long wait. I told you it was a one-night thing only.'

'You also told me that we would never know each other's names. Never meet again.'

He paused just long enough for the shocking impact of those words to hit home hard with the realisation that both of them had now been disproved.

'And *I* told you that I never do one-night stands. It's a personal rule I have.'

'Well, then, it's a rule that you're just going to have to break this time. Because I have no intention of renewing our—acquaintance in any way. One night was more than enough for me and that's the way I want things to stay.'

'Is that so?'

His arms folded across his chest, Theo looked her up and down with coldly contemptuous black eyes.

'Well, let's see.'

Before Skye had a moment to realise just what was in his thoughts, he had moved forward, taking her chin in one powerful hand and wrenching her face up towards his. She had just one split second in which to recognise the ruthless intent in his eyes, but not long enough to voice the protest that formed in her mind.

Her mouth was still opening to try and speak as his came down, hard and determined, crushing the objection straight back down her throat.

As a kiss, it was cruel and passionless, but as an act of punishment for rejecting his demand out of hand, it was perfect. There was nothing of affection or warmth in it, only a cold-blooded determination to show her who was in control here.

But it didn't stay that way.

Because something happened in the moment that their lips touched. Something that charged the atmosphere, changed the truth of that kiss into something very new and very different.

From something meant to control and be controlled, in the space of a heartbeat it flared into something totally *out* of control. Heat burned; hunger woke and demanded appeasement; need broke free of all restraint.

Skye swayed forwards, melting against Theo's hard form, and his arms came out to enclose her, imprison her along the length of him. Skin seemed to blend with skin, arms, legs, bodies entangled. Their heartbeats lurched, quickened, raced, thudding in time with each other, drowning out all other sounds beyond the pulse of molten blood in their veins. Their only breathing was the quickly snatched gasps of urgent passion, grabbed at frantically to avoid oblivion, but allowing for only the briefest moments away from the clinging, teasing, openly demanding mouth of the other.

'Skye—beauty—*agape mou*…'

Theo's voice was thick and rough with lust, his hands as clumsy as they tugged at the barrier of soft towelling that came between them, pulling the insecure knot loose in seconds, the white folds tumbling to the ground at their feet.

'You may have had enough but I have not. I want this—'

Skye's mouth opened under his in a gasp of shocked delight as his hand skimmed over her straining body, heat searing through the white Lycra, inflaming her hunger even more.

'And I want this…'

That searching hand found the swell of one breast where the betraying nipple pulsed against the restraint of the clinging material, his thumb catching and circling the hardened bud, making her moan aloud in wild expression of her need.

'Oh, yes, this.'

It was a low, dark undertone, with fiendish laughter running through it. Laughter that darkened even further as his urgent fingers tugged at the strap of her costume, wrenching it down over her shoulder, imprisoning her arm against her side and exposing the white slope of her upper breast.

While the hard warmth of his hand supported the soft weight, his hungry mouth sought the exposed flesh, kissing, licking, even nipping lightly at the smooth skin until Skye flung back her head and moaned aloud.

'This is what I want,' he muttered harshly against her. 'And it's what you want too. What we both want more than all the world. It's what's between us, lady. You can't fight it, and neither can I.'

The only response Skye could manage was a wild, indeterminate sound that could have been either acceptance or denial, but clearly Theo took it as acceptance.

'Come with me, my lovely. Come with me now…'

'No!'

Skye had no idea just what it was that jolted her out of the heated fantasy into which she'd fallen. She didn't know if it was some faint, unexpected sound that intruded in her mental delirium, or the way that Theo's mouth had left her breast or the sudden cooling touch of a tiny breeze that wafted its way across her exposed skin. She only knew that some unexpected sneaking coldness had slipped into her mind, dousing the heat that raged, stunning her into shocked realisation of just what she was doing.

'I said no!'

Desperation gave her a strength she hadn't known she possessed so that she could push him away, hard, the force of the movement driving him almost to the edge of the pool. But he recovered in a second, whirling back to face her, black eyes glittering in cold rage.

'What do you mean—?'

'Oh, come on!'

The frantic tattoo her heart was beating at the thought of the narrow escape she had just had, the shivering sensation brought by the realisation of how close she had come to total disaster, made Skye's voice range up and down in panic, but at least she sounded strong enough and determined enough to make him stop and listen to her.

'What part of no don't you understand? You may be Greek, *Kyrios* Antonakos, but your English isn't as bad as that. You know exactly what I meant!'

'I know what you *said*,' Theo flung back venomously. 'But that isn't exactly what you *meant*. And I don't need to know any English at all to differentiate between the two. I have other ways of interpreting that.'

'Other ways?'

For a moment Skye simply gaped in blank confusion, but then he gave a slow, deliberate glance from those polished jet eyes, away from her face and dropping down to rest on her still-exposed breast—and the betraying tightness of the pouting nipple, blatant evidence to anyone who wanted to look of the hunger he had roused in her. A hunger that was still clawing at her insides, making it almost impossible to think beyond the burning sense of need.

But she *had* to think. She had to stop feeling and force her mind to concentrate on what really mattered. She had almost ruined everything. Almost destroyed her chances of rescuing her family from the total disaster that faced them. The man before her, tall and strong, with the sunlight playing on the silken black hair, the bronzed skin of his face and chest, might be everything she most wanted in the world right now, but she had to force that weak, indulgent feeling from her mind and *think*.

And what she had to think was that this must not, could not, happen.

If she wanted to save her family, then Theo Antonakos was forbidden to her.

And so she wrenched up the dangling strap of the swimming costume, wincing in distress as the white Lycra scraped over the sensitised tip of her aching breast. Pulling the little clothing she had as high as it would go, she forced herself to face Theo's cold-eyed fury with what she hoped looked like a degree of calm she was far from feeling.

'I don't give a damn about your "other ways"!' she managed, the brutal control she was exerting over her voice making it sound high and tight, and absolutely cold with rejection. 'The one thing you listen to is what I *say*! And what I say is *no*—got that? N-O. No! I'm saying no and I *mean* no.'

For one fearful second there was such a maelstrom of rage in his face, blazing in his eyes, that she actually feared he would ignore her and reach out, grab her once again. She had nerved herself for flight when she saw him recollect himself, shake his head faintly and impose a degree of control over his actions that she had to admire even as she welcomed it with a shaking rush of relief.

But if Theo had controlled his physical impulses, he had not yet restrained his tongue.

'You say that now, sweetheart,' he declared with brutal

cynicism, 'but that no was a long time coming. So tell me, my lovely, what was it that forced the rejection from you? Was it the thought that someone else might see us—your mama perhaps?'

'Mama?' Skye echoed blankly, unable to believe he had used the word. Had he really said…?

'Because if that's what it was, my angel, then I'm certain you don't need to worry. I'm sure she'd be perfectly happy for us both.'

'Happy?'

Just what was he talking about? Every word confused her even more. What had her mother to do with this? Did Theo know…?

'Keep it in the family, so to speak. Your mother, my father—you and me.'

Your mother, my father…

Skye's thoughts reeled sickeningly. He thought her mother was his father's fiancée! He actually believed that she was here with her mother and that her mother was the one about to marry Cyril Antonakos!

'Well?'

Skye's silence, the stunned look on her face, puzzled Theo. Defiance he could understand; even anger would be perfectly explicable. But all the anger that had burned in her seemed to have fizzled out, subsiding like a damp squib that had never actually exploded.

And in a way that disappointed him.

He was spoiling for a fight. Had been ever since she had tried to claim that she didn't want him any more. It stung his pride to hear her declare that, especially when a tension in the sexy body in the clinging white swimsuit and a particular light in the depths of those dove-grey eyes revealed the statement for the lie that it was.

She couldn't have been more aware of him if she had been a nervous young deer who had come upon a hunting tiger in the middle of a clearing. She seemed unaware of the way that she was uneasily shifting her weight from one foot to another, her eyes warily watching his slightest move. Even the fine nostrils seemed to flare in apprehension every time he moved or spoke.

Like hell, she'd had enough of him! Just as there was no way that he had ever tired of her.

Anger and hurt pride had pushed him into action, making him pull her close. And her reaction had been everything that he had anticipated. Everything he had wanted. She had turned to flames in his arms, going up like the driest of kindling laid at the base of a fire, her passion so fierce that he had almost felt his skin might have melted in the heat of it. She had responded to his kiss with all the hunger and the desire that he'd dreamed of.

And he had been lost. Swamped by heat and desire; his body hardening in a second. He had lost all awareness of where he was.

He had thought that he had taken her along with him. Her responses had been everything he could have wanted, her kisses adding fuel to the fires blazing within him. He had been so sure that she was his. That once more he would have her in his bed—and that this time he would make sure it was for much longer than one night.

One night with her had already taught him that it was nowhere near long enough to sate himself on her body. One night had only made him realise what hunger really was and how much he wanted this woman in his bed. Finding her here like this, after his vain search for her in London, had been such an unexpected thrill and he was prepared to do whatever it took to keep her here.

The fight, the tension between them had only added to the electrical current of desire that sparked his appetite for her. And her sudden rejection of him, the way she had pulled away, had left him fiercely frustrated, his aroused body ready to take the satisfaction it needed.

Now she had just backed down.

Apparently with nothing to say, she was simply staring at him as if he had suddenly grown an extra head, her big eyes wide and clouded with something that looked like shock.

'Well?' he repeated. 'What do you say?'

'I…' she began, but her voice trailed off, dying into silence once again.

Theo's hands clamped tight shut at his sides, struggling to resist the urge to shake her from this trance she seemed to have fallen into.

'Skye!'

But as he spoke another voice came from the direction of the house, breaking into what he had been about to say and silencing him too.

'Theo! There you are! Amalthea said you had arrived.'

Taken by surprise, Theo muttered a dark curse under his breath. His father's appearance was the last thing he wanted right now.

After five years' estrangement, not speaking, not even sending letters, this first meeting with Cyril was going to be awkward enough without anyone else there. The presence of someone else—and just who that someone was— was a complication he could do without.

'*Pateras.*'

A sudden movement drew his eyes from the dark, heavy-set man now approaching and back to Skye. She had snatched up the white towel from the ground and was once more knotting it hastily round her body. Such unexpected modesty on her part frankly surprised him. And so did her sudden loss of colour. Every trace of blood had ebbed from her cheeks, leaving her looking strained and almost ill, the wide grey eyes huge pools above the ashen cheeks.

'Skye?'

It came out on an undertone of concern, keeping the low-voiced question from his father's hearing. Theo knew better than most that the older man could be difficult and autocratic in his business dealings and with other men. But with women—particularly young, attractive women—he was usually a practised charmer, unlikely to cause such a panic-stricken reaction in any member of the opposite sex.

So was there some tension between his father and Skye Marston that he knew nothing about? It was going to make for an awkward relationship between Cyril and his about-to-be stepdaughter if that was the case.

But Skye had already turned away from him and was watching Cyril's approach, her face hidden so that he couldn't read any further changes in her expression.

'So you two have met already.'

If there was something wrong, then clearly Cyril wasn't aware of it as he directed a smile straight into Skye's face. His greeting of his son was more restrained, his expression several degrees short of warm, but he took the hand that Theo offered him and shook it hard.

'Good to have you back under my roof again, boy.'

That 'boy' grated as Theo was sure it was supposed to. His father had never accepted that he had grown up long ago. That had been one of the reasons for their estrangement.

But he had promised himself that this time he would really try to keep the peace.

'I couldn't miss the wedding,' he said, unable to erase the stiffness from his tone.

'Of course not. And you had to meet your new step-mother—which I see you've already done.'

Already done?

Thoughts spinning, Theo tried to force the words to make

sense, but failed completely. There was no logic to them—not unless...

Hell—no! His mind revolted at the thought. He refused to accept the way he was thinking. It was impossible—had to be.

But his father's arm had gone around Skye's waist, and he was turning her round to face his son. 'Still, I'll do the formal introductions now.'

No! Theo wanted to shout it at the top of his voice to drown out what was coming. He wanted to put his hands over his father's mouth to stop him speaking—anything—stem the flow of words that seemed to be leading inexorably to the most appalling conclusion.

It couldn't be—*Theos,* let it not be possible.

But Skye's cheeks seemed to have grown even paler. And her huge light grey eyes looked anywhere but into his face as his father continued blithely with his announcement, totally unaware of the impact it was having.

'Theo, I want you to meet Skye Marston, soon to be Skye Antonakos. Your new stepmother-to-be and, of course, my fiancée.'

CHAPTER SIX

IF LOOKS could kill then she would have died a thousand times over tonight, Skye thought miserably as she tried once more to make a pretence of eating the meal that had been put in front of her. The cold blaze of fury in the black eyes of the man sitting opposite felt as if it had the power to shrivel her into nothing where she sat, reducing her to just a small bundle of ashes on her chair.

She wished that the earth would just open and swallow her up, anything so that she didn't have to be here. She would much rather have escaped to her room and stayed hidden there all night.

But there was no escape. Cyril Antonakos liked a formal dinner in the evenings and he expected his family and guests to dress up for it. So she had been forced to put on the elegant peacock-blue silk dress he had told her to wear, pin her hair up into an elegant roll at the back of her head and sit down at the big wooden table to endure the worst sort of torture by food.

She had no idea at all what she was supposed to be eating, only that it had as much taste and texture as stewed sawdust and that it was impossible to swallow anything because her throat seemed to have closed up completely.

And the all the time Theo Antonakos was watching her like a hawk eyeing its prey, watching, waiting, judging the best time to swoop down and pounce. And just like some tiny, shivering dormouse cowering on the ground and watching the shadow of the predator's wings circling overhead, she had no doubt that when he did decide to act, then the attack would be swift, merciless—and totally lethal.

She was just surprised that he hadn't denounced her to his father from the first moment he had realised who she was. She had fully expected the condemnation to come as soon as the introduction had been made and her heart had stopped beating, her breath catching in her throat as she'd waited for the words that would ruin her and her family and bring the whole delicate structure of Cyril's unexpected offer to rescue them tumbling down around her.

But to her astonishment it hadn't happened. Somehow Theo had controlled the burn of fury deep inside him, though, seeing the anger that had blazed in his eyes, Skye had recognised that it was there and only the most savage and ruthless control was what held it back, kept it from showing in his voice when he had replied to his father's introduction.

'Ms Marston and I had just made ourselves known to each other,' he said smoothly. So smoothly that Skye actually blinked hard in shock at the skilful way he managed to fake an easy calm that he was clearly so very far from feeling. 'You're a lucky man, Father, to have such a beautiful fiancée.'

And then, when she was least expecting it, and when she certainly wasn't at all emotionally prepared, he shocked her rigid by holding out his hand to her in a pretence of a formal greeting.

'It's a pleasure to meet you, Ms Marston.'

That 'pleasure' was laced with a darkly sardonic intonation that turned it into a mockery of the true meaning of the word.

And it made Skye recall, so unwillingly, the way that earlier he had taunted her, 'Do we shake hands formally and really do everything totally back to front?'

The memory almost made her snatch her hand away, jumping back from the burn of his skin against hers, the pressure of palm on palm. But to do that was to risk alerting his father to the fact that something was wrong. At the moment, Cyril Antonakos was beaming with proud satisfaction as he watched what he believed was the first meeting between his fiancée and the estranged son who had newly returned home. How quickly that smile would fade, his mood changing rapidly if he was even to suspect that they had met before—never mind realising in what circumstances that meeting had taken place.

Just thinking of it made Skye's hand shudder still within Theo's grasp, and feeling it he tightened his grip on her cruelly. Looking into the black depths of his eyes, she saw the danger that smouldered there, searing over her face in a look of pure contempt. It was as if he was sending her a wordless message through the merciless pressure on her fingers.

'I can break you as quickly and easily as I can crush your hand,' he seemed to be saying. 'And I will—as and when I want to.'

She had been waiting for him to act ever since. All through the painfully awkward moments after Cyril's arrival, and Theo's realisation of just what her position in his family was. Then she had had to go to her room to shower and change, and get ready for the evening. She had had to leave father and son alone then, unable to find any excuse to stay with them, but she had rushed through her preparations, terrified by the thought that when she returned to the main living room Theo might have decided to tell his father the truth, and all hell would have broken loose.

She had nerved herself to see a dark scowl on the older man's face. A smug, cruel satisfaction lighting his son's black eyes. Struggling with the fear that gripped her at the thought that she might be told to pack her bags and go home—and that her father, her family, could rot in hell—she had found that her legs were trembling so hard they would barely support her as she'd made her way from her bedroom on the lower floor and into the airy white-painted living room.

But Theo had said nothing, it seemed. If he had then Cyril would not have come forward with a smile to give her his usual peck on the cheek, and offer her a drink.

'We're having champagne tonight, my dear,' he said. 'It is, after all, a time for celebration.'

'The return of the prodigal son,' Theo supplied dryly.

Like his father, he got up from his seat as she came into the room and was holding out to her a delicate crystal flute filled with bubbling pale wine.

'And of course to celebrate your own arrival into the family.'

He was so close to her that there was no way his father could have seen the cold black stare that accompanied the apparently welcoming words. But Skye saw it, and as a result her hand shook so violently as she took her drink that some of the champagne slopped over the edge and spilled onto the fine silk of her skirt.

'Careful,' Theo said. 'You don't want to spoil things.'

He smiled as he spoke, but the icy glitter of his eyes, and the soft but deadly menace of his tone, left Skye in no doubt at all that the warning was meant in a way that was very different from a concern about her dress.

As a result she had been desperately on edge all evening, waiting for the axe to fall, for Theo to speak out and reveal the dark secret that would ruin everything.

But for now he was clearly biding his time, and hiding his cruel intent behind a smiling mask.

'So how did you two meet?' he asked now, pushing aside his plate and leaning back in his chair, a glass of rich red wine in one hand.

It was an innocent enough question—on the surface at least. But underneath the lazily drawled words lurked so many dangerous rocks that could sink her totally if she wasn't careful.

Instinctively Skye turned to Cyril, conceding to him automatically. When he had come up with his proposal, he had insisted on absolute secrecy. Their marriage was to look genuine, with no hint of the deal behind it, and of course both Skye and her father had been only too glad to agree.

'Business,' was what he said, helping himself to another portion of the rich baklava that had formed their dessert. 'Skye's father runs a couple of my hotels in England.'

'In London?' Both Theo's tone and his eyes had sharpened and Skye shivered faintly, knowing where his thoughts were heading.

'No—Suffolk. Country house hotels—part of the group but out of the capital.'

'But Suffolk isn't far from London, is it?'

Theo raised his glass to his lips, sipped slowly, black eyes moving to lock with grey over the top of it. His fierce, unwavering gaze held hers mesmerically.

'Do you go into London very often, *Kyria* Marston?'

'Skye, please.'

She forced it from between lips that felt as if they were carved from wood.

'And, no—I don't go into London.'

'Not at all?'

Careful! Skye warned herself. One false step and he would swoop like that hunting eagle. But she didn't want him to think he had her on the run. It might feel like that, of course—she was very definitely trapped with her back against a wall, but she was damned if she was going to run away in panic and leave the field to him. She might just as well surrender right here and now and tell Cyril the truth about their meeting herself.

She could at least give Theo Antonakos a run for his money.

Deliberately she picked up her own glass, swirled the wine around in the bottom of it, then looked him straight in the eye again.

'Well, obviously, I do go to London every now and then—but not often. And to tell you the truth, I can't remember the last time I was there.'

Her defiance caught his attention. One black brow lifted sharply in sardonic response and he inclined his dark head in a small acknowledgement of the way she had parried his attack.

Oh, but she was good, Theo admitted to himself. This Skye Marston was a superb actress—so good that, if he didn't now know exactly what was going on, he would have been totally convinced by her performance.

He had met her precisely twice—for less than a day at a time—and on those occasions she had been perhaps half a dozen different women, changing her personality and her behaviour as quickly and easily as he changed his clothes.

Looking at her now, no one would ever guess that she had been that nervous, distressed creature in the London bar, let alone the wild, passionate woman who had been in his bed that night.

Now here she was the picture of cool elegance in that sleek turquoise silk dress, sleeveless and with a deep vee neckline. Silver glittered at her ears and around the long graceful neck, exposed by the way she had piled that glorious rich coloured hair up at the back of her neck, and she looked calm, relaxed and totally in control.

But she couldn't really be in control, any more than he could. She had to know that their shared secret was there, between them, like a dark shadow.

He lifted his glass again to drink, then reconsidered and only pretended to sip from it. His head was clouded enough. His thoughts had been reeling since the instant in which his father's announcement had hit him like a punch to his jaw, and he still hadn't decided what to do about it.

'You don't want to go out—to clubs—or bars?'

He wasn't quite sure who was watching whom—only that it seemed to him as if there were no one in the room but the two of them. His father might have disappeared completely, and the quiet, decorous presence of a couple of maids barely impinged on his consciousness.

'Skye doesn't frequent clubs and such.'

It was Cyril who answered, reminding Theo sharply of the fact that he was there, at the head of the table. That this was his house—his father's home—and the woman opposite was his father's future bride.

'That's one of the things that attracted me to her. Her innocence. She's not like so many modern young women.'

This time Theo really did have to gulp down a large mouthful of his wine, if only to stop himself from laughing out loud, or making some cynical comment, revealing just precisely how he felt about that statement.

So she had his father totally conned. The old man had no idea at all what she was really like.

So why didn't he just tell him? Why didn't he just open his mouth and say the words?

Your fiancée is not at all the woman you think she is.

The words sounded so clearly inside his head that for one heart-stopping moment he almost thought he'd said them aloud and froze, waiting for the explosion that would follow.

But nothing happened. The declaration had just been in his imagination and the conversation continued just as before—his father blithely ignorant of the emotional grenade that had almost exploded right in his face.

Because that was the effect it would have had. In one

split second, Cyril Antonakos would have gone from being the proudly possessive fiancé of a beautiful, stylish, sexy...

Oh, *Theos,* so devastatingly sexy...

A gorgeous, glamorous, much younger woman.

One moment, Cyril would have been the envy of all men with such a woman on his arm—the next he would have known the sordid truth.

'Her mother has been unwell. So Skye spends most of her time at home, caring for her.'

Except when she's out trawling bars, picking up strange men...

Once more Theo had to bite down hard on his lower lip to stop the words from escaping.

Skye's stunning eyes had dropped, staring down at her hands on the table, and it was all he could do not to laugh out loud in cynical admiration. As a pose of innocent modesty, it was damn near perfect—except that he knew it was a lie and so did she.

So why didn't he just admit it? Why didn't he announce to his father that the woman Cyril thought was a sweet, unworldly, family type wasn't anything of the sort?

Because if he did then, as well as damning her, he would destroy himself in his father's eyes. In fact, he would probably end up painted as the villain of the piece and Cyril would turn his back on him once and for all—for good this time. His father would cut him out of his life without a second thought.

And he had vowed that if his father ever held out an olive branch of peace he would grab it with both hands. That he would do everything in his power to repair the breach that had come between them; end the estrangement if he possibly could.

That was why he was here now. Why he had come to be the best man at the wedding—unaware of just who the bride his father had chosen was. He knew what interpretation his father would probably put on it. That he had come crawling back because he thought that doing so would change Cyril's mind about cutting him out of his will.

Well, if that was the case, then he would take a great delight in letting the old man know that he had no need at all of anyone else's money. He had more than enough of his own.

But this island was a very different matter. Helikos had come to Cyril through his first wife—Theo's mother. It had been in her family for centuries. Calista Antonakos had been buried here, as had both her father and mother before her. It was Theo's rightful inheritance, and one he would fight for with the last strength in his body. He certainly didn't intend to lose it because of some little gold-digger who had caught his father's attention. This year's wife who, if she followed the example of every other *Kyria* Antonakos, would be here and gone again in the space of a couple of years.

'That is unusual,' he managed, knowing from the tiny flicker of a glance in his direction that Skye was unable to control that the acid tone of the words hadn't been lost on her. 'I have to admit that in anyone else I might find it hard to accept about any modern young woman. But, having met your lovely fiancée, I can believe anything of her. Why, when I first encountered her this afternoon, she was embarrassed at being caught in just her swimming costume— in spite of the fact that it was a far more modest design than so many I have seen.'

She was listening hard again. All her attention was focused on his face, and the way those slender, elegant hands were nervously folding her napkin over and over on itself betrayed the inner tension that she had managed to smooth from her expression. She was not at all sure just in what direction he was going to take this and that thought gave him an intense, dark satisfaction.

He waited a nicely calculated moment before continuing with deliberate casualness.

'In fact, there was one woman I met last weekend… She was exactly Skye's age—and build—but the skirt she wore was barely there. She was probably showing far more flesh than you were this afternoon, Stepmama.'

Oh, she didn't like that! She had definitely winced at that 'Stepmama', flinching back in her chair at his tone.

'So it was hardly surprising that she got herself into trouble with some roughs in a bar—'

But Skye had clearly had enough. Dropping the napkin down on the table, she suddenly met his mocking gaze head on, a new flame of bravado in her soft grey eyes.

'That's precisely why I never go into bars or clubs if I can help it!' she declared defiantly. 'You can never tell what sort of thug you might meet there.'

Thug! It was meant to sting and it did.

Whatever else he had been that night, *thug* didn't describe it. He had treated her as well as she had any right to expect, when she had come on to him as she had. But of course she would want to make out that she had been the innocent in all this, to win the sympathy vote, just in case Cyril ever found out the truth.

A black tide of rage swamped his mind, drowning all rational thought, and his hand clenched so tightly on the stem of the wineglass that he was within an inch of snapping it sharply in two.

He couldn't stand to be in the room with the lying, conniving little bitch any longer. He had to get out of here or explode. And if he did lose his temper, then he would take Skye Marston and her calculated play-acting with him. He would tell the truth about their meeting—give his father every single gory detail, and then walk out while the shock waves were reverberating round the house.

But those shock waves would damage his world too.

They would take the fragile peace he had made with his father and shatter it irrevocably into tiny, irreparable pieces. If he took Skye Marston down, then she would take his last chance of inheriting Helikos with her. And he wasn't prepared to let that go.

Not for a cheap little tramp who was clearly well practised in lying through her teeth.

'Well, you don't need to worry about getting rid of me,' he said, tossing down his own napkin and getting to his feet. He directed what he hoped was obviously a fake smile of understanding, his gaze going to where his father's hand still rested on her arm.

'I can see that you two would obviously like to be alone—and I'd hate to intrude. Besides, I'm expecting a call from a young lady.'

It was only his secretary with news of a contract he was working on, but hell would freeze over before he would admit to that.

'So I'll say goodnight, Father—Stepmama. And I'll see you in the morning.'

He was proud of the way that he managed to stroll from the room. Pleased with the fact that he didn't pause or look back, or even show that he gave a damn about what he was leaving behind him. He knew he appeared relaxed, casual and totally at ease.

The truth couldn't be more different.

Because, no matter how much he might tell himself that he had kept quiet only because of Helikos, he knew that the real truth was much more complicated than that. Ever since that night they had spent together in London he hadn't been able to get the searingly erotic images of Skye Marston out of his thoughts—and he still couldn't. Just sitting opposite her had set off a string of heated images that circled over and over in his thoughts until he felt he would go mad.

He didn't want to think of them—didn't want to think of her.

But the truth was that he could think of nothing else.

CHAPTER SEVEN

HE MIGHT as well face facts; he was never going to sleep.

Theo finally admitted to himself that he had no chance at all of drifting into the welcome unconsciousness of slumber, no matter how hard he tried.

He had been tossing and turning in his bed for an hour or more now, and even working on the intensely boring business documents he had tried to use to numb his mind into sleeping had not had the desired effect. He was as wide awake as he had been when he'd left the dining table—wider, in fact, as his struggle not to think of Skye Marston had left him feeling more and more restless with each second that passed.

Eventually he gave up completely, tossed the file down onto the floor, flung himself out of bed and dragged on the pair of swimming shorts that he had discarded earlier.

He had wanted to swim earlier and had been frustrated. Finding Skye in the pool had driven every other thought from his head.

But now he felt so restless and edgy, with a tension building up inside him like the growing oppression before a storm. He had to act or explode. He had to do *something*! And exercise was the sanest, the safest thing he could think of.

Swimming in the still of the night, with only the moon for light, was a calming, relaxing experience. There was no one around, only the sound of an owl hooting once or twice to disturb the silence. Theo swam the length of the pool over and over and over again, backwards and forwards. Long, powerful strokes swept through the water, his mus-

cular legs kicked again and again, until at last he felt a
degree of peace descend on him.

Slowly, he began to tire, but still he pushed himself
harder and further until his muscles ached and his breathing
had a raw edge to it.

'Enough,' he muttered at one last turn. 'Enough.'

Now, at last, he felt he might sleep.

If he could just keep Skye Marston from his mind then
he might actually get some rest. It was after one in the
morning, time to go to bed.

The single-storeyed pool house was in darkness. Only a
small lamp by the door glowed to break up the pitch-black
that came from being so far out in the country without a
single street lamp for miles. But Theo knew his way around
from growing up here as a boy. Shaking the water drops
from his soaked hair, he padded into the hall, confident and
sure on bare feet. Pausing only to snatch up a towel from
a hook in the shower room, he made his way to the kitchen,
rubbing himself dry as he went.

The light switch was to his left. Not even needing to
look, he reached out a hand and clicked it on.

And froze in shock at the sight of the silent female figure
sitting at the kitchen table, her face pale, her back stiffly
upright, and her hands folded on the surface in front of her.

She was dressed in just a simple white tee shirt and jeans,
her feet bare. The long red hair was loose and fell unstyled
over her shoulders and down her back; there was no trace
of make-up at all that he could see on her pale, soft face,
and she looked stunning.

So stunning that he cursed the kick his heart gave just
at the sight of her. The next moment he instinctively moved
the towel he was holding so that it fell down in front of
him, hiding the instant hardness that strained against the
front of his shorts. How could he still respond to just the

sight of this woman like this when he now knew just what she was?

An hour's swim in the cool water of the swimming pool and he still felt like this! Hot and hungry in the space of a heartbeat. He was frankly surprised that the remains of the water on his body weren't evaporating from the heat of his skin in a cloud of steam. What he needed was to go and plunge back into the water.

That or a very long, very cold shower.

'What the hell are you doing here?'

'Waiting for you,' Skye said quietly. 'We have to talk.'

'No, we don't. I don't have to do anything I don't want and I don't want to talk to you.'

Skye drew in a deep breath and carefully tried to adjust her thoughts, find the new approach that would fit better with this obviously truculent mood he was in.

'I need to talk to you.'

'Maybe you do—though I don't see why. Seems to me you made your decision about things a week ago when you decided to use me for a one-night stand and then disappear out of my life—back to my father's bed.'

'Oh, no!'

That brought her head up sharply. She couldn't have him believing that! The situation was bad enough as it was, but she couldn't let him continue to think that way.

'I never—I mean—we never... We don't share a bed, your father and I. And we've never...'

Her voice trailed off as Theo slashed a hand through the air in a brutal silencing gesture.

'Enough!' he declared harshly. 'Way too much information. Though at least I'm spared the worry that my papa might start banging on the door, demanding to be let in, having woken in the middle of the night and found that his fiancée has crept away from his bed for a midnight assignation with his son.'

There was such savage anger in the last words that Skye
found herself flinching back in her chair, fearful of the cold
fury in his voice. But Theo made no move towards her. In
fact, from the moment that he had come in the door and
found her sitting here, he hadn't moved an inch. Instead he
was standing stock still, just as he had when he'd flicked
on the light to see her.

'N-no—that won't happen.'

The shake in her voice didn't come from the moment of
fear. Instead, it was all purely feminine awareness. She desperately needed to get her thoughts and her feelings under
control so that she could function properly. But functioning
at all was almost beyond her; functioning *properly* was entirely out of the question. And it became more difficult with
every second that passed simply because of the way that
Theo looked.

She knew he'd been swimming because she'd heard the
faint splashing of the water as she'd made her way up from
the lower level where her bedroom was to the main terrace.
She hadn't dared use the lift inside the house in case
Cyril woke and heard its faint hum and came to see what
was going on, so she had used the outdoor stairs that were
carved into the rock of the cliffside, moving hesitantly in
the dimly lit darkness.

The moon had been shining down on the swimming pool
as she'd passed it, keeping closely to the shadows so as not
to be seen. And in the pale light she had seen Theo's dark
head, the flash of his muscular arms as he powered through
the water, from one end to the next—a swift, neat turn, and
back again. Again and again.

The moonlight had turned him into an eerie, almost un-
earthly being. His broad chest and back had been bathed
with silver, gleaming and beautiful, making her think of a
dolphin she had seen out in the bay only that morning. She
had stayed there for a few stolen minutes, watching hyp-

notised, unable to turn away. Her mouth had dried and her heart felt as if it were beating a rapid tattoo in her chest. She could have stayed there all night, but the sudden fear of being seen, either by the man in the pool or his father, had pushed her into action. Fear had sent her hurrying to the pool house where she had waited, nerves stretched taut with apprehension, until she had heard Theo come in the door.

When he'd switched the light on, all the feelings she had experienced outside had flooded back in full force. But in a very different way.

Where outside he had been silver and darkness, elemental, ethereal, a fantasy of a merman, here he was heat and light and physical strength. He was a real man with warm, bronzed skin, still spattered lightly with sparkling water drops. His black eyes burned under lush, thick lashes, and the blood that pulsed through his veins made his body glow with health and masculine vigour.

The moon man had made her heart catch in admiration and astonishment, but she had only wanted to watch and keep her distance from him. This man made her think of life and passion and sex and her own blood heated at the memory of how it had felt to be held in his arms, her head pillowed on the hard, warm width of that chest.

'Your father is fast asleep. I heard him snoring. He had plenty to drink at dinner.'

'So did I, but it didn't exactly guarantee a night's sleep.'

Theo rubbed the towel over his still wet hair, ruffling it in a way that Skye found shockingly endearing. He looked suddenly young and almost boyish in a way that she would be all kinds of a fool to even think of believing. Theo Antonakos was no boy—and she would do well to remember that. He was all man—and hard and dangerous with it.

'If it had, you wouldn't have found the house empty when you arrived.'

He paused, cold black eyes searing over her in sharp assessment.

'Or was that the idea? Did you have plans of sneaking into my bed and seducing—?'

'No!'

She couldn't even let him finish the appalling sentence. Couldn't let him allow even the *thought* of such a thing into his mind.

'No way! That wasn't what I had in mind at all. As I said, I came to talk.'

Theo's sigh was weary, resigned, as he raked a hand through his damp hair and slicked it back from his face.

'Then can it wait until I put some clothes on?'

'Oh—yes—sorry—of course.'

She was gabbling like an idiot, wondering if he had caught her watching him like a child in a sweet shop, almost drooling over the delights on show.

She must *not* think like that. Think practical, Skye. Find something to *do*—to distract you. If she even let in the thought of him stripping off those clinging swimming shorts, rubbing the big body dry...

No!

Such thoughts were far too dangerous to her peace of mind.

What peace of mind? She hadn't known any such thing since *that night,* when Theo Antonakos had come into her life like a nuclear explosion. And now she was struggling to deal with the devastation that was the aftermath.

'Of course. You go and change. Shall I make some coffee?'

'You really do want to make sure that I have no chance at all of sleeping tonight, don't you? No coffee. And no wine. Seems to me I'm going to need a clear head for this. There's some mineral water in the fridge. Glasses in the cupboard above it.'

He had disappeared in the direction of the bedroom by the time that any of his comments really registered on Skye's already jumbled brain.

You really do want to make sure that I have no chance at all of sleeping tonight, don't you?

Had he meant that, like her, he had been lying awake, unable to sleep? Was that why he had taken to swimming in the middle of the night?

And if so, then what sort of thoughts had kept him awake and restless?

Don't go there! she told herself. Don't risk it!

Because the truth was that she didn't know which was the greater risk to her mental balance: knowing that Theo had lain awake thinking of her—or knowing that he had *not*.

She didn't have time to think, anyway. She had barely found the water and the glasses before Theo was back with her.

He had pulled on a loose navy tee shirt and a pair of jogging trousers. Both items were old and baggy and shouldn't have been sexy at all. But it didn't matter what this man wore, he still took her breath away. Perhaps it was because she knew, and remembered so well, just what the body underneath the clothes was like, so that he could have worn an old sack and still have had the impact of a blow to her heart.

She had a nasty little fight with herself to keep her hand from shaking as she filled a glass with the sparkling water and held it out to him. The faint brush of his fingers as he took it from her sent a sensation like an electric shock shooting up her arm and to disguise the betraying reaction she reached for her own glass and gulped down half of it without pausing for breath.

'So talk.' Theo had barely touched his own drink before putting the glass back down on the table. He leaned against the wall and folded his arms across his chest, narrowed eyes focusing tightly on her face. 'You said you wanted to talk— so talk.'

'Are you going to say anything?'

Oh, damn, she hadn't meant it to come out like that. She'd planned on being calm and reasonable. On coming round to the point gradually. Instead she'd just blurted out what was uppermost in her mind without a second's thought.

'About what?'

'Oh, don't play games! You know very well about what! Are you going to say anything to your father?'

Theo's dark head went back, resting against the door post, his black, gleaming stare impenetrable and impassive in a coldly inscrutable face.

'My father...' he said at last, drawling the words out with a slow deliberation that tightened nerves already close to snapping until she felt she wanted to scream. 'Why should I tell him anything?'

'Oh!'

The unexpected answer was such a relief that all the tension left Skye in a sudden rush so that she sagged against the nearest chair like a puppet whose strings had been cut. The release from tension was so great that her head was spinning with it and she was totally unable to think of anything beyond the feeling of elation that rushed through her like a flood tide.

'Oh, thank you!' She gasped. 'Thank you! Thank...'

The words shrivelled on her lips as her vision cleared and she caught the way he was looking at her. She saw the dark frown that drew his black brows together, the cold, assessing glance from those jet eyes, and suddenly knew she had made a terrible mistake.

'You...'

'*I'm* not going to tell my father anything,' Theo stated icily. 'I think that's your responsibility.'

'What?'

Skye had been swallowing a sip of water as he spoke and she knew a moment of real horror as her throat seemed to close around the drink, threatening to choke her. It was only with a struggle that she managed to regain control, and gulp it down. But even then her voice on the question was shrill and raw, as if her vocal cords were still tightly twisted.

'What do you mean?'

'I know you heard what I said.'

Theo levered himself away from the wall and moved into the adjoining sitting room, flinging himself down into a chair and leaning back, stretching out long legs on the wooden floor in front of him.

'And I'm damn sure you understood it. So why ask for an explanation? You know this is what you have to do.'

'But—yes, of course I understand, but…'

Theo's sigh was a masterpiece—a perfect blend of irritation, impatience and a ruthless control and his eyes were cold as ice floes as he turned them on her.

'You weren't thinking of doing anything else?'

'But I can't!'

Nightmare visions of the disastrous consequences that would follow if she did as Theo expected filled Skye's thoughts, leaving her shaking and fighting back tears.

Her whole world would fall apart. No, there would be no world for her if that was to happen. Her family would be destroyed—her father in prison…her mother…

'I won't do it! I can't!'

'You don't have any alternative,' Theo stated with unyielding brutality. 'Either you tell him or I do.'

Skye closed her eyes against the fear that crawled along her spine. He didn't know what he was asking. But she couldn't tell him. She had given her word to Cyril that she would never reveal to anyone the real reason for their marriage, and if she broke it then her father would be in trouble—but her mother would be the one who would suffer.

'Please don't do this,' she whispered. 'Please.'

'So what would you prefer I did?' Theo enquired with dark cynicism. 'Let my father live a lie—and live one myself by watching him marry you? Dance at your wedding?'

The acid on the words was so savage she felt it would strip the skin from her bones. She wanted to run—to take to her heels and flee, never looking back. But the time for that was long gone; if, indeed, she had ever had a chance. She only had one hope of salvaging anything for her family from this; though even that was impossible if Theo carried out his threat.

'I'm not asking that.'

Putting down her glass with a hand that shook so much she barely avoided dropping it right onto the wooden floor, she moved to his side, perching herself on the arm of the chair and looking deep into his dark, closed face.

'But please don't do this, Theo.'

Something flickered in the blackness of his eyes but, whatever it was, it was definitely not a sign of any weakening or even any concession.

Instead, he regarded her with his face still set in that cold, stony expression, rejection of her plea radiating from him like a force. Talking to him was like banging her head hard against a rough, unyielding wall. It hurt—and it was clearly having very little effect.

But she still had to try.

'I'm begging you.'

Impulsively she reached forward, grabbed at both his hands, holding them in her own, willing him to listen.

'Please, Theo.'

Was this the man who had come to her rescue on that

night in London? The man who had held her so warmly, who had kissed her so gently. The man who had made love to her so passionately and so wonderfully. Could he even be the same man?

But inside he must remember—inside he must surely still feel...

His face was just inches away from hers now. She could feel his breath on her cheek, sense the sudden change in his heart rate under the worn navy cotton of his tee shirt. As she watched she saw him snatch an uneven breath, saw his tongue sneak out and, very briefly, touch the sensual lips that, she suddenly realised, were surprisingly dry.

So he wasn't as armoured against her as she had thought! And she most definitely wasn't immune to him. Sitting this close to him, feeling the warmth of his body, knowing the scent of his skin, she felt the deep, primal hunger beating an erotic pulse through her bloodstream.

And the hunger that he seemed to spark in her just by existing was back, gnawing at her inside, scrambling her thoughts into chaos...

'*Theos! Ochi!* Damn you to hell—*ochi! No!*'

Hard hands clamped around her arms, bruising as they lifted her, wrenched her away from him. She hadn't realised that she had leaned so close and she was still stumbling mentally through the shocking confusion, not knowing what was happening to her, not understanding, when he stood up abruptly and forcefully.

'What do you think I am?'

It was a savage roar, one that brought her head up fast—only to drop her gaze just as quickly when she saw the black rage that burned in his face. His height and strength were impressive enough when she was able to face him, standing upright, but now, when his full height towered over her, he was awe-inspiring and more than a little terrifying.

'Theo…' she began tentatively, her voice breaking on his name, but she wasn't sure if he even heard her; and the black blaze of his eyes in the strong-boned face shrivelled any other words in her mouth.

'What do you think I am?' he demanded again, low and savage, making her shrink back against the chair, wishing she could become invisible, or disappear. 'I may not have been on the best of terms with my father over the past years—but do you think I would betray him with you?'

'No—no—I never meant…' Skye tried to interject, horrified at the way he had misinterpreted her actions, seeing an attempt at seduction in the way she had been unable to hide her feelings. But he ignored her in his rage and swept on heedlessly.

'How low do you think I would stoop? How far would you lower yourself to get what you want?'

'I never—'

'No?'

A violent, angry gesture dismissed her weak attempt at a protest, almost as if he were throwing her words right out the window.

'Then what the hell was all that? "Oh, please, Theo… please…"'

Skye could only blink in stunned horror as he suddenly switched to a frighteningly near-accurate copy of her own words, her own voice, and to her shock and distress she caught the note of husky seduction mixed in with the pleading she had aimed for.

'"I'm begging you, Theo…" Oh, yes—you were begging, all right!'

To her total astonishment he suddenly came forward and held out a hand, clearly intending to help her up. Stunned and bemused, Skye could only take the hand he offered, finding herself wrenched to her feet with a force that almost had her flying to the opposite side of the room.

But Theo caught her, whirled her round back to face him, yanked her close. For a long, long moment he simply stared into her face, but then he reached out his free hand, tracing the side of her face, the contours of her cheek, before he pushed his long, powerful fingers into the fall of her burnished red hair.

'Oh, I know what you were begging for. What you wanted was this…'

The kiss he dragged her into was hard and rough, cruelly punishing, devastating. It was meant to tell her exactly what he thought of her and it did. It humiliated, angered, shattered her. And it left her shaking in her shoes at just the thought of what was in his mind.

But then just as suddenly that kiss stopped.

It stopped and Theo lifted his head for a moment, drew in a raw, ragged breath. Molten jet eyes blazed down into hers, searing right through to her soul.

'Oh, yes, my sweet,' he murmured, soft as a deadly snake. '*That's* what you want. What you respond to. What you use to try to entice me into doing as you want.'

'It wasn't like that…' Skye tried to whisper, but her tongue seemed to have frozen in her mouth, unable to speak a word, and he either didn't hear her or ignored her attempt and pushed straight on.

'And do you know what I hate—what I despise the most? It's that even now, when I know that everything you are is a lie, that the woman I met, the woman I slept with, was as false as she could be, that she was promised to someone else—to my own father!—you still can't stop! You still think that you can seduce me round to your way of thinking—to doing what you want me to do. That by offering me your body—'

'No!'

'Yes,' Theo returned harshly. 'Oh, yes. But it won't work, *agape mou*. You don't catch me that way again. I

may have been duped at our first meeting—but I don't put
my head into the noose a second time. Not for anyone—
and certainly not for a conniving, scheming little tramp like
you've proved yourself to be.'

'No...' It was all she could manage; all she could think
of to say.

But even as she spoke she knew that it was all pointless,
that she might just as well have saved herself the effort.
Theo wasn't going to listen to her, and, even if he did,
there was no way she could refute the appalling accusations
he was throwing at her, not unless she offered him some
alternative explanation.

And the only explanation she could offer was the truth.
A truth that she was forbidden to tell anyone, that she had
sworn to keep to herself. If she let it out, she would ruin
so many other lives.

While keeping silent only ruined her own.

'No?' Theo scorned. 'Well, I'm sorry, my angel, but I
just don't believe you.'

His hand came out, slowly, carefully, so that she didn't
have time to react or flinch away.

With the back of one long finger he traced the line of
her face, from her temple, down her cheek, along the curve
of her jaw. Just for a second, his touch lingered on her
mouth, stroking softly, and even though she knew it was
impossible, that she was just deceiving herself, in that second, despairingly, Skye would have sworn that the bleak
black eyes had been touched with a tiny gleam of regret.

But she had to have been imagining things because the
next moment he snatched his hand away, shaking it faintly
as if to remove the contamination of her touch. Whatever
had been in his eyes vanished completely as his face closed
up, harsh and severe, in total rejection of her.

'You have three days,' he told her, each word cold and clear and totally obdurate. 'Three days in which to tell my father the truth. And at the end of that time, if you still haven't told him—then I promise you I will.'

CHAPTER EIGHT

THREE days.

It hadn't sounded long when Theo had given Skye the ultimatum. In fact it hadn't sounded like any time at all.

Three days—just seventy-two hours—in which to find the courage to face Cyril and admit to him what had happened. She didn't know how she could do it. She only knew that somehow—God knew how—she *had* to.

But that had been the day before yesterday. Now more than forty-eight hours of the seventy-two had passed—gone. And she was no nearer to bringing herself to do as Theo had ordered.

If anything, she was further away from it than she had ever been.

For one thing, Cyril hadn't even been in the house most of the time. He had spent a large amount of yesterday in the village and had returned in such a dreadful mood that Skye had hurriedly retired to her room and left him to himself. This morning he had ordered the helicopter to take him to Athens at what seemed like the crack of dawn and hadn't been seen since.

Skye could only be thankful that Theo too had made himself scarce. The thought of facing him and the inevitable reaction when he discovered that she still hadn't given in to his demands and told his father the truth made her shiver in genuine fear.

The future seemed dark and bleak, without a single glimmer of hope on the horizon, and she had no idea which way to turn.

If she didn't tell Cyril, then Theo would. But how could

she tell Cyril when doing so would inevitably mean that he would call off the whole engagement and the wedding that was supposed to follow it?

And without that wedding, then her father had no chance of avoiding arrest, because if thwarted then Cyril would surely press charges even more vehemently. And if he was arrested, then her mother…

'Oh, heaven help me!'

Skye sank down onto the nearest chair and buried her face in her hands, giving in to despair.

She had never felt so lost and alone. So totally abandoned by everyone.

'Is there a problem?'

She recognised the husky male voice immediately. It was the one that had haunted her dreams, sounded in her head all day long ever since she had heard it issuing the brutal ultimatum that threatened to shatter her life, and that of all the people she loved.

'Oh, no, there's no problem!' she flung at him, her head coming up sharply, auburn hair tossed back over her shoulder, grey eyes blazing defiance. 'No problem at all! Only the fact that my life finally seemed to be back on some sort of track—one that I could at least cope with. But then I had the misfortune to meet you and now everything's blown up in my face!'

'You haven't told him.' It was a statement, not a question, but Skye still felt he was waiting for a response to it.

'No, I haven't told him!'

If he'd been around in the house, he would have known that. But for his own private reasons Theo had made himself scarce for the past couple of days. Having delivered his ultimatum, he had backed off and left her alone with his father.

Of course, she knew why. He was expecting her to use the time to tell Cyril everything. She supposed that he thought he was being fair—even considerate—by giving her the space and the quiet in which to broach the subject.

Well, he might not have been actually putting pressure on her directly with his words and his presence, but the knowledge that he was there, waiting, watching, like some cruel hunter lurking in the shadows, waiting to pounce if she didn't do as he ordered, had kept her in a permanent state of shivering terror, never knowing when his dark patience would run out and he would move in for the kill.

'For one thing, I haven't had an opportunity, and for another—well, I just don't know how he's going to react.'

'That's something you should have considered before you leapt into bed with a complete stranger.'

The cynicism in Theo's tone seemed all the worse when Skye admitted to herself just how wonderful he looked. With the afternoon sunlight shining on the glossy black hair, making the dark eyes gleam spectacularly between their frame of thick, lush lashes, he was a Greek god come to life in modern dress. The long, lean legs were clothed in jeans so tight they were positively indecent, and the power of his chest and shoulders was emphasised by the loving cling of the soft tee shirt to the muscled contours. The white material threw the colour of his bronzed skin into sharp relief, his tan already deepened by several days in the Greek sun, and the whole picture was one that made her mouth dry in purely sensual delight.

'I had no idea that the complete stranger was going to turn out to be my fiancé's son!'

'No, I don't suppose you did,' Theo drawled, strolling into the room and dropping down into a chair opposite with indolent ease. 'That was rather unfortunate for you.'

'Unfortunate!' Skye echoed sourly. 'That has to be the understatement of the year!'

'But would it have made things any more justifiable if I'd been a perfect stranger? You would still have been unfaithful to the man you were engaged to. Or are you one of those people who believe that the crime is not in the actual action, but in getting found out?'

'Not at all!' Skye denied his words furiously 'I don't expect you to believe me, but I don't make a habit of indulging in one-night stands with complete strangers!'

'You'd be wrong about that—I do believe you.'

'And I wasn't exactly *engaged* to your father at the time—'

The sudden realisation of the words he had inserted quietly into her tirade pulled her up sharp, her head spinning in shock.

She couldn't be hearing properly. Had he said…?

'*What* did you say?' she demanded rawly.

'That I believe you. That you're not the type who makes a habit of indulging in one-night stands with complete strangers.'

'You—you do?'

'Absolutely.'

Stunned relief and delight flooded through her. Her heart leapt, her spirits lifted. A smile she couldn't suppress spread wide across her face.

'That's wonderful! Fantastic! You can't imagine the relief that makes me feel…'

But something was wrong.

Very wrong.

The smile slipped a bit, faded, as she realised that there was no answering lightening of Theo's expression. Instead, his features remained set in the sombre, unyielding cast that they had displayed from the moment he had come into the room.

As sudden doubt crept into her mind and took an uncomfortable hold Skye felt her world tilt on its balance, swaying sickeningly.

'You didn't mean it?' she questioned hesitantly.

'Oh, yes, I meant it. I could hardly think otherwise—could I? After all, I am only too aware that there hadn't been any man before me. You were a virgin that night.'

Another statement. A flat, blank-toned question that rocked her back in her seat, making her stare into his dark, shuttered face. Had she failed so completely in her attempt to look and act sophisticated and experienced?

'I—what—you knew?'

The look Theo shot her was dark with cynical mockery. A black humour that wasn't echoed in any lightening of his expression, not even the tiniest hint of a curve to his sensual mouth.

'Oh, yes, I knew. Do you know what that did to me?'

'You're angry about that?'

She couldn't understand his reaction, couldn't understand what was going through his head at all, and the confusion and uncertainty made her too uncomfortable to sit still. Pushing herself to her feet, she prowled about the room, agonisingly conscious of those deep, dark eyes following her every move until she felt like some specimen under a microscope or a caged animal being closely observed by some coldly analytical scientist.

'I don't get it! I don't understand at all! I—I thought it was a deep-seated male fantasy to be some woman's first lover. To be the one who took her virginity…'

But she'd hit quite the wrong note there. In trying for a levity she was far from feeling, her words had had the effect of lighting the blue touch-paper and failing to stand well back while the whole multicoloured explosion roared into life right in her face.

Theo hurled himself to his feet in a movement that was so expressive of barely controlled violence that it had her stumbling back behind a chair for protection. His face was twisted into a savage scowl that added to her sense of fearful apprehension.

'In a sordid one-night stand in a cheap hotel?' he snarled viciously. 'Oh, yeah—some fantasy! Your—a woman's—first time should be something special—something to remember. Not just thrown away!'

He *meant* it! Skye could hardly believe what she was seeing. Theo truly meant this. It was in his eyes, in his voice.

'Can't you see?' she pleaded with him. 'That's why I did it—why I was with you. I didn't want your—my wedding night to be the first. That's why I was there.'

She'd thought she could make things better by explaining, but to judge from the change of expression, the searing burn of those deep-set eyes, she'd only managed the exact opposite.

'To throw it away on any man you met?'

He was taking it exactly the wrong way.

'Not just any man…'

And it had been special, she told him in the privacy of her thoughts, not daring to let on just *how* special that night had been. It was bad enough knowing it herself, but if she admitted to even a tiny part of it then she knew that it would rip her to pieces inside.

'Oh, don't tell me that you met me and instantly knew I was the love of your life,' Theo scorned.

'No—I'm not saying that.'

'I could have been just anyone.'

'No!' *Never.* 'And the hotel wasn't that cheap!'

Oh, why couldn't she stop? It had been obvious from the start that her attempts to pretend that that night hadn't mattered so much had failed painfully. Theo's scowl, the way his black brows were drawn tightly together, the black eyes blazing beneath them were warning enough that she was blundering blindly into a dangerous minefield where at any moment things might blow up in her face. But still she couldn't help herself. Couldn't stop herself from blurting out totally inappropriate remarks that were only making matters worse.

'It was to me!'

The savage declaration made her jump like a startled rabbit. In fact, that was exactly what she felt like as he came towards her—a small, frightened rabbit, transfixed in the beam of a car's headlights, wishing desperately that she could move.

'I did exactly what you wanted. Took you exactly where you asked. ''A quiet, decent hotel'',' Theo said, and Skye realised that he was quoting her exactly.

'But, of course, I didn't know who you were then. If I had, then I might have…'

Something about the icy glare he turned on her froze the words on her tongue, cutting them off completely. In dawning horror, she realised just what she was saying, the impression she was giving. A hot tide of red swept right across her face and her hands crept up to cover her mouth, trying to hold the dreadful words back.

But of course it was far too late.

'If you'd known who I was then what, Skye?' Theo pounced on the foolish sentence. 'Would you have held out for more, is that it, hmm? Would you have insisted on a five-star place, or asked for more? Traded your virginity for a night in a penthouse suite, perhaps—or a little room service?'

'I didn't ask for anything from you!'

'Only a night of meaningless sex with an anonymous man.'

'Yes! Yes, that was exactly what I was looking for!'

Skye winced inside at the way that sounded. But she was beyond controlling her voice. Because the truth was that Theo was not reacting in any way as she had anticipated.

Not that she had ever *anticipated* meeting up with the man with whom she had spent that crazy night in London ever again! She had thought that her one night of breaking out into the freedom that soon would be lost to her for ever would be her secret, and hers alone. That it would be totally anonymous, and no one would know.

But there were two problems with that. One was that in no way at all could the sex have been described as 'meaningless'. It had been wild; it had been wonderful. It had pitched her straight from blind innocence and ignorance into a world of sensation, of knowing—and of hunger.

It had been special—so very special.

And it had left an indelible mark on her for ever.

But at least she had managed to keep the anonymous part to exactly that. And as a result she had been quite safe. Until she had come here to Helikos and come face to face with a black twist of fate in the form of Theo Antonakos.

'And that was exactly what I got—and what you got as well. It was what you wanted too! Wasn't it?'

Had she actually been hoping for something else? If she had, then the stupid thought was crushed out of her by his swift retort.

'Well, I sure as hell wasn't looking for marriage!'

'So there you are—we both got exactly what we were looking for. So why can't you leave it at that?'

'You know damn well why!' he flung at her. 'Because it can't be left at that!'

'Why not? Surely if we just put it all behind us and move on, then it can all be over and done with.'

For Theo at least.

'That isn't going to work,' Theo muttered, shaking his dark head slowly.

'Why can't it?'

'Because of who we are—who you are.'

'Me?'

'You're my father's fiancée. That's what makes the difference—all the difference in the world.'

'But it doesn't have to,' Skye protested. 'Only if we let it.'

'*Skye!*'

Her name was a violent sound of outraged fury on his tongue and he raked his hands through his hair, pressing them against the bones of his skull in exasperation.

'Can't you see that there is no "if we let it"?'

'I don't know what you mean.'

'We have no choice but to let it!' Theo told her fiercely. 'You are going to marry my father…and…'

'And?' Skye prompted when he fell silent, seeming to hunt for the words.

'*Theos!* Can you not see it? Can you not feel it?'

'F-feel what?' Skye stammered, though she had a terrible feeling that she knew what was in his thoughts. She knew what she had been hiding from for days and the thought of bringing it out into the open terrified her.

'This thing that's between us.'

'There's nothing between us,' Skye put in hastily, terrified to even let the idea into her mind. 'Nothing at all. I don't know what you're talking about!'

Liar! his look said. *You know exactly what I mean. Exactly what there is.*

'There's an atmosphere—almost an electricity that's in the air between us. I can't keep my eyes—my hands—off you!'

She actually turned white at the words. He watched the blood drain from her cheeks, leaving them pallid and ashen.

He knew exactly how she was feeling. He'd tried to deny it himself at first. But then, like a fool, he'd kissed her. He'd kissed her in anger and contempt, but it hadn't stayed that way. Other, more primitive feelings had swept through him like a tidal wave and he'd known just why he couldn't leave the situation that way—why he couldn't leave the island though, God help him, he'd tried!

He still wanted her. Wanted her more than ever. He didn't care if she was a gold-digger, didn't care about anything but having her back in his bed again.

But she was promised to his father. And he had never taken another man's woman in his life. He didn't intend to start now.

But if she were to leave Cyril...

'It isn't over between us and you know it.'

'It is!' It was a cry of panic, of desperation. 'It is over! It has to be—I'm marrying your father!'

'Then don't!'

There, it was out. Theo told himself. The thing that had been preying on his thoughts all day, every day since the moment he had realised just who she was and why she was here on Helikos. The words that he had been trying not to say, words he had sworn that he would never say, but even as he had done so he had known that he would inevitably one day. He would have to.

For days he'd fought with himself. Fought to stay away from her. Fought the need to be with her. He had set himself to a gruelling regime of exercise, running on the seashore, swimming endless laps of the pool, lifting weights in the small gym his father had had built but had very obviously never used. It had kept him out of her way and it had exhausted his body, but his mind had stayed wide awake.

And at night, in the darkness, the memories had come.

Heated memories of the night they had spent together. The one night when he had known all the sweetness and the passion that her glorious body could offer.

And he had known he wanted more.

The sweetness he wanted to taste all over again. The passion he longed to sate himself on once more.

He had barely managed to cope with the past two days as it was. He had only kept himself from giving in to the magnetic pull her body had for his by telling himself over and over again that she wasn't available, that she was engaged—to his *father,* for God's sake!

She was not only not available, she was forbidden!

But even knowing that, he had endured two nights without sleep. Spent two long days fighting the need to see her. Fighting his body's need to bury himself in her again.

He knew now that that was why he had been so insistent that she tell his father about the night they had spent together. He didn't just want the truth out in the open; he wanted her free from this impossible engagement.

He wanted her all to himself. And he felt he would go mad if he didn't have her.

'Don't marry my father. You can't marry him feeling the way you do about—'

'About you?' Skye inserted swiftly, jerkily. 'I don't feel anything for you!'

'But you do.' Theo dismissed her protest with a contemptuous flick of his hand. 'You feel just the way I do— I can see it in your face. In your eyes whenever I'm near.'

'You arrogant…'

The negligent shrug of broad shoulders under the white tee shirt showed how little he cared about her accusation.

'I may be arrogant, but at least I'm honest.'

Deliberately he took a slow step forward, then another, his eyes fixed on her face, watching every flicker of reaction that she was unable to hide. He saw the way her head went back, the sudden change in her breathing, the darkness of her eyes.

'See?' was all he said, but he knew she'd got the message. Ruthlessly he pressed home his advantage. 'Damn you, Skye, think about this—about what will happen when my father finds out…'

'Why should he find out?'

Her voice had changed again and there was a note in it

now that he couldn't even begin to read. He didn't know what to feel either. His emotions seemed to be running on a loop of anger, through concern, exasperation, and an irrational, overwhelming desire to grab her, haul her into his arms and kiss her senseless. Kissing seemed to be the only function of that soft, sexy mouth that was simple, uncomplicated—and totally understandable.

Oh, who was he trying to kid? Kissing her might start out as the most straightforward thing in this whole tangle of knots that simply being with Skye tied him up in, but it would very rapidly turn into the most complex and problematical situation before he had time to breathe. He couldn't kiss Skye while she was with his father; and, for her own personal, private reasons, she seemed determined to try to hold fast to this appalling engagement.

'I can't believe you're asking me that question.'

'I could pretend—'

'Oh, hell, yes, you could!'

Theo couldn't hold back the cynical laughter that escaped him at the thought.

'You could pretend, all right—but if you wanted to be convincing you'd have to turn in a performance that's a damn sight better than the one you're giving me!'

He'd actually silenced her. For the first time since he'd come into the room and found her sitting on the chair with her head in her hands, she was finally stunned into silence, staring up at him, her face frozen in shock.

'There's something else, isn't there? Something you're not telling me. Damnation, Skye, just what is going on here?'

Her eyes flinched away from his, dropping down to stare at the carpet with an impossibly fierce concentration.

'I don't know what you mean.'

'Don't give me that!'

Dropping to one knee in front of her, he caught her chin

in his hand, pushing it up so that she was forced to meet his gaze. When she tried to pull away he simply clamped his fingers more tightly around her jaw and drew her back inexorably to face him.

'Tell me!' he commanded. 'I want to know just why you are so determined to marry my father.'

CHAPTER NINE

How could she ever answer that? Skye asked herself. She was trapped, no matter which way she turned. Tied by so many different promises to so many people, and knowing she had no way out. There was the promise she had made to her father—others to Cyril…

But the one promise that truly mattered to her was the one that she had made in her heart to her mother. Claire Marston knew nothing of the real reasons why her daughter was suddenly going to marry a much older Greek millionaire; she would have been horrified if she did. But in her heart Skye had promised that she would do anything—everything—she could to ensure that her mother had the health and strength to enjoy as much of life as she could. And if that meant giving up some of her own life, her own happiness, in return, then she believed it was worth it.

So now she had only one choice open to her, one path she could possibly follow.

And she took it.

'Why?' she echoed with what she hoped was a deceptively lightweight and flippant air. She had started on this coldly casual act to protect herself; she couldn't afford to let it slip now. 'Isn't it obvious? Because he asked me.'

Once again, Theo's response surprised her. She had expected anger. She had expected contempt. She had expected that he would simply toss her aside—mentally at least—and just walk out. So she was stunned when he shook his head in total rejection of what she was saying.

'Not good enough,' he stated with a cold finality.

His absolute calmness was somehow more disturbing

than if he had lost his temper and shouted at her. A sudden, scary feeling that she was fighting for her life pushed her towards an even more outrageous declaration.

'You don't think that's good enough? Why ever not?'

Her pause was supposed to give him time to respond, but he didn't take it. Instead, he seemed to be waiting for her to speak again.

But what could she say? If he only knew it, she had spoken the exact truth when she had given him her answer. Cyril had offered marriage as a way out of the appalling problems that beset her family, and, in despair, with no way to turn, she had accepted him.

'What's so difficult to believe about it?' she demanded, the anguish in her heart putting a sharpness on her tongue that she couldn't have managed if she'd planned it. 'Who in their right mind would want to turn down this?' She waved a hand in an all-encompassing gesture that took in the whole room, the patio out beyond the doors, and the blue water of the swimming pool beyond that. 'I certainly wasn't going to.'

It was only when his face changed, his expression hardening, eyes turning to black flint, that she realised how a moment before he had had an entirely different look. She had been near to some sympathy, some understanding from him, and now he had backed away again. Physically as well as mentally.

He had moved back from her; his grip on her jaw loosening. The barriers were up between them once more and it hurt so badly that she had to blink back tears.

But it was better this way.

Safer.

The implications of that word, 'safer', were ones she flinched away from admitting to herself. They gave her an idea, though. If she tried to defend herself from Theo's questions, then she very rapidly found herself with her back against the wall. It was time to stand up for herself—go on the attack instead.

Wrenching her chin free from his loosened grasp, she tried to push Theo aside, get to her feet. But the barrier of his big body offered far more resistance than she had ever imagined. Her push had no effect whatsoever on him, but it made her fingers curl in shock at the sensations that fizzed up her nerves as they encountered the heat and hardness of his powerful chest.

Giving up the attempt to make him move, she scrambled inelegantly off the chair over its arm, turning hastily to confront him while she had the advantage of height because he still knelt on the floor.

'Why does it matter so much to you what happens between me and your father? I understood that you and he weren't exactly close.'

She'd got under his guard with that one. She saw it register in the depths of his eyes and knew a shiver of apprehension as his jaw tightened and a muscle in his cheek tugged sharply.

'Who told you that?'

'Your father, of course.'

Her throat dried as Theo uncoiled his long body and slowly stood up. Perhaps it was the fact that she had no shoes on and in bare feet was inches smaller, but Skye felt that never before had he seemed so tall, so imposing, so *big* as when he towered over her now. Her toes curled on the polished wooden floor as she fought against the craven impulse to turn and run.

'And what did he tell you about it?'

'That—that you had a disagreement.'

'Which is something of an understatement.'

The bitter irony of Theo's response made it plain that it had been anything but a 'disagreement'.

'What was it about?'

'Do you really want to know?' Theo demanded sharply. 'Really?'

'Yes, I do.' Skye tried to sound much more certain than she actually felt. 'It might make me understand things more.'

Something in Theo's expression warned her that that was a vain hope. But she had taken this path now. She was determined to see it through.

'Tell me,' she said unevenly.

Theo pushed his hands deep into the pockets of his jeans and strolled away towards the open patio doors where he stood, staring out at the clear blue water of the pool glinting in the sun.

'My father disowned me because I wouldn't marry the bride of his choice.'

'What?' Skye was stunned. 'You're kidding!'

Theo swung round to face her again and the deadly serious cast of his stunning features made the half-laughing protest and disbelief fade rapidly from her face.

'Do I look as if I am joking?' he demanded haughtily, his accent sounding very pronounced on the question. 'Believe me, it is not a topic I would be flippant about.'

'But—he—I mean—why?'

Theo's mouth curved into a grim travesty of a smile that had no trace of humour at all in it.

'My father has always tried to run my life,' he said at last. 'When I was small he took control completely—I could barely breathe without his permission. My mother died when I was five—two years later I was sent to boarding-school in England.'

'At seven?'

She looked truly shocked, Theo reflected. Shocked, and something else he couldn't quite interpret. If he'd been caught in a weak moment he might have called it sympathetic, but he would probably be fooling himself to even consider it.

'I wasn't the only one,' he returned dryly. 'I was in a class of boys that age. My father was determined that I should get the best education possible—for him that meant an English public school, then an English university. Then, of course, working with him in the Antonakos Corporation.'

'He had your life all mapped out for you.'

Theo's mouth twisted cynically.

'Right down to the woman I should marry.'

Skye perched on the arm of one of the big chairs. Her eyes still had that strange shadowed look in them. Concentrate on that, he told himself fiercely. At least if he kept his gaze—and his attention—focused on her eyes, then he would stop himself from thinking too much about the rest of her.

About the slide of her hair over the bare, lightly tanned shoulder exposed by the slender straps of her lilac-coloured dress. About the way that sitting on the edge of the chair had pulled the already short skirt up even higher on the slim, elegant legs. About the sway of soft breasts clearly not confined in some restricting contraption of satin and Lycra, but moving with each slight gesture she made.

When she lifted a hand to push through her hair his blood pressure mounted to an alarming degree. And the memory of those legs wrapped around his waist like hot silk as she writhed underneath him threatened his ability to think so badly that he barely heard her next comment and had to force his attention back to the present before he lost track of things completely.

'You didn't like her?'

'You really don't know my father too well, do you? I never saw her—and neither, I believe, did he.'

There was no mistaking the emotion that widened her

eyes now. It was total consternation—mixed with a touch of disbelief.

'You'd never even met her?'

Theo shook his head firmly. 'It was to be an arranged marriage. A cold-blooded financial arrangement between my father and hers.'

'And you had no say in the matter?'

'My father certainly didn't intend that I should. I was twenty-seven—more than old enough to start providing him with grandchildren. He had surveyed all the families with daughters of marriageable age, and Agna's father owned land he wanted. That, together with the fact that she was just nineteen, a virgin, and the family fortune, though no match for the Antonakos wealth, was far from inadequate, made her the perfect choice as far as he was concerned.'

'So this Agna didn't get a choice either?'

'Why should she? She was only a daughter, and as far as two greedy old men were concerned she had one real purpose to serve—to marry well, improve the family fortunes, and bear an heir to the combined estate.'

'Oh, don't! You make her sound like a brood mare!'

Skye's voice broke uncontrollably on the words as a result of the bleak thoughts that flooded her mind. At first she been feeling so uptight that she had almost let his explanation of the rift with his father slip by in a haze of shocked disbelief, without registering the impact it had on her personally. All she had thought of was the way *Theo* had been treated, when she should have looked at what it meant for her.

And what it meant for her was an added brutal twist to the knife in her heart, an added sense of being used.

She was only a daughter, and as far as two greedy old men were concerned she had one purpose to serve—to marry well, improve the family fortunes, and bear an heir to the combined estate.

The words seemed to gather an added sense of bitterness with each repetition inside her head. Theo's father had not managed to get his way, by marrying his son off, so he had done the next best thing by taking a young wife who, in her own words, would have to act as 'a brood mare'.

'Not me, sweetheart,' Theo returned harshly. 'I was the one who turned her down, remember. I had no wish to get married. And I lost my own inheritance as a result.'

'He really disinherited you? Cut you out of his will without a penny?'

'That is what the term usually means. Though that "without a penny" isn't strictly accurate. I'd already formed my own company—one with an income my father couldn't touch. No, the part of my inheritance I really lost was this island.'

'Helikos?'

The grim set to Theo's mouth as he nodded twisted her nerves into even more painful knots.

'It was my mother's and it should have come to me. But anything else—forget it! In the five years since I rebelled against the idea of becoming a married man, I've more than doubled my profits. I expect my personal fortune will match my father's now. So you needn't worry that I lost out on the deal.'

'I never...' Skye began, but she was interrupted by the sound of the telephone shrilling through the room. She glanced in the direction of the sound, but it was more important that Theo should know she hadn't been shocked at his father's treatment of him because of the money he had lost.

'That wasn't what was on my mind!' she continued. 'I—'

Once more the sound of the phone cut into her words.

'Aren't you going to answer that?' Theo asked.

'I'm not sure I should. Your father...'

Cyril had made it plain that she was not to interfere in his life. That she was only to be a decorative wife on his arm and in his bed.

'It will probably be him anyway. And if it isn't—well, the reason you're here is that you will be *Kyria* Antonakos in a matter of weeks. So if you're determined to go through with it, you'd better get a taste for acting as the mistress of the house.'

He made a point of walking away to the open doors again, giving her time and privacy for the call.

It *was* Cyril and what he had to say, the tone he used, made icy footsteps dance up and down her spine. He had never, obviously, treated her with much affection, but now his tone was positively brusque, his need to get away quickly desperately worrying.

Skye was suddenly a prey to a terrible fear that something had gone wrong. Had something happened to make Cyril change his mind so that even the sacrifice she was prepared to make wasn't enough? The thought made her realise just how terribly isolated she was, how alone. But with Theo so close at hand she didn't dare to ask, and Cyril issued his last order and switched off the phone even as she was struggling to find a reply.

When Theo swung round again to face her she was still standing by the table, sharp teeth digging into her lower lip, a frown of concern between her brows.

'Theo will look after you,' Cyril had said, and right at this moment she couldn't even begin to think which was worse—this terrible, dragging sense of loneliness and fear, or the thought of being alone with Theo once more.

'He's staying in Athens tonight,' she said flatly when she saw that Theo was looking at her. 'Not coming back till tomorrow. He—he said you'd look after me.'

She lifted her eyes as she spoke, her dove-grey gaze

locking with his, and Theo wondered sharply just what was going through her mind.

He knew what was going through *his*.

His father was not coming back until tomorrow. Twenty-four hours alone with Skye.

Twenty-four hours alone with temptation. A *night* of temptation.

He said you'd look after me.

Oh, *Theos*! His father had no suspicion at all just how he would like to *look after* this woman, or he wouldn't have left her in his care.

He had already been fighting himself desperately for more than forty-eight hours. Could he manage to keep his feelings on a tight rein for another day, here, on his own in the house with her?

It was not something he wanted to risk.

'I have things I need to do.'

'All right.'

She wouldn't look at him as she spoke, but seemed absorbed in a painting that hung on the far wall, concentrating fiercely on the image of Persephone.

'You'll be all right?'

'I'll be fine.'

It was less certain this time, the words faintly uneven. But she still wouldn't look at him.

Was there a thickness in her voice? And the only time he had ever seen anyone blink that hard it had been because they were blinking back...

'Skye?'

Perversely, now that he had what he wanted, Theo found he was more than reluctant to leave. A faint flicker of a smile touched Skye's mouth as she watched him hesitate. But it was a cynical, disturbingly weary smile. And at last she looked at him, or at least she turned her head in his direction, but her unfocused gaze seemed to go straight over his shoulder, avoiding his eyes.

'What are you trying to do?' she questioned with a rough-edged note to the words, as if her words were un-ravelling as she spoke. 'Do you want to prove that I can't let you go? That that…electricity that you think is between us will make it impossible to part from you?'

'I'd be a fool to think that,' he said with dark softness, 'when I know only too well that you could walk out with-out a second thought. You've already done it once.'

'I told you it was just for that night.'

'And I told you I don't do one-night stands.'

This time when she blinked her gaze seemed to come back into focus and her dark, cloudy eyes met his just once, then flinched away again.

'Are you claiming you wanted more?'

'It was certainly an experience that I would have liked to repeat if you hadn't bolted out of there like a frightened rabbit before I even had time to wake up.'

'I did not *bolt*!'

'You sure as hell didn't hang around. What was it, sweet Skye? A sudden realisation that you had a conscience after all?'

'It wasn't that at all.'

Skye aimed for defiance, almost made it, but her voice slipped a little on the last couple of words. But she felt as if she were fighting for her life here and she had no inten-tion of letting him see it.

The acid burn of misery ate into her soul at the memory of the way she had felt when she had left that hotel room. At the time she had thought that nothing could make her feel worse. Now she knew how wrong she had been.

'I said at the time that it was my way or nothing. And you agreed.'

'I went along with what you said,' Theo corrected coldly.

'I don't recall signing any agreement in blood. I was fool enough to think you might wait around at least for breakfast.'

'I told you how it would be. Why should you complain when I stuck to my word?'

'I didn't like the way it made me feel.'

'And that was?'

'Used.'

It was the last thing she had expected and the single word made her thoughts reel in shock.

Used.

He had felt *used*?

How did he think his father had made her feel?

'Join the club!' she flashed back, her spinning brain unable to think of anything less provocative in the few seconds that were at her disposal.

'What?'

For a moment she thought that once more Theo's grasp of English had failed him and that was why he was frowning his lack of comprehension. But the next second she realised how dangerously close she had come to giving away the true details of her situation.

'Well, you have to admit it's unusual for a man to feel that way...' She covered her tracks hastily. 'That's how most women feel when a man only wants a one-night stand. It doesn't do any harm for you to get a taste of your own medicine.'

'I did not *use* you!'

'We both used each other. It was just—what was it you said? A night of meaningless passion.'

'Meaningless is the truth. You couldn't get out of there quick enough!'

Oh, if only he knew the reality of it!

Skye felt tears threaten and fought against them hard,

tightening her jaw and clamping her mouth tight shut against the little cry of distress that almost escaped her.

If only he knew how she had felt that morning when she had woken to find herself curled up close to his long, warm body, clasped tight in the strength of his arms.

For a few, wonderful moments reality hadn't quite sunk in and she had lain there, keeping her eyes closed, a small, ridiculous smile on her face, just enjoying the sensation of being held like this. How she had wished that she could just stay there, held close, and never, ever move again.

And when she had finally left the room, her face had been streaked with tears. Tears of loss for a man who hadn't even known who she was and—if fate was kind—would never know.

But of course fate had not been kind. The truth was that fate had been at its cruellest that night, and again when it had brought her here, to this island just three days ago.

Because it had brought her face to face with the man who had stolen part of her soul on that single night in a London hotel. The man whom she had tried to convince herself she never wanted to meet ever again. But the man whom she knew, deep down in her heart, she most longed to see in the entire world.

Until he had appeared in Helikos in the form of the one man that she must never, ever, even dream of getting close to. The man who was totally forbidden to her, and had to stay that way for the rest of her life.

CHAPTER TEN

'I'M SORRY.'

Skye felt obliged to say it.

'I never meant you to feel used.'

The truth was that it was the last thing she had expected.

'But can't we forget about that night—put it behind us?'

'You know damn well that we can't!'

Theo's voice was rough and husky and his eyes burned like polished jet as they scoured her face.

'It's still there—between us. I can't forget about it—can you?'

Never in her life, Skye acknowledged, but she was going to have to try. There was no way she and her family could have a future if she didn't escape from the past.

'I have to,' she said with what she hoped sounded like conviction. 'We have to. Nothing can happen between us. I'm marrying your father. We have to live as if we'd never met before. As if we'd never...'

'And you can do that, can you?' Theo put in when her voice failed her, lacking the courage to complete the sentence. His tone was dark with cynical scepticism, making his disbelief all too plain. 'You can pretend that we were never lovers—that we have only ever been stepmother and stepson?'

No! No, I can't do it—I can't bear it! Skye's heart felt as if it were being ripped in two at just the thought. She didn't want to be Theo's stepmother. She didn't feel at all motherly towards him. She wanted...

But she couldn't have what she wanted. That was forbidden to her. She had to put even the dream of it out of her mind and learn, somehow, to live with what was real.

She found the strength to straighten her back, lift her head. She even managed to look him straight in the face, meeting the black-ice stare of those coldly assessing eyes.

'Yes,' she managed, and was stunned to hear an assurance that she could never have felt actually sounding in her voice.

But was it enough to convince Theo? He *had* to be convinced. She didn't know how she could go on if he wasn't.

He didn't look convinced. But then she didn't know what he *did* look. She couldn't read his still, inscrutable expression. Couldn't tell a single thought that was passing through his coolly assessing brain. She could only hope and pray.

Still with his eyes fixed on her face, Theo stirred slightly. He drew in a long, thoughtful breath, inclined his head to one side, ever so slightly.

'Prove it,' he said.

'What?'

'Prove it,' Theo repeated, with a harder, slashing emphasis. 'If you're so convinced that you can act as if we've never been lovers—as if there is nothing between us—then do it. And get some practice in before my father comes home. He said I would look after you; I think I'd better start doing that.'

'But…' Skye tried to protest, but Theo cut through her stumbling attempt to speak.

'Spend the rest of the day with me. We'll do a guided tour of the island—that seems like the sort of thing a good stepson would do. Be my stepmother—nothing more. And if at the end of the day you can still say you can live with things that way, then I swear I'll leave you alone—for good.'

I'll leave you alone—for good.

Skye's mind swung violently between hope and despair;

agreement and total, desolate rejection of his suggestion. One part of her wanted to do this so that he would leave her in peace—and yet the thing she most wanted in all the world was that he would never leave her. But the way she wanted that was what was totally forbidden to her.

She was going to have to learn to live with that. And perhaps the way that Theo had suggested—the idea of practising, of trying to get used to the idea, without the fear of having Cyril's eyes following every move—might just work.

She didn't know. But the one thing she was sure of was that the ruthless, determined set of Theo's hard features made it only too plain that if she refused then he would put his own interpretation on that fact. An interpretation that spelt death to her hopes of any peace of mind in the future.

It seemed to her that she had only one possible choice.

'All right,' she said slowly. 'I'll do it.'

Was he really going through with this? Theo asked himself when they were in the car and heading down the rough, winding road that led away from the house. What had happened to his doubts, to the private acknowledgement of the risks he ran, the temptation he would have to endure if he stayed?

The truth was that he *wanted* that temptation. He couldn't turn away and just leave it. When he was with Skye he felt more involved with everything, more *alive* than ever before, and he wasn't going to abandon a chance to experience that sensation once more, even if it was for the last time.

Besides, he hadn't been back to Helikos in all the five years he had been apart from his father. He wanted to reacquaint himself with the place, revisit his favourite spots, the places he had loved as a boy. And he would enjoy seeing them afresh through her eyes.

'We'll follow the coast road first,' he told her. 'That way we can visit the ruined monastery and take a look at some of the caves before we head for the village. I know a wonderful little *taverna* where we can eat dinner. The people who own it were like family to me.'

And almost more than family, he recalled. Berenice, the oldest daughter, a woman not much more than five years older than himself, had had an intense affair with his father at about the time that the old man had tried to push his son into an unwanted marriage. He remembered how, in one of the last conversations he had had with Cyril, he had flung the fact into the older man's face.

'If you're so desperate to have more heirs,' he had shouted, 'then why don't you marry your mistress? Start a new family with her!'

'I might just do that!' Cyril had responded.

But it seemed that now Berenice was out of the picture. Obviously, his father had thought twice about making a simple village woman the fifth Mrs Antonakos.

Instead he had chosen this English girl who was less than half his age. A girl who was not at all the type his father usually went for.

Berenice was much more his father's type. Cyril Antonakos was drawn to that small, black-haired, dark-eyed, full-bosomed type of woman. Not the tall, slim, Titian-haired seductress that Skye Marston was.

A woman who, simply by existing, made Theo live in a state of constant hunger, of a desire so hot and painful that it was an agony of frustration to sit so close to her in the confined space of the car. An agony of yearning to inhale the delicate fragrance of her skin with every breath he took, and not do anything about it.

A woman who made him want to slam on the brakes,

bring the car to a screeching halt and turn in his seat, reaching out for her in desperation. Made him want to drag her into his arms, haul her close and take her mouth, kissing her hard and long, demandingly, until they were both senseless with heady desire, an explosive cocktail of hunger and frantic passion impossible to control.

'*Theos...*' Cursing under his breath, Theo gripped the steering wheel so tightly that the knuckles on his hands showed white under the tanned skin. Pebbles flew up from underneath the tyres, clanging against the underside of the car and making Skye look up in stunned confusion.

'Is there a problem?'

'I forgot how primitive the island roads can be. You can't afford to let your concentration slip for a moment.'

'The view has much the same effect,' she smiled. 'I never knew the sea could be so many wonderful shades of blue.'

If she smiled at him like that once more, then he was lost. Theo forced his attention back to the road

'This is October. You should see it in the summer—it's like the most brilliant jewel in all the world then.'

'I'd love to see it.'

Skye's voice had an odd little break in it, one that made it sound suddenly vulnerable and dangerously appealing so that Theo had to clench his jaw tight against the way that that softness twisted in his guts.

'You will do,' he said, the fight he was having with himself making his words come out far more harshly than he wanted. 'You'll be living here then—as my stepmama.'

If he had reached out and slapped her hard across the face, it couldn't have had a more dramatic effect on her. She shrank back inside herself like a small, frightened rabbit retreating into the protection of its burrow. The sudden clouding of her eyes and the way that her sharp white teeth dug into the softness of her mouth were like a reproach to him, making him curse himself for the roughness of his reply.

But at least she had lost that tempting smile. And the way that she turned from him, fixing her concentration back onto the azure spread of the ocean at the bottom of the dramatic fall of the cliffs, meant that temptation no longer tormented him with thoughts of the softness of her breasts beneath the lilac dress, the shortness of her skirt.

If she kept her back turned to him, her gaze on the view before her, then he might just be able to keep a grip on the hunger; stop it from running away with the last bit of sense he possessed.

If she kept her back turned to him, her gaze on the view before her, then she might just be able to keep a grip on her emotions, Skye told herself. She had made a near fatal mistake in turning, in smiling at him, as she had.

Turning had brought her too close to him. It had made her so intensely aware of his physical presence beside her. She had inhaled the scent of his body with her swiftly indrawn breath, and her smile had been directed straight into those watchful black eyes. And she was sure there had been some flicker of response in them that had had her holding her breath in disbelief.

But then suddenly he had changed. She had seen it in his face, heard it in the tone of his voice as he had drawled cruelly, 'You'll be living here then—as my stepmama.'

Did he know how much it hurt to be slapped in the face by that reminder? He had to. It was why he had done it. He was making sure that she remembered exactly where she would stand with him if she went through with the marriage to his father.

A marriage she *had* to go through with if she was to have any chance of ensuring her parents' future.

And any chance of saving her mother's life. The memory of the phone call she had had with her father last night invaded her head, dragging dark shadows with it. She had wanted to speak to her mother, but Claire Marston had been sleeping. They weren't prepared to wake her…

A tiny gasping sob escaped her, impossible to hold back. She had been a fool to think that she could ever go through with this stepmother act.

'What's wrong?'

The hard demand sliced through the atmosphere inside the car like a slashing knife, making her jump with the force of it.

'Nothing.'

Her heart lurched painfully as she heard his muttered curse and felt the car come to an abrupt halt, spraying pebbles wildly around the tyres.

'Something has upset you and I want to know what.'

'Do you really have to ask?' Skye twisted in her seat, turning back to face him, blinking ferociously to drive away the weak and revealing tears in her eyes.

'I mean—I'm sure you know only too well. Or can guess. Why are you so determined that I shouldn't marry your father?' she demanded when she saw his dark frown of incomprehension. 'Why does it matter so much to you?'

'Because you would be living a lie—we both would.'

'We had one night together! It doesn't have to affect the rest of our lives.'

'One night I can't forget. And I don't believe you can either.'

There was no hint of yielding in his face. His features were set in hard, ruthless lines, his eyes glittering with the coldest anger.

'You were a virgin—you know what they say about always remembering your first.'

That burned so much into her already wounded soul that Skye closed her eyes briefly against the pain. But then she immediately forced them open again, dragging herself back into the role of careless indifference she had chosen for her own protection.

'Well, don't flatter yourself that that's true for me. You might want to imagine that you were unforgettable, but I'm afraid that's just not the case.'

Not true, her outraged conscience reproached her, crying out against the betrayal of the truth. She hadn't forgotten Theo's touch, his kisses, his lovemaking. The vivid intensity of her memories, the blazing Technicolor brilliance of her dreams, left her in no doubt at all that the images would never fade.

She'd insulted him savagely too. She could see it in the flaring rage in the black brilliance of his eyes, the tightness of every muscle in his face that scored white lines of fury around his nose and mouth, stretched the skin ferociously over the broad cheekbones. It hurt to see what she had done, and she longed to open her mouth and protest sharply, to take back the terrible words. But even as her conscience lashed at her for the lies, her sense of self-protection recognised the need for it; the shield she had put up against the dangers of letting this man get too close.

But he was already too close, she admitted miserably. He was in her mind all day, every day. In her dreams each night.

In her heart.

But *no*! She wouldn't allow herself to let that idea into her head. She couldn't risk it, didn't dare to even consider the possibility that she had come to care for Theo Antonakos more than was safe.

'Is that why you bolted? Because I was so *forgettable*?'

He was starting the car again as he spoke. Starting it with a roar and a crunch of gears that, even after such a short acquaintance with his driving techniques, she knew was completely non-typical of him.

He was beyond angry. He was furious—coldly furious.

But while she shivered inside at the thought of his rage, she also welcomed it. His loss of temper had distracted him, taken him away from the thought of probing into why she had been so upset. It had stopped him from asking any more questions that she would find impossible to answer and so, while she couldn't relax, she could at least feel that she only had one thing to concentrate on. Theo's obvious dislike of and contempt for the woman she was pretending to be, the mask she was hiding behind, was hard enough to cope with. But at least it kept him from digging any deeper into areas that she couldn't even begin to explain.

'Or was it that you were shocked rigid at the discovery of your own sensuality and you were running scared?'

'I wasn't scared! What is there to be scared of?'

'What?'

Once more the car screeched to a halt on the deserted road. Theo had barely had time to yank on the brake before he had flung off his seat belt and was turning towards her, grabbing hold of her arms and pulling her towards him with a force that made her own seat belt lock, holding her immobile.

Cursing savagely, he stabbed a long finger on the button that released the strap, catching her as she tumbled into his arms.

'What is there to be scared of? I'll show you...'

Arms like steels bands fastened around her, twisting her in her seat as he hauled her up against him. His mouth came down on hers with a savage demand, crushing her lips cruelly and forcing them open under the pressure of his.

But then, in the space of a single, jerking heartbeat, everything changed. Her mouth wasn't crushed open, but yielding swiftly and softly, letting him in rather than having no option. The taste of him was as intoxicating as fine wine, rushing straight to her head, coiling along her senses so that she couldn't get enough of him. Her tongue tangled with his, taking in more of him, inviting, offering more of herself. And he took it. He took her mouth, he took her senses, he took her hunger and fed it, making it grow and rage out of control.

His hands were moving over her body, stroking, caressing, tantalising. Never once demanding, and yet the yearning ache, the throbbing pulse that woke between her thighs created a stinging need that was a fiendish combination of the darkest pleasure and the sharpest pain. Her fingers were clawing at his chest, fastening over his shoulder, digging into hard, taut muscle under the smooth cotton of his shirt. But she couldn't keep them still. Sliding upwards, they tangled in his hair, twisting in the black silken strands, holding him prisoner, his mouth still on hers, when she feared he would move away.

She didn't want this to end. She couldn't bear it if it had to stop. She felt she would die, or at least some vital part of her would cease to exist. She wished she were anywhere but here, in the cramped discomfort of the luxurious car's front seat, where the brake handle and other controls poked into her side, her hips, prevented her from getting just as close as she most wanted.

She wanted to be somewhere where she could take this further—where he could take *her*. Where they could take each other. Her heated, frenzied fantasies were already forming images of forcing open the car door, and tumbling out onto the grass verge at the side of the road, dragging Theo with her, when, with a low, protesting moan, he wrenched himself free, pulling his mouth from hers and flinging himself back in his seat.

His chest was heaving raggedly, his breath snatched in, rough and raw. His head was thrown back, exposing the long, tanned line of his throat, his hair wildly tousled from the effects of her clutching hands, and his eyes were closed, clamped tight as if he didn't *want* to see. Didn't want to face reality, but to concentrate instead on the blazing inner world that had sent flame searing through his senses, wild as the smallest spark through bone-dry tinder.

'*Theos!*'

The word was barely formed. It was just a gasping sound, forced from a throat that was raw and dry and as husky as if it pained him desperately to speak.

'You ask what there is to be afraid of! *That's* what! And if it doesn't scare you, then it sure as hell scares the life out of me! It makes me forget what I believe is right—the way I believe I should act...'

Skye didn't know if she was shaking with fear at his reaction or with the ferocity of the sensual response he had drawn from her. She was trembling like a leaf and yet at the same time she had never felt more alive in her whole life. Her whole body was in a state of stinging awareness, so much so that to have been pushed away from him as she had felt like a little death, a terrible loss that left her feeling bereft and desolated.

'*That's* why you can't marry my father—admit it, damn you!'

Skye couldn't say a word. Couldn't open her mouth or she would give herself away. Just her tone would reveal how devastated she was, how true his words were. He wouldn't even need to challenge her to admit it—her voice alone would betray her.

And so she kept silent. But so did Theo.

And there was something about his silence—some fierce, withdrawn, brutally controlled quality that twisted in her heart and added a whole new dimension to her despair.

She hadn't meant to entangle him in all this. Hadn't ever thought that he would become involved in her own private hell. And she didn't want to make him feel this way. The terrible sense of frustration and guilt and scorching, blazing need was bad enough when she was enduring it herself. The thought of having forced someone else to go through it—and to know that there was no way she could do anything about it—appalled her right to her soul.

'Theo…'

With a shaking hand she reached out to touch his thigh, only to have him snap upright, knocking her hand away from him with a rough, jerky movement.

'Don't!' he commanded in a voice that still carried the echoes of the sensual storm that had shaken them both. 'Don't ever touch me again! You see what happens when we touch! We both go up in flames! We're not safe to be together.'

Shadowed dark eyes slid sideways to study her face, the question she didn't want him to ask burning deep inside them.

'Not if you're determined to stick to this mad idea of marriage.'

How did she answer that? There was only one possible response she could give, even if her heart rebelled against it all the way.

'Are you still set on marrying my father?'

'If he'll have me.'

'Then stay the hell away from me.'

Theo didn't care if he was being unfair. He knew she would only have to say that she hadn't come anywhere near him—that he was the one who had pounced on *her*—and he wouldn't have a leg to stand on. But right now he wasn't feeling at all fair. He wasn't even feeling in the least bit in control.

The sensual storm that had exploded in his body had taken his mind with it. And he was still having to fight the raging need that turned his body to fire, made his blood run molten through his veins.

He didn't even dare to look at her straight. If he did he

would see her soft mouth swollen with his kisses, the glorious red-gold hair mussed and tangled, her jacket awry, skirt pulled up over her thighs. If he did, then the fires he was struggling to damp down in a body that was still hard and aching with need would flare up again in a second, and this time he might not be able to hold them back.

'I told you—we're not safe to be together.'

'Then you'd better turn this car right round and take me back.'

'I thought you wanted to see the island.'

'I did. But...'

Theo shook himself inwardly, trying to bring some sense to his whirling thoughts.

'I said I'd show you the island.' His voice was rigid with control. 'If we stay out in the open—stick to public places—we should be okay. It has to be a damn sight safer than going back to the villa.'

He wanted to show her Helikos, damn it! He wanted her to see his favourite places—the beach where he had run wild as a child, the ruined monastery where he had played games of imaginary knights and dragons, and where his mother and her family were buried. The village where he had made friends with a few, forbidden village boys and where later—in his adolescence—he had learned more about the opposite sex than his father ever suspected.

He wanted to see those places anew through her eyes. And, yes, if he told the truth, he wanted to be the one who showed them to her, not his father.

It was time he admitted the truth. He was jealous as hell of his own father. Jealous of the fact that the old man was engaged to this stunning woman—that she seemed determined to marry him, even if only for her own mercenary reasons. It might be weak, it might be foolish—it might be downright crassly stupid—but right now he reckoned he'd settle for being used for his money if it meant having Skye Marston in his bed once again.

Admit it, he told himself: he'd do anything—sell his soul if necessary—for that. But his only chance of convincing her that she didn't need to marry his father was to spend time with her. And if the constant ache in his groin and the raging nag of frustration was the cost of that time, then he'd pay that too. If it was that or nothing, then he wasn't going to settle for nothing.

'Just think of me as your private tour guide,' he managed to say with a reasonable degree of conviction. 'I'll be the soul of discretion. I promise.'

The look she shot him was sidelong and filled with disbelieving scepticism.

'You have my word,' Theo assured her. 'I'll behave just as I should when I'm out with my stepmother-to-be.'

He meant it too. Meant it all the more because of the way that her face changed when he said those last three words.

And the fact that she clearly hated being described as his future stepmother just as much as he hated describing her that way gave Theo such a personal satisfaction that he smiled secretly to himself as he put the car in motion again.

He'd behave like the perfect stepson, all right. He wouldn't put a foot wrong. And if the lovely Skye found that she didn't like being treated that way—well, that suited him down to the ground.

CHAPTER ELEVEN

THEO stuck to his word for almost all the afternoon. He was the perfect escort, and the perfect stepson. He was cool, polite, attentive, but not too attentive, considerate, helpful…and nothing more.

At least externally.

Inside his head it was a completely different matter.

No stepson should ever harbour the thoughts about his stepmother that he did. He certainly shouldn't notice the sway of her breasts under the soft cotton of her dress, or the way her legs tightened as she climbed the cliff walk to the ruined monastery. He shouldn't notice how slender and soft her feet were when she pulled off her shoes to walk barefoot over the sand and paddle her toes in the sea that lapped against the beach. And he most definitely shouldn't have wanted to swing her into his arms and kiss her senseless, carrying her away from the shore, to find a secret hidden place where he could strip the clothes from her body and make mad, passionate love to her until they were both too dazed even to think.

But those thoughts were the ones he kept hidden inside his mind. To Skye's face he was totally in control, driving her all around the island, telling her the history of the places they visited, and adding personal tales of his own childhood to entertain her. He taught her words of his language here and there and finally, as the shadows of the gathering dusk began to fall about them, he took her to the small *taverna* in the village where he introduced her to the best of the local food.

'This is wonderful!' Skye exclaimed, washing down the

last morsel of a tasty filo roll stuffed with spinach with a swallow of crisp white wine. 'What did you say it was called again?'

'*Bourekakia*,' Theo told her, smiling in response to her enthusiasm.

It was impossible not to smile when she looked at him like that, her eyes sparkling in the light from the candles that stood on every scrubbed wood table top. Her skin glowed after the afternoon spent in the open air, colour washed into her cheeks by the wind that had blown in from the sea. She had caught her hair back loosely, tying it with a turquoise silk scarf, and silver earrings gleamed on the lobes of her exposed ears.

'*Bourekakia*.' Skye struggled to get her tongue around the syllables. 'I must definitely have those again! They were delicious. And to think that until now the only thing I ever ate that was Greek was a feta salad.'

The earrings danced as she laughed. Earrings he had bought for her in one of the tiny shops in the village; little more than a single room where craftsmen worked to traditional designs handed down from father to son over a century or more. She had fallen in love with the tiny silver dolphins on sight and he hadn't been able to resist making an excuse to go back and buy them when she had been distracted by an array of belts at a leather goods stall.

It wasn't breaking his promise to stick to the rules, he told himself. He would have done the same for a prospective stepmother who was much closer to his father's age if she had expressed the same delight in the jewellery. The earrings wouldn't have looked as stunning on anyone else, though. The beautifully curved shaped of the dolphins' bodies accentuated the graceful lines of Skye's slender neck, and the polished silver gleamed softly against the glorious colour of her hair.

The temptation to reach out and touch the delicate silver,

using it as an excuse to stroke his fingers down the equally elegant length of her throat, was almost irresistible and he had to reach for his own glass in order to distract himself from the dangerous appeal.

'Oh, Iannis can make you a salad if you want. But I think that what you've ordered for your main course…'

His voice trailed off as he spotted a waitress bringing a bottle of wine to a nearby table.

'Berenice!'

The woman who had been his father's mistress.

'Excuse me.'

'Of course.'

What else could she say? Skye asked herself as Theo tossed down his napkin, pushing back his chair as he did so. *No? Of course I won't excuse you—not if you're going to speak to her!*

She had no right to say any such thing. No excuse for keeping him here at the table with her and nothing to explain the automatic protest that leapt to her lips and could only just be swallowed down in time before she opened her mouth and let it out, giving herself away in the process.

She didn't want him to leave her. Certainly not if he was going to speak to another woman—especially one as stunning and sensually feminine as this sloe-eyed, black-haired beauty who was smiling a warm and open welcome as Theo approached.

But the only justification for the feelings she had came tangled up in a word that she didn't want to let into her thoughts. A word that she knew was the one that described what she felt, but that she didn't want to acknowledge because the emotions behind it were too dangerous, too threatening, too overwhelmingly terrifying to be able to cope with right here and now.

That word was *jealousy*.

She was jealous of the woman whose appearance had

pulled Theo to his feet with such speed. She was jealous of the smile that had lit his face, sparking in his eyes as he had recognised her, said her name. And she was jealous of the answering smile on this Berenice's lips and the evident warmth of her greeting.

She was jealous.

She was more than just jealous. She was eaten up with the horrible feeling. Fighting to stay in her seat and not jump up and march over to where Theo and this Berenice were engaged in an animated conversation.

Leave him alone! He's mine!

'Oh, no!'

The words escaped in a shocked whisper and Skye reached for her wineglass, swallowing down a large mouthful as the shock of her thoughts rocked her sense of reality, triggering off a series of shivering explosions along her skin and down her spine, making her shudder in fearful response.

It couldn't have happened to her—could it?

But another swift glance across the room, meant to calm her, to convince her that nothing had happened, that her fears were only imaginary, had the exact opposite effect.

The first impact was physical. It was as if she were seeing him again with brand new eyes. Seeing the tall, powerful form, the straight shoulders, strong chest tapering down to a narrow waist and long, muscular legs. In the flickering light of the many candles that lit the *taverna,* his strongly carved features and deep-set black eyes looked like the face on one of the statues of the ancient gods of mythology. And the glossy black hair fell forward over his forehead as he bent towards Berenice, his attention fixed totally on her.

And it was that attention, the absolute concentration on her and what she was saying, that made Skye realise something else. Something much more shocking and disturbing to her mental balance.

She couldn't bear to see Theo with another woman. Couldn't bear to see this Berenice looking up into his face, big dark eyes locking with his as she spoke softly and rapidly in Greek.

The sudden sombreness of his expression, his total stillness, told her that the two of them were discussing something important, something they didn't want Skye to share, and that knowledge twisted sharply in her suddenly devastated heart. And when Theo leaned forward, kissing the other woman lightly on the cheek, she felt her eyes burn with tears. Tears that made the image before her blur and swim disturbingly, like an out-of-focus film.

Her hands went up to the lobes of her ears where the delicate silver earrings hung.

Theo had bought her those. She had adored them on sight but, always conscious of the need not to spend money she didn't have, had reluctantly left them where they were. She hadn't even been aware of the fact that Theo had noticed how much she had liked them until they had sat down at the table in this *taverna* and he had slid a small package across the table to her.

'A souvenir of your first visit to Helikos,' he'd said in a casual, almost throw-away tone.

Foolishly she'd taken the gift out of all proportion. She been so thrilled that she had worn the earrings right away, twisting and turning her wineglass to try and see the effect they had in her reflection, and all the while grinning like an excited child.

And all that Theo had said was, 'I'm glad you like them.'

The earrings might have been out of her price range, but to a man of Theo's wealth they were simply a cheap trinket, something he could have bought a thousand times over and not even missed the cost.

But to Skye they meant so much more.

And that 'more' now forced her to face exactly why she was feeling the way she was.

She was jealous because she had fallen in love. She had fallen head over heels in love with Theo Antonakos, the man she could never have, the man who was totally forbidden to her.

She loved the son of the man she had to marry.

'Oh, no!' she whispered to herself, mentally falling headlong into the deepest, darkest pit of despair. 'Oh, please, please—no!'

But Theo was heading back towards the table and she had to collect herself, hide the way she was feeling.

'Sorry about that.'

He offered the apology in an abstracted, unfocused tone, one that jarred on Skye's already over-sensitised mood.

'No problem,' she mumbled.

She couldn't look him in the face. How did you look at a man in the moment that you had realised you were in love with him? And how could she look at the man she loved and know that he was lost to her for ever because she was going to—had to—marry his father?

But even though her whole body was singing in newly heightened response to the potent physical presence of the man opposite, it was obvious that he didn't feel the same. Glancing up through her eyelashes, she could see that Theo's attention wasn't on her. He was frowning down into his glass, black brows drawn sharply together and one strong hand tapping restlessly on the table, beating out a tattoo of impatience and irritation that she could find no explanation for.

But of course it was because of Berenice. He had been pleased to see her, but something the Greek woman had said to him had changed his mood totally.

What was she to him? Just a friend? From his initial reaction she had seemed more than that.

Was it possible that Theo could be seeing someone else and still make a play for her as he had?

Of course he could!

Reaching for her glass again, she emptied it in one swift, unwise swallow, feeling the wine hit her senses almost instantly.

Had that moment in the car at the beginning of the afternoon told her nothing? Had she learned nothing from the way that Theo had reached for her, the ferocious sensuality of his kiss, the savage passion that had flared between them instantly?

'What is there to be scared of?' she had asked him.

And he had shown her.

He had taken her into his arms and he had kissed her cruelly, ruthlessly, with a kiss that had nothing of caring or tenderness in it, but only of the determination to exert power, to control. To show her just what there was between them—blinding sexual passion, and nothing else.

He might as well have branded her with his mark of possession, like a slave of long ago; it would have had the same effect. She wore that brand on her heart anyway, knowing that she was his, and could never be anything else. Theo could feel for another woman, because his physical hunger for Skye was unleavened with any degree of caring. But Skye herself could only love him and, because her heart was given entirely into his hands, she could never feel for anyone else.

'We're going home.'

Theo's voice, rough and harsh, dragged her from the misery of her thoughts, her startled grey eyes flying to his face, seeing the shadows in the spectacular eyes. Shadows that had nothing to do with the flickering light of the candle flames.

'But we haven't eaten—the main course...'

'Are you hungry?' he demanded brusquely.

'Well—no—not really.'

The truth was that every scrap of the appetite she had had at the beginning of the meal had gone. Her earlier enthusiasm for the food now seemed light years away, and her stomach heaved nauseously at even the thought of it.

'Then we're going home.'

It wasn't up for debate, his tone said. And the way he pushed back his chair, the legs making an ugly, scraping sound on the tiled floor, emphasised that. He had decided, and he expected her to do as he said. But she didn't feel strong enough to fight his autocratic assumption that she would jump when he said, 'Jump.' And the truth was that if she did, then her protests would soon be revealed as the lies they were when their meals were brought and she couldn't eat any of it.

So she reached for her jacket from the back of her own chair and got up too. Theo dropped money onto the table top without even counting it, and then he was striding towards the door.

Unlike the way he had behaved on their way in, he didn't take Skye's arm to escort her, neither did he look back to see if she was following him. Whatever Berenice had said, it had clearly angered him terribly, and Skye shivered inwardly at the thought of just what might happen, what sort of mood he might be in when they were alone and in the privacy of the car.

To her astonishment her fears were unfounded. The fact was that Theo said nothing at all as he drove the car at a speed that was positively terrifying all the way back to the villa.

Even there he didn't speak, but left the car, slamming its door behind him, and marched straight into the living room where he poured himself a glass of brandy and took a large swallow, clearly making up for the way he had stuck strictly to water over dinner.

'Okay—so you're in a bad mood.' Pushed beyond the need for caution by the painful knots in her stomach, Skye surveyed him from the safety of the doorway. 'So are you going to explain?'

'You don't know what you're asking,' Theo returned flatly.

'I'm asking for an explanation. I reckon you owe me one after suddenly abandoning me in the middle of our meal together and going to talk to some other woman!'

No, that was totally unwise. She sounded like an insecure and jealous girlfriend. She sounded exactly as she *felt*. But not as she had any right to be.

'And then dragging me away from my meal before I'd even had a chance to taste it—'

'You said you weren't hungry.'

'Well, of course I wasn't hungry—not then. Who could have any appetite when you were glaring at them like a storm cloud from across the table?'

'My apologies.' He made it sound like anything but an apology. 'But I didn't want to stay there.'

'Then I think you owe me at least a reason for all this!'

'I owe you nothing!' Theo snarled, splashing another measure of brandy into his glass. 'All I promised was a trip around my island.'

'I'm not talking about the tour of your precious island!'

Something was wrong there.

Some sudden reaction, a tiny movement that he couldn't quite control, revealed Theo's feelings when she knew he would rather have died than let them show. There was a new wariness in the glittering black eyes, a tautness about his mouth and jaw that revealed she had come close to hitting home.

'Your island…' Skye said slowly as a whole new set of thoughts filtered down into her bewildered mind.

'My island,' Theo echoed darkly, watching her through narrowed eyes. 'What about my island, sweet Skye?'

It was his tone that convinced her. The cynically drawling way he spoke, the harsh emphasis on that 'my island'. It confirmed the way a suspicion had been eating away at her thoughts all the way through the trip around the island.

It was my mother's and it should have come to me. Theo's voice, dark with bitterness, rang inside her head from earlier that afternoon.

'Your father—he disinherited you.'

His only response was a hard, swift nod of his dark head, burning eyes still fixed on her face.

'Before your falling out, as his heir, you would have inherited Helikos. But now…'

'Now what, *agape mou*?' Theo prompted harshly when she hesitated, struggling with thoughts that stabbed at her like daggers. 'Just what is going through your fanciful little mind now?'

It was that 'fanciful' that pushed her into it. If he hadn't said that she might have chickened out, backtracking desperately and coming up with some other cover story to explain her reaction. But…'fanciful' he had said, and the sardonic way the word had left his mouth, the cruelly mocking smile that had curved his sensual lips, incensed her, driving her over the top from cautious sense and into reckless determination.

'That's what's really behind all this, isn't it? Why you want to ruin things between your father and me. Why you want to make sure I never marry him. When your father disinherited you, you lost the chance to own this island at some time in the future. But as long as there was no one else, then there was always the chance that Cyril might change his mind…'

She was running out of steam, faltering in front of the steely-eyed glare that seemed to sear the skin from her face.

'Go on,' Theo prompted icily when she hesitated. 'I'm finding this all fascinating.'

'But—but if he married again, and had another child, then that child would become his heir in your place. You're determined to break up your father and me so that we don't marry—don't have children—and no one will come between you and your precious inheritance, Helikos.'

Catching her breath after the rush through the explanation, Skye fell silent and waited, her heart thumping cruelly, for Theo's reaction.

It was not what she expected.

He laughed. He actually threw back his head and laughed out loud. But it was not a kind laugh, not at all warm, and it definitely had no real humour in it. It was cold and cruel and deeply cynical, filled with dark mockery at her outburst.

'Oh, my dear Skye, if you really think that then you don't know me at all. If I was trying to stop my father from begetting another child, then I would be sorely disappointed. Because he already has a new heir—or he will have soon.'

'He can't! I mean—'

'Oh, I know that you told me that you and my father had never slept together. But one thing you should know, *agape mou,* is that my father has never, to my knowledge, ever been faithful to any one woman in his life. And he isn't starting now. He has a mistress. Her name is Berenice.'

He had put the glass down on the nearest table and Skye had the strangest idea that he had done so because he expected her to react in some way. But she couldn't. At least, not in the way that he was evidently expecting.

It was true it was a struggle to hold back on the feelings that were whirling inside her, pushing for expression, beating at her mind. But the emotions she was fighting not to express were far from the ones that Theo was expecting.

Berenice was *Cyril's* lover. She had nothing to do with Theo—except as his father's mistress!

Skye knew she was supposed to be shocked—perhaps Theo even expected her to be upset, but inside her head her thoughts were bubbling in wild relief and happiness.

'That woman in the *taverna*?' she managed, and her voice was as shaky as Theo might have expected, if for totally opposite reasons.

'The woman in the *taverna*,' he confirmed. 'She's been my father's mistress for years—since before I left Helikos, in fact. But she always feared she was barren—that she couldn't have any children.'

'But now…' Skye supplied when he hesitated. Because obviously there was a 'but' to come.

'Now she knows that's not the case,' Theo replied soberly. 'Berenice is three months pregnant and the child is my father's.'

CHAPTER TWELVE

'YOUR father's?'

Skye had gone so white that Theo feared she might faint. In fact she was swaying weakly where she stood, as if her legs were about to give way beneath her.

'Skye?'

His voice was raw with concern. The truth was that he had never actually expected her to react like this. If he'd even suspected it, he would never have told her the truth quite so baldly and directly. But the way she had reacted to the fact that his father had a mistress had been so understated, almost as if she had been expecting it, that he had been more convinced than ever that she cared nothing for Cyril, and that she wouldn't care either to know about the baby that Berenice was expecting.

'Here—sit down.'

He moved to her side hastily, half leading, half carrying her to the settee and lowering her into it, coming down beside her on the soft cushions.

'I'm sorry—I shouldn't—'

''S all right,' Skye mumbled in a voice that made it blatantly plain it was not.

'No, it isn't. I—oh, hell, Skye!'

She had glanced at him as he spoke, looking up at him without the fall of her long auburn hair to hide her face. So he had seen the revealing sheen that glistened on her soft grey eyes.

'Tears?'

'No!'

149

She was stiffly defiant, her head coming up high and her smooth chin lifting determinedly.

But the mutinous expression and tone were completely ruined by the quaver in her voice. She had to struggle to control her mouth too, trying to clamp it into a hard line and failing abjectly. Somehow she had kept any tears from falling, but the wet drops had turned her long, lush lashes into damp, spiky clumps.

'Not tears!'

'Not tears?' Theo echoed softly. Lifting a finger to the corner of her eye, he brushed it against the softness of her lashes and brought it away wet. 'Then what are these?'

Skye's blurred gaze dropped to the hand he held out, focused on the moisture glistening on that finger. She stared at it as long, silent seconds ticked by, and he could almost feel the struggle she was having with herself not to reveal anything of what she was thinking.

But she couldn't hide the tiny, betraying signs. The way her throat worked as she swallowed. The small, undignified sniff.

And then a single tear fell onto his hand, hot and wet and desperately revealing.

'Oh, Skye!'

She muttered something, so low and thick with tears that he didn't catch it. But then she repeated it and this time there was no mistaking the desperation in the words.

'I can't...' Her voice broke on the word. 'I can't go through with this. I really can't!'

Theo couldn't put a name to the feelings that exploded inside him. Concern was there, and a powerful sense of sympathy for what she was going through. A need to understand—to know just what she meant—ran through everything like a seam of gold through the hardest rock. But there were other thoughts, less honourable ones, but ones he wouldn't have been human if he didn't admit to.

There was the sudden upsurge of triumph at the thought that he had finally got through to her—that he was finally seeing the real Skye after all. And surely tears meant that the real Skye was not quite as mercenary and corrupt as her declarations of why she had agreed to marry his father had made her appear.

But the one feeling he couldn't subdue was the way that he wanted—needed—her to say that what she couldn't go through with was the marriage to his father. For the first time he admitted to himself how much he had been waiting for just that moment.

'What?' he asked, still not moving, still not touching her.

He couldn't touch, not until he was sure. Because if he touched, then he would never, ever be able to let go again.

'What did you say?'

Her response came on a huge, gasping sigh. 'I can't...'

'You can't go through with this—with what? Skye, tell me—what can't you do?'

'I can't go through with this marriage!'

High and wild, the words were a wail of despair.

'I can't marry your father! I *won't*!'

And then, at last, the tears came with a vengeance. They welled up inside her eyes, drowning the shadowed grey, and turning it to glistening, blurring silver. The crystal drops spilled over, tumbled down her cheeks and dripped onto his hand, onto her dress, leaving dark, uneven splodges of moisture, soaking into the material.

But still she was totally silent. The tears streamed down her face, sheening her cheeks, dampening her hair, but she didn't make a sound.

And Theo found that that appalled him. Other women he had known had wept loudly, noisily, with great gasping sobs, and heaving breaths. Skye seemed like a marble statue, pale and still and totally silent.

Just the tears. The endless tears. And a terrible desolation in her eyes.

He couldn't hold back any longer.

'Come here!'

He enfolded her in his arms, hugged her to him. She buried her face in his shirt, resting her cheek on his chest. Her shoulders shook and the tears still came.

'Hush,' he soothed, stroking one hand down over the silky rope of her hair, feeling its springing softness beneath his fingers. 'Hush, *agape mou*...'

He found he was crooning to her in his own language, using soft words in Greek that he never would have said to her if he had thought that she might understand. In Greek he could call her sweet, and darling, he could tell her how beautiful he thought her, how he wanted to look after her, how he *wanted* her. Words that he could never use in her own language, to her face, because she would laugh, scorning them, and she would tell him that she had only wanted him for one night—nothing more.

And he had been right to think he must not touch her. From the moment that he had made contact with her slender body, he had known that he had stepped over the invisible line that was drawn between them. Between what was right and what was wrong. What they could and could not do. He had touched her and the feel of her softness, of the warmth of her skin, seemed to burn right up his fingers, searing along every nerve and setting it tingling as if from some wild electrical shock.

She seemed so small and fragile suddenly, the curve of her neck where her head rested against his chest so delicate and pale that it made his heart ache in longing. The scent of her skin and the sweet floral essence of her perfume coiled up around his senses, making his head swim with desire, tormenting him, driving him crazy with response. And the hard, cruel kick of sexual need that hardened his body, tightening sharply, was so primal a force that it almost made him groan aloud in yearning hunger.

She had stopped weeping now. The only way he knew it was that her shoulders had stopped shaking and she had seemed to freeze against him, totally still. But she wasn't moving away, and she kept her head pressed to his chest, her face hidden from view.

'Skye...' he said, stroking a hand down over her hair, tracing the line of fine bones at the point where her neck met her spine. Her name was almost indistinguishable in a voice that was thickened and rough with the arousal he could no longer hide.

She sighed and stirred faintly, but that was all. He sensed the warmth of her breath through the material of her shirt and it made his heart clench in sharp desire.

'Skye...'

This time her name was part sound, part caress against her skin as he kissed along the same path that his fingers had traced a moment before. His tongue touched her skin and he knew that nothing in the world had ever tasted so wonderful, so exceptional, unique. His fingers tugged at the silk scarf that fastened her hair, pulling it loose and letting it fall like a scented curtain all around them.

And then, in that secret world, he found he could ask. He could say the words.

'Did you mean that? When you said you couldn't marry my father?'

Under the burnished hair her head moved in a silent nod of acquiescence. His heart clenched cruelly, but that was not enough.

'Then say it! Say it, *agape mou*. Tell me *why*.'

'I can't marry your father because...'

It was so low that he might have missed it if he hadn't been straining to catch every tiny sound she made. But he caught it and the roar of his blood was like the sound of thunder inside his skull.

'Because it's you that I want.'

He needed no second urging. His dark head swept down, his mouth taking hers. They clung together, hands, bodies, lips, crushed so tight, so close that it seemed impossible to tell where the man ended and the woman began, her hair swirled around them, caught and clung to the roughness of his end-of-the-day stubble and held him prisoner like finest chains of silk.

Her mouth had opened under his, no hesitation, no restraint. But no yielding either. She was all need, fire and lightning and total abandon. And he couldn't wait any longer.

'Skye, my beautiful Skye, will you come to me now— come to my bed?'

'Yes,' she sighed against his lips, her body giving him the answer as she clung to him in need. 'Yes—please. But not here.'

Not here. He knew what she was saying. Not in his father's house.

Jackknifing to his feet, he scooped her up in his arms and lifted her from her seat. Carrying her with an ease that came from a sense of wild exultation, he shouldered his way out the door and into the shadowed darkness of the night. He carried her across the tiled courtyard where the water of the pool lapped against the sides, all colour drained from it in the moonlight.

The door to the pool house was left unlocked—no one ever came out this far into the countryside—and he kicked it open, marching in. Long strides made swift work of the short journey across the kitchen, the tiny living room, through another door.

And then they were in his bedroom where he lowered her to the bed and came down beside her, reaching for her, fingers twisting in the tangled hair, his hands cupping the fine bones of her skull as he brought his mouth down onto hers.

He had been afraid that the short trip from the house, the slight cooling touch of the night, might have dampened down some of the fire in her, lessening her ardour, but he need not have worried. If anything she met him with more enthusiasm than before, returned his kiss with a fervour that made his thoughts spin, and he threw himself down on top of her, crushing her underneath the hungry weight of his body.

Skye welcomed the heat and pressure that enclosed her. For a few heart-shaking seconds as Theo had carried her across the courtyard she had feared that the touch of the night air would cool his passion or hers, bring both of them to their senses with a rush. And whatever happened now, whatever the consequences, she didn't want to lose this wild delirium, the feeling of total right, total conviction.

She had no idea where this would lead. She didn't dare even to *think* of any such thing. All she knew was that she wanted this, wanted it more than anything else in her whole life, in her whole world. She didn't have any idea what would happen in the future—or if she even had a future— but right now she didn't care.

Knowing that no matter what happened she could never marry Cyril gave her a wild sort of freedom. She couldn't marry him, not if there was a baby to be considered, another woman who needed him, a child who needed a father.

What she would do about her family, her father's predicament, she didn't know. Somehow she would find a way. She would beg Cyril—do anything! But tonight she couldn't think about that. She couldn't think about anything but what she had right here and now. Tomorrow would have to take care of itself. She had tonight.

They had tonight.

It was nothing like that first time. Nothing like *that night* in London. There was none of the apprehension, none of the nervous worry.

She didn't feel any embarrassment at being almost naked with Theo, only wanted to touch and stroke and feel. She was tugging at his clothing before he had even dealt with hers, making him mutter in Greek in dark impatience when she stopped him from unfastening her bra because she wanted to rip his tee shirt off him, wanted the feel of his skin beneath her hands.

'Skye...'

The sound of her name was thick and sensual, a rough-edged, raw-toned mutter of impatient protest that made laughter bubble up inside her at the thought that she could reduce this big, powerful man to a state where he shook at her touch.

'Theo...' she returned, echoing both his accent and his intonation.

'Witch!'

He grabbed at her, turned her over until she was face down in the softness of the pillows. Holding her down with one hand, he wouldn't let her move until he had undone the strap of her bra one-handed, pulled it free and tossed it over his shoulder into the room. The sliver of white silk that was her only other covering proved trickier to remove single-handed, but he solved the problem by straddling her back and kissing his way down her spine. This created a sensation so erotically pleasurable that all she could do was lie still and submit, too given over to the delight of his touch to care that the last bit of her clothing was being eased down her legs as his kisses moved lower.

It was when she felt the heated pressure of his mouth on the softness of her buttocks that she moaned aloud in delight. His laughter was a warm sensation against her skin and he caught hold of her again, turned her back to face him.

'Now, you little temptress…'

But even as he laughed out the words, his mood changed dramatically.

Skye caught her breath in shock at the ferocity of the desire that blazed in his black eyes. His breath came harshly and a faint burn of red scored the line of his high cheek-bones.

'You are beautiful.'

It was a sigh of pure sensuality and his hands had a faint tremor in them as he touched her face, traced the line of her cheeks. Those hard, knowing hands smoothed down either side of her neck, curved along her shoulders, then slid underneath her breasts to cup and hold their soft full-ness, his thumbs stroking each pink, raised nipple in delib-erate provocation.

'Oh, Theo…'

Sensation speared along every nerve, making her twist and arch under the pinioning weight of his body, and she saw his smile grow darker, deeper as he lowered himself onto her, his mouth taking hers in a hard, demanding kiss. Her need for him was a hot, heavy pulse between her thighs, the honeyed ache that this time she knew was only the beginning.

This time she recognised the start of sensations that could only grow—that would build and build until she was out of her mind with delight. And she wanted that. Wanted it so much that she pulled Theo down to her, taking all that his mouth could give while her impatient hands were busy with his belt, unfastening the button at his waist, sliding down his zip…

'*Agape mou…*' Theo choked as her seeking fingers found their goal, the heated hardness of him springing free of his clothing and into the welcoming embrace of her touch.

She curled her hands around the rigid shaft, instinctively stroking, teasing until he groaned in near desperate protest.

'You will spoil things for yourself, sweetheart,' he muttered against her ear. 'You're destroying my control.'

'And who said I wanted control?' she teased, letting her tongue trace the curving top of his ear, down the softness of its lobe. 'That's not what I'm looking for tonight.'

'Is that so? Then I think we are both looking for the same thing.'

He turned the removal of the last of his clothes into a sensual art, sliding his long body over hers as she eased away his jeans, his underwear. The powerful length of his legs came between hers, parting her thighs, opening her to him.

And at the same time his mouth tormented her sensitised and aching breasts. Hot hands lifted them towards him, his tongue coiling round and round each nipple in turn, bringing them to stinging, burning awareness, before taking first one and then the other into the warmth of his mouth, suckling softly, sending rivulets of fire running along the pathways of her nerves to pool in molten hunger at the core of her femininity.

'Theo!'

This time his name was an urgent reproach and she lifted her body to his, pushing herself against him, enticing, inviting, demanding.

A demand he had no hesitation in answering.

One fierce, wild thrust brought his body into hers, hard and sure. So hard, so sure that Skye flung back her head against the pillows and closed her eyes, concentrating all her being on the sensation of him filling her, being with her, taking her...

'*Ochi*—no!'

His sudden harsh protest stunned her, shocking her eyes

back open again. His hard face was directly above her, black eyes burning down into her startled grey ones.

'This time you do not close your eyes!' he told her roughly. 'This time you stay with me right to the very last moment. This time you *know* who is making love to you.'

Didn't he know? Couldn't he tell? Surely it was obvious that she couldn't be more aware of just whom she was with, who was making love to her? She had only ever given herself to one man like this. And she could only ever give herself in this way once in her life.

Tonight was the night that she made love with the man she loved. And if tonight was the only night she had left with him for the rest of her life, then no other night—no other man—would ever match it.

'I know who you are,' she tried, then lost the words in a moan of pleasure as he moved deep within her, pushing harder, further into her needy body. 'And I wouldn't want anyone else.'

'I'm glad to hear that.'

Theo's reply was a tiger's purr of triumph, rich and dark and husky with a blend of need and the deepest satisfaction.

'Because tonight I intend to spoil you for any other lover. After tonight you'll only be able to think of me.'

'I already do…'

Skye spoke fast to push away the bitter sting of that 'any other lover'. How could she know any other lover after this? How could she want any other man?

But then Theo moved again, his hand sliding intimately between their joined bodies, a knowing finger stroking her, exciting her with devastating effect. And at the same time his mouth closed over one erect nipple, faintly grazing it with his teeth, making her toss her head frantically on the pillow, her hair tangling wildly beneath her.

'Say my name,' he ordered thickly. 'Say my name.'

'Theo,' Skye responded in immediate obedience, incapable of any other reaction. 'Theo—Theo—*Theo*!'

Her voice rose almost to a scream on the last word, barely able to get the sound out. The combined assault upon her senses was driving her to the edge of distraction. She was so close that she could almost taste it…almost…

'Only me,' Theo muttered roughly against her yearning flesh. 'Only me.'

'Only you,' Skye echoed, not even knowing if her voice could be heard or not as she lost herself in the spiralling, whirling haze of need. 'Oh, yes—only…'

But the rest of her words were lost on a high, keening cry of fulfilment as she felt her senses soar and splinter into the final golden oblivion of ecstasy.

CHAPTER THIRTEEN

IT WAS the phone that woke them late the next morning.

It was ringing in the main house, but there was an extension that was switched through to the pool house when there was no one at home, and the sound of it shrilling through the small apartment dragged them from the sleep of exhaustion.

Cursing softly, Theo padded through into the living room to answer it while Skye still struggled to wake properly, forcing her heavy lids to open reluctantly. But only moments later he was back, holding out the phone to her.

'For you,' he said flatly. 'From England. Your father.'

Skye didn't understand the look on his face, or the blank tone of his voice, but her need for news of her mother overrode all other thoughts so she almost grabbed at the phone, putting it hastily to her ear.

'Dad?'

Theo moved away into the other room—to give her privacy, Skye assumed. She heard the sound of the kettle being switched on, the clink of a spoon in a mug, but then something her father said forced her to concentrate hard.

It was ten minutes later that, having finished her call, switched off the phone and waited for Theo to come back, she realised that he was not in fact still being tactful. He was deliberately staying away and she had no idea why.

Throwing back the covers, she snatched at the nearest thing to hand that would cover her nakedness. It turned out to be the tee shirt Theo had been wearing last night, still bearing his imprint in the scent of his body that permeated the soft material. It was just long enough to reach to the tops of her thighs, exposing large amounts of slender leg. But there was no point in false modesty. Theo had seen— and touched, and *kissed*—every last inch of her throughout the night. There was little point in covering up now. Brushing her hands through her tangled hair in a vague attempt to restore it to some sort of order, she made her way into the living room.

Theo was standing by the open patio doors, staring out at the hazy mist that blurred the far horizon. He had pulled on a pair of jeans but nothing else, and she was shocked to see the way that the bronzed skin of his broad back still bore the marks of her nails where she had caught him in the throes of one particularly mind-blowing orgasm in the middle of the night.

'Theo?'

He didn't hear her, he was so absorbed in whatever occupied his thoughts. Padding silently on bare feet, she crossed the room unnoticed, lifting a soft hand to touch one of the small red weals.

'I'm sorry,' she said quietly. Then, 'Sorry!' more emphatically as he spun round in sudden shock.

Her tone changed abruptly as she saw his expression.

'Is something wrong?'

'I don't know.'

There was a worrying stiffness in his reply and the black eyes were opaque and distant. No longer those of the ardent lover of the night before.

'Why don't you tell me?'

'Tell you what? What do you want to know?'

Theo looked down at the still-full mug of coffee that was in his hand. Clearly he had made it and then forgotten to drink it, letting it grow cold as he became absorbed in whatever thoughts had preoccupied him out here while she was on the phone.

Grimacing in distaste, he tossed the unappetising liquid

out onto the stone paving beyond the window and dumped the empty mug on a nearby bookshelf.

'Why don't you start with why your parents aren't here?'

The mention of her parents made her tense instinctively. Even the tiny hairs at the back of her neck lifted in the instinctive reaction of a wary cat as she wondered if in fact he had been listening to her phone conversation after all.

With that phone call all the wild euphoria of the night before had evaporated like mist before the sun. Cold, hard reality had slammed home, rocking her world and sending her spinning into a yawning chasm of despair. All her fantasies of escape, of freedom, lay shattered at her feet, and her own foolish actions had made the situation so much worse. Now she had no idea which way to turn.

'If you are supposed to be marrying my father soon, then wouldn't your parents want to be at the wedding?'

That at least was easy to answer.

'My mother is ill—her heart. She's in hospital and too weak to travel.'

She tried to just make it a statement of fact, but the news she had just had from her father made that impossible. Her voice caught on the words, broke revealingly towards the end.

And Theo's keen hearing picked up on it straight away.

'It's bad?' he asked sharply.

This time Skye's voice deserted her and she could only nod silently as she struggled with the tears that burned in her throat, stung at the back of her eyes.

'How bad?'

'This operation that she's in for is her last hope.'

And now her foolishness of last night might just have destroyed all hope of the current treatment being successful. Last night, in a state of shock at the discovery of Cyril's mistress and her pregnancy, she'd thought only of the needs of that unborn child. This morning, with the news of her mother's condition far worse than she had anticipated, she had to consider her own family's needs. But there was no way that one could win out without destroying the hopes of the other.

'If it doesn't work then she'll—she'll need a transplant.'

'Then what the hell are you doing here? Why aren't you with her?'

'I wish I could be—but your father wanted me here.'

Sensing the next question, she rushed into answering it before Theo even had time to ask it.

'He wanted the marriage to take place as soon as possible...' Her voice trailed off, failing her once again as she saw the disbelief harden in his eyes, watched him shake his head in adamant rejection of her words.

'Surely even my father would wait. Skye—what is it that you're not telling me?'

Suddenly, ridiculously, Skye was desperately aware of her state of undress. The tee shirt that had seemed a reasonably adequate covering now seemed impossibly skimpy and revealing. Not at all the right sort of clothing in which to be having this sort of conversation.

But then, what sort of clothing *was* suitable for this sort of conversation?

Nervously she tugged at the hem of the shirt, painfully conscious of the fact that it did nothing to bring it any further down her thighs. All it did do was to draw Theo's black-eyed gaze to the point where her clothing ended and her legs began.

'There's something wrong here,' Theo went on, his tone making her shiver inside. 'And I want to know what it is.'

His face was set into lines of ruthless determination, telling her without words that there was no point in trying to appeal to his better nature—he just wasn't prepared to let this go.

Her heart felt as if it were breaking inside her. If he

pushed, she would have to answer. But she couldn't tell him the whole truth.

The truth that wasn't hers to tell.

And her father's phone call had just been a brutal reminder of how much that truth mattered. So she would have to go back to dealing in half-truths again. The terrible thing was that half-truths were also half-lies.

'Skye…'

The dangerous note in Theo's use of her name shocked her onto the defensive. She would have to go back to the cold, brittle role that had been her protection up to now.

'Th-there's nothing to tell.'

'No?'

If there was one thing Theo hated it was being lied to—and Skye was lying through her pretty teeth right now. He was convinced of that. Her beautiful eyes wouldn't quite meet his and she was shifting from one foot to another uneasily.

It would help him think more clearly if she weren't so distractingly dressed. He found it almost impossible to concentrate when she was standing there wearing nothing but the tee shirt he had discarded last night. The memory of the way she had stripped him of it, of the feel of her soft hands on his skin, on the most intimate parts of his body, made hot blood flood his veins so that he had to clamp down hard on the impulse to let his thoughts run riot.

'I don't believe you. And I want to find out just what's going on.'

'Nothing—' Skye began again, but Theo had had enough.

'All right!' he exploded, flinging out his hands in a gesture of wild exasperation. 'All right—so there's *nothing* there that you want to explain about. Well, we'll come back to that. Let's try a different tack instead.'

He'd caught her off balance there, that was obvious. Her

expression had changed, the defiant wariness in her eyes changing to a look of shocked confusion. She had even taken a step backwards, like a cornered animal.

'What—?' she began fearfully, but he didn't give her the chance to speak.

'There are other questions I want answering—questions you might find easier to answer, so we'll start with one of those, shall we? How about telling me about the night we first met?'

She was definitely on edge now. So much so that she was poised on the balls of her feet, looking as if she was about to run at any moment.

'What about that night?'

'You said that you agreed to marry my father because you wanted a wealthy husband.'

'I knew he could keep me in the manner to which I'd like to become accustomed.'

Skye's interjection sounded so unconcerned, so blasé, that for a moment he stopped dead, appalled by her carelessness. But then he looked into her eyes once more and saw the shadows that darkened their soft grey, the struggle she was having to meet his scrutiny, and he knew that he had to go on until he found out just what she was hiding.

'So, if that's the case, then why me? If you wanted a sugar-daddy for the rest of your life, why didn't you make sure of that before you went off the rails? Why the hell did you risk it all to sleep with me?'

Her chin came up higher, her eyes clashing with his in open defiance.

'You helped me—you came to my rescue. I was grateful.'

'Grateful!'

Theo echoed the word in bleak disgust.

'And so you slept with me! So tell me, my lovely Skye, is that how you plan to thank everyone, how you pay all your debts? Which makes me wonder—what the hell did my father do for you?'

She was backing away again, forcing him to move towards her if he was to keep this conversation going. All the colour had faded from her cheeks so that her hair was almost unbearably vivid, the deep pools of her eyes looking like bruises against the ashen white of her skin.

'I can't! It's none of your business!'

'I'm making it my business! Skye—tell me! What—?'

'Money!'

She flung the word into his face in a sort of wild despair. And then suddenly it was as if, having broken through some barrier, she could no longer hold anything back and the words just came pouring out.

'I told you—I needed money! There are debts—really bad debts. Debts I'll never meet on my own.'

'And my father said he'd pay them? But surely your parents...?'

'They have no more than I have! Less! And even if they could help me—do you think I'd ask? With my mother as ill as she is—it would kill her! So when your father offered marriage...'

'You snatched at his offer before he could change his mind.'

It had the dreadful ring of truth. And knowing his father, he could see that Cyril would not have been able to resist the macho prestige of being able to acquire a bride younger than his own son—even if he had to buy her to make it happen.

'It was my only way out. I couldn't see any other alternative. And he—he offered so much...'

'I'll bet he did. And so what was my part in all this?'

If it were possible, he would have sworn that she had gone even whiter. There wasn't a trace of blood left in her translucent skin.

'I—you—that was my last night of freedom. Your—Cyril was waiting for my answer. I had to give it to him the next day. I knew I was going to have to say yes—that from then on my life wouldn't be my own—and so I—I was looking for some…'

She seemed to struggle to find the right word, to get it out.

'Some fun.'

'*Fun!*'

The realisation that he had been nothing more than an act of rebellion against her upcoming marriage of convenience stuck in his throat, making him want to retch.

'That's all it was to you—some fun?'

'That's what it was supposed to be!'

There was an odd note in her voice. He was trying to get a handle on what it meant when she destroyed his concentration by adding, 'I hadn't reckoned on you turning up here afterwards.'

'I'll bet you didn't! And if I hadn't turned up, what would you have done? Lied?'

She actually flinched away from his words—or from the fury with which he flung them at her.

He felt furious. Furious with her for proving herself to have been as shallow and as grasping as he had feared she would be. And furious with himself because, even now, seeing her as she was, he still couldn't let go.

He had wanted that first night with her to prove to her that they could have more than the one-night stand that was all she had been prepared to offer him. Then he had wanted just one *more* night, to gorge himself on her, sate himself until he could walk away and not look back. Or that was what he had told himself.

But it hadn't worked out like that. Once again, a night with her had left him wanting, left him hungry. And like a fool he still wanted more. He couldn't let her go.

'You father asked for a bride. I would have been that bride.'

'Because he promised to pay off your debts? But you didn't expect the marriage to be any *fun*. Is that right? You could have played your cards better than that, sweetheart.'

'I don't know what you mean!'

'You had a better hand than you thought,' Theo elaborated cruelly. 'That night—when you chose me to have your *fun* with—if you'd been a little more clever, a little more wily, you could have found out more about me. You could have got yourself a husband who would give you more of what you wanted.'

Skye could hardly believe what she was hearing.

'A husband—are you saying that...?'

She couldn't frame the words. They just didn't seem possible.

'That if I'd known you needed a rich husband I would have applied for the job? That's exactly what I'm saying. I still am.'

No. Skye shook her head sharply. She couldn't have heard *that*. It was too much; too cruel.

'No?'

She heard Theo's mocking voice through a buzzing haze inside her head.

'Is that no, you didn't know—or no, you won't have me? Surely you're not going to turn down a husband who'll pay off your debts and not ask awkward questions about your virginity—and I think we've proved that we can provide that essential element of *fun* in bed.'

This couldn't be happening. Skye wanted to wrap her arms around her body to hold herself together. She was trembling in reaction and desperately wanted to hide the fact from him.

'Tempted?' Theo asked.

Tempted didn't describe it. It was all that she could ever have hoped for—all she had dreamed of since that night in London. She had dreamed that the man she had met and made love with—the man she had given her heart to—would somehow find her and come back into her life. That he would rescue her from the situation that had trapped her—tell her he loved her, and ask her to marry him.

Now it seemed that all her dreams had come true, but in the most bitterly ironic way possible. Theo was back in her life, he had asked her to marry him—but everything conspired to make sure that she couldn't say yes.

He didn't love her, for one thing. The most important, most essential thing. And even if she had felt she might be able to commit herself to a loveless marriage—as she had been prepared to endure with his father—it just wasn't possible. Theo might be able to pay off the debts her family owed, but there was so much more to the situation than just the money.

She had promised to marry Cyril in order to save her father from jail and if she didn't marry him then he would prosecute. That was the other reason why Andrew Marston had phoned her this morning. She could still hear his words ringing inside her head.

'You will go through with this, Skye, won't you? Promise me you will! I can't go to prison—it will kill me—and it will certainly kill your mother!'

A sound from outside caught her attention, bringing her head swinging round. The roar of a powerful car in the distance, coming up the road from the village.

Theo had heard it too.

'My father's back. When he finds you're not in the house, he'll come looking for you. It's decision time, *agape mou*. Which one is it to be—marriage to my father or to me?'

But Skye couldn't find any words to answer him. She was already dashing back to the bedroom, snatching up her crumpled dress. It took only seconds to discard Theo's shirt and pull on her clothes and by the time he appeared in the doorway she was tugging down the lilac cotton and pushing her feet into her shoes at the same time.

'I don't believe it!'

The contempt in his voice lashed at her and she winced away from the brutal pain it brought to her already desolated heart.

'I have to do this,' she told him, grabbing a brush from the top of a chest and dragging it roughly through her hair. 'Please understand!'

'Oh, I understand all right,' Theo declared, his tone harsh enough to strip away a protective layer of skin. 'But you'd better understand one thing too. I will wait one minute for you to change your mind—and, if you do, then we'll go to my father together. I'll tell him what happened—say I seduced you.'

'You'd do that for me?'

In a morning of shocks, this was the most unbelievable. The last thing she would ever have thought she would hear him say.

'But if you walk out of that door without me, then you walk out for good. You never come back—is that understood?'

Skye nodded miserably. She could be in no doubt that Theo meant the threat. She could also be in no doubt that she was going to have to make him carry it out. She couldn't tell him the truth and because of that she could never do anything but leave.

'I'm sorry,' was all she could manage as she turned to go.

For one appalling moment she thought that he was not going to move, that he would not let her past. His strong arm barred the way, one hand resting on the opposite side of the door frame, blocking her path. Her heart slowed almost to a stop as burning black eyes clashed with troubled grey, Theo seeming to search for something in her face. She didn't know what he found there, but at last he lowered his arm to his side and stood back.

'You don't come back,' he repeated emphatically.

Knowing there was nothing she could say, Skye slipped past him and headed towards the door. Theo simply watched her go, arms folded across his chest and his face set like stone.

Tears blurred her eyes, almost blinding her as she stumbled her way across the courtyard, down the stone steps at the side of the house and into her room on the lower level.

She had barely closed the door behind her when Cyril's big car turned in at the gates.

CHAPTER FOURTEEN

SKYE put the last of her clothes into the suitcase and closed the lid. That was the final job done; there was nothing left to keep her there.

A long, desolate sigh escaped her. It was all she was capable of. No more tears. She was all cried out. At least for now.

She had no doubt that when she got home there would be more tears, more distress. She would have to try to explain things to her father, and she would have to take care of her mother. She didn't know how she would do it. She only knew she had to.

She had tried so hard to find a way out of this, but she knew that there wasn't one. Only the way that Cyril had offered and that was the one thing she knew she couldn't do.

Anything else she might have considered. But not that.

The car that Cyril had promised would take her to the helicopter was waiting at the door, a uniformed chauffeur standing beside it, cap pulled down low over his eyes. He took her case, saw her into the back seat, and closed the door, all without a word. Which was exactly the way she wanted it.

The truth was that she was barely conscious of her surroundings, of anything. She didn't have a word to say to anyone. The only man she wanted to speak to was determinedly absent, locked into the pool house, and she hadn't seen a sign of him since he had offered that dreadful ultimatum and watched her walk out.

And now she would never see him again. Ever.

The trip from the house to the helicopter pad was only a matter of minutes in the powerful car, and too soon, well before she was emotionally ready, they swung round the last bend and their destination came into sight. Clenching her hands tight over the handles of her bag, Skye forced herself to straighten in her seat, and prepare for their arrival.

Only to gasp in shock as the chauffeur brought the car to a smooth halt, still some distance away from the official parking place.

'What's the matter?'

The long hours of strain showed in her voice, making it raw and husky.

'Is something wrong? Do I have to walk from here?'

'No, that won't be necessary,' was the reply in a voice that made her heart stop violently in her chest, then launch back into action at double-quick time. 'I'll take you right to the launch pad if you like—and if you decide you want to go.'

Skye was too stunned to speak. Her tongue wouldn't work, her heart was now racing high up in her throat and her breath was snatched in raw, uneven gasps.

'*You?*' was all she managed to croak.

It didn't seem possible—it couldn't be true. But even as she forced out the question the man in the driving seat pulled off his cap and tossed it aside as he swivelled round to face her.

'*Kalimera,* Skye,' Theo said calmly.

'Wh-what are you doing here?'

It was hopelessly inane, but inanity was all she was capable of.

'I came to see you.'

'But you said that if I walked out—'

'I know.' Theo's voice was low. 'And I was a total fool to do so.'

He'd known he was a fool even as he'd been saying the

words. Known that the only, inevitable result of throwing out such an ultimatum was that it would blow up right in his face, leaving him with his life turned upside down and everything working out in the opposite way to what he wanted.

He wanted Skye to stay—there, he'd admitted it to himself once and for all. He wanted her to stay, and the last thing he needed was for her to walk away from him and never come back.

So what had he done?

Like a fool, he'd made it impossible for her to do anything else. He'd created a situation in which she was going to have to walk away because she had no choice. Hurt and angry, he'd pushed her into a corner from which she'd only had one possible escape route and then he'd been even more hurt and angry that she'd taken it. And he'd had to watch her walk away and known that he'd set up the whole situation in the first place.

The sense of loss—a real, tearing pain, far worse than the hurt pride that had pushed him into this—had wanted him to call her back. But anger, black, destructive anger, had kept him silent as he'd watched her walk away.

And when she'd gone he'd snatched up the coffee mug from the shelf where he'd placed it and hurled it against the wall, cursing savagely as he'd watched it splinter into a thousand tiny pieces.

'I put you in an impossible situation and then hated you when you reacted against it.'

'I had to talk to your father.' Skye's voice was very low.

'I know that now. I knew it as soon as I calmed down. But at the time I was just too damn blind to see. What can I say?'

He spread his hands in a gesture of resigned defeat.

'I was jealous. Jealousy does weird things to your mind.'

He'd shocked her there. She was sitting back in her seat,

wide grey eyes huge in a pale face. Wide grey, *red-rimmed* eyes. He hated himself for that evidence of tears just as he welcomed it as a sign of hope.

'Jealous?' she questioned now, a definite hesitancy on the word. 'Of who?'

'Of my father.'

Since she'd sat back, he couldn't see her properly, so he unclasped the seat belt quickly, freeing himself to turn enough to face her full on. He had to see her face. To know what she was feeling, if not what she was thinking. At least that way he might have some clue as to how to handle this.

'Hell, I reckon I've been jealous of every man in the world since I met you. But most of all my father.'

That was better. There had been a genuine flash of delight across her face when he'd said that. But it had been there and gone too quickly, too carefully masked for his liking.

'Why?'

'Isn't it obvious? Because I wanted you so much.'

It was more than that. Much more. He'd known how much from the way it had felt to watch her walk away and out of his life. But he wasn't ready to admit that yet.

'You made that clear.'

At least there was a flare of life in what she said. But was that life amusement or cynicism? The truth was that her tone was a mixture of both.

'Theo—the pilot is waiting.'

Was she so anxious to be gone? The thought rocked him, making him realise how much he was still taking for granted. He knew what he felt, but he had no idea what was going through *her* mind at all.

'No, he isn't,' he growled. 'Because there isn't a pilot.'

'Then how am I going to get off the island?'

'I'll fly you myself. If you have to go.'

'Of course I have to go! You know that I can't stay! Your father—'

'My father told me he'd ordered the pilot to get the helicopter ready, but I cancelled it.'

'You spoke to your father?'

'Of course I did. How do you think I knew when you were leaving?'

Skye felt as if the car must be rocking from side to side with the force of her emotions, first up and then down, until she no longer knew just where she was.

If he had spoken to his father, then she knew why he was here.

Cyril must have offered him the same sort of deal that he had offered her. A deal she had had to refuse. For the second time that day she had been offered a chance to have what she most wanted, most dreamed of in life, but under conditions that meant she had no alternative but to turn it down. Surely fate wouldn't be so cruel as to make her have to go through that again. Not when she was already having to endure this meeting as well.

Having resigned herself so unhappily to the fact that she was never going to see Theo again and then nerved herself for the journey home, it had been a stunning shock to find both resolutions overturned in a matter of seconds. It was too cruel of Theo—or fate, or whoever had decided it—to give her this one last look at his beloved face and know that she was going to have to leave him. Having said goodbye to him in her heart had been torment enough. But having to go through it all over again in reality was more than she could bear.

'Theo, please let me go! If you don't want me...'

'Damn it, woman! Weren't you listening? I just said that I wanted you—too much!'

'I know you did,' Skye admitted. 'But I think that what

you mean by *want* and what I mean are two very different things.'

In the seat in front, Theo stirred restlessly, one hand clenching into a fist and slamming down onto the leather covered back.

'Are you trying to deny that you wanted me every bit as much? Because if you are, then I don't believe—'

'No,' Skye cut in sadly. 'No, of course I'm not going to deny that. I'd be a fool to even try.'

'Then you do still want me?'

'Want?'

It was a shaken laugh and just for a second she leaned forward in her seat, acting on a foolish impulse to reach out and touch him. His face was just within reach, the lean line of his jaw faintly shadowed with dark stubble even at this time of the morning...

But she was forgetting about her seat belt, which snapped into place to hold her back, and she collapsed down in her seat again, letting out a sigh that was a blend of deep regret and a double-edged relief.

Regret because she longed to let her fingers rest on his dear face, to feel the satin warmth of his skin just once more, and relief because deep down inside she knew that if she *had* made contact, it wouldn't have stopped at that. There was no way she could have touched him and then done nothing more.

'Oh, yes, I want you,' she breathed. 'But if you've spoken to your father, then you know it won't work.'

In the darkness at the back of her thoughts, she could hear Cyril's words when she had finally got to see him earlier. She had decided to tell him everything—about her meeting with Theo that first time and what had happened ever since. She had been prepared to beg, to plead with him to help her father even if he wouldn't marry her. She'd offer to be his servant, nursemaid to the baby Berenice was expecting—anything.

She hadn't been able to say a word.

Cyril already knew about the baby, it seemed. That was why he had been so distant over the past few days; why he had gone to Athens to talk to his lawyer.

He had only planned to marry her in order to father a child. He had a child now and he was going to marry its mother, Berenice. So the arranged marriage between them would now not take place.

He was quite calm, totally businesslike about it.

But he had a proposition to put to Skye. One that would solve her problems—and those of her family.

'I've seen the way my son looks at you,' he said. 'He has a gleam in his eyes that gives away what he's thinking. He wants you, any man can see that. If you marry him, then our deal still stands...'

'Why didn't you tell me?'

Theo's voice interrupted her unhappy reflections, dragging her back to the present. He was leaning even further over the seat, black eyes burning into her face, and his voice was huskily intent.

'Why didn't you tell me about your father's problems?'

'They weren't mine to tell! I promised Dad I'd—'

She broke off sharply as he muttered something dark and dangerous in his native Greek.

'What did you say?'

Theo obviously made an effort to pull his black mood under control.

'I said that your father does not deserve your loyalty. What sort of man is he to let you go through this for his sake?'

'I said I would! And I was doing it for Mum as well. If my father goes to prison then it will kill her. She needs him so badly...'

Emotion forced her to stop, gulping down the tears that were welling up inside before she felt strong enough to go on.

'And Dad—Dad adores her so much that he would rather that I was unhappy than that he should lose her. He wouldn't want to live.'

'Now that I can understand,' Theo murmured, but Skye noticed that he did not loosen the strong hands that had clenched into tight, dangerous-looking fists on the back of the car seat. 'But I still cannot forgive.'

Forgive.

It was the last word that she expected and it drew her eyes to his face again. Looking more closely, looking beyond the grim set of his mouth, the tight muscles in his jaw, she saw unexpected shadows in the once brilliant dark eyes. It was as if, once the anger he had shown earlier had receded, it had left some sort of emotional bruising behind, marking his face with it. Just seeing that made her feel that perhaps she might dare open up to him a little more.

After all, what harm could it do? She and her family had nothing left to lose.

'Your father couldn't forgive either,' she said sadly. 'I don't know how I'm going to be able to tell Dad that— and Mum…'

This time she had to dig her teeth down hard into her bottom lip to hold back the tears and her eyes blurred so much that she didn't see Theo move.

'Don't!' he said sharply, suddenly leaning over the back of the seat and reaching out to stroke a soft thumb over the damaged lip. 'Don't do that.'

His tone took her breath away, froze her in her seat. Shock cleared her gaze so that she found herself looking into dark, deep eyes. Eyes that no longer seemed as hard as polished jet, but melting and liquid.

She was dreaming. She had to be. There was no way she

could trust her own vision. She was seeing things—or at least putting the interpretation she wanted on things that were really not that way.

'I'm forgetting…'

The soothing hand was snatched away so quickly that Skye almost moaned aloud, her own fingers coming up to cover the spot where his touch had rested. Under cover of their concealment, she savoured the taste of his skin on her mouth, then blinked hard in stunned amazement as Theo pulled a long white envelope from his pocket and tossed it onto the seat beside her.

'What's this?'

'Open it and see.'

It was the fact that he so clearly tried for nonchalance and failed that set her nerves jangling. Unfastening the uncomfortably restraining seat belt, she picked up the envelope and thumbed it open.

Inside was a single thick sheet of paper, printed on one side, with several signatures at the bottom. Disturbingly conscious of Theo's jet eyes on her, Skye skimmed through it hastily, then paused, frowning in shock, and went back to read it again.

It still didn't make any sense.

'I don't understand! This seems to say that your father isn't going to inform the police.'

'That's exactly what it does say.'

'But why? And what does this mean? This bit about "all accounts having been repaid…"'

'It means that your father's debts have been cleared.'

'By whom?'

She saw the answer in his eyes.

'Oh, no! Please don't say that you—'

'Of course, me.'

Theo couldn't believe her reaction. She actually looked

horrified at what he had done. When all the time he had been expecting—dreaming—planning…

If she truly was appalled, then where did that leave his next move? Unable to stay still in the confined space of the car any longer, he flung open the door and swung himself out into the crisp morning air. With a rough movement he pulled open the door to where she sat and leaned down to come face to face with her.

'Just what is wrong with that? Why the hell shouldn't I pay off your father's debts? And why shouldn't *my* father agree not to press charges? You don't really think that he would want to see my wife's father in jail for—'

'Your what?' Skye inserted in sharp question.

'My father-in-law,' Theo returned. 'Isn't it obvious my father wouldn't—?'

His words failed him when he saw the blank bewilderment on her face. Bewilderment mixed with total rejection of what he had just said.

'Don't you think you should ask me first?' she said in a tone so stiff that he half expected to be slapped in the face by the words as they came out.

It didn't surprise him, though. He'd blundered in, messing things up. He had to do this properly.

'I'm sorry—I rushed in—I was coming to that. I—'

There was only one thing for it. He was lowering himself to one knee outside the car, taking her hand in his.

'Skye. Will you—?'

But the look on her face was even more appalled than before. She snatched her hand back, cradling it to her as if it were burned.

'No—don't!' she gasped. 'Just don't! Don't do this— anything but this! Please, if you want payment, I'll pay you back if it takes my lifetime—but don't pretend you want to marry me! Please don't!'

If she had punched him hard in the face, Theo couldn't

have reeled back any more violently. He almost fell, but struggled to keep his balance and then got to his feet. Because he still held onto her hand, Skye had to go with him, scrambling awkwardly out of her seat and coming to stand beside him, facing him over the open car door.

'Just what—?' he began, but then broke off sharply.

What sort of an idiot was he? What did it take to get it through his thick skull? She didn't want to marry him; that was obvious. The best thing he could hope for now was to get out with some pride intact.

'I'm sorry,' he said, letting go of her hand and stepping back. 'I must have read the signals all wrong. I'm sorry.'

Skye's head was spinning. She didn't know what to believe.

Theo's proposal, his arrogant assumption that she would just fall in with his plans because they made her father his father-in-law, had been more than she could bear. Did he think that she didn't know *why* he was doing it? That his father hadn't talked of his plans with her?

And yet there had been that moment before he had let her hand drop when just for a moment he had closed his eyes as if to blot out the scene before him. And in that moment she had seen the flash of something very deep and very dark in his eyes.

In someone else she would have called it pain—but in Theo?

'I'm sorry too,' she said, stumbling over the words as she tried to get them out. 'I wish I could—you've been so kind…'

'*Kind?*' Theo echoed in a tone so savage it made her flinch from it. But she couldn't let herself be stopped now. She had to say this.

'I know that you think this way you'll get everything you want, and I'm sorry about the island, but—'

'Just a second,' Theo cut in. 'What the hell do you mean I'll get everything I want?'

'What your father promised. If you married me, you'd get your inheritance—get Helikos. I wish I could have done that for you. But I know how you felt when your father tried to force you into marriage before. If you married me, in time you'd regret it and—'

The expression on his face got through to her. He couldn't fake that look of blank confusion.

'You don't know what I'm talking about, do you?'

Theo shook his dark head slowly.

'Not an idea.'

'Your father never said that—that—if you married me he'd give you your inheritance—the island?'

'He'd have a problem—I already refused to have anything from him.'

Skye barely heard Theo's response, she was so determined to tell him everything.

'I knew how you hated it that first time when he wanted to tell you who to marry. I couldn't put you through that again. And I—I couldn't face the prospect that if you went into an arranged marriage with me then one day you might regret it so badly...'

'You're right. I would,' Theo inserted soberly.

'I thought s-so.'

It was a struggle to speak. The pain was so bad that it was tearing her apart inside.

But Theo hadn't finished.

'If I married you because my father dictated it and for no other reason, then, yes, I would regret it. Because that first time he tried, there was one thing it taught me—and that was I was so opposed to an arranged marriage because I only ever wanted to marry someone I loved. Someone I could share the rest of my life with. Someone I could grow old with.'

'I—I hope you find her.' It took all her strength to say it.

'I already have,' Theo responded softly.

He sounded totally strong, totally sure. She was falling apart. But then she saw the way he was looking at her.

'Who?' she had to ask.

'You,' he replied simply.

She couldn't have heard right. Her foolish, weak mind must have put the thought into her head. It couldn't be true! And yet...

'You—you said you'd already refused to have anything from your father?'

'That's right. As soon as I realised he was going to try to use Helikos as a bargaining tool, I knew I wanted nothing to do with it. If you thought that I was asking you to marry me because of what I would get out of it, then how would you ever know I adore you? And I do love you, Skye. I love you more than all the world.'

It was too much, too huge, too wonderful to take in.

'But you—I've seen how you love Helikos.'

'I love you more. And if I gained the island and lost you, then I would have lost the world. An island won't love me back, but I hope—pray—that one day you might find it in your heart to love me.'

'I already do.' Skye couldn't hold the words back any longer. 'I—'

But she got no further as Theo swept her up into a wild embrace, bringing his mouth down hard on hers in a kiss like no other they had ever shared. And as the world spun out of focus and into a golden haze of delight, Skye recognised just why it felt this way.

It was a kiss that was every bit as ardent and passionate and demanding as so many others they had shared. But this time, it was also a kiss of love.

When he finally released her, her eyes were sparkling

with tears. But they were tears of joy, of pure delight, of sheer, unadulterated happiness. Theo hugged her close, one hand coming softly under her chin to turn her face up to his, and his burning black eyes looked down into her glowing grey ones.

'So will you marry me, my love? Marry me and stay with me for the rest of my life so that I can spend my days showing you how much I care?'

Too full of joy to speak, she could only nod her heartfelt response, knowing that the way she was feeling couldn't be put into words, but showed in her face. And, just to make sure, she put her feelings into another long, glorious kiss.

'Tell me something,' she whispered when they finally found the strength to move apart—just a little. 'If I'd insisted on leaving, would you really have flown me away from here?'

'If I had to. But wherever you went, I would have gone too. I would never have let you out of my sight until I persuaded you to believe in my love for you—and to marry me.'

'Really?'

'Let me show you.'

Taking her hand, he led her to the back of the car and opened the boot. There beside her luggage was his case too.

'I'm packed and ready to go, my love,' Theo told her. 'I told my father I didn't want anything from him—except that pardon for your father. That's his wedding present to us and all I'll ever want from him. If I have you then I could never want for more.'

Reaching into the car, he pulled out the cases, then led her towards where the helicopter stood. And only now did she realise that the aircraft carried Theo's insignia on the side, not that of his father's corporation.

With the cases safely stowed, he turned to her once more and held out his hand.

'So, Skye, my love, will you come with me now? Come with me and start a new life—our married life?'

'It's what I want most in all the world,' she assured him.

A few moments later the engine roared, the blades spun and they took off from the island and headed into the bright light of their future. Together.

AT THE GREEK
TYCOON'S BIDDING

BY
CATHY WILLIAMS

Cathy Williams is originally from Trinidad, but has lived in England for a number of years. She currently has a house in Warwickshire, which she shares with her husband Richard, her three daughters, Charlotte, Olivia and Emma, and their pet cat, Salem. She adores writing romantic fiction and would love one of her girls to become a writer – although at the moment she is happy enough if they do their homework and agree not to bicker with one another!

Don't miss Cathy Williams's exciting new novel, *Hired for the Boss's Bedroom*, available this month from Mills & Boon® Modern™.

CHAPTER ONE

THEO was in the middle of reading a financial report when he heard the crash. The sound catapulted through the empty corridors of the office with ear-splitting intensity. Any other person would have reacted in shock, and probably fear. After all, it was late, and even with security guards there was no building in London that could be termed fully safe from someone determined to break and enter. Not Theo Miquel. Without bothering to arm himself with the prerequisite heavy object, dark brows knitted into an impatient frown at being interrupted, he strode out of his plush designer office, activating the switch that flooded the darkness outside with brilliant fluorescent light.

Theo Miquel was not a man to run scared of anything, least of all a would-be intruder who was clumsy enough to signal his arrival by crashing into something.

It didn't take long for him to pinpoint the origin of the interruption, for sprawled in the corridor was a trolley, the contents of which were scattered across the marble-tiled floor. Cleaning fluids, broom, mop—and a bucket of water which was slowly spreading along the tiles towards the carpeted offices on either side.

As his eyes took in the chaotic sight he heard the clamour

of feet pounding up the stairs, and then the security guard was there, out of breath and bristling with apologies. They converged at the scene of the crime at roughly the same time, although it was Theo who was the first to kneel next to the inert body of the girl who had collapsed on the floor.

'So sorry, sir,' Sid stammered, watching as Theo felt for a pulse. 'I came as fast as I could—as soon as I heard the noise. I can take over from here, sir.'

'Get this stuff cleared away.'

'Of course, sir. I'm very sorry… She looked a little pale when she came in this evening, but I had no idea…'

'Stop babbling and tidy this mess up,' Theo commanded sharply.

He barely registered the flustered guard squeezing dry the mop and soaking up the spilt water before it could intrude into the expensive offices and wreak yet more havoc.

At least the girl hadn't been inconsiderate enough to die on his premises. There was a pulse, and she might be as pale as hell but she was breathing. She had fainted—probably pregnant. A symptom of the times. Controlling his irritation, he scooped her up, oblivious to the frantic worry pasted on the security guard's face. He was dimly aware that his employees, whatever their rank, treated him with a certain amount of subservience. He was unaware that this subservience teetered precariously on the brink of downright fear, so he was vastly exasperated when he glanced across to find Sid virtually wringing his hands.

'I can take care of her, sir… No need for you to get involved… Not a problem…'

'Just make sure this place is cleaned up and then you can return to duty. If I need you, I'll call.'

This was an interruption he could well have done without.

It was Friday. It was after nine in the night and there was still half a report to get through if he was to e-mail the corrected copy to his counterpart on the other side of the world before their high-level meeting the following Monday.

He kicked open the door to his office and deposited the now stirring body on the long burgundy sofa which occupied one entire wall of the large room. He had not had a hand in designing the décor of his office. If he had, he would probably have chosen the barest of furnishings—after all, an office was a place to work and not a cosy sitting room in which to luxuriate—but he had found over the years, and to his surprise, that the grand, heavy opulence of the room was strangely conducive to concentration. The oak-panelled walls would have been more at home in a gentleman's club, but there was still something warm about them, filled as they were with books on finance, economics and naturally the accounts of the vast shipping empire that was the very basis of his huge inherited wealth. His desk, fashioned in a time before computers, lacked the convenient set-up to accommodate modems and fax machines and all the various appendages of twenty-first-century living, but it was pleasing to look at and did its job. The windows were floor to ceiling, and lacked the smoked glass effect of the taller, more modern offices all around, but they were charming. In the crazy rush of the city his offices, housed in a grand Victorian house, were a touch of old-world sanity.

It was more than he was currently feeling as he stared down at the girl, whose eyelids were beginning to flutter as consciousness crawled back.

She was solidly built beneath the blue and white striped overalls which covered a choice of clothing Theo would have found offensive on any woman. A thick cardigan of some indiscriminate brown colour and jeans that were frayed at the hems, their only merit being that they partially concealed heavy-duty shoes that would have been more suitable for a man working on a building site than a woman.

He waited, standing over her, arms folded, his body language informing her in no uncertain terms that, while he might have rescued her, he wasn't about to allow the act of charity to overstay its limited welcome.

And while he waited, impatience mounting, his eyes roved over her face, taking in the short, straight nose, the wide mouth, and eyebrows that were surprisingly defined and at odds with the pale curly hair that had escaped its restraints.

As her eyes fluttered open he could only assume that he had been taken by surprise, because for a few seconds a confusing surge of awareness rushed through him. She had amazing eyes. The purest and deepest of blues. Then she blinked, disoriented, and the moment was lost as reality took over. The reality of his work being interrupted when time was not on his side.

'It would appear that you fainted,' Theo informed her as she struggled into a sitting position.

Heather gazed up at the man staring down at her and felt her throat tighten. For the past six months she had worked in his offices, coming in at six-thirty when she could begin cleaning, after the bulk of the employees had left. From a distance, she had watched him out of the corner of her eye, watched as he worked behind his desk, his door flung open—although she knew, from snatches of conversation she had overheard over the months, that very few would risk popping in for a light chat. She had felt herself thrill to the tones of his dark, deep voice when he happened to talk to one of his employees. He intimidated everyone, but as far as she was concerned he was the most beautiful man she had ever laid eyes on.

The lines of his face were strong—harsh, even—but he possessed a classic beauty that was still aggressively and ruggedly masculine. Midnight-dark hair swept back from his powerful face, curling against the nape of his neck, and even though she had never had the courage to look him in the face she had glimpsed enough to know that his eyes were dark and fathomless, and fringed with lashes that most women would have given their eye teeth for. She supposed that if she had worked for him she might well have found him as forbidding as everyone else seemed to, but he had no influence over the course of her life and so she could appreciate him without fear.

Not that she was by nature the type of girl who cowered in the presence of anyone. By nature she was of a sunny disposition, and was a great believer that she was equal to everyone else, whatever her social standing might temporarily be and however broke she was. What counted lay inside and not in the outer packaging.

While her mind had been wandering down the extraordinary path that had found her lying on the sofa in his office, Theo had taken himself to his drinks cabinet and returned with a small glass of brown liquid.

'Drink some of this.'

Heather blinked and tried not to stare too hard at him. 'What is it?' she asked.

'Brandy.'

'I can't.'

'I beg your pardon?'

'I can't. It's against company policy to drink while on the job. I could get the sack and I need the money.'

As far as Theo was concerned this was far too much information. All he wanted was for her to guzzle a bit of the brandy, which would have her up and running, leaving him with sufficient time to get through what he had to do if he were to avoid an argument with the latest of his dates, whose temper had already been tested to the limit by the frequency of his cancellations.

'Drink,' he ordered, holding the glass close to her lips, and Heather nervously obeyed, taking the tiniest of sips and flushing with guilt.

'Oh, for goodness' sake!' Theo exclaimed. 'You've just fainted! One sip of brandy isn't selling your soul to the devil!'

'I've never fainted before,' Heather said. 'Mum used to tell me that I wasn't the fainting sort. Fainting was for undernourished girls, not for fatties like me. Claire fainted a lot when we were growing up. Well, not exactly *a lot,* but a few times. Which is a lot by anyone's standards…'

Theo experienced the novel sensation of being bombarded on all fronts. For a few seconds he literally lost the power of speech.

'Perhaps I'm coming down with something,' Heather remarked, frowning. She sincerely hoped not. She couldn't afford to start taking time off work because of ill health. Her night job with the cleaning company was on a temporary basis. No sick leave. And her day job as assistant teacher at a school near where she lived just wasn't sufficient for her to really make ends meet. She felt the colour drain away from her face.

Theo watched, fascinated by this transparent display of emotion, before urgently pressing the glass to her lips. The last thing he needed was another attack of the vapours.

'You need more than just a sip of this. It'll restore some of your energy.'

Heather took a bigger mouthful and felt the alcohol burn pleasantly in the pit of her stomach.

'You don't recognise me, do you?'

'Recognise you? Why on earth should I recognise you?

Look,' Theo said decisively, 'I have a lot of work to get through before I leave here tonight. You can sit on the sofa till you feel rested enough to leave, but if you'll excuse me I'm going to have to return to work.' He was struck by a bright idea. 'If you like I can get that security guard chap to come and take you downstairs.'

'Sid.'

'Sorry?'

'His name's Sid. The "security guard chap". Shouldn't you know that?' Heather asked curiously. 'He's been working for you for over three years!' But, like with her, he would have seen him and not registered his face. To a man like Theo Miquel he was literally invisible.

Not liking the accusatory tone to her voice, Theo momentarily forgot the half-read financial report lying on his desk.

'It beats me why I should know the name of every security guard who's ever worked here…'

'You employ him!'

'I employ lots of people. And anyway, this is a ridiculous conversation. I have work to do and…'

'I'm an interruption. I'm sorry.' Heather sighed and felt tears well up as she contemplated the disappearance of her job should she be ill. It was the middle of January. There were a million and one viruses flying about, most of them apparently winging their way from the Far East in an attempt to find more victims.

'You're not about to cry, are you?' Theo demanded. He fished into his trouser pocket and extracted a handkerchief, cursing himself for his good nature in carrying the girl into his office. A complete stranger, no less, who now seemed intent on chatting to him as though he wasn't a very important man—a man whose valuable time was money!

'Sorry.' Heather took the handkerchief and sniffled miserably into it. She blew her nose, which made her feel light-headed all over again. 'Perhaps I'm just hungry,' she offered, thinking aloud.

Theo ran his fingers through his hair and cast one despairing glance at the report on the desk. 'Hungry?' he said flatly.

'Doesn't that sometimes bring about fainting spells?' Heather asked, looking at him questioningly.

'I haven't quite got to that part of my nutrition course as yet,' Theo said with thick sarcasm, and she smiled. It was a smile that lit up her face. Could have lit up an entire room, for that matter. He felt inordinately pleased at having engineered this response in her. With a stifled sigh of resignation, he decided to put the report on hold for few minutes.

'I have a call to make,' he said, walking away even as he took his mobile phone from his pocket. 'I'm going to give you the land line. Use it to call for some food.'

'Oh, no! I couldn't just *order food in*!' She shuddered at the cost involved.

'You can and you will.' He looked across at her in the middle of handing her the telephone. 'If you're hungry then you have to eat something, and there's no fridge in my office with a handy supply of food. So just order whatever you like. Call the Savoy. Tell them who I am. They'll deliver whatever you want.'

'*The Savoy*?' Heather squeaked in consternation.

'On the house, Miss… Miss… I don't know your name…'

'Heather. Heather Ross.' She smiled shyly at him, marvelling at his patience and consideration, especially when you considered that from what she'd gathered, people found him scary.

Theo, she noticed, did not bother to give her his name, but perhaps he assumed that she would already know it—as indeed she did. She saw it every evening in gold plate on his door. Buoyed up by the kick from the brandy, and the realisation that hunger had brought on her unaccountable loss of strength, Heather dialled through to the Savoy, even though the practical streak in her knew that it was a ridiculous nonsense when all she probably needed was a cheese sandwich and a bottle of water. She was vaguely aware, in the background, that an urgent and hushed conversation was being conducted, one to which he clearly did not want her to be a party, and as soon as he was off the phone she turned to him with stricken eyes.

'I've messed up your arrangements for this evening, haven't I?'

She could tell that this line of conversation was not falling upon fertile ground, but her tendency to blurt out what happened to be in her head did not go hand in hand with the silent approach he clearly wanted. He would order in food for her, or rather get her to order in her own food—which she had sensibly confined to sandwiches, astounded at the effect his name had had on whoever was in charge of the reception desk at the Savoy—but beyond that he did not want her chatter.

'No matter.' He shrugged. 'I couldn't make it anyway.' Not that Claudia had seen it in quite that light. In fact, his ears were still ringing from the sound of the telephone being banged down at the other end, and he could hardly blame her. He consoled himself with the absolute fact that the minute a woman started making demands on his time it was almost certainly the time to dispose of her. In this case, the woman in question had disposed of herself.

'Was it important?' Heather asked anxiously.

'What's important is lying on my desk, waiting to be read, so if you don't mind…' He half expected her to launch into another conversation, but to his relief she maintained an obedient silence, though he couldn't stop his eyes from straying towards her every so often, distracting him from the task at hand.

By the time the food arrived—couriered over—Theo had abandoned all hope of finishing the report, at least until he had escorted her out of the building.

'Why have you not been eating?' he asked, watching as she plunged into her sandwich with the gusto of someone suddenly released from a starvation diet.

'There's no need for you to make polite conversation,' Heather said, tucking into sandwich number two. 'I know you have heaps of work to do. These sandwiches are fantastic, by the way.'

'I'll get back to work once you've gone.'

'Oh, I feel fine now. I might as well finish what I came to do.' She glanced across at him and then quickly reverted her attention back to the diminishing pile of sandwiches, just in case she found herself staring again.

'And encourage another fainting fit? I don't think that's a good idea.'

'You mean in case I cause more hassle?'

Theo didn't immediately answer. He was mesmerised by the sight of a woman eating so much. Judging by the women he knew, eating was fast becoming a dying art form. They nibbled at salad leaves or else pushed food around their plates as if one calorie too many might lead to sudden obesity.

'I'm hungry,' Heather said defensively. 'Normally I'm a very light eater, as a matter of fact. I should really be rake-thin. But I have a very stubborn metabolism. It refuses to do its job.'

'What's the name of this firm you work for? I'll call them and let them know that you're in no fit state to continue here tonight.' He reached for the telephone and was halted by her sudden squeak of panic.

'You can't do that!'

'Why not?' Black eyes narrowed shrewdly on her face. 'I take it you *are* legally registered with the company, and not involved in any moonlighting as a tax dodge…'

'Of course I'm not moonlighting!' Heather denied hotly.

'Then what's the problem?'

'The problem is that I *need* to complete this job because I *need* my time sheet to be signed downstairs! I can't afford to go home just because I felt a little sick!' Awareness of her situation rushed through her and she slung her legs over the side of the sofa. All at once, released from the temporary daze of being in his presence and no longer feeling light-headed, she realised what an unappealing sight she must make. Hair everywhere, her robust frame encased in the least flattering garment known to mankind. She hardly presented the storybook image of a fragile, appealing damsel in distress. She ran her fingers self-consciously through her hair, feeling for the elastic band that had gone a bit askew and repositioning her ponytail back to where it should be, along with all the other rebellious curls that had managed to fall out.

'Give me a minute,' she said, sucking in a few deep lungfuls of air, 'and I'll be on my way.' She stood up, and sat back down. She looked at him miserably. 'Maybe I need a few minutes,' she suggested. 'I can wait outside. I don't mind sitting on the ground—just till I gather myself. Honestly, I don't know what the matter is…'

'Are you pregnant?' Theo asked abruptly.

Heather raised horrified eyes to him. 'Pregnant? Of course I'm not pregnant! Why on earth would you think that? Oh…I know why. I'm young, I fainted, and I'm involved in manual work…therefore I must be a brainless bimbo who's stupidly managed to get herself pregnant…'

'That wasn't my reason for suggesting it...' Theo lied, discomfited by her accurate assessment of his thought processes.

'Well, then...' Another thought lodged in her head and she blushed painfully. 'It's because I'm fat, isn't it?'

Not wanting to encourage this line of conversation, and seriously concerned that getting rid of the girl might prove more difficult than he had anticipated, Theo adroitly changed the subject.

'I can't have you collapsing on my premises.' He walked over to her and looked down at the discreet name label pinned to the front of her overall. Distantly he registered that she certainly was on the plump side. Her breasts, pushing against the unyielding fabric, appeared to be voluminous. In every respect she was physically the antithesis of the women he dated, who were always leggy, brunette, flat chested and ultra-glamorous. 'Hills Cleaning Services,' he murmured to himself. 'What's the telephone number?'

Heather reluctantly provided him with the information and waited with a sinking heart as he called and explained the situation to her employer at the other end of the line.

'I've been sacked, haven't I?' she asked gloomily, the minute he was off the phone.

'Apparently there have been two incidents recently...?'

'Oh, not fainting incidents,' Heather expanded quickly, just in case he began thinking that she was one of those pathetic women who couldn't take care of themselves. 'You haven't told me what they said...'

'I thought I just had. In a roundabout way.' Unusual for him to say anything in a roundabout way, but he was reluctantly beginning to feel sorry for the woman. Overweight, insecure, and clearly ill equipped to do any other job. Thanks to him, she would now have to find alternative employment. He felt an uncustomary twinge of guilt. 'They seem to think that you're a liability…'

'That's silly,' Heather said miserably. 'I'm not a liability. I admit a couple of times I got home from work and fell asleep. I just meant to put my feet up for five minutes with a cup of tea, but you know how it is. I nodded off, and by the time I woke up it was too late to do the cleaning job…'

'You do *two* jobs…?' Theo asked in astonishment.

'I'm sorry. I know you thought you were doing the right thing, and I know you mightn't have wanted me around just in case I fainted again—which I wouldn't have, by the way—but thanks to you I'm now out of pocket. They probably won't even pay me for the hour and a half I've been here.' She stared despondently into the abyss of imminent poverty. Of course there were other night jobs. She could always do that bar one at the local pub. Tom would have her in a minute. But bar work was gruelling and exhausting. At least with the cleaning job she could switch to automatic and get through her work with her mind pleasantly drifting off to a comforting fantasy land in which she actually completed the illustration course she wanted and became famous designing the covers for children's books.

'What's the day job?' Theo asked curiously. She was now strong enough to sit up. He wasn't really interested in hearing the ins and outs of her life, but a few minutes' chat wouldn't kill him, and it would give her a bit more time to gather her resources. Her hands rested limply on her lap and she was staring into the distance, no doubt contemplating the horror of not earning minimum wages by doing a job that was draining her of all her energy. Thus far, only two women he had dated had held down jobs, and neither had actually seen their jobs as anything more than an interruption of their leisure time—something to do as an amusing distraction from the daily grind of shopping, self-pampering and lunches with their friends.

'Oh. Day job.' Heather refocused on the man looking at her and was hit by the realisation that this would probably be the last time she had the pleasure of seeing him. She felt an uncomfortable little void open up in the pit of her stomach. 'I'm an assistant teacher at the school just around the corner from me,' she said dully.

'You're an *assistant teacher*?'

His shocked tone managed to raise a smile from her. She could easily have been offended by the implied insult, but she knew that from the Olympian summits which he occupied he would simply have assumed that, as a cleaner, she would be incapable of achieving much else—just as he had assumed that her fainting fit had been brought on by pregnancy.

'I know. Incredible, isn't it?' she replied, grinning, regaining some of her lost spirit. Now she just wanted to drag the conversation out for as long as possible, bearing in mind that she wouldn't be clapping eyes on him again.

'Why do you clean offices if you have a perfectly viable daytime job?'

'Because my "perfectly viable daytime job" just about manages to pay the rent on my room and the bills and I need to save some money up so that I can afford to carry on with my studies.' Well, he might not have known her from Adam before, but he certainly appeared confounded by her revelation now—the revelation that she actually had a brain. 'You see,' she continued, enjoying his undivided attention while she had it, 'I left school quite young. At sixteen, as a matter of fact. I don't know why, but all my friends were doing that—leaving to get jobs. Not that there were a whole heap of jobs for school-leavers in the Yorkshire village I came from. But, anyway, it seemed a good idea at the time, and earning money was great. It helped out with Mum, and Claire couldn't help out there. She wanted to head to London and get into acting…'

'Claire…?'

'My sister. The skinny, beautiful one I mentioned to you?' Heather's eyes misted over with pride. 'Long blonde hair… big green eyes… She needed all the money Mum could spare so that she could get started in her career…'

This woman, Theo thought, was an open book. Had no one ever told her that the allure of the female sex lay in the ability to be mysterious? To stimulate the chase with teasing pieces of information dropped here and there? Her frankness was beyond belief. Now she was telling him all about her sister and the fabulous career that had taken her across the Atlantic, where she was now modelling and already getting bit parts in daytime soaps.

Theo held up his hand to put a stop to the deluge of personal chatter.

He hardened himself against the immediate dismay that brought a flush of pink colour to her cheeks.

'You seem to be fully recovered,' he informed her. 'I'm very sorry that you no longer have your job with the cleaning firm, but it's probably for the best if you're physically not up to it…' He stood up, decisively bringing her presence in his office to an end, and waited until she had followed suit. Her hair was still continuing to rebel against the clips and elastic band, and now she was standing up he could see that she was shorter than he had thought—at best five foot four. She smoothed down her unflattering overall and he resisted the urge to give her a piece of good advice. Namely that she would probably be able to get a decent well-paid job if she paid a bit more attention to how she looked. Employers tended to look at the general appearance of their employees and were often influenced by it, unfair though it was.

'Maybe you're right. I guess I shall just have to go and work for Tom. He won't mind if I oversleep now and again. He likes me, and he'll pay me just so long as I give him what he wants...'

Theo paused in mid-stride, holding the door open while Heather walked past him, oblivious to the horror on his face. Ever the optimist, she was already working out the pros of the job she had previously dismissed out of hand. For starters, it was close, and would involve no public transport travel—which was always a concern to her, bearing in mind what you read in the newspapers. Also, Tom would be much more lenient than the cleaning company if she accidentally skipped an evening's work. And maybe, just maybe, she could drop the name of the pub into this conversation and casually mention that Theo might like to come along and patronise it some time.

She opened her mouth to voice that tantalising suggestion, only to discover that she had been walking towards the elevator on her own. He was still standing by his door and staring at her as though she had mutated into another form of life.

'Oh!' Heather blinked, disappointed that he wasn't at least walking her to the lift, then she chastised herself for being silly. Prior to this evening the man hadn't even known of her existence, even though he must have at least glimpsed her off and on over the previous months! He had been good enough to look after her in his office, interrupting his own busy work schedule, which he had not been obliged to do. Crazy to think that he would accompany her on her journey down! She gave him a little wave. 'Thank you for being so kind and looking after me,' she said, raising her voice to cover the yawning distance between them. 'I'll just be off!'

Theo had no idea how he had managed to become unwittingly embroiled in the concerns of a perfect stranger, but, having been instrumental in getting her the sack, he felt morally obliged to question her decision about taking on a job that sounded very insalubrious indeed. Who was this Tom character? he wondered. Probably some sad old man who thought he could pay for the services of a naïve young girl in desperate need of cash. And naïve she most certainly was. Theo couldn't remember a time when he had been confronted by someone so green around the ears.

'Give me a minute.' He returned to the office, hesitated for a few seconds in front of his computer before shutting it down, grabbed his coat, his laptop and his briefcase and then exited, switching off the light behind him before closing and locking his door.

Heather was still there by the lift, looking utterly bemused. A revelation of his own sentiments, he thought wryly. No time to fulfil his commitment to Claudia, but now perversely driven to accompany this stranger to her house because she had succeeded in rousing some kind of a sense of duty in him. He likened it to the sentiment someone might feel when confronted by a defenceless animal accidentally caught under the wheels of a car and in need of a vet.

'Are you leaving work?' Heather asked in surprise, looking up at him, wishing, for once, that she wasn't quite as short as she was. Short and stocky and stupidly thrilled just to be taking the elevator down with him. 'It's just that you don't normally leave this early.'

Theo paused to stare at her.

'You know what time I leave work in the evenings…?' He pressed the elevator button and the doors opened smoothly, as though the lift had been sitting there, just waiting for him to appear and summon it into immediate action.

Heather blushed. 'No! I mean,' she continued, dragging out the syllable, 'I just know that you usually leave after I've finished cleaning most of the directors' floor.' She laughed airily as the lift doors shut on them, locking her into a weird feeling of imposed intimacy. 'When you do something as monotonous as cleaning, you start paying attention to the silliest of details. I guess it just makes the time go past a little quicker! I know you're usually the last to leave in the evenings, along with Jimmy and a couple of others who work on the floor below.' Best change the subject, she thought. She was beginning to sound sad. 'Do you know,' she confided, 'that sandwich has done me the world of good? I feel fantastic. Do you often send out for food from the Savoy?' She sneaked a little sideways glance at him and found that he was looking at her in a very odd manner. 'Sorry. I'm chatting too much. Have you got plans for this evening?'

'Only ones that involve dropping you back to wherever it is you live…'

Heather's mouth dropped open.

'Deprived of the power of speech?' Theo said dryly. 'That must surely be a first for you.'

'You're dropping me back to my house?' Heather squeaked. Now she really *did* feel guilty. 'Please don't. There's no need.' She laid her small hand tentatively on his arm as the doors opened and they stepped outside. The contact with his forearm, even though it was through a layer of shirt, sent a burning sensation running through her and she quickly removed her hand. 'I'm not as feeble as you seem to think I am. Can't you tell from my girth that I'm a bonny lass?' She laughed self-deprecatingly but he didn't laugh back. Didn't even crack a smile.

Theo was not a man accustomed to delving into the female psyche. He had always prided himself on pretty much knowing how women operated. They expressed their interest in a certain way—the lowered eyes, the coy smile, the slight inclination of the head—and then came the game of hide and seek, a game he thoroughly enjoyed. It was only after that things took a downturn, when inevitably they began questioning the amount of time he put into his work, insinuating that he would be far better amused if he paid them more attention, because after all wasn't that what relationships were all about? They were all about trying to build a relationship with him, trying to pin him down. Insecurities never raised their heads, although in truth none of them had ever had anything much to be insecure about.

Now it occurred to him that this girl had insecurities about her weight and Lord only knew what else. Insecurities that had made her the sort of gullible woman who might be tempted by a man for all the wrong reasons.

'Your coat,' he said, 'and then I shall take you out and feed you…'

CHAPTER TWO

BECAUSE there was no convenient underground car park for the office, most of the employees who chose to drive in—willing to pay the Congestion Charge because it gave them flexibility to leave London at the drop of the hat to attend meetings elsewhere—parked at the nearest multi-storey car park.

Theo, however, had a chauffeur permanently on call. Within minutes of speaking into his mobile phone, a long, sleek Mercedes had pulled up outside the building, engine gently throbbing as it waited for them to get in.

Heather had moved on from protesting about the need to be dropped home to protesting about his invitation to dinner, which was unnecessary considering she had just eaten sandwiches courtesy of the Savoy.

She found herself ushered into the back seat of the car and slid across to make space for him.

'It's very good of you, Mr Miquel...'

'Considering you fainted on my doorstep, so to speak, I think you can call me by my first name—Theo.'

'Well, all right. But I still don't need taking anywhere. You don't have to feel responsible for me, although I'm very grateful for your help...'

Theo turned to look at her, his massive body lounging indolently against the car door.

'I can't remember the last time I was so comprehensively turned down for dinner by a woman.'

Heather squirmed, and wondered how she could temper her protests in case he thought that she was being offensive and ungrateful after all he had done for her. And she had to admit that the thought of having dinner with him was disconcerting but also exciting.

'I'm not exactly dressed for dinner,' she said, staring down at her workmanlike shoes and the thick black coat which did its job very efficiently but which also made her look a little like a ship in full sail.

'No, you're not,' Theo agreed, 'but I'm sure Henri won't mind.'

'Henri?' So he agreed she looked a complete mess. Well, her success rate with the opposite sex had never been that sparkling. At least not when it came to the sexual side of things. She had grown up in the shadow of her beautiful sister and from an early age had resigned herself to the inevitability of always taking second place. Boys had been her best mates, but they had been enthralled by Claire. That was simply life, and she had never let it get her down.

Right now it *was* getting her down.

'The proprietor at a little French bistro I go to quite often,' Theo was explaining. 'We go back a long way.'

'Oh, yes? How's that?' She wondered whether she might be able to sneak into the bathroom at the 'little French bistro' and do something with her hair, somehow glue it into submission.

'I helped him out a long time ago—financed him for the restaurant he wanted to open.'

'I knew you had a soft side!' Heather exclaimed impulsively, smiling at him.

Good Lord, Theo thought, the woman needed protecting from her own good nature!

'It was a sensible business arrangement,' Theo corrected, not much liking the image of him as having a *soft side*. If he had, he'd certainly never seen evidence of it, nor had any of those kings of finance who deferred to him the minute he opened his mouth. 'To dispel the myth, I made money out of the deal.'

'But I'm sure you would have invested in him even if you hadn't thought that you were going to. I guess that's what friendship's all about, isn't it?'

'I really have not given it much thought,' Theo said deflatingly. 'We are here.' He nodded as the car slowed down, and Heather glanced around to see that the little bistro was more of a chic restaurant—the sort of place that gathered trendy people who all sat around with glasses of white wine looking at everybody else.

She groaned aloud and shot him a frantic look.

'I can't go in there.'

'Why not?' Theo asked with a trace of irritation. He was beginning to wonder what demonic urge had impelled him into taking this dippy woman out. Yes, sure he was concerned by her ominous remarks about her future job—but, really, what business was it of his? Adults chose to do what they wanted to do with their lives. He decided right there and then that this would be his one truly good deed for the year.

'Look at me!' Heather squeaked, her face flushed with panic.

Theo looked. 'No one will pay you the slightest bit of attention.' That was the best he could do at consoling her without resort to outright lying.

'*Everyone* is going to look!' Heather contradicted in a high voice. 'I mean, just look at the people in there.' The wide gold-fish-bowl-style restaurant offered an obliging view of a crowd of people smartly dressed and relaxing in an atmosphere of self-congratulation. They seemed to be making the statement that they were all beautiful, and thank goodness for that.

The car had now stopped and Theo's chauffeur had smoothly moved round to the passenger door, which he was opening for her.

Next to Theo, Heather felt even more of an embarrass-ment. She raised imploring eyes to him and he shook his head impatiently.

'You're too self-conscious about your appearance.'

'That's all right for *you* to say,' she informed him. 'You happen to be blessed with amazing good looks.'

'Do you always say what's on your mind?' Theo asked, a little taken aback by her blunt statement.

Heather ignored that. She was too busy hovering. He had to propel her through the door, and he might not notice a thing, but she certainly did. All those faces turned in their di-rection. The women sniggered, she was certain of it, before feasting their eyes on the man by her side.

The men shot her quick disparaging looks, and then they, too, looked at Theo, wondering whether they should recog-nise him. Heather felt worse than invisible. Indeed, invisible would have been a much more acceptable option. As it was, she stared down at the shiny wooden floor which made the most of highlighting her practical line in footwear.

'We're over there,' Theo murmured, bending down. 'Would you like me to lead you or are you prepared to look up and make your way to the table unaided?'

'Very funny,' Heather whispered back at him. 'Do you

notice how everyone's staring at me, wondering what on earth I'm doing here?'

'No one's staring at you.'

'Well, they *were*,' Heather informed him, reaching her chair with deep relief and sinking into it.

'Your mother has a lot to blame herself for in letting whatever complexes you have about your sister get out of hand.' He picked up the menu on the table but gave it only a scant perusal, obviously knowing in advance what he intended to order.

Heather leaned forward and looked at him earnestly. 'It wasn't Mum's fault that she happened to give birth to a swan and an ugly duckling.'

'Point proved. Is she aware that you constantly make comparisons between yourself and your sister?'

'Mum died seven years ago.' She waited for the meaningless expressions of regret but none were forthcoming. Instead, Theo held her gaze thoughtfully before giving her a quick nod. 'She was ill for about two years before she finally passed away. That's why I never finished my education. I needed to get working.'

'And what was your sister doing at the time?'

'Claire was in London, doing an acting course and some waitressing.'

'And you were left no assets that would have helped you with your own ambitions?' Against his will, he was curious about the dynamics of her family. Without looking away from her, he ordered a bottle of wine and the fish of the day, which she ordered as well.

Heather flushed. 'Claire needed what little there was far more than I did at the time. She promised that when she made it big she would pay me back—not that the money ever mattered. Mum was gone and I didn't really care about dividing what she'd left us, which wasn't very much anyway.'

'And has she made it big?' Theo asked casually, knowing what answer he would receive. Sure enough, it was no surprise to discover that dreams of stardom were languishing across the Atlantic. No surprise either to discover that the money had never managed to wing its way back to its original owner, who seemed stunningly content with the situation.

'So you are happy to compare yourself unfavourably to someone whose only claim to fame apparently lies in her looks?' Theo mused over a glass of wine.

'She also happens to be a very warm person,' Heather defended hotly. Mostly, she conceded to herself, when she was getting her own way. Her selfishness had always been a combination of infuriating and endearing. It had been hard to lose her temper with Claire, and the few times that she had she had met with a brick wall of plaintive incomprehension. 'Anyway, I don't *compare* myself to Claire. I just admire her looks. Don't you have brothers you sometimes compare yourself to?' It was such a ridiculous notion that she couldn't help but grin. 'No. I can't picture you comparing yourself unfavourably to anybody. You're way too self-confident for that. I guess you'd expect people to compare themselves to *you*.'

'No siblings,' Theo informed her flatly, his tone of voice warning her away from any further probing into his personal life, but Heather was gazing at him thoughtfully.

'That's very sad for you. I know that Claire doesn't live here, but it's just good knowing that she's with me in spirit, so to speak. What about your parents? Where do they live? Over here? They must be very proud of you, what with you being so successful in your job…'

Women didn't make a habit of probing into Theo's personal life. In fact, women knew when to back off without having to be told. Something in his expression had always been very good at warning them about the boundaries he laid down. He wined them and dined them and treated them with extravagant gestures that were wildly out of most people's orbit. In return he asked only for relationships without complications. His life was hectic enough without having to deal with demands from the opposite sex.

Heather didn't appear to have the correct instincts warning her to drop the subject. In fact, she was looking at him with the keen enthusiasm of a puppy dog waiting for a treat.

Just as well she was of no interest to him sexually. Theo was convinced that if you fed women with too much personal information, it engendered illusions of permanence. They thought that they had somehow crawled under your skin and were therefore in the right position to stage a complete takeover.

Since this woman was not in the category of a fisherman trawling a net in the hope of netting the fish, he didn't immediately succumb to the automatic instinct to shut down. Instead, he returned her gaze and shrugged.

'My father died when I was a boy and my mother does not live over here. She lives in Greece.'

'Which, of course, is where you're from…'

Theo permitted himself a faint smile. 'Why *of course*…?'

'Oh, all those stereotypes of Greek men being tall, dark and handsome.' Heather grinned at the bemused expression on his face. She was just teasing, but she wondered how many times in his life he had ever been teased. 'Does your mother come and visit you often?'

'You ask a lot of questions.'

Their food arrived and was placed in front of them; their glasses were refilled with wine which Heather felt quite free to drink considering she was now out of a job.

'People have interesting stories. How else do you find out

who they are if you don't ask questions?' Her appetite, which should have been sated after the sandwiches, stirred into life. Naturally she wasn't going to guzzle the lot, but it wasn't often that she found herself sitting in a restaurant of this calibre. Somehow it would have seemed rude to be dismissive of the food.

'So does she?' Heather persisted.

'What are you talking about?'

'Your mother. Does she come over and visit?'

Theo shook his head in pure exasperation. 'Occasionally,' he finally conceded. 'She visits my country house, and when she does I commute to London. She hates the city. In fact, she has never been here. There—satisfied?'

Heather nodded. *For the moment*, she wanted to say, before remembering that there would be no more moments, that in fact she was only here because he felt duty-bound to send her on her way with a bit more concern than he would probably otherwise have shown because he had effectively cost her her cleaning job. Which suddenly brought her back down to earth and the reality of losing an income, small though it was, which was necessary to her. She closed her knife and fork on the half-eaten plate of food and cupped her chin in one hand.

'You're finished?' Theo asked in amazement.

Heather felt a little jab of hurt coil deep inside her. Through the shield of her naturally sunny disposition she suddenly had a bleak vision of an alternative reality. The reality that was coldly pointing out that while she had nurtured pleasant fantasies about this tall, aggressively handsome man, while she had always made sure to clean his floor when she knew that he was going to be around, he had never once glanced in her direction—would not have recognised her if she had landed opposite him on a desert island. And while she luxuriated in the thrill of being in his company now, unexpected as it was, the thrill was not mutual. To him she was nothing but an overweight woman whose company he was probably itching to get away from.

'Did you think that I would carry on eating till I exploded?' Heather said, far more sharply than she had intended. She softened her uncharacteristically sarcastic reply with a rueful smile. 'Sorry, I was just thinking about what I shall do now that I no longer have a job to go to in the evenings.'

'I can't believe that you really have to hold down two jobs to survive. Surely you can cut back on one or two luxuries…make ends meet that way…?'

Heather laughed. Rich, warm laughter that had a few heads turning in her direction.

'You don't live in the real world, Mr Miquel…'

'Theo…'

'Well, you don't. I don't *have* any luxuries to cut back on. Friends come over for meals and we watch television and maybe drink a couple of bottles of wine on a Saturday night, and in summer we go on picnics in the park. I don't do theatres or restaurants or even cinemas very often. Actually, I don't have an awful lot of free time anyway, which is probably a good thing when it comes to balancing my finances…' The look of horror on his face was growing by the second, but Heather was unfazed by that. Of course he wouldn't understand the world she lived in. Why should he? She probably only had a vague inkling of his. 'I prefer to save up for my course rather than blow money on clothes and entertainment.'

'And I thought being young was all about being reckless,' Theo drawled. With a spurt of surprise, he realised that he was having fun. Not quite the same fun that he normally had in the company of a woman, but he felt invigorated. Maybe his jaded palette needed novelty more often.

Heather lifted one shoulder dismissively. 'Maybe it is, if you can support a reckless lifestyle. Anyway, I'm not a reckless kind of person.'

'Then perhaps you should reconsider your job with this man…'

'Tom?' She looked at him in surprise. 'What's so reckless about working behind a bar a few nights every week? Just so long as I laugh a lot and chat to the punters, Tom will be more than happy with me.'

Theo looked down and did a rapid rethink on his original assumption, which seemed ridiculous now that he thought about it. 'Long hours?' was all he said, and she nodded.

'Very long and very tiring, which was why I turned down his offer all those months ago. But needs must. There aren't that many jobs a girl can do at night, and I can't fit anything else into my days.' She sighed. How helpful it would have been if Claire had been true to her word and sent back some of that money she had borrowed all that time ago. But it had been two months since she had spoken to her sister, and a lot longer since they had physically met up. It would be crazy when contact was so limited and precious, to start asking for her loan back.

'Anyway, no point moaning about all of that.' She smiled. 'The food was delicious. Thank you. I'm glad I came.'

'Even though you couldn't bear the thought of everyone staring at you?' He poured her another glass of wine, finishing the bottle, and wondered whether he should order another. If novelty had been what he was after, then he had certainly found it in this woman who was prepared to eat and drink without fear of the consequences. He also realised that it would be no hardship to prolong the evening a bit. After all, his current girlfriend was no longer around, and issues of work would wait until the morning, when he would return to his office to complete what he had started.

'More wine?' he asked, signalling to the waiter as he waited for her response.

Heather's face felt flushed. In fact, she felt quite warm, and would have removed her jumper but for the fact that the old tee shirt she was wearing underneath was even more of an eyesore than the thick grey sweater she had hurriedly stuck on when she had left the house earlier in the evening.

'Aren't I keeping you from something?' She looked at him earnestly.

'Like what?'

'Oh, I don't know. Don't you have somewhere to go? A date or something?'

'My date cancelled on me when I told her that I was running late.'

So that had been the urgent phone call which she had glimpsed out of the corner of her eye. Heather felt a rush of guilt and she reddened.

'That's awful!' She half stood up but he waved her back down, nodding at the waiter to pour the wine he had ordered. 'I can't be the cause of a row between you and your girlfriend. I'm sorry.'

'Sit back down,' Theo ordered, amused at her attack of conscience. 'You simply helped along the inevitable, if it's any consolation. Sit! People will stare. You don't want that, do you?'

Heather grudgingly took her seat, but her eyes were still anxiously focused on his face. 'What do you mean?' She gulped a mouthful of wine and then pushed the glass away from her.

'I mean—' he leant towards her '—I can see the group of people behind you, and they're just waiting to see if you're about to commit social suicide by causing a scene…'

'That's not what I meant!'

'I'm aware of that.'

'Oh!' She pushed some flyaway hair out of her face. 'Then what *did* you mean? About me helping along the inevitable? Were you going to dump her?'

'Sooner or later.' He sprawled back into his chair, folded his arms and stared at her transparently distraught face. Who would have imagined that the girl cleaning his office would have proved such a refreshing companion for the evening? He could hardly believe it himself.

'Oh.' Heather fell back on the single word. 'Why would she break up with you just because you were running late?' She frowned, puzzled. Yes, relationships could be transitory, but wasn't that taking it too far? She herself had only been in one long-standing relationship and even when they had both reached the point of recognising that things weren't going anywhere between them they had still taken many long evenings to finally cut the ties. 'And why would you have dumped her sooner or later? Weren't you serious about her?'

That, as far as Theo was concerned, was one question too far. He called for the bill and then leant forward, resting his elbows on the table.

'I think we've reached the point where you're asking about things that are none of your business.'

For a few charged moments Heather glimpsed the man everyone tiptoed around. The man with the steel hand in the velvet glove. She shrugged. 'Okay. I apologise. Sometimes I talk too much.'

'Sometimes you do,' Theo agreed unsmilingly. He settled

the bill and, eager to return their last snatches of conversation to a less tense footing, Heather smiled brightly.

'I would offer to pay my way, but my finances…'

'Can barely run to a cinema show. I know.' He stood up and wondered again why such an ungainly girl would wear clothes that deliberately emphasised her girth.

Heather stood up quickly, too quickly, because suddenly the effects of having drunk too much of the very cold, very good white wine took their toll and she teetered slightly on her feet.

The ground had definitely felt more stable when she was sitting down.

And now she had to make her way across the even more crowded room.

'That's the problem with good wine,' Theo said lazily. 'Too easy to drink.' He moved over to where she was standing in panicked indecision and slipped his arm around her waist.

That contact seemed to electrify every inch of her body. She was aware of the heated racing of her pulses and a deep, steady throb that began somewhere in the pit of her stomach and flooded outwards, obliterating every ounce of common sense in its path.

A vague girlish crush…one night talking, the briefest of touches that meant absolutely zero to him…and she felt her head spinning like a woman in love.

She barely heard him talking to her as he ushered her through the room and out towards the exit, pausing *en route* to exchange a few pleasantries with Henri, who had materialised out of thin air and found time for banter even though he clearly had plenty of work to do.

Lord, but she wanted to curve her body into his! Had she ever felt this way with Johnny? She couldn't remember. She didn't think so.

As soon as they were outside he released her, and she took

a couple of steps back, just to recover from that giddy sensation. The cold air was good. As was the safe, comforting bulk of her coat, which he had somehow managed to get her into.

His chauffeur was parked a few metres up, but before he started walking her towards the car Heather looked at him and gave a watery smile.

'I'll be fine to make my way back from here,' she said, enunciating every word very carefully. She stuck her hands firmly into the deep pockets of her coat and clenched her fists.

'Don't be ridiculous. Where do you live?'

'Honestly. I'm fine. You've done too much already.' She was aware that there was just the smallest hint of her words being slurred. When he placed his hand on her elbow she knew that she would capitulate.

'You've gone very quiet…'

'I feel a bit wobbly…tired…' As soon as she was in the car she rested her head back and closed her eyes. She was dimly aware of giving Theo her address, and the next time she opened her eyes it was to find that they had arrived at the house which she shared with four other girls, all of whom were out. For the first time she realised that she must be the only person under the age of twenty-five, single and in London, who wasn't out doing something on a Friday night. Except she *had* done something!

He walked her to the door, took her bag from her when she couldn't locate her keys and managed to find them. This after pulling out everything bar the kitchen sink from her voluminous sack. When he stepped inside the house Heather didn't protest. Yes, he had done his duty, and he was keen to be off, but, no, she didn't want him to leave. Not just yet. Not when she wouldn't be seeing him again.

'Would you like some coffee?' Heather asked awkwardly.

'How many of you share this place?'

'Four.' She hiccupped, and covered her mouth with her hand.

'I think you probably need the coffee more than I do. Go and sit down and I'll make you some.'

Well, Theo reasoned, his evening had gone wildly wrong starting from the moment he'd heard that crash outside his office, so why not wrap it up doing something he rarely did? Waiting on a woman who was the worse for wear and had probably collapsed into a snoring heap on her sofa?

Theo wasn't a brutish male chauvinist. However, he had been spoilt by the attention lavished on him by members of the opposite sex. His looks, his charisma and his vast wealth had always been a powerful magnetic pull for women who heeded his slightest whim. He had never particularly had to put himself out. In fact, he couldn't recall the last time he had taken care of a woman in the manner in which he was now taking care of the one who had fallen asleep beside him in the car when he had been in the middle of a sentence.

He made his way to the back of the house, observing the chaos in which four people apparently lived with no pressing desire to tidy up behind themselves. The kitchen sported the detritus of breakfast eaten on the run and not cleared away. Jumpers were slung in odd places and shoes were randomly scattered. On the window ledge a row of cards suggested a birthday had come and gone.

Coffee made, he reached the sitting room to find that Heather had fallen asleep. She had stripped off her jumper and was sprawled on the sofa with one arm raised, half covering her face and dipping over the arm of the chair.

She had kicked off her shoes, revealing thick grey socks.

Theo stood for a few seconds, drawing in a sharp breath, because the shapeless figure wasn't quite as shapeless as he had imagined. Her breasts were big, succulently generous, but there was proportion to her body and the sliver of skin he glimpsed where the tee shirt rose up was surprisingly firm.

He rubbed his eyes to dispel the uneasy sensation of staring at her, and the even more uneasy suspicion that he would have liked to move closer so that he could appreciate those curves a bit more.

Without waking her up, he deposited the coffee on the table by the sofa and, after a few seconds' hesitation, pulled out his pen and hunted around for some paper. He wasn't going to wake her, but walking away without saying goodbye somehow felt wrong. So he jotted down a couple of lines, wishing her luck in getting a new job, then he left, resisting the terrible urge to look back over his shoulder at her softly breathing body.

Once outside, he laughed at the insanity that had possessed him for a few fleeting seconds. He had looked at her and *had been turned on*! He almost called Claudia, knowing that some sweet talk would have her running back into his arms, but instead he switched off his mobile phone and forced his highly disciplined brain to concentrate on the work he had had to defer to the following morning.

Heather, surfacing the next day to the sounds of one of her room-mates clattering about in the kitchen, had a few seconds of blissful oblivion during which she imagined the sounds to be Theo, making her that cup of coffee.

The cup of coffee lying cold on the table by her. Next to a note which she now read. It said nothing at all. A few polite words scribbled down before he left the house, doubtless relieved that there was no need for him to continue the charade of entertaining her.

Heather sat up and buried her head in her hands. He hadn't

woken her up! She had fallen asleep and lost her opportunity to spend a few more minutes in his company.

The sun seemed to have gone out of her life. It was only when, after a week, one of her friends in the house mentioned it that Heather gave herself a stiff lecture. Moping around over a man she had known for roughly three hours was insane.

'Am I insane?' she asked her reflection. 'No. Because you know,' she added, wagging her finger censoriously at herself, 'only a complete loony would lose sleep over a man like Theo!'

She pulled herself together and accepted the job at Tom's pub. It was, as she had predicted, hard work but sociable, and was suited to her temperament. The hours might have been longer, and her exhaustion levels might have been higher, but she was at least eating regularly, and she took Fridays off. Theo's remark about being young and enjoying life had stuck in her head.

Not, even after six weeks, that any of those fun-packed Friday evenings with her friends could compare to that one night that had sprung from nothing and disappeared before she could hold onto it.

And his image kept slipping into her head. She couldn't seem to help it. One minute she would be laughing at something and the next minute there he was, released from the restraints she kept trying to put on him. She went to bed with him at night and woke up to him the following morning, and she just couldn't help it. It was involuntary. The man haunted her.

Of course it would end. Time had a wonderful way of healing, and she cheerfully resigned herself to due process. She was so resigned, in fact, that when, two months after she had last laid eyes on him, she picked up her telephone to hear his voice on the other end, she almost didn't recognise it.

Then she sat down, flapping her arm madly so that Beth

would turn the television down, which she did, making sure she remained where she was to overhear the conversation. Heather could feel her heart start racing. He had managed to get her name from the firm of cleaners she had worked for, apparently. Heather assumed his influence must have unlocked her personnel file, since its contents were confidential. Not that she cared. She just wanted him to tell her why he had called.

'I have a proposition to put to you,' he finally said, when pleasantries had been exhausted.

'Really?' She tried to keep the stomach-turning curiosity out of her voice.

'My housekeeper has gone. Her sister in Scotland has fallen ill and needs looking after. The job has become vacant and I thought of you.' He briefly explained what it entailed. It could even, he informed her, be a live-in post. His apartment had a separate wing and he was rarely there anyway. He preferred to spend as many of his free weekends as he could in the country. He told her how much she would be earning and the figure made her gasp. It was far and away more than she was currently earning with both her jobs combined. She would be able to save and, if she decided to live in, would be able to afford her course within months, instead of the tortuous years she had anticipated.

Not that financial considerations played much of a part in her decision.

'I accept,' she told him promptly, making him smile at the other end of the line. 'Just tell me when you want me to start...'

CHAPTER THREE

'So,' BETH said sternly, 'what happens next?'

Eighteen months on and they were sitting in the usual place they met, an all-day French wine bar and restaurant which never seemed particularly bothered about serving cappuccinos to people who had zero intention of eating but would still manage to occupy valuable seats for hours at a stretch.

Heather bit her lower lip nervously, because she knew exactly what was coming. She managed to buy herself a few seconds of thinking time by taking a sip of her coffee, but the question was still there when she met her friend's concerned, probing brown eyes.

'What do you mean?' she dodged unsuccessfully.

To start with Beth had been overjoyed at her friend's sudden run of good luck. To be asked to do something as undemanding as looking after a house that would be very clean most of the time anyway, considering its owner wasn't often there, at a salary that was way over the going rate, sure beat the hell out of working in Tom's rowdy pub till all hours of the morning. Giving up the assistant teaching job would be a wrench, but, heck, she would be able to complete her course and then get started on the career ladder.

As far as Beth was concerned, a woman was defined by

her career. She herself had wanted to be a lawyer from the age of five, if she was to be believed, and had got on with turning her dream into reality without ever deviating from her route.

Heather deeply admired her friend's ambitious streak. So much so that she had tried very hard in the beginning not to let on that her real reason for accepting Theo's generous offer was her own inarticulated need to be near him. But, not being secretive by nature, she had soon lapsed into easy confidences, and ever since had had to endure her friend's occasionally withering remarks about being used.

'I *mean*,' Beth said, leaning forward with the concerned frown of one friend trying to impart to another friend what should have been self-evident, 'now that your course has finished, are you going to move out and get a job with that publishing company? The one you sent your application off to? You *did* send that application off, didn't you?'

Heather wilted in the face of this direct line of questioning and mumbled something about needing to add a few finishing touches to it. In truth, the envelope had been lying in her bag for a fortnight while she fought off the sickening prospect of leaving behind a situation that was going nowhere but happened to be working very nicely for her.

While she continued to fan the flames of her infatuation, Theo was as far removed from being interested in her sexually as he ever had been. Theirs was an evolving situation. She had evolved into emotional dependency and he had evolved into having the perfect housekeeper. Indeed, her housekeeping duties were now virtually non-existent. She did some light cleaning, mostly in her own wing, some even lighter cooking to accommodate him when he happened to be in for supper, but mostly she had become a curious mixture of out-of-hours secretary and general do-it-all.

He talked to her about work issues, no longer reminding her that everything he told her was always in the strictest confidence. She'd used to laugh at his frowning secrecy, gently informing him that she personally didn't know a single person who would have been remotely interested in offshore deals involving companies they had never heard of. He would watch her as she pottered around his kitchen, chatting about her friends and what they got up to.

He found her relaxing and amusing and, more importantly, undemanding. Unlike the women he continued to wine and dine, she showed none of the clinginess that some of them displayed, and she had never nurtured ambitions beyond her reach. In his eyes, they had the perfect relationship. He paid her handsomely, and had increased her already generous salary every three months in direct proportion to the level of duties she took on. In return she helped him in ways far beyond what he would have expected his own secretary at work to do.

She never minded running through e-mails with him, or typing up letters that had to be done late at night after he had left the office. Nor did she balk at buying expensive jewellery for girlfriends, or even ordering the customary bunch of red roses he would have delivered when a relationship was nearing the end of its natural life span.

On a couple of occasions, when he had been out of the country and way too busy to shop, she had even purchased gifts for his mother, which she'd had couriered over to Greece. She could be relied upon to choose just the right thing. He should know. He had seen the reactions of the recipients.

There was nothing Beth could tell her that Heather didn't already know. This time, though, it was different. She had finished her illustration course and had come top of her class.

She no longer needed to save madly. In fact Theo's generous salary, and the fact that she paid no rent—at his insistence—meant that she had managed to foot the bill for the course, buy all her coursework material, even take herself off on various excursions to exhibitions of interest, and still have money in the bank. Not enough to put down for buying her own place, but more than enough to rent somewhere on her own.

Every word Beth was telling her now made sense. Confronted by too much of the truth to be palatable, Heather took refuge in vague answers.

'I actually know of an apartment…' Beth casually announced, glancing at her watch because her lunch hour had extended well beyond its time limit. 'It's in my block. It's not as big as mine, just the one bedroom, but you'll love it, and you wouldn't have someone knocking on your door in the late hours of the night, expecting you to fling on a dressing gown and follow him so that you can transcribe some letter that he could easily get his secretary to do the next day…'

But I never mind doing that, Heather wanted to say. She knew better, though. So she nodded distantly and tried to look enthusiastic. 'I could have a look…' she compromised.

Beth took that for a definite *yes* and stood up and reached for her briefcase. 'Good. Let me know when you're free and I'll sort out an appointment for you. But I'm telling you now that you won't be able to sit around and think about things, because it'll be snapped up in no time at all.' As if aware of the preaching tone of her voice, she grinned sheepishly and gave Heather a friendly hug. 'I care about you,' she said.

'I know.'

'And I hate to think of you languishing in that man's house, desperately waiting for him to notice you while you busy yourself doing his dirty errands.'

'I don't—'

'Of course you do!' Beth cut short the protest briskly. Heather, she had decided long ago, had an amazing knack for justifying Theo's bad behaviour and her responses to it. She had met him a few times in the past and knew, realistically, that hell would freeze over before he looked at Heather in any way aside from that of one lucky employer who had a doting employee at his beck and call. He liked his women tall, thin and vacant. Heather resoundingly didn't fit into any of those categories, and as far as Beth was concerned she let herself down by feeding the illusion that one day he might see her with different eyes.

'I'm off now, darling. You take care—and *phone me*. Okay?'

'Okay,' Heather agreed readily, not quite dismissing the option of moving out, but not giving it much importance either.

Fate had brought her together with Theo, in a manner of speaking, and fate wasn't quite ready to take her away.

But the application in her handbag, the possibility of a flat and Beth's stern little talk did have her thinking as she made her way back to Theo's place.

On the way back she stopped off and bought a few things from the delicatessen at the corner—things she knew he would like. He would be away for the weekend, but tonight he would be in. She would make him some spaghetti Bolognese, to which he was very partial.

As she approached the apartment block she tried not to think of his weekend activities. He was seeing yet another of his impossibly beautiful brunettes. This one was called Venetia, and she suited the name. She was almost as tall as he was in heels, only wore designer clothes, and on the one occasion she had met Heather had treated her with the slightly disdainful superiority of someone very beautiful in the presence of a troll.

That Heather was jealous was something she would never have revealed to Theo.

But, on top of everything else, it filtered into her system now like poison.

It was no longer enough to content herself with the silly delusion that enjoying him was enough. Yes, she found him endlessly fascinating, with his endearing arrogance, his sharp wit and his moments of real thoughtfulness. But was it really enough?

She had completed her course two weeks ago, and in its wake the grinding clang of time was left marching on, reminding her, in the sudden void, that she had a life to be getting on with—and not a life that revolved around one man who really didn't pay her a scrap of attention even though she knew, in some inexplicable way, that she was virtually indispensable to him.

Or are you? a nasty little voice in her head said, making her pause in her tracks. *You'd like to think you are, but don't we all believe the things we want to believe and discard the rest?*

It was with a heavy heart that Heather walked up to his apartment. She had started that as a form of exercise over the past few weeks—as a way of counteracting her love of chocolate and all things sweet and therefore calorie laden.

Theo lived on the top floor of a high-specification block of penthouse apartments in the very heart of Knightsbridge. Typically, his was by far the largest, encompassing the entire upper floor of the building. It was as big as any conventional house, although laid out in a contemporary fashion, and he had not stinted in its decoration. In fact, he had told her, as she'd traipsed her way through in awestruck silence on her very first day, he had simply employed the top designer in London to come in and have his way with it. His only constraints had involved colour—as little of it as possible—and no plants which would require looking after.

Over the months Heather had done nothing about the colour, but she *had* brought in plants, which she religiously tended.

She had also brightened up the walls with some of her illustrations, unruffled by Theo's initial grunting response and then gratified by his occasional appreciative remarks.

Her interest in hanging a few more, which she had been looking forward to choosing from her portfolio, had been squashed under her uncustomary downward spiral of thoughts.

She let herself into the apartment, dumped the food in the fridge and, still reeling from the depressing effect of Beth's opinions, headed for the shower.

It was wonderfully refreshing. Although summer was on its last legs, and had been a particularly uneventful one even by English standards, it had been a muggy day and she had built up a healthy sweat trekking up the flights of stairs with a fairly heavy carrier bag.

The sound of the doorbell being rung insistently only just managed to penetrate the sound of the shower and the clamour of her thoughts.

Of course it wouldn't be Theo. Theo never, but never, got back before seven in the evening. He also possessed his own key, which he would never be scatty enough to misplace. But even so…who else could it be? The porter on the ground floor would never allow any salesperson to go up the elevator. It would have been more than his life was worth. Very rich people hugged their privacy and would have been horrified at the thought that any old person could come knocking on their door demanding their attention. In fact, sightings of neighbours were few and far between. Heather was convinced that the super-rich possessed some kind of special radar that warned them when to venture out of their apartments and when not to.

She felt her heartbeat quicken at the thought that she might open the door to see Theo standing there.

It wasn't Theo. And it wasn't a salesperson, unlikely as that option had been. It was a short, dark-haired woman in her sixties, with a face that should have been fierce but just looked exhausted.

Heather didn't know who was more surprised to see whom. They broke the silence at the same time, one speaking voluble Greek, the other stuttering out a bewildered request for some identity. Eventually, they both fell silent once more, until Heather said, her natural friendliness kicking in, 'I'm sorry, but would you mind telling me who you are? It's just that…well… not many people are allowed up unless they're expected…' She smiled to offset any offence that might have been taken. Not having had time to change into anything else, she clutched the cord of her bathrobe tightly around her and was self-consciously aware of bright black eyes appraising her.

'Who are *you*?' The woman peered around Heather. 'Where is my son? Is my son here? The man at the desk said that there would be someone to open up for me. I thought he was talking about Theo. Where is he? Who are you?'

Heather gaped. Theo had mentioned his mother now and again—the mother for whom he had the deepest respect and admiration, the mother who never ventured to London because the crowds confused her.

'Please—come in, Mrs Miquel.' A shy smile. 'I'm so glad to meet you. I'm Heather…'

'Heather? Heather who? Theo never mentioned a Heather

to me, but then my son never talks about his girlfriends. I was beginning to think he had none! Or maybe too many…eh?' She bustled into the apartment and immediately headed for the sofa, where she sat down with a sigh of relief. 'Come over here, child. Let me see you.'

'Oh, but you've got the wrong—'

'Shh!' Theo's mother placed one finger commandingly over her lips. 'Humour an old woman who has been praying so long for her son to find a nice girl to settle down with. And this could not have come at a better time for me, my child. Yes. You look plump and well fed.'

'I'm on a diet…' Heather mumbled, aghast at the other woman's misconceptions and determined to set things straight. 'Well, soon will be…cabbages…soup… I'll shed pounds… But, you know, I think… Well…I'm sorry to disappoint you…but…'

'Disappointed? Of course I am not disappointed, my child…!' The old face suddenly lit up with a smile and Heather helplessly smiled back. 'Theo likes to think that I am old-fashioned…maybe that is why he did not tell me about you…he thought that I would disapprove of you two living together…'

'No, Mrs Miquel…' Heather urgently positioned herself on the sofa, acutely conscious that her state of dress was doing nothing to further the truth. 'I mean, we *are* living together…*technically*…'

'And, while I am an old woman, I am not that old that I do not realise how times have changed. In my day—well…we did things differently. But that is not to say that I do not understand how young people do things…' She unexpectedly reached out to cup the side of Heather's face with her hand. 'I am just happy that my beloved Theo has found someone, and I can tell you are a kind person. It is in your eyes.'

Heather wondered how kindness could be so easily confused with panic.

'And you must not call me Mrs Miquel, my child. My name is Litsa.'

'Theo didn't say anything about you coming over...'

'I had hoped to...' Her face fell into anxious lines of worry. 'It is best if I explain to him in person... Now, I am tired...perhaps you could call Theo...explain that I am here...?'

'Of course!' Since Litsa's eyelids were fluttering shut, and her strength was clearly sapped, Heather didn't feel it appropriate to embark on a lengthy explanation of how it was that she came to be occupying Theo's flat, currently dressed in a bathrobe, and what her real role was. She decided that it was perhaps best to leave that little nugget of disillusionment to Theo.

In the meantime she would escort Litsa to one of the spare rooms, make sure that she was settled into bed, and bring her something to eat—although, after that first outburst of curiosity, she now seemed to have wilted.

Thankfully, the sprawling apartment had several spare bedrooms, two with *en suite* bathrooms, and Heather showed her to one of these. How she had managed to accomplish a trip to London was a mystery, because she suddenly seemed very fragile, like a piece of china that could be easily broken. She was asleep before Heather had finished removing her jacket and shoes. Making as little noise as possible, she closed the curtains and tucked her underneath the covers.

However, she felt sure that anyone who wasn't stone deaf would have heard her heart beating like a steam engine.

Her fingers were trembling as she dialled Theo's mobile phone. He answered immediately, his tone of voice implying that she had interrupted him in the middle of something important. She took a deep breath and spoke quickly, just in case he decided to hang up on her without giving her the benefit of the doubt. When it came to matters of work Theo did not possess a sense of humour. Heather had worked sufficiently with him to have spotted the change that came over him the minute he lost himself in anything to do with his job.

'What are you talking about?' he snapped. 'I can't understand a word you're saying.'

'I'm saying that *your mother is here*, Theo.'

'Hold on.' There was a few seconds of silence, then he was back on the line. 'Now speak.'

Heather knew that her words were leaping over each other. Several times he had to ask her to slow down. No, she didn't know *why* Litsa had shown up…but she was asleep now and *he had to drop whatever he was doing and come back to the apartment immediately*.

There was nothing Theo hated more than any distraction from work, and right now he was in the middle of a high-level conference, but for the first time he felt something more powerful than the magnetic pull of his work. He felt fear. It fizzed in his blood like acid as he hurtled out of his office, urgently calling his chauffeur to have his car ready and waiting outside.

Typically for Heather, who had never learned the art of economising with her speech, she had babbled on in a confused manner about needing to set his mother straight about something or other, but he had barely heard. His brain had already leapt to possibilities that did not bear thinking about.

His mother *never* came to London, never mind without any prior warning. To have travelled over without first informing him was unthinkable.

Indeed, Theo could think of no reason why his mother should not have warned him of her arrival. He briefly wondered whether she *had*, whether he had misfiled the information somewhere in his head, but he immediately discounted that. He forgot nothing—and certainly nothing as important as his mother coming to England.

The car had not quite stopped before he was opening the passenger door and heading towards the apartment block.

He burst through the door of his apartment to find Heather anxiously waiting for him, dressed in her usual garb of leggings and a baggy tee shirt with broad stripes.

'She's sound asleep,' Heather said, leaping to her feet and catching him by the arm before he could storm into the bedroom to ask questions.

His eyes looked wild and she relaxed her hold into something more reassuring. 'Let me make you some coffee. We need to talk.'

For a few seconds she thought he was going to shrug her hand off and head for the bedroom, but instead he ran his fingers through his hair and nodded.

He watched as she meticulously made some coffee. Along with all the other amazing and under-used high-tech gadgets in his kitchen was a cappuccino maker which he had never learnt to use. Heather, ditzy as she was, had sussed it out in no time, and now she handed him a cup of frothy coffee and sat opposite him at the chrome and glass kitchen table.

'Is there a problem?' Theo demanded. 'My mother never makes unannounced visits to this country so I am assuming that there is. What exactly did she say?'

'You mean did she tell me why she had come over?'

'That's right. Did she?'

Heather shook her head slowly and tried to figure out how to break it to him that his mother had rushed into some pretty horrendous misconceptions. She had tried on the telephone but her words had come out all jumbled, and anyway he hadn't been listening. Even from the other end of the line she had managed to glean that much.

'Theo. Is she all right? I mean, physically? She looked a little…frail…'

Theo's eyes darkened and he leant towards her. 'Explain.'

'She just seemed delicate…'

'And you would have been able to see that all in the space of what…half an hour? Because you're not actually doing an art course at all? Because you're actually studying to become a doctor?' He gave a bark of laughter under which Heather could pick up the strains of fear and her eyes widened sympathetically.

Theo stood up abruptly and pushed his chair back, then he leaned both hands on the table and shot her a hard, cold look. 'And spare me the compassion. I'm not in the mood for it.'

'Okay.' She felt the sting of tears at the back of her eyes and bit her lip.

Theo looked at her downbent head and knew that he had been unnecessarily cruel, but the apology he felt obliged to offer refused to come to his lips. Did she have any idea how her passing glib remark had consolidated all the nebulous fears that had been swimming about in his head? He banged his fist on the table and Heather jumped.

'I'm sorry,' she whispered.

'Sorry about what?' Theo snarled back. 'About offering your opinion when it hasn't been asked for?'

'Sorry that you're scared.' She met his eyes bravely and was relieved when he at least deigned to sit back down. She had never seen him scared before, had never seen him even close to it. If he wanted to take it out on her, then so be it. Wasn't that what love was all about? And didn't she love him?

However, she instinctively knew that dwelling on it wasn't a good idea, so she gave him a watery smile and sighed.

'There's something else,' she volunteered tentatively. 'I did try explaining to you on the phone, but I'm not sure you understood what I was trying to say. You know how sometimes I say stuff and it doesn't come out the way I mean…'

In the face of this prosaic understatement Theo felt some of the tension drain away from him and he smiled grudgingly. 'I've noticed.'

'Well…when your mother rang the doorbell I was in the shower…'

Theo frowned and tried to make sense of this random statement. He couldn't, so he waited patiently for her to continue. Given sufficient time, Heather's ramblings usually led to a fairly coherent place.

'I know you're probably thinking that it was a pretty odd time to have a shower, in the middle of the afternoon, but I'd decided to climb the stairs with some shopping… Anyway… Yes, I was in the shower and I went to answer the door in my bathrobe…'

'Do you plan on getting to the point any time this year?'

'Forget about the bathrobe…it doesn't matter. The *point* is…and I know you're going to be angry at this but it *wasn't my fault*…your mother wasn't expecting to see me.'

'Why didn't she ask Hal to let her up if she wasn't expecting to find anyone in the apartment?'

'Because Hal told her that someone would be here…she just expected that someone to be *you*…'

'At four-thirty in the afternoon?'

Heather ignored this rhetorical question and fixed him with a pleading stare which immediately sent alarm bells clanging in his head.

'I'm afraid she got the wrong impression…'

'Got the wrong impression? What impression did she get?'

'That I was…somehow involved with you…'

'You *are* involved with me. You're my housekeeper, amongst other things.'

'Not that kind of involved, Theo. Involved, *involved*. On a romantic level involved. As in your girlfriend.'

Theo's reaction was unexpected. He burst out laughing.

'I know it's incredible,' Heather said tightly. 'I know I'm not the sort of woman you would glance at twice…'

Theo stopped laughing and looked at her narrowly, faintly uneasy about her tone of voice, but she had already progressed to the main body of the story and he was now getting the picture loud and clear.

He had kept his mother in the dark about his frequent liaisons—half to protect her, half to spare himself the inevitable disappointment he knew he would read on her face—and now she had walked in on a woman in a bathrobe, sharing his apartment, and had jumped to all the wrong conclusions.

'But you told her the truth, didn't you?' he interrupted.

'I couldn't.'

'You couldn't? Run that by me, Heather. My mother starts telling you how pleased she is that her son has finally found himself a good woman and you *don't find it possible to point her in the right direction*?' He was beginning to wonder how a day at the office could end up going so monstrously wrong.

'She didn't let me get a word in edgeways, Theo, and then she just sort of…lost all her steam—as though energy had been drained out of her—and I just didn't have the heart to shake her and tell her that she'd made a mistake…'

'Well, I'll sort that out.' He took a sip of his coffee and regarded Heather over the rim of his cup. Heather? Girlfriend? Ridiculous notion. His eyes drifted over her face, with its finely defined features and expressive eyes, then downwards to the striped tee shirt that did absolutely nothing for her and seemed to belong to a range of clothing specifically chosen for that purpose.

Yes, sure, she might have a personality—quite a bit of a personality, as he had discovered over time—but personality wasn't high on Theo's list of desirable qualities in a woman.

'Shouldn't be a problem,' he continued.

'You mean because no one in their right mind would ever think that I might be attractive?' Heather heard the words come out of her with a start of surprise, and she carried on quickly, not giving him time to latch onto their significance. 'Perhaps you ought to go and check on her…she seems to have been asleep for a while…'

'Where did *that* come from?' Theo asked with a frown. Heather might not be a candidate for a modelling contract, but then again he had never once seen her succumb to any real insecurities about her appearance. She joked about her figure now and again, and always seemed to be on some diet or another, but that was as far as it went. 'Has some man insulted you?' He felt a flare of sudden overpowering rage.

'Don't be silly, Theo. I'm just…in a weird mood. Must be your mother showing up…'

Which brought him back to what his mother was doing here, and he nodded and stood up. 'I'm going to go and check on her.'

'Don't wake her up if she's still asleep,' Heather urged. 'She looked as though she needed the rest. Perhaps she came over here to relax.' That made no sense at all, but she couldn't bear to see the sudden lines of strain etched on his darkly handsome features. It was funny how successfully he had always managed to promote his own invincibility. To see him vulnerable hurt her in ways she couldn't define. Nor could she express how she felt, because he would have rejected her sympathy as fiercely as if she had offered him a cup of arsenic.

'You don't have to patronise me,' Theo said dryly, but at least, Heather thought, he wasn't angry, and she smiled.

'I do if it stops you worrying so much.'

'Why?'

'Because…' She felt *terra firma* begin to shift worryingly under her feet. 'Because I would do it for anyone.' Which was a version of the truth at any rate. 'I can't bear to see anyone hurting.'

'A good Samaritan?' Theo said, still looking at her intently. 'Well, now I'm going to see my mother, and I shall end up being the bad Samaritan when I inform her that her notions about us are a load of rubbish.' He laughed and shook his head, as if still incredulous that such an error of judgement might have been made in the first place.

It left Heather thinking how important it was now to leave. She couldn't blame Theo for the fact that he found any idea of them being connected romantically a complete joke. The joke, she miserably pondered, was on her. She had harboured a ridiculous unfounded infatuation with him virtually from the very first moment she had clapped eyes on him, sitting behind his desk, brow furrowed in concentration, barely aware of her existence as she cleaned around him. And that had eventually led her here, to his apartment, entrenched in feelings that would never be reciprocated. Beth had been right all along. She needed to control her life and set it in the direction she wanted to take—instead of passively allowing her emotions to dictate to her.

It all made perfect sense to her in the forty-five minutes she spent in the kitchen, waiting for Theo to emerge and wondering whether it was appropriate for her to wait at all.

When he eventually did come out, she knew from his expression that the news wasn't going to be good.

'I need something stronger than coffee,' was the first thing he said as he sat at the kitchen table and wearily pressed his thumbs on his eyes. 'And I suggest,' he added, 'that you have something as well.'

Occasionally Heather had wine with Theo when she happened to have cooked for him, but actually she was on an alcohol-free diet, guaranteed to shed several pounds in combination with rigorous exercise—which she planned on getting down to very soon. The look on his face put paid to that. She poured them both a glass and sat down facing him.

'She did not want to worry me,' Theo said at last. 'The chest pains began a while ago, but she put it down to old age, wear and tear. Eventually, she made an appointment with her doctor, who referred her to his colleague in London, a specialist in heart surgery.'

Heather gasped. 'And you had no idea…?'

'If I had, do you think that I would have allowed her to carry that burden on her own?' Theo snapped irritably. She had tapped into his own dark guilt—guilt that he had been so wrapped up in his own fast-moving life that he barely surfaced to see what was going on around him. 'She took the private jet over to London, visited with the doctor, who did a few tests, and she was then told that flying back to Greece was not a realistic option. Which was when she decided to come here, to my flat. Which was when she met you…'

CHAPTER FOUR

HEATHER waited for an improvement on this flatly spoken statement, which had carried just a hint of accusation with it. None was forthcoming.

'Look,' she said, drawing in a deep breath, 'I've been thinking…and…' The prospect of saying goodbye loomed ahead of her like a yawning Black Hole, but she ducked down and ploughed on. 'And now your mother's here…and, well…*especially as she seemed to get the wrong impression of me*…it wouldn't be appropriate…for me to stay on here…' She could feel her cheeks reddening under his silent watchful gaze, and the wrenching in her gut as she absorbed the enormity of what she was doing. Not that it wasn't the *right* thing to do— because it absolutely was!

'I've finished my course now, and it's time I moved on…with a proper job. Not that it hasn't been great being here… Well, Beth has a flat in mind for me, actually…it's in the same block as hers. Just small, of course, because I won't be able to afford that much to start with…' As usual she could hear herself turning one small statement of fact into several bewildering thousands, and she forced herself to shut up and smile.

Theo shrugged. 'It is naturally up to you if you feel inclined to move out…'

Heather fought the undermining temptation to retract her rash statement and buy herself just a little more time, just a few more months. 'I think it's for the best,' she mumbled.

'So might it be. Just not yet.'

For a few wild seconds her heart leapt as she translated those three words into what she wanted to hear. *Need, love, want!* Then reality sank its teeth into her and she looked at him, bemused.

'Permit me to clarify,' he said, finishing his wine and helping himself to another glass. 'As I said, my mother has a heart problem. She's explained it to me as best as she can and it would appear that it is not life threatening. Of course I will talk to her consultant in depth about that.' He frowned, and Heather could read his thoughts as if they were written on his forehead in large neon lettering. She felt sorry for the consultant. 'But, at any rate, it is imperative that she is spared any stress.'

'Naturally,' Heather nodded, relieved. Things might have been a lot worse.

'Which brings me to you,' Theo said smoothly. He sat back and tapped the table with one thoughtful forefinger. 'My mother, as you pointed out, is under the illusion that we are involved with one another, that I have finally found the woman I want to settle down with. In her head, you are living in my apartment, and therefore we are conducting a serious relationship...'

'You mean *you haven't told her the truth*?'

'It was impossible,' Theo informed her flatly, and Heather gaped at him in consternation. 'She's in a very fragile state of health at the moment. If I tell her the truth, then there is no telling how it might affect her current situation.'

'But you have to!' Heather cried.

'Not necessarily.'

'Not necessarily? I plan on *moving out*, Theo! Don't you think she might suspect that something's not quite right when your so-called serious relationship rents a flat on the other side of town? Anyway,' she continued, 'it wouldn't be right to deceive an old woman…'

'It wouldn't be right to burden her with stress she cannot handle…'

'How can you assume that your mother wouldn't be able to handle the truth, Theo?' She leaned forward, so that her hands were lying flat on the table between them. 'You're not thinking straight.'

'I know I'm not,' Theo said simply. 'But I'm afraid to take the chance.'

As easily as that he managed to slice through all her protests and appeal to her on the most basic of levels, and although there was absolute sincerity in his eyes, she wouldn't have been surprised if he had deliberately used the ploy because he knew her well enough to realise that her emotions were her downfall. This was a girl who sobbed during the sad bits in films, who would give her last coins to a busker on the underground and who continued to have faith in a sister who had taken her money and headed for the hills.

Theo watched the sudden indecision in her eyes and breathed an inward sigh of relief.

'It won't be for long,' he promised. 'A couple of weeks—no more. Just until she's strong enough to travel back to Greece…'

'And you'll break it to her then…?'

'I'll break to her gently, over time. Put it this way, your role will soon be over. After that you can get your proper job and find your proper flat and start your proper life.' He didn't know why the thought of that made him ever so slightly angry, but it did. Since he didn't care to analyse the emotion, he let it go. There were far more pressing things to think about.

How easy it was for him to say that, Heather thought sadly. She could easily be replaced. There weren't many who would bite a hand willing to part with generous sums of money for very easy work.

She thought of the times when she had foolishly bought presents for his girlfriends, while the pain of being the helpful employee in the background had twisted inside her like a knife. Well, if she had thought that fate hadn't quite finished with her, how right she had been!

'I think I'll go to my room now,' Heather said, standing up. 'I'll come out a bit later, if your mother wakes up, but I'm not very hungry.'

'Another one of your crazy diets?' Theo asked, and she replied with a smile that was neither friendly nor hostile. She felt as though the stuffing had been knocked out of her. But before she could leave the room he was talking again, telling her as if it was the most normal thing in the world that his mother expected them to be sharing a bedroom.

Heather spun round and looked at him, aghast. '*Share a room*?' she squeaked, walking towards him. '*With you*?'

'It's a very big bedroom,' Theo said placatingly. 'With a sofa.'

'Out of the question!'

'Why?' He raised his eyebrows in what was the first indication of amusement since he had walked into the flat a couple of hours previously. 'What do you think I'm going to do?'

'I don't think *anything*!'

'Then why the sudden outburst?' he asked curiously. 'Unless you think I might be tempted to touch…?' A sudden image of her flashed through his head, a picture of her lying on the sofa many months ago, after he had delivered her back to the house she had been sharing at the time…lying with her hand flung back and her breasts, full and heavy, gently rising and falling as she breathed.

'It just doesn't seem right,' Heather muttered, blushing furiously. She could tell that he was laughing at her and was bitterly hurt and angry.

Theo's voice was more brusque than he intended. 'I know it's not ideal, but it won't be for long. Now, you'll have to clear your belongings into my bedroom—or at least some of them. Enough to…'

'Perpetuate the charade?' Heather heard herself say tightly. She couldn't remember ever speaking to him like that, with real anger in her voice, not even when she had been feeling angry inside. It was as though she was looking at herself for the first time and watching someone else—someone who had been prepared to do as he asked, like a puppy following its master, because the pure pleasure of being around him now and again had outweighed everything else. Every last ounce of common sense.

Now fate had played one last trick on her, and she was being punished in the most cruel way possible.

'Why can't you get Venetia to come and stay with you?' Heather asked in a more normal voice. 'That way, at least you won't be lying.' And that, more than anything else, would force her to make a decision and move out, because knowing that he was in his room with his current girlfriend would have taken the knife-twisting a step too far.

Theo had never brought a woman back to his apartment to sleep. Heather had correctly read this as his way of ensuring that no woman got her foot through the door and started nurturing impossible ideas of permanence. He didn't mind *her* living under the same roof because as far as he was concerned Heather wasn't a threat to his precious independence. She wondered what he would have done had he ever suspected that she was addicted to him. Thrown her out without a backward glance, she imagined.

'Venetia isn't the sort of woman my mother would approve of,' Theo was telling her now, eyebrows raised in amusement at the very thought of it. 'And besides…' He paused thoughtfully. 'I wouldn't like Venetia to think that a brief spell of moving in might lead to something more concrete. With you it would be completely different. You would know the boundaries and wouldn't be stupid enough to think that they could be overstepped. Anyway—' he shrugged '—my mother's taken to you. She thinks you're very sweet and jolly.'

Heather couldn't think of two adjectives she would have found more insulting, even though she knew that insulting her was the last thing on Theo's mind. He was simply stating a fact.

'Of course I'll compensate you financially for doing this, Heather. Even I realise that it's a favour way beyond the normal call of duty.'

An hour later and Heather was still in a daze at the progression of events. She had moved a select amount of her belongings into his room, choosing to stuff as much as she could into the drawers of the room she currently occupied.

Just standing there, looking around her, made her feel slightly sick. She had always found his bedroom enormous, way too big for one person, with its own small sitting area and a bathroom that could have accommodated a small family. However, with the prospect of sharing it in mind, it suddenly seemed painfully small. Was it her imagination or had the proportions shrunk to the size of a doll's house?

She wouldn't dwell on it, she decided. In a funny way his unconscious insults, the offer of payment, the assumption that she would know her place because she was, after all, no more than a valued housekeeper who happened to be in the wrong place at the wrong time, would strengthen her. He had effectively managed to put her in her place, and as soon as his mother left she would finally have the backbone to walk away.

Having always been a firm believer in the truism that every cloud had a silver lining, Heather now clung to this salutary theory with the tenacity of a drowning man clinging to a lifebelt.

It didn't help that his mother was such a nice person. Over a light supper, she briefly explained to them both what her doctor in Greece had advised, but it was clear that she was much more interested in learning about the new addition to her son's life.

'I have worried about him,' she told Heather in a conspiratorial whisper that was meant to be overheard. 'Too much success with the girls from an early age is not always a good thing for a young boy! It can turn him into a playboy, if that is the correct word!'

Faced with the glorious opportunity to somehow get back at him, Heather smiled and glanced at Theo. He looked uncomfortable and hunted.

'Theo? Oh, no, Theo *would never* see women as playthings—would you?'

The look he shot her from under his lashes was worth every second of the dig, accompanied as it was by a wide-eyed stare of complete innocence. With an inarticulate grunt, he began clearing away the dishes.

'It is very important for a man to settle down,' Litsa was saying, watching approvingly as her son gave off the totally inaccurate impression of someone who habitually helped around the kitchen. 'A good wife is necessary to train a man into being civilised!' She laughed and gave him an affectionate look, while Heather chewed over the ridiculous notion of any woman being able to train Theo Miquel.

'You seem to be flagging, Mama,' he said, shooting Heather a warning glance which she ignored. 'Perhaps it is time for you to retire now. Big day tomorrow. I shall come with you to see the consultant, so you needn't worry yourself unnecessarily.'

He had successfully managed to divert the conversation, but his respite was transitory. Litsa Miquel spent the next forty-five minutes in pleasurable contemplation of her son's settled love life, obviously relieved that she could now share her past concerns about him with someone who understood, and Heather picked up the reins of the conversation with gusto.

It was a unique experience for him to be on the receiving end of female banter that made him squirm, and squirm he did, as childhood escapades were dredged up, until eventually he vaulted to his feet and insisted that he take his mother to her room.

As they disappeared in the direction of the bedroom Heather could feel her ebullient mood evaporating under the weight of reality. Reality was his dismissal of her, made all the more cruel because he wasn't aware of it. It was the bitter emptiness of realising just how far she had sunk in her own estimation—sunk to the level of someone who had been prepared to scramble for the crumbs he had carelessly tossed at her. Reality was the bedroom waiting for her. That thought galvanised her into immediate action. She didn't know how long it would take him to settle his mother, but it wouldn't give her much time to get into her pyjamas and fling herself under the covers, lights off.

For someone who had never seen the allure of strenuous exercise, Heather now discovered that she could move at the speed of light.

She let herself into his bedroom with wings on the soles
of her feet and completed her ablutions in five seconds flat.
Then, with the door of the bathroom firmly locked, she
speedily changed into her pyjamas, which consisted of a pair
of small shorts and a vest top. Since she had not heard the
sound of a door opening and closing, she assumed he was still
with his mother, leaving the coast clear for her to sprint to the
bed, leap in, and then switch off the light by the bed.

She dearly wished that she had had the foresight to stack
some spare linen on the sofa, but there was no way she was
going to risk a trip to the laundry cupboard—and anyway he
could get it himself. He did precious little around the house as
it was, never mind his persuasive acting earlier on when he had
strode around the kitchen, tidying up, teacloth draped over one
shoulder, for all the world as though he did it on a regular basis.

After one hour of coiled tension, body on red-hot alert for the
sound of the door opening, sleep began to take its toll, and by
the time Theo did enter the bedroom Heather was sound asleep.

He had been working. His conversation with his mother
had been to his mind over-long, despite his fruitless attempts
to convince her that she was exhausted and needed to get to
sleep immediately. He had never realised just how much she
worried about him—about the pressure he was under from
work, about his single state. With a fictitious relationship now
on the scene, a dam of maternal concerns had been unleashed,
and he had left the bedroom feeling slightly battered.

Then had come an awkward conversation with Venetia, as
he cancelled plans.

After that, work had seemed to be the only thing, and so he
had remained in his office for well over an hour, replying to
e-mails that could have easily waited until a more civilised hour.

The sight of Heather in his bed rendered him momentarily disconcerted. She was lying just as she had been months ago, on that sofa, with one arm flung wide. He very much doubted that she had originally lain down in that position of utter abandonment.

Making as little noise as possible, Theo advanced into the bedroom, his eyes getting accustomed to the darkness as he walked tentatively towards the bed, unbuttoning his shirt *en route* before stripping it off and discarding it.

When he had mentioned the sofa, his implication had been that *she* would sleep on it. A faint smile curved the corners of his mouth as he stood over her, watching her as she slept. Fair's fair, he thought wryly. He had twisted her arm to help him out. As far as she was concerned he could take the sofa—or, judging from her deep reluctance to participate in his plan, the floor, and never mind any bedlinen.

He showered quickly, finding himself preoccupied more with the woman lying on his bed and what he would do about her than anything else.

She stirred as he walked back into the room, stark naked. Now he could see the shapely bend of her leg, protruding from under the quilt, and, from the looks of it, whatever she was wearing there wasn't a great deal of it. Was she one of those women who covered themselves up like a nun during the day but then wore sexy little bits of nothing at night? The thought kick-started something in him, some reaction that felt as though it had been waiting there all along for the right time to leap out. He sucked in his breath sharply and turned away, aware of his body's reaction proclaiming a sexual response that was as powerful as it was unexpected.

The sofa, of course, would kill any uninvited thoughts, but he glanced at it, dismissing it as quickly as he saw it.

She was sound asleep, and his bed was infinitely more comfortable than any sofa, especially one that required making up and thus a hunt for bedlinen which would take for ever, considering he had no idea where it was stored.

He soundlessly slipped under the covers and lay down completely still, willing his arousal to subside.

When she restlessly turned over, so that she was now facing in his direction, Theo almost groaned. The small vest left little to the imagination, revealing as it did a generous cleavage which he had never before glimpsed under her daily uniform of baggy tops. His breathing was ragged as he raked her flushed face, her slightly parted lips and the tousle of soft blonde hair framing her face.

He didn't trust himself to look any lower, just in case he lost control.

Lord only knew how long he would have remained there, relishing the pleasurable novelty of wanting a woman with no possibility of having her, if she hadn't stretched—a very small movement that brought her hand into immediate contact with his chest.

He froze as her eyes flew open, and then she shrieked, drawing back from him in horror.

'Keep it down!' he snapped.

'What are you doing here!'

'This is my bedroom, remember? The one you agreed to share?'

'I didn't agree to *share the bed*!' Heather's nervous system was in a state of wild disarray as her eyes locked with his. At the back of her mind, the information was sinking in that he wasn't wearing anything above his waist. What her hand had come into contact with had *not* been the comforting touch of sensible flannelette pyjamas. *Was he wearing anything below*?

Her whole body began to burn as her imagination dived off its springboard and took flight.

'The sofa isn't made up,' Theo informed her. Far from staunching his erection, the shadows and angles of her flustered face were proving an even bigger turn-on.

'Then *go and make it up*! You can't stay in this bed with me! You promised…'

'I never promised anything,' Theo breathed unevenly. 'And stop getting so worked up. It's a big bed.' Which didn't explain why they were lying a matter of ten inches away from one another. He had made no attempt to widen the distance between them. She had certainly tried, but to go any further back would result in her falling off the edge. He could feel her body quivering with tension and ordered himself to get a grip.

'Are you wearing anything?' Heather heard herself stutter, and his silence was telling. 'You're not, are you?'

'I don't possess any pyjamas. I've never seen the point of them.'

'How could you be so…so…*disrespectful?*' Heather whispered, tears gathering at the back of her eyes.

'*Disrespectful?*' Theo was flabbergasted. 'I have no idea what you're talking about.'

'Oh, yes, you do!' Heather said bitterly. 'You're so contemptuous of me that you don't care whether I'm in this bed or not! You don't even care whether you're wearing anything or not! Because as far as you're concerned I might just as well be a…a…*sack of potatoes*!'

In the tense silence that greeted this remark Theo reached out and took her hand.

'Except,' he whispered roughly, 'a sack of potatoes wouldn't have this effect on me!'

Heather felt the hard throb of his erection, and for a few seconds time seemed to stand still. The sexual awareness which had been kept under tabs for so long broke through its flimsy barriers and rushed through her like a tidal wave.

She could hear her own uneven breathing, like someone who has completed a marathon uphill. Every muscle in her body was quivering. He still had his hand covering hers, forcing her to feel for herself the effect of her proximity.

'Well?' he prompted. 'I don't think what you're feeling is the result of a man who is contemptuous of you…'

'You need…need to go and sleep somewhere else…'

'And then pretend in the morning that none of this happened? Why would I do that?' He released her hand, but only so that he could smooth his fingers over her waist, then under the small cropped vest to the bountiful curve of her breast.

Theo groaned. Take away the shapeless garments and she was all woman, all voluptuous, curvy woman, with breasts a man could lose himself in.

With one swift movement he angled his body up so that he was looking down at her.

In the half-light he looked devilishly sexy. His arms were strongly muscled and his beautiful mouth…his beautiful mouth was drawing closer.

With a stifled, hungry gasp, Heather closed her eyes and was lost in his urgent, devouring kiss. With a will of their own her arms curved around his neck, pulling him towards her, and her body writhed, pleading to be stilled.

Eventually, Theo drew back from the kiss—but only so that he could transfer his attention to her neck.

Had he wanted this all along? Had he watched her without even realising it himself? Created fantasies around her? He didn't think so, but if he hadn't why was it now that his body was acting as though attaining the conquest of some private yearning?

He roughly pushed up her vest and then kneeled back on his haunches, the better to appreciate what he had known all along. She wasn't built along the lines of those stick insects he went out with. As a connoisseur of women's bodies, he could say with his hand on his heart that he had never before set eyes on such gloriously abundant breasts. He reached down and felt the weight of them in his hands, and then, very slowly, appreciating every second of the experience, he rubbed the pads of his thumbs over her defined nipples. The tips were hard and he watched, fascinated and unbearably turned on, as she wriggled under his touch, her eyes still firmly closed and her hands balled into fists.

'You have amazing breasts,' he breathed shakily, and her eyes flickered open.

'By that, I take it you mean *big*?' She had never, ever associated the word *big* with anything complimentary, at least not when it came to her body, but the way he was looking at her now was making her feel very sexy, very proud of the breasts she had become accustomed to concealing.

'Amazing,' he corrected. He bent down and tenderly began to suckle on one full nipple, licking and drawing the swollen bud into his mouth until she was moaning with pleasure.

Heather feverishly lifted the vest over her head while he continued his assault on her breasts, dividing his attention between the two until she thought she was literally going to pass out from ecstasy. During those long nights when she had wistfully wondered what it would be like to have him make love to her, see her as a woman instead of someone he had grown accustomed to having around, the way you might grow accustomed to having a pot plant around, during those nights she had never dreamed that the reality would be so exquisitely more fulfilling.

With every fibre of her body she responded to his caress.

She reached to touch him, to feel him, and shuddered with a heady sense of power when he groaned in response.

So this was what it felt like to have this beautiful, wonderful, clever man surrender! To see him shed that formidable control! She arched up and he wrenched the shorts off her, hands hot and urgent.

Heather shifted and felt his hands cover her down there, then his fingers were exploring her telling wetness, rubbing and pressing against the pulsating sensitised bud that sent shock waves of pleasure racing through her.

With a feeling of aching, pounding anticipation, she felt his mouth travel over the flat planes of her stomach—the stomach she had always unfavourably compared to her sister's, the stomach he didn't seem repulsed by—until he was nuzzling into the soft downy hair that veiled her womanhood.

'You can't!' Heather gasped, and he looked up and met her eyes with an amused smile.

'Have you never been touched there before?'

'Not in *that* way!'

'What way?' Her look was a mixture of innocence and excitement, and it slammed straight through him, making his blood boil with desire. For one brief moment Theo wondered where all this suffocating sexual tension was coming from. For a man who prided himself on being an expert lover, a lover who took his time and was a master of finesse, he seemed to have been reduced to a wild animal with only one thought on his mind—possession.

Submitting to primal urges he thought he had mastered a

long time ago, Theo breathed in her erotic, musky smell and tenderly flicked his tongue into her.

It took a superhuman feat of will-power not to rise up and thrust into her. Her wetness was driving him crazy, as was her wanton writhing as he explored her with his mouth. Her soft femininity was slippery, and the sweetest thing he had ever tasted. He knew when she was about to tip over the brink, and before she could do that, he quickly and efficiently took the necessary precautions.

By the time he took her, Heather was well on the way to cresting the peak, and just a few deep thrusts sent her hurtling into a sensory experience that was unique for her. Her whole body shuddered as she surrendered to the waves of pleasure that crashed through her, eventually subsiding into a warm glow of pure contentment.

From restless slumber, she was now fully awake. Actually, her body felt charged in a way it never had before. To think that this beautiful man had brought her to such heights, had sated himself in her, filled her with absolute joy.

She turned to him and sighed. 'That was wonderful.' A tiny frown creased her forehead. 'Was it okay for you? I mean,' she continued anxiously, 'I'm not very experienced…'

'You turn me on just the way you are,' Theo growled, pulling her closer to him and possessively draping one leg over hers.

'Did you mean for this to happen?' Heather asked. 'No, of course you didn't. So why did you make love to me?'

Faced with this direct question, Theo was lost for an answer.

'I mean, was it just because I happened to be in your bed? I know you probably think I'm crazy,' Heather continued, suddenly aware that this might not quite qualify as lazy post coital conversation, 'but I really need to know, Theo.'

'Why? Didn't you enjoy it?' He stroked her hair away from her face, touched by her anxiety.

'I thought it was the most wonderful experience I've ever had,' she answered truthfully, and that was enough to send a charge of pure masculine pride soaring through him.

'The *most* wonderful…?' he teased, smiling when she nodded. 'That puts a lot of pressure on me,' he said gravely.

In a split second Heather realised the error of her ways. She had succumbed to him without so much as a struggle. A few half-hearted protests, but then she had foolishly yielded—of course he would now be looking at the whole situation with a sense of mounting alarm.

Theo did not like women who clung. Nor, she imagined, would he like women who behaved like inexperienced, infatuated adolescents. He would want them cool and carefully controlled. She wondered how to backtrack and, even more importantly, how she could assume the façade of being cool and controlled when she had never been either.

'I'm sorry,' Heather apologised stiffly.

'Why be sorry? We just shared a mind-blowing experience.' And out of nowhere, Theo mused. Which just went to prove the point that around every corner a surprise lay in wait. Who would have thought that the woman whose company he had found utterly relaxing and unthreatening could conceal such depths of fire?

'Which,' he added lazily, 'is why I feel under such pressure. I mean, how am I going to top my first performance?'

Heather felt herself go weak with relief. Why would he say that if his intention was to curse himself for his weakness and chuck her out?

Thoughts of moving on with her independent life flew out of her head faster than water pouring down a plughole. She loved this man. They had made love and it had been, in his very own words, a *mind-blowing* experience. She felt as though she was suddenly walking on the clouds. Giddy with joy, she curled against him.

'You have a very sexy body,' Theo murmured, filling his hand with her lush breast. 'Why do you spend so much time covering it up?'

'You should know, Theo,' Heather said shyly, barely able to believe her ears. 'Aren't you supposed to be a connoisseur of women? I'm not built…well, along the lines of a model, am I?'

Theo didn't answer. He was finding it difficult to remember why he had ever been attracted to his past models. He slid his hand along her side, enjoying the womanly dip of her waist and the full, smooth rise of her hip.

'You don't know what it's like going through your teenage years without the advantages of being thin.' Especially, Heather thought, when you had a sister who looked like hers. 'Boys made snide remarks at school and my girlfriends felt sorry for me. It just wasn't cool to have a figure like mine, so I learned to cover it up.'

For the first time she felt truly proud of her curves, especially when he so blatantly enjoyed them. He pushed her gently onto her back and pleasured himself at her breasts. A man could lose himself in them!

Heather sighed with enjoyment and languorously squirmed under his exploring mouth. The heat that had subsided was building up again, and with a soft moan of anticipation she parted her legs so that he could touch her.

Want, need, love and utter fulfilment bathed her in warm joy, and as she curled her fingers into his hair she gave herself up utterly to the experience.

CHAPTER FIVE

OBSERVING his own situation through detached eyes—something Theo was remarkably good at—he knew that he should be feeling trapped and restless. He was, after all, currently occupying his own private vision of hell. His working hours had been severely curtailed. The past fortnight had seen him first at the hospital, where his mother had been recuperating after heart surgery, and then latterly at his apartment, where he had insisted she remain for at least another couple of weeks, until she was strong enough to venture back to Greece.

She had dutifully grumbled, but had given in without too much persuasion.

Theo suspected that his mother was secretly enjoying the relaxation of being pampered. Heather spent part of her day working on her portfolio, but seemed content to sacrifice the remainder to taking his mother for little walks and experimenting with Greek food in the kitchen under Litsa's eagle-eyed tutelage.

'It helps me,' his mother said tetchily, when he tried to convince her that she needed to take it easy. 'And I am not doing the cooking, Theo. Just supervising. What would you want me to do? Lie in bed all day like an invalid?'

He had diplomatically refrained from pointing out that she *was* an invalid, whether she chose to accept the fact or not.

Litsa had never been one to sit around doing nothing, and she wasn't about to change the habits of a lifetime. She was also in her element, bonding with the woman she imagined to be her future daughter-in-law—and Theo couldn't blame her. She had, after all, waited long enough.

The fact that his mother was dealing with an illusion was something that only impinged slightly on his conscience. The advantages of the situation as far as his mother's health was involved were too self-evident. Her progress, the consultant had told him a few days earlier, had been really impressive. Theo didn't think that would have been the case had she been sitting in his flat from dawn till dusk on her own, with nothing but her own worries and doubts for company.

No, Heather had been good for her—as had the pleasantly warming thought that she was dealing with her son's significant other.

And at the moment, it happened to suit him as well. Even though the invasion of his working life should have had him fuming.

He snapped shut the lid of his laptop computer and headed for the jacket hanging in the wardrobe of his office.

Jackie, his personal assistant, popped her head around the door and surreptitiously glanced at her watch. She knew that his mother was staying with him, and that there had been a minor medical problem which had been dealt with, but it still shocked her whenever she walked into his office at five-thirty to find him getting ready to go.

'Whatever it is, Jackie,' Theo said, without looking around, 'you'll have to cancel it. I'm on my way out.'

'Yes, but…'

'No buts.' He slipped on his jacket and turned to her. 'After five-thirty I'm off duty, until my mother is on her feet and back in Greece.' He began packing his computer into its leather case. He could use his mother as his excuse for the temporary derailment of his working hours, and, yes, he knew that he had to be there for her, that waltzing in at ridiculous hours, long after she would have retired for the night, just wasn't on, but the prospect of Heather waiting for him back at the apartment was an enticing one.

And why not enjoy the holiday? Theo decided, irritably aware that Jackie was still hovering.

'Why don't you head home as well, Jackie?' he said kindly. 'The reports can wait till tomorrow.'

Jackie grinned at him. She hadn't lasted three years as his PA without having a good sense of humour and an ability to speak her mind in the face of any gathering thunder clouds.

'I think I'll make that remark a special entry in my diary tonight,' she said tartly. 'Considering it's the first time you've ever been known to admit that *anything* can actually wait until tomorrow.'

'Keeping diaries is a very sad hobby for a woman in her forties,' Theo informed her gravely.

'Well, I hope you've managed to keep in *your* diary a certain date for tomorrow evening.'

Theo frowned and opened his mouth to issue an instruction that all meetings should be off the agenda until he advised otherwise, but Jackie was already continuing in a firm voice, 'It's the annual company do.' She handed him the standard invitation which he had, naturally, committed to memory. 'Everyone will be expecting you to attend.'

Theo knew what the event would be like. His employees would all be waiting to see which bombshell he brought, and far too much alcohol would be consumed, but the food would be good, and as far as morale-boosting went the annual event was always a winner. He would give a short but salutary speech about company profits and bonuses in the pipeline, and would make sure that he stayed for the duration, even though his dates invariably got bored halfway through and began making complaining little noises shortly after dessert was served.

'Wouldn't miss it for the world,' Theo murmured, pocketing the invitation.

'And will you be bringing one of your gorgeous dates?'

'Wait and see, Jackie. Now, clear off. You have diaries to maintain, a husband to feed and children to sort out.'

'I know! Don't I lead a wildly exciting life?'

On the way home, Theo mused on his own less than wildly exciting life. Under normal circumstances he would have left the office no earlier than eight, and would have probably been looking forward to dinner with some extravagantly stunning creature followed by all the sex his heart could desire.

Normal circumstances were lying just round the corner, as far as he was concerned, but in the meantime...

By the time he arrived at the apartment his head was full of images of Heather, who would probably have cooked something and would be waiting for him with his mother, doubtless absorbed in one of those intensely irritating reality shows which seemed to cross all language barriers.

He was whistling as he let himself in.

Heather rose from the chair to greet him, her face wreathed in smiles. 'You mother is much better today, Theo.' She reached up to kiss him, enjoying the lingering feel of his mouth on hers. 'We went for a walk and stopped off at the corner shop to buy some stuff. I've been showing her a typical English meal.' She looked over her shoulder to Litsa, who was smiling at them from the comfort of the sofa. 'Would you like a drink?'

'I'll tell you what I'd like a bit later on, when we're alone.' He brushed his hand casually across her breast and watched her face go bright red.

Heather happily contemplated the night ahead. Life was so wonderful at the moment! A few weeks and whatever rebellious spark she'd had had been extinguished under Theo's lazy caresses at night, his magical, sensitive, amazing lovemaking. She adored his mother, who was brave and wise and gentle…and that said something, didn't it? How many women actually *liked* their boyfriend's mothers?

Because that was what she told herself she was. Theo's girlfriend. And, yes, it had started off as a pretence, but that was then and this was now. And right now she fell into his arms at night, loving every bit of him, and he found her irresistible. He'd told her so himself.

Life couldn't be better!

She had put her career on hold, at least for the moment, and had managed to fob off Beth's exasperation at her lack of direction. The flat, apparently, was still available, but Heather wasn't in the least interested.

She was just too busy enjoying the bliss of living the dream.

When, later, Theo invited her to his company do, Heather closed her eyes with pure happiness and accepted.

Amused at the rapturous expression on her face, Theo felt obliged to tell her that she could expect a very prosaic event. Lots of food and drink and the usual horseplay between the younger members of staff.

Heather barely heard. 'What shall I wear?'

'Go out and buy yourself something,' Theo told her, fast losing interest. He had been looking forward to getting her into bed all evening, and had no intention of wasting time in a pointless female conversation about clothes.

He levered himself up so that he was looking down on her, and really the sight was one he could not get enough of.

He kissed her lingeringly, taking his time. Tonight he would take her to the limits, and then, when she had eventually climbed down, he would carry her there again. He trailed delicate feathery kisses across her neck, and as he bent to lose himself in the wonder of her breasts she tugged him gently by his hair,

'You could come shopping with me…'

'Mmm. Why not?' Theo murmured, breaking his stride to give her one of those ravishing sexy smiles that could turn her limbs to water.

Heather sighed with pure pleasure and gave herself over to enjoying the night.

Theo awoke to find her staring at him intently from the other side of the bed, and he grinned. He had never known a woman so open in her sexual attraction, and it pleased him.

'What time is it?' He flung back the covers and Heather watched, fascinated as always by the sinewy strength of his body. Morning light lovingly showed every flex and movement of his limbs as he slung his legs over the side of the bed before lying back down and pulling her towards him.

'Not quite late enough,' Theo growled, as the covers slipped down, exposing rosy nipples just perfect for sucking.

'Uh-uh.' She primly yanked the covers back up, half tempted to dump the promised shopping expedition in exchange for an hour longer in bed with the man of her dreams. 'Shopping. Remember?'

'Remember what?'

'You said that you would come shopping with me today. I haven't got anything I could possibly wear to a company do, and I'm no good at shopping on my own. I always end up buying the wrong clothes.'

'Did I promise to do that?' Theo frowned, perplexed. 'I honestly don't remember.' He drew back, hating himself for having to dash cold water over her but knowing that taking a day out to shop with a woman, however sexy that woman was, was just a bit too much. 'Well, I'm sorry, Heather. I really can't.'

Heather smiled. At least she tried very hard to. He didn't even remember! He had been so caught up in the business of wanting her that he couldn't even recall something he had said to her, something he had promised. She had gone to sleep wrapped up in the warm, comforting glow of thinking that the following day would bring him out with her, doing something normal couples did, maybe even having lunch out somewhere, and he had gone to sleep, sexually sated and without a thought of her in his head.

'Okay. No problem.' She rolled over, climbed out of bed, and walked self-consciously to the bathroom, her back towards him and tears gathering at a pace in her eyes.

She returned twenty minutes later to find him dressed and waiting for her.

For a heartbeat of a second she hoped that he had had a change of mind, even though she knew that nurturing such a hope was no more than yet another sign of her weakness. Instead he handed her a credit card and told her to go to Harrods, buy whatever she wanted, and put it on his account. He would phone ahead and let them know that she would be coming.

'Right.' Heather took the card, although she had no intention of using it. Hadn't she enough money in her bank account, thanks to him?

'Maybe I can meet you somewhere for lunch,' Theo compromised. For once he was having a struggle with his conscience—although she seemed fine now. He had had an uncomfortable feeling earlier on that she was going to burst into tears, but fortunately he had been mistaken. Tears were not Theo's thing.

'No.' Heather smiled brightly. 'I'll see if I can meet Beth for lunch. I'd like to take your mother, to shop for a few things before she goes back to Greece on Sunday, but I don't think the crowds would do her any good.'

Litsa was going back and Heather wondered what was going to happen to them. Without having to keep up the pretense, would he expect her to return to her jack of all trades status? An hour earlier she would have denied any such possibility, but doubts were beginning to break through the rosy, unrealistic haze of her dreams.

She stood, willing him to try and talk her out of that, but instead he smiled and moved over to her so that he could kiss her on the mouth, and with a pathetic moan of surrender she tugged the lapels of his jacket, pulling him into her.

Satisfied, Theo smiled and wondered where that chill of unease had come from earlier on. He was as safe in the knowledge that she wanted him as much as any man could be safe about anything in this life.

Three hours later Heather left the apartment, and ran full-tilt into the full-blown storm of Beth's misgivings.

'It'll end in tears,' she warned, which was just the thing Heather didn't want to hear. 'If you'd had any sense at all you would never have gone into any ridiculous pretend relationship with the man. He's bad news.'

'It's not a *pretend relationship* now,' Heather defended herself half-heartedly. 'I love him, and I know he feels something for me…'

'Because you were stupid enough to sleep with him?' Beth laughed, but not unkindly. 'Look, Heather, you've got to come back down to Planet Earth and realise that what you have is no more real than any of the other relationships he's had in the past, with all those glamorous women you lost sleep over. Do you remember them? The ones with legs to their armpits and IQs roughly on a par with their ages? Remember them? You should, you know. You bought the goodbye bunches of roses for most of them.'

'Yes, I know, but…' But she was different—wasn't she? She spent nights with him in his bed, in his apartment…she had met his mother…didn't that count for anything? She remembered the way he had dismissed her earlier on, and the burgeoning doubts pushed a little harder against the romantic dreams she had so optimistically and hopefully spun in her head.

'I'm just saying that you've got to be realistic, Heather,' Beth said, determined that she would carry the torch for realism even if her friend was reluctant to. Heather was sweetly and endearingly disingenuous, but Beth had had sufficient experience of men like Theo to know that they could be seriously hazardous to a woman's health.

Beth's version of reality was to drop all stupid notions about for ever after with Theo, and living in his big country house—which, she reminded Heather, she had never been invited to visit—with the happy sounds of kiddies' footsteps clattering across the floors. Reality was to stop spinning fantasies and to start thinking ahead, and the way forward was to include the probability that once Litsa had gone her role with Theo would be effectively over.

'You make him sound like a monster,' Heather cried, appalled because she knew that the man she had fallen in love with could be tremendously funny and thoughtful when he chose to be. She wished that she hadn't bothered to enlist Beth's help in choosing her outfit. She had hoped for some sound advice about colours and styles, maybe a bit of shared excitement that she was going somewhere with Theo—somewhere that involved the people he worked with. She had hoped to find support for her theory that *it meant something*. Instead, she had opened up by confessing that Theo had reneged on his promise to accompany her and it had been downhill ever since.

Beth had taken the afternoon off to help her out, which was very good of her because her lifestyle was frantic, and, having committed to the gesture, she now seemed determined to control the time booked as efficiently as possible.

Heather would have got annoyed, but annoyance was something she only ever attained when pushed to the absolute limit and she knew that her friend was just rooting for her.

So, once lunch and the sermons were over, she greeted the afternoon's shopping spree with a little sigh of resignation.

'First off,' Beth said, after insisting on paying the bill—presumably, Heather thought, in advance sympathy for the chucking out and inevitable poverty which was due to come to her shortly, 'you tell me what sort of clothes you have in mind, and then I'll tell you what I have in mind.'

Heather gave the matter careful thought. A dark colour, she decided, would be right for her figure. Something elegant and straight, so that she didn't stand out. She would be meeting people she didn't know from Adam, and her take on the situation was to blend effortlessly into the background, which she had usually found the safest place to be. She voiced her suggestions hesitantly, making sure to qualify each suggestion with a foolproof reason.

'Wrong, wrong—all wrong,' Beth said with satisfaction, making Heather feel as though she had been unwittingly led into a trap.

Right, right, all right turned out to be a cunning selection of clothes that Heather quailed at the thought of trying on, never mind actually wearing. Shoes would be purchased for style and wow factor, not for comfort. Her hair was going to be tamed, possibly even trimmed, and make-up was going to make a statement—and that statement did not include the concept of looking as though none had been applied. In other words, Heather heard with a sinking heart, a total makeover was on the cards.

'And what's more,' Beth announced, one hand imperiously outstretched to attract a taxi as she looked at her friend over her shoulder, 'you're going to surprise the bastard with this get-up, which means you're going to meet him at the venue. You can change at my place and I'll drop you.'

'Theo's not a bastard.' The rest of the sentence was slowly filtering into her brain with sickening remorselessness.

Beth was on a roll, and once in the taxi she ticked off all the reasons why Heather should follow her lead. She needed to strike out for herself, to prove to Theo that she was her own woman and not the doormat he assumed she was. She needed to break her habit of a lifetime of always, but *always*, dressing down, because the sea was actually teeming with fish—colourful, playful, easygoing fish—and there was no need to get tied up to the biggest shark in town. The day was coming, Beth warned, in the tones of a soothsayer ominously forced to predict the inevitable, when she would be out there on her own, when she could no longer hide away and make do with fairytale dreams. Where would she be if she took flight from reality and cowered inside her flat? Only emerging in clothes that made her invisible? Would she ever be able to find a partner?

Heather was suitably alarmed at the picture painted. 'I don't look good in bright colours,' she ventured. 'And I can't camp out at your place until it's time to go.'

'Why not?'

'Because…' The thought of confidently walking into a venue packed with people she didn't know terrified her. She had managed to live her entire life without ever having to undergo the experience. At least if she arrived with Theo she could hide behind him.

'You'll be fine,' Beth said encouragingly. 'Better than fine. Trust me. Go on. Phone Theo now, before you chicken out.'

Beth's voice was the consistency of honey, and Heather shot her a wry look, but really what she said—*everything* she had said—made sense in a way Heather had always recognised but had never confronted. As soon as she stepped away from her emotional interpretation of the scenario, she could see it for what it was. A pretend relationship that hadn't become real at all. Because Theo hadn't fallen madly in love with her. The pretend relationship had simply become one that involved sex. Apparently, and for reasons she couldn't begin to fathom, he was physically attracted to her. But that meant nothing. As Beth had very kindly pointed out, Theo was attracted to any manner of woman and saw nothing wrong in having sexual relationships that were utterly devoid of significance.

Heather wanted significance. She had been willing to pretend that making love with him was just step one in attaining it. Maybe it was, but probably it wasn't—and anyway, surely it wouldn't be such a bad thing if Theo had a wake-up call? She indulged in the pleasant fantasy of shocking him and realised that Beth had thrust her mobile phone into her hand.

The call to Theo only served to harden her resolve. What had seemed a horrific idea at the time now offered distinct advantages. She was put through to Theo at what was obviously a highly inconvenient time. His voice, when he picked up, was curt. Heather got the feeling that she could have taken a rocket and landed on the moon for all he cared. He was in a meeting, he had no time to talk, and he wasn't about to make time.

'I probably won't be able to get back to the apartment in time to leave with you…'

She could feel herself straining to hear him reject any such thing out of hand, but he didn't. All he said was, *'Fine, you can meet me there. You're a big girl now anyway.'*

A mountain of defeat settled on her shoulders like lead, although she fought to give him the benefit of the doubt in her mind. He was busy. He literally had no time to reassure her or even to chat. And that wasn't his fault. She had hovered around him long enough to know that work was an all-consuming force in his life. She depressed the 'end call' button, blinking away the urge to burst into tears.

'Well?'

'I'm in your hands!'

Beth grinned broadly. 'Good. And don't expect any rest breaks.'

There were none.

Clothes came first. Of course with restrictions on the price, because there was no way that Heather was going to touch the Harrods account card that nestled like a bad omen in her purse. But price restrictions were of no matter to Beth, who confidently declared that youth was all about getting away with wearing cheap because youth could pull it off.

When Heather tried to argue the challenges of her generous figure she was waved down and pulled into shops where clothes of every hue and every cut were tried on and dismissed, or tried on and considered, maybe to return to later.

After dress three, Heather gave up squealing with horror at the amount of flesh being exposed and gave herself over to the experience of being transformed. By outfit six she was beginning to think that she really didn't look too bad with less on. The breasts she had shamefully hidden from the age of thirteen suited the low cut necks of the trendy dresses, and her legs weren't half bad. Yes, her figure was hourglass, but that wasn't necessarily a bad thing. Claire had the model figure, but she had her own physical charm.

She lost count of how many outfits she had tried on before they finally decided on the right one. The fabric was soft and swirly, and clung to her body without cutting into her, and the cut of the dress, with its teasingly daring neckline, revealed a cleavage that most women, Beth assured her, would have died for.

Heather allowed herself to be reassured.

It was also a vibrant turquoise, and against that striking colour her skin looked radiantly healthy and her hair looked more positively fair.

It took less time to find the shoes.

'I'll never be able to actually walk in these,' Heather said, eyeing them sceptically. They were cream and high, and reminded her of the delicate things Claire had used to wear as a teenager—shoes she had always thought she was way too heavy for.

'You don't need to walk. You need to *sashay.*'

Heather decided that sashaying would be just about all she could manage. Hopefully there wouldn't be a fire alarm at any point.

She was beginning to feel transformed already, and, although she wouldn't have dreamt of saying so to Beth, she hoped that Theo would sit up and take notice, maybe have his head turned. She played with the thought as she sat through a stint at the hair-dressers, which had been booked earlier in the day.

Her fair hair was dyed to an impossible blonde, although

Simon—very camp and very theatrical—left the rebellious curls, deciding in consultation with Beth that it gave her a provocatively wild look, at odds with her look of wide-eyed innocence.

She laughed when he asked whether she had a brother, but really the makeover had boosted her confidence enormously.

Three hours previously Beth had told her to switch off her mobile phone. Now she itched to switch it back on, so that she could share some of her happiness with Theo. She didn't. She went back to the apartment with Beth, studiously avoiding any talk about the one that was still vacant. That momentary depression had lifted, like clouds on a summer day, and as the time drew nearer not even the tingling of nerves in her stomach could stanch the healthy appreciation of how she looked.

Beth let out a long whistle as Heather stood in front of the full-length mirror and gaped at the stranger staring back at her.

She was striking. The opposite of invisible. Beth had applied her make-up and it was bold without being clownish. Grey eyeshadow, mascara, blusher, lipstick and eyeliner. She looked…*sexy*!

There was a list of *don't*s to accompany the look. *Don't walk fast, don't get drunk, don't talk too much, don't talk too little, don't flirt with the juniors, and, most of all, don't sleep with the boss!*

'This was a good idea,' she confided to Beth, as the car pulled up in front of the hotel. 'I mean, I'm terrified of going in on my own, but…'

'But you need to do that once in a while. It's called independence. Now, *shoo*!'

Heather walked into the hotel, with very small steps for fear of spoiling her new-found image by toppling over on her heels, and discovered for the first time in her life that eyes were swivelling round to look at her.

So this was what it felt like! To walk into a place with your head held high and feel those sidelong interested glances! Instead of shuffling in, hiding behind a group of people, self-consciously aware of your unappealing outfit and hideously aware of what was underneath. Ashamed not to be skinny.

She was shown to the rooms that had been booked for the night, and already crowds were spilling out. A typical office crowd of mixed people, ranging from early twenties to near retirement.

Heather walked in and peered around, and spotted Theo almost immediately. He was standing in a group of people, doing his thing for the younger members of the organisation who were either laughing because they genuinely appreciated his wit or else laughing because they were in the company of the Great Man.

She shimmered through the crowds, noting that the interested glances hadn't stopped, until she was standing directly in Theo's line of vision.

As he registered her presence, Heather gave fulsome thanks to her friend for having ridden roughshod over her wishes and engineered a look that she had tried her hardest to avoid. It was worth every second of those embarrassing moments in dressing rooms, squeezing herself into outfits she would never have considered in a thousand years. Because the way he was looking at her now made it all worthwhile.

Then he was introducing her to the group, moving on to introduce her to fellow directors, and to his personal assistant Jackie, who grinned and whispered to her at some point during the evening, when the drink was beginning to get the better of everyone, that it was such a change to meet one of Theo's dates who actually had something to say for herself.

Heather was in her element. She couldn't remember why

she had been so gutted earlier on, because as the evening wore on she could feel his eyes restlessly roving over her, and when, towards the end of the evening, he growled into her ear that if they didn't leave soon he might have to excuse them both to the nearest cloakrooms, so that he could have his wicked way with her, she thought she might die on the spot.

She had obeyed Beth's instructions to the letter, and had made sure not to drink too much, but the little amount of the wine she had imbibed, combined with the fizzing excitement running through her, had put her on a high.

They left towards the very end, after the witching hour. Theo had booked his driver, who was waiting patiently outside.

'You were brilliant,' he murmured, massaging the back of her neck with his thumb. She had been, too. No boredom or whingeing about wanting to leave, no shying away from mixing with his employees from the highest to the lowest. She had stalked into the room looking magnificent, and he had been impressed and amused to see how she had handled the evening. He also hadn't failed to notice the looks she'd got from some of the guys when they'd thought it was safe to look.

Of course he was comfortably safe in the knowledge that no one would have dared make a pass at her, or even flirt, however tempting she looked. And she certainly *had* looked tempting.

Once in the car, he said something to his driver and slid the dark screen across, enclosing them in a cocoon of privacy.

'So,' Heather said smugly, 'you thought I was *brilliant?* Did the outfit have anything to do with it?'

'You mixed like a trouper,' Theo drawled, pulling her towards him. Not only clothes, but perfume as well. A light, delicate aroma that was subtly tantalising. 'And, yes, the outfit is definitely...' he slid his hand across her waist, curving it up towards the tempting cleavage pouting at him '...very striking indeed...'

Heather shuddered in pleasant expectation of being touched—in the back of a car no less, another first experience for her. He had, he whispered into her ear, as his hand traced the exposed cleft between her breasts, told his driver to take the long route back to his apartment, the *very* long route.

Theo's lovemaking was slow and languorous, though stopping short of full sexual intercourse, which he said would be an uncomfortable shambles because he was simply too big a man to do anything effective in the back of a car, no matter that the car was a big one.

Nor were any clothes shed—which just went to show how erotic touching could be over a forty-five-minute period, at the end of which Heather thought she was going to swoon from being teased with such expertise.

Through the flimsy fabric of her dress he'd managed to send her erogenous zones into hot overdrive. She squirmed, trying to quell the urgent demands her body was making on her, and he continued, ruthlessly turning her on.

It was just as well that Litsa wasn't a particularly light sleeper, and that her room was not too close in proximity to Theo's, because their arrival back at the apartment was a hasty dash towards the bedroom, peeling clothes off along the way, both of them greedy for what had been promised on that very long ride back home.

CHAPTER SIX

HEATHER tried hard to bury the doubts that had sprung up after her shopping trip with Beth. With Litsa ready to leave, they surfaced thick and fast. Just as quickly, she told herself that, yes, she really would address them, but not just yet—not until Theo's mother had left.

She had half hoped that at some point Litsa would decide to tread on unexplored territory and ask Theo what his intentions were, which might have given Heather an opportunity to gauge the ground, but no such luck. Having counted her blessings in seeing her son involved in a relationship with a woman of whom she approved, Litsa was discreet enough not to venture further with her questioning.

And there was no convenient airport wait during which the conversation might have been broached. She was returning to Greece on the family's private jet.

Her heart went out to Theo as he quizzed her on her health, asking her repeatedly whether she wanted to return to Greece, whether it might not be an idea to stay on in London for just a short while longer. But Litsa, like so many older people, missed the familiarity of her normal surroundings. She wanted to return to the peace of the Greek countryside and the routine of friends and old family members.

Theo had arranged for someone to come in daily and take care of her, but he was still worried. Heather wanted to reach out and take his hand, just to give him a bit of reassurance, but she was too uncertain as to how this simple gesture might be greeted.

Which said a lot, she thought. Yet another indication of her doubts, but she succeeded in squashing it.

Hadn't they just spent the most wonderful couple of days? By day, they had capitalised on the few remaining hours of his mother's stay, but the nights had belonged to them, and they'd slaked their passion through into the early hours of the morning.

Now, watching as Theo helped his mother out of the car, Heather attempted to convince herself, yet again, that their soaring passion must surely be a pointer to emotions as yet undisclosed. She smiled brightly at Litsa, pleased that she looked so much better than she had a few weeks ago and sorry that she was leaving.

The hug they gave one another was one of genuine warmth.

'Now, you take good care of my son for me,' Litsa murmured, and Heather's eyes flew to meet Theo's, which were regarding her with some amusement.

'I think it's safe to say that I'm capable of taking care of myself, Mama,' he drawled.

'Every man needs a woman,' Litsa said stoutly, in the tone of someone flatly stating a certainty. 'He may not realise it, but he does. And I am very glad that you have found someone.' Her voice lowered with gentle pleasure.

Heather, watching Theo's face closely, was trying to see how those words were affecting him, but if they were at all then he was keeping it to himself.

'I will be on the phone to you every day, Mama, and don't think that you can tell any untruths about how you are feeling because I will also be on the phone to the nursemaid that I've hired, and to both my uncles.'

'Spied on as though I am not capable of taking care of myself!' Litsa grumbled, allowing herself to be assisted onto the plane. She gave Heather one last backward glance, and they shared a moment of amusement at Theo's authoritarian voice. 'And when will I be seeing you both again?' Litsa demanded. Heather breathed a sigh of relief that some kind of target question had been finally asked.

'Let's jump one hurdle at a time,' Theo murmured. 'Get fully better before you begin issuing invitations.' He broke his non-answer with a smile. 'I have been to enough of your little get-togethers to know that you spend far too much time catering for your guests yourself while your caterers relax with cups of espresso and enjoy the scenery.'

They watched the jet from a distance as it taxied and took flight, and when it finally disappeared into the vast blueness of the sky Heather felt nervous tension swamp her in a way it hadn't done before. She had spent a long time living under the same roof as him, adoring him from a respectable distance, working for him and not once had she felt this sudden terrifying awareness of his proximity. But, then again, when things had been on a safe footing she had been able to exercise a certain control over her emotions.

Even when they had become lovers, thrown into the same bed by circumstances thrust upon them, his mother had always been there as an invisible chaperone against her fragile peace of mind.

No mother now, and no more safety of a relationship that knew its limits. She was in uncharted territory and it scared her to death.

'I hope your mother is all right when she gets over to Greece,' Heather said, to break the suffocating silence.

Theo, focusing on the road, frowned. 'Why should she not be?' He glanced over at her. 'I have arranged everything. She will be met by one of my uncles and the woman I have employed to look after her, and there will be no need for her to lift a finger to do anything.'

'She'll miss having you around, I guess.'

'But she understands that I work here and find it very difficult to get away for holidays.'

Heather chewed her lip and applied herself to thinking of something light-hearted she could say. It was crazy that she had shared so much with him and yet…

The silence between them seemed thunderous. She took a deep breath and began chatting aimlessly about Greece, asking questions about his mother's house and what it was like. When it dawned on her that he might think she was inveigling for an invitation, she branched out, embarrassed, and began to talk about holidays in general.

Meanwhile, under the surface of her chatter, she was aware of the tension building up inside her. She had no idea whether he was feeling the same, but she doubted it. He seemed a little distracted, but that was all, and that was fully explainable considering he had just put his mother on a plane back to Greece and was probably thinking about her, whatever he said about the expertise of his arrangements.

Walking back into the apartment notched up the tension levels substantially higher.

The bedroom they had shared for the past few weeks was just there, to her right. She was aware of it even if she wasn't actually looking at the bed.

Over time, most of her clothes had found their way into his room—a natural migration because it was so much easier changing there, especially when there was no longer any reason not to. She thought of the intimacy of her toothbrush next to his and felt a little sick at what she knew she had to do.

'Drink?' Theo asked, heading towards the kitchen while Heather trailed along behind him in anxious thoughtful silence.

It was a little after six-thirty. Too early for her to be contemplating wine. But she needed it. She nodded and sat down at the kitchen counter on one of the bar stools.

She waited until he had handed her a glass and then she blurted it out—no preparation, no thinking about how she would phrase what she wanted to say.

'Theo, what happens next?'

Theo paused for the merest breath of a second and looked at her over the rim of his wine glass.

'What do you *want* to happen?' he asked mildly.

Heather met his gorgeous eyes and willed herself not to weaken. 'Your mother's gone now, Theo. There's no need for us to…'

'Carry on being lovers?'

Put like that, their relationship, which meant so much to her, seemed reduced to the level of two consenting adults sharing a bed for the fun of it. Force of habit and her own upbeat nature immediately kicked in, allowing her to put the most forgiving spin on his baldly enunciated statement. Words of affection did not come easily to a man like Theo. He was depressed, as well, over the whole business with his mother, even though it was something he had not shared with her.

She had to will herself to stop.

'You do me a disservice if you imagine that the only reason I slept with you was to perpetuate a charade for the sake of my mother. You also do yourself a disservice.'

Heather smiled, relieved. 'I'm so glad you said that, Theo. I thought that perhaps…'

'What we have would come to a premature end?' His sexy mouth curved into one of those devastating smiles that could knock her sideways. Heather gulped down a mouthful of wine to steady herself against the temptation to let the conversation go. It was shockingly easy to lose focus when Theo turned on the charm, just like he was doing now, as he strolled towards her, eyes locked into hers, every movement confident of his own massive sex appeal.

Trying to concentrate was like trying to remain upright in a pool of treacle.

He gently removed the wine glass from her hands and leant on the counter separating them so that he could kiss her. This wasn't one of his hot, urgent kisses. There was something touchingly gentle about it, and Heather lost herself in his caressing mouth, distracted for a while from her ground plans.

When he finally drew back her eyes were brimming with compassion.

'I know you were shocked by what happened to your mother, Theo. We never expect any harm to come to our parents, and even when we do we're still never quite ready for it. But she's going to be fine. I know it.'

Coming from anyone else, this expression of sympathy would have been unacceptable and would have immediately frozen his passion, but he looked into her huge blue eyes and was touched by what he saw there.

'I'm so glad I have my very own fortune teller living with me,' he murmured, but not unkindly. 'Would you like to express your sympathy more than just verbally?' He drew back, finished his wine in one long mouthful, and smiled at her with lazy intent.

Heather's determination became a little fuzzy. When he headed towards the bedroom she found that she was following him, as though propelled by legs that had a mind of their own.

'It seems odd…' she said, looking around the bedroom that bore little traces of her everywhere. Her alarm clock, which sat on the table by her side of the bed, the vase of flowers she had put by the window to brighten up the room, the furry bedroom slippers that were tucked under the chair.

'What seems odd?' Theo had moved over to the window to stare outside for a few seconds, before spinning back round to face her.

'Being here without your mother around…'

He laughed. 'Most women might have found it odd the other way around.'

He began stripping off his shirt. Only when he was half naked did he realise that she was still hovering by the door, hands clasped behind her back, when she should have been coming to him, revealing the spectacular body once more hidden under her baggy camouflage clothing.

'Do you want me to do a striptease for you?' he enquired softly. Thoughts of taking her were releasing him from the coiled tension of seeing his mother off. He would never have admitted it in so many words, but he had been worried to death that she was leaving too soon, that she would have been better off recuperating in London, where he could keep an eye on her. He wanted to find sanctuary from his anxious thoughts in the arms of the woman standing in front of him—a fully clothed woman who seemed oddly hesitant.

With the superb arrogance of the utterly self-confident, Theo brushed aside all thought that Heather might actually not want to hop into bed with him. His hand hovered over the buckle of his belt, which he slowly pulled through the loops of his trousers.

Heather licked her lips nervously. She knew that if she went any closer to him she would be sucked in, like a fly getting just a bit too close to the spider's web. Like a gifted magician, Theo had the amazing ability to banish thought from her head and turn her into his obedient puppet.

Heather struggled with the recognition that she couldn't allow that to happen this time. She had been gifted a golden opportunity to find out what she meant to him, whether they could take what they had a stage further now that his mother had gone. She wasn't going to pass the chance up.

'Actually, Theo, I'd quite like just to talk…'

Theo greeted this with narrowed eyes. 'Talk? Talk about what? You've already done the sympathy thing. There's no need to go over old ground. I assure you that I am not about to collapse because I am apprehensive about my mother's health. I will telephone the relevant people on a daily basis, and if I get the slightest whiff of concern then it would be no problem for me to fly to Greece.'

'I'm sure it wouldn't,' Heather said, maintaining her position by the door. It felt safe there. It gave her the illusion that she could do a runner if the conversation got too much for her to handle. 'But actually I wasn't going to talk about your mother.'

'Ah.' Comprehension dawned. 'You want to pick up where we left off earlier on. Is that it? You want my reassurance that I want you, that sleeping with you wasn't just an artificial situation generated by necessity.' He smiled slowly and walked towards her. 'I didn't imagine that I would have to prove my desire to you. You have seen first hand that what you do to my body has nothing to do with make-believe. Oh, no…'

Heather was struggling to breathe. When he was standing right in front of her, she closed her eyes to steady herself. Without the benefit of one lot of senses, she might just be able to control the other four. No good. She might shut him out of her line of vision, but she could still see him in her head. She opened her eyes and took a deep breath.

'I just want to know what happens next…you know…for us…'

Theo wasn't thick. The significance of her words was the verbal equivalent of a very long, very cold shower, or a dip in the North Sea. All traces of passion left his body in a staggering rush, replaced by a cool appraisal of her flushed face.

'I thought you had already asked that question,' he said coolly.

'I know. But you didn't give me an answer.' She risked a quick look at his face and her stomach churned queasily at the expression of icy withdrawal she saw there.

Theo didn't immediately answer. Instead he walked over to where he had dropped his shirt and shrugged it back on. Very good. Half clothed, he was just too distracting. He also remained where he was, by the window, which was very good for her state of mind.

She found that she could actually breathe now.

'Okay.' Theo shrugged. 'The truth is that, yes, we both owe what we have to an unforeseen combination of circumstances. Were it not for my mother arriving, finding you *in situ* and jumping to all the wrong conclusions, then we would never have slept together. However, now that we have, I see no need to disturb the arrangement as it stands.'

Heather was winded, and deeply hurt by his casual assumption that without the intervention of fate in the form of his ill mother he would never have looked at her twice. She had spent almost two years hovering in the background, feeding off the crumbs he had dropped for her, always imagining a day when he would finally see her for the woman that she was. Now she knew that she had been living a dream. She clasped her arms around her and looked down. She was sure the whole world, if it had listened, hard, would have heard the sound of her hammering heart.

Irritated by her continuing silence, Theo frowned. 'Well?' he demanded. 'I might have expected something more by way of response.'

'Something like what, Theo?' All the nebulous feelings she had had since her afternoon with Beth crystallised into a hard knot of miserable realization—the sort of miserable realisation that no amount of self-justifying internal clap-trap could cure.

She had waddled around him for years, invisible underneath her camouflage clothing, and then she had somehow landed up naked in his bed. He had happened to like what he had seen, and therefore had made full use of it.

Moreover, she could hardly blame him when she had been an eager and willing pupil.

'This conversation is beginning to bore me,' Theo announced, strolling out of the room.

Heather, who actually just wanted to find somewhere dark and hide away, knew that she couldn't leave things where they lay. Much as she didn't want to follow him, she did—to find him helping himself to something stronger than wine.

'I'm sorry if I'm boring you, Theo. I know you like to keep things superficial with women…'

'There's nothing superficial about sex!' he thundered, banging his glass on the counter with such force that some of its contents splashed and formed a little puddle. He swore silently and grabbed a teatowel, which he proceeded to dump on the spreading patch.

'Well, no…not when it's part of a meaningful relationship…'

He met her eyes steadily. 'Not when it's part of an *enjoyable* relationship. There's the nub, Heather. Relationships can be enjoyable without necessarily being *meaningful*.'

They were both tiptoeing around the central issue. She could either agree with him and back off, take the little he was offering which was a whole lot more than she had ever had in the past, or she could stick to her guns and probably get blown apart in the process.

'I just need to know where we're going, Theo. I mean, is there any kind of future for us?'

Theo, swirling what was left of his drink, could barely believe his ears. He had just offered her something he had never offered another woman before—the chance to have a live-in relationship with him—and what was her response to that? Questions about longevity, musings about that woolly thing called *a future,* which seemed to occupy women's minds with disproportionate significance.

'I think you've been a little too influenced by my mother.' He poured some of his drink down his throat and then refilled the glass. 'Somewhere along the line you have allowed the myth to become reality. Let me clarify the situation for you, Heather…'

Heather did not want him to clarify the situation for her. Nor did she want to see him looking at her with the cold eyes of a stranger. She wanted him back, the man she loved and knew. But in the space of a second it became perfectly clear that she would never have that man back, because the nature of their relationship had been altered. Like someone trapped on a dizzying, nightmarish rollercoaster ride, Heather felt herself being catapulted towards an inevitable conclusion. There was no getting off the ride now that it had taken off.

Like a rabbit caught in the dazzling headlights of an oncoming car, she stood there, eyes wide, looking at him, half praying that he wouldn't say any more. Her legs felt weak and she sat on a stool, resting her arms on the counter and staring through him and past him.

'Any notion of permanence between us was something created for my mother's benefit. She was weak, and I didn't feel that launching into an explanation of what you were doing living under my roof would have helped her along the road to recovery. She has wanted to see me settled for a long time—too long—and she saw you and flew to the conclusions she wanted to… She still comes from a time when two people living together constituted a relationship…'

'We *have* got a relationship, Theo…' Heather wondered whether he could hear the note of pleading in her voice as clearly as she could.

'We have,' he agreed smoothly. 'But one of a purely sexual nature. It's something I hadn't expected, and I'm quite willing for it to continue, but that is all it will ever be.'

'And when will you tell your mother the truth?' Neediness had jumped on her from behind and grabbed her by the throat, and she hated it. Somehow she had waltzed through life without ever really being under the control of anyone or anything. Yes, she had needed to work, but no job had ever meant so much that the thought of losing it had lost her sleep. And, yes, she had friends, and she enjoyed them, but *need*…? No. Now, as she was trampled under the remorseless march of Theo's cool, dispassionate summary of what they had, she could feel her need rising up and making her say things she knew she shouldn't.

'That is something that need not concern you,' Theo answered indifferently. 'When my mother has fully recovered, then I shall tell her that you are no longer a part of my life…that things simply did not work out…we were incompatible…'

Heather nodded dully, fighting back the insane desire to

argue her stand, to tell him that they *were* compatible. Hadn't she lived with him for months and months? Hadn't she seen him in his worst lights and his best? Thankfully good sense prevailed and she remained silent.

'She will be disappointed, but she will recover,' Theo continued, with sweeping confidence.

'And will you ever settle down, Theo? Or are there just too many women in the world left to explore?'

Theo didn't care for that at all. Just because he was not ready for commitment it did not mean that he was shallow in his dealings with women. He looked at her through narrowed eyes and told himself that, yes, what was happening was for the best. It had been foolhardy to extend his invitation for them to continue sleeping with one another. Already she was beginning to tap her feet to the invisible sound of wedding bells, and that would never do.

'My life's ambition,' he drawled, with every semblance of boredom, 'is not to sleep with as many women as I can before I die, believe it or not…'

'No, you'll only sleep with them if they can give you a cast-iron guarantee of non-involvement. Not many of those around, Theo.'

Theo was flabbergasted. When had it all changed? If he could have staked money on the one woman who would have been immune to thoughts of marriage, it would have been her. Hadn't she worked for him for nearly two years? Hadn't she seen first hand his views on commitment?

'I cannot believe that you, of all people, can be sitting here and telling me this.'

Since Heather couldn't quite believe it either, she didn't say anything.

'I am not looking for a life partner because at this point in time I need the freedom to pursue my career. I would not be unfair enough to any woman to marry her with the illusion that she would be anything but second place in my life, and what woman would want that?'

Heather almost laughed out loud at that piece of verbal dexterity. So now she was meant to believe that poor Theo was only thinking of the woman—doing her a favour, in fact, by never promising more than what he could deliver that day. And in return all he asked was not to be plagued by anyone being so thoughtless as to suggest that she might be concerned with what happened beyond a twenty-four-hour period!

She wasn't going to have a great long debate with him about that, though. He was as skilful with his words as he was with everything else, and she knew that whatever argument she put forward he would proceed to knock it down, because he wanted to remain in an ivory tower and that was, quite simply, that.

'You're right,' she agreed wearily. 'No woman.'

Theo felt a surge of anger tear through him and fought it down, surprised by his irrational response. He was just doing what he usually did when a woman started fantasising about the impossible. He willed himself to get back in control of his scattered thoughts, and a lifetime of self-discipline came to his rescue.

'Don't you ever get tired, Theo?' Heather asked curiously.

'Tired? Tired of what?'

'Oh, I don't know…tired of the different faces, of playing the field…new dates, new women, new conversation…'

'I thrive on variety.' Theo stood up abruptly and headed towards the sofa. He liked this line of conversation almost as little as he had liked her implication that he was somehow superficial in his dealings with the opposite sex.

That seemed to be a closing statement, and Heather

remained on the stool, blinking back her tears. Eventually she stood up and started walking towards the bedroom.

'Reconsidering my offer?' Theo asked casually, and she rounded on him, fury replacing the misery of a few seconds earlier.

'No, *I am not*!' After everything he had said, his arrogance to think that she would even consider some short-lived vacancy as his mistress was just too much. 'I wouldn't *dream* of sleeping in your bed, knowing that at any minute I might be chucked out because you'd got bored and decided it was moving-on time!'

'Then why did you sleep with me in the first place?'

'Your mother assumed…'

'My mother *assumed* that we were in a relationship, which doesn't answer my question… Ah…I see…'

'What do you see…?' Heather blinked in confusion. She had been led into a trap and now he knew what she was all about—knew that she had fallen in love with him. Well, there could be nothing more terrifying for him. Love would have him running that mile even faster than he already was! She had hoped to leave with at least her dignity intact, but now she could see that had been a wild hope.

'I see someone who spotted an opportunity and seized it with both hands.' There was a tone to his voice that Heather had never heard before. It was as flat and as hard as a slab of steel, and she stared at him in speechless bewilderment.

Into the silence, Theo moved onwards, his voice growing colder by the second as he contemplated the full spectre of her deceit. 'I asked myself earlier how things could have changed so drastically between us. For months you were as reliable as the day was long. You took care of the house, you helped me with my work when I needed it, and most of all you never complained. Now here you are, demanding promises of a future…'

'I wasn't *demanding*…I was—'

'*Shut up!*' His voice was like a whip, subduing her into sudden shocked silence once more. In the past, when she had witnessed his anger over something to do with work, he had shown it by stalking round the room, dictating something to her in staccato bursts, his movements restless and fuelled. Now he was perfectly still, and all the more intimidating for that.

'Was it when you supposedly *allowed* yourself to be tempted into bed with me that you started thinking what a good catch I might be? Started thinking that maybe, just maybe, if you played your cards right, you would be in with a chance?'

All colour leached from Heather's face, and her eyes widened in horror at his massive misinterpretation of events.

'Wh-what…?' she stuttered.

'Did you think that if you buttered up my mother you would somehow get one foot over the winning line? After all, you knew that no other woman had ever been in a position to meet any member of my family. Maybe you imagined that circumstances had played right into your hands… You once told me that you believed in fate. Well, what better display of fate than to closet you with my mother for weeks on end?'

'No! None of what you're saying is true!' Heather said, appalled.

Theo, a runaway train gathering momentum, ignored the interruption.

'Sleeping with me, knowing that I lusted after you, must have seemed the icing on the cake!' He thought of the way he had looked forward to stepping through the door, craved the nights when he could make love to her, feel every curve of her body, and he hated himself for the weakness. 'You must have known that I am like any red-blooded male. Throw a naked desirable woman at me and I find it hard to resist.'

With every word he trampled over her fragile hopes, and he was right. She *had* seen his mother's sudden appearance on the scene as a sign of fate. Hadn't she been in the process of really thinking about moving out? And, yes, she *had* hoped that she would come to mean something to him after they had slept together, that he might see her really and truly for the first time. Naïve expectations had found fertile ground in her romantic heart, and time had done the rest.

'When did you first begin to think that I might be worth hunting down? Was it when you first stepped into this place and saw it for the first time?' He remembered her awestruck, wide-eyed pleasure and could have kicked himself for never once thinking that his money might have inspired gold-digging ambitions. At the time he had been amused!

'I don't know how you can sit there and say those things, Theo.'

'Because I am a very practical man. I am also an extremely rich one. And rich, practical men have suspicious minds. You should have taken that into account.'

'This is like a bad dream,' Heather whispered. She felt as though she had been cheerfully living in a house, thinking the walls secure, only to find that the house was made of straw and susceptible to a puff of wind.

'People wake up from bad dreams, Heather. This is no dream. This is reality.'

'Yes. Yes, it is.' And she'd brought it on herself. She blindly turned away, scrambled away from those cold, distant eyes into the bedroom, where she frantically began pulling all her possessions out of drawers, out of cupboards, throwing them on the bed in a heap.

Strains of classical music wafted through the door, a beautiful sound that was incongruous with what she was feeling. Deed done, she assumed that he was now relaxing.

She didn't look in his direction when she walked past towards her old room and the suitcase lying under the bed. She had come with very little and she was leaving with far less. She didn't much care whether her clothes disappeared in a puff of smoke. She hated them, but she made herself pack them. The few that were in her old bedroom and then the rest.

Somewhere along the line he had disappeared, although the CD player was still softly playing Vivaldi. She assumed he would be in the office. Away from her. After so long with him, he was happy to let her leave his apartment without even bothering to say goodbye.

In a daze, and with her suitcase, her portfolio and some assorted bags at her feet, Heather stood by the front door, not knowing whether to try and find him or not.

In the end there seemed no point. He had said what he had to say and he would never believe that she wasn't an opportunist.

Instead, she hastily scribbled a note, thanking him for the job he had given her, which had enabled her to fund her course, and leaving him the key to his apartment.

From the sanctuary of his office Theo heard the click of the door being shut, and scowled at the laptop winking in front of him. She would have wondered whether to disturb him to say goodbye and would have hesitated. He knew that because he seemed to know her so well. Not surprising, considering they had shared the same space for such a long time. Big mistake now, in retrospect.

He pushed himself away from the desk and walked through

to the kitchen. Of course this was the natural and only conclusion. It needn't have been, if she had agreed to continue their dalliance, but, no, like all women she had wanted him to pay lip service to the non-existent significance of what they had shared. He felt a wall of frustration slam into him. Why she couldn't have accepted what was on offer was a mystery to him, but she hadn't, and so she had to go. He neither needed nor wanted the clutter of a woman in his life—a woman nurturing thoughts of permanence.

Give it a couple of weeks, he told himself, and his head would be clear of her. Until then he would work his guts out and paper over the rough patch with a few dinner dates. Everything back to normal. The way it should be.

CHAPTER SEVEN

SHE had to get out of the flat. Beth had given Heather this piece of advice in a tone of voice that brooked no argument. It had been three weeks, she had pointed out, and three weeks was plenty long enough to pine for a man who had used her.

'I *am* getting out of the flat,' Heather replied, choosing to go with the literal interpretation of her friend's statement. 'I'm toting my portfolio to every publisher and advertising agency in the city. In fact, I'm hardly ever *in*. Actually—' she dangled a carrot tantalisingly in front of Beth, hoping to play the Distraction Card '—I have a second interview with the MacBride agency on Monday. Maybe you could help me shop for a successful interview outfit on the weekend…?'

Beth's response to that was to announce to her friend that she had found her a date. As if, Heather had thought wildly, she was a charitable organisation in need of government aid.

'My counterpart in Dublin, as a matter of fact,' she continued, pleased with herself. 'I've met him a couple of times and he's perfect. Tall, blond, going places…'

Heather would have to wear something stunning, something along the lines of what she had worn for the office party with the GTB, which was Beth's abbreviation for Theo—the

Greek Tycoon Bastard. And why not do something with her hair? Some highlights, maybe?

And, as always, Heather found herself half protesting, half glumly acknowledging the sense behind what her friend was saying. And, as always, the half she didn't want to win invariably won.

Which was why she was now, on a Saturday night, standing in front of Beth's floor-to-ceiling mirror in her bedroom, being inspected by her friend like a microbe under a magnifying glass.

And a very satisfying specimen at that, Beth considered with satisfaction. She stood back and gave a low whistle of appreciation. Heather might think that she had been dragged, kicking and screaming, into a date with someone she wasn't interested in meeting, but she needed to get out. Three and a half weeks had seen her drop weight and her normally sunny nature had become worryingly flat. Yes, she had dutifully gone from agency to agency in search of work, just as she had dutifully moved into the vacant flat next to Beth's, and she had obligingly summoned up a pretence of light-heartedness. But underneath she was as empty as a shell.

Whether she appreciated it or not, as far as Beth was concerned, her friend needed to go out and have a good time.

Beth did not believe in letting the grass grow under her feet. Yes, time was a great healer, but with a bit of careful forward planning the healing process could be brought forward in leaps and bounds, and she had approached the problem of her friend with the same logical precision that she applied to her work.

The odd meal out and nights in with girlie chats hadn't worked. Heather had listened whenever Beth broached the subject of Theo, but had stubbornly refused to participate in the cleansing process of conversation. She had listened and resolutely changed the subject.

So step one was to get her friend out in the company of a man. And step two was to show her that there was life beyond Theo Miquel, that he wasn't worth pining over. And what better way to demonstrate that inescapable truth than to manoeuvre her into a position from which she could glean all the evidence with her own eyes?

With breathtaking ease, Beth had arranged the evening out with military precision.

London, for the energetic networker, was a village. It had been relatively easy to find out where Theo Miquel would be on a given Saturday evening. It was prime time and already, with his relationship with Heather not even cold, he was back on the playing field. Beth had even met his latest acquisition— a tall, languid brunette—at a legal do a few months previously, dripping diamonds and hanging on to the arm of one of the law partners in a rival company. Although she wouldn't have dreamt of telling Heather that.

And his weekends with women were not private, romantic one-on-ones for Theo. He would be going to a very expensive, very elite, smoky little jazz club in Notting Hill.

And so would Heather and her hunky dinner date. Beth had arranged it.

'You look wonderful,' she said truthfully. 'Very glamorous. Scott's going to be knocked for six.'

'Is he desperate?' Heather demanded.

'Far from it. He's quite a catch.'

'Then how is it he hasn't been caught yet?' Not that Heather had any intention of catching anyone, but neither was she thrilled to be going out with a rampant serial womaniser just for the sake of it. She thought of Theo, felt her lips wobble and pulled herself together.

'Hasn't found the right woman,' Beth said patiently. 'But he's good company, and a very kind person.'

'Theo could be very kind, you know.'

Beth ignored that. 'The highlights look good on you. Blonde and copper. I'd never have thought of that combination, but it suits you. And your eyes look enormous with that make-up.'

Heather gave herself a desultory glance in the mirror. Three months ago she wouldn't have recognised the woman staring back at her. Gone was the background blob in dark colours with frazzled hair permanently tied up. In its place stood an attractive, now curvaceous woman—thanks to the shedding of nearly half a stone because misery had no appetite. Her outfit was unrevealing, but very clingy. A black dress, pinched in at the waist with a belt, and high black shoes. Beth had lent her a coat, a *faux* fur affair that looked wickedly luxurious.

At her insistence, Scott would be meeting her at the club: some place she had never heard of in Notting Hill, which, aside from the open-air market, was not somewhere she frequented. But she hadn't wanted Scott in her own personal space.

Beth walked her to the door like a clucking, fussy mother hen, leaving her with strict instructions to phone first thing in the morning with an update.

It was a relief to be in the back of a taxi and no longer obliged to try and show excitement. She didn't feel excited. Nothing excited her much nowadays. Not even the prospect of a very good job which she had been given to understand was hers but for the formalities. She thought of Theo constantly, wondering what he was up to and whether he thought of her.

The prospect of spending hours in the company of

someone she didn't know, who would expect her to be brimming over with good cheer, seemed like an exhausting uphill struggle.

It would almost not be such a bad thing if she was stood up. But she arrived to find Scott there, waiting as promised in the outside lobby, and exactly as Beth had described him.

A little over six foot, fair wavy hair, and a warm, pleasant face. He smiled at Heather, and she relaxed and smiled back because there was nothing insolent or threatening in the blue eyes that ran appreciatively over her.

'I thought I might wear a white carnation,' he said, helping her with her coat, 'just in case you missed me. But it seemed a bit corny.'

His voice was as pleasant as his looks, and up close he smelled of some clean, male fragrance.

'Beth gave me quite a detailed description.' Heather smiled again. 'I think she almost wished she'd had a photograph— just in case…'

'I can imagine.' He laughed good-humouredly. 'Beth leaves nothing to chance. It's why she's so good at what she does. Been here before?'

'The club scene's passed me by, I'm afraid…' They had entered the darkly lit cosy confines of a room that curled informally in a U shape around a small stage, in the centre of which a jazz band was playing some whimsical, vaguely familiar tune.

'Tell me about it!'

And, surprisingly, she did. After half a bottle of wine, she even confided her doubts about the evening, and about whether she was ready to start back on the dating scene.

'I'm relieved you said that,' Scott told her, leaning towards her so that he could be heard over the sound of the music, 'because I've just crawled out of a relationship and I'm taking it easy myself. No involvement equals no broken heart.'

'Beth never mentioned it…'

'No?' He laughed and shook his head. 'Clearly taking her matchmaking skills a bit too seriously for her own good.'

'But she means well…'

'And I can't say that I'm having a miserable time. Are you?'

'No.' Heather surprised herself. 'I'm not.'

'Good. Nice to know that I'm not the hard work you expected!' He linked his fingers through hers and gave her hand a friendly squeeze which felt just right, comfortable.

This was just the sort of man she should be falling head over heels with, Heather thought, cupping her face in her hand and thinking about Theo. Someone nice. Someone who was recovering from a broken heart which meant that he had a heart in there somewhere.

She had opened her mouth to share something of what she was thinking with him when she heard the cutting drawl of a familiar voice and her whole body went rigid with shocked awareness.

'Well, well, well…'

Heather twisted round and followed Theo with her eyes until he was standing right in front of them.

She had to blink several times, because it was so surreal seeing him in the flesh. And a few weeks of absence had done nothing to diminish the devastating effect of his sex appeal.

Belatedly she realised that Scott was still clasping her fingers, but when she tried to wriggle free he tightened his grip, before releasing her so that he could stand up and extend his hand in greeting.

It was ignored as Theo glanced away and focused his attention on Heather, who reluctantly stood up and managed a smile.

The palms of her hands felt horrible, sweaty. She pressed them against her sides and widened her smile. 'Theo! What a surprise.'

'Isn't it just?' Theo answered with deadly politeness. 'I had no idea that you came to places like this. I always got the impression that you were content to stay at home, doing your artwork and catching up on TV soaps.'

Heather flushed. If he had intended to make her sound as dull as dishwater, then he had succeeded. Normally slow to anger, she felt a fire begin to burn inside her, and she took a few deep breaths, feeling sorry for Scott—who had been deliberately sidelined by Theo.

'Just the sort of woman I appreciate,' Scott said, joining in the conversation. Although the look he received from Theo was hardly encouraging. 'I'm not much of a club man myself. Much prefer a night in with the television—although documentaries are more my style. Name's Scott, by the way.'

Flustered, Heather completed the introductions, but she was uncomfortably aware that Theo's attention was focused solely on her flaming face.

'It's good to see you, Theo…you're looking well. But I don't want to keep you…'

'You're looking well, too…' His eyes brazenly appraised her with lingering, insolent thoroughness. 'Nice dress.'

'Thank you… Are you here with someone…? Perhaps you should be getting back to your party…' Heather looked around, but the club was dark and crowded.

'Oh, I'm not here with a party…' Theo drawled.

'Right.'

'Michelle's waiting at a table over there, at the back…'

Heather involuntarily followed the direction of his brief nod, and miraculously the crowds seemed to fade into the background—leaving her a clear and unimpeded view of a rake-thin, tall, dark-haired woman sitting on her own, with a flute of champagne in one hand and wearing a scarlet dress that exposed a hell of a lot more than it concealed.

Heather hadn't seriously thought that Theo would spend too long on his own after she had left, but seeing the evidence of just how quickly he had moved on made her stiffen with unaccustomed bitterness.

She suddenly felt deeply grateful that she was with Scott, and viciously pleased that Theo would see for himself that she, too, wasn't sitting in, counting the seconds go by. Even if that was exactly what she *had* been doing.

'She looks lonely, Theo.' Heather glanced warmly at Scott and then back to Theo. 'I suggest you hurry back to her before someone else comes along and snaps her up. These sorts of places can attract men on the prowl, in case you didn't know.'

'Are you speaking from experience?' He glanced over at Scott questioningly.

'I don't prowl around for women,' Scott said mildly, placing one arm affectionately over Heather's shoulders. 'I'm way too discriminating for that.' He laughed. 'In fact, my friends say I'm too discriminating for my own good. I only settle for…the best…'

Heather flashed him a grateful smile and sank down into her chair, followed by Scott, leaving Theo towering over them both.

Instead of taking the hint and going, though, he leaned forward and planted his hands squarely on the table.

'I myself prefer variety,' he said with a wolfish smile. 'But each to their own. Now, Heather and I haven't seen each other in a while, so would you mind if I stole her away from you for a dance? I promise to return her to you in one piece.'

'I think we'll let Heather decide whether she wants to dance with you,' Scott said, turning to her.

Theo obviously had a less gentlemanly option in mind, because he didn't give her a chance to voice an opinion. He reached out and clasped her hand in his, and before Heather could protest she was on her feet and being led towards the dance floor, one solicitous hand firmly placed at her elbow.

'How dare you?' Heather whispered, feeling her body react with unwelcome heat to the big, masculine body now pressing uncomfortably close to hers. 'I don't want to dance with you! My date's sitting on his own at the table and it's very rude to abandon him!'

'He didn't seem to mind,' Theo replied dismissively.

He pulled her a little closer. Through the thin little number she was wearing he could feel everything. The thrust of her generous breasts, the small curve of her spine. It enraged him to consider how much he had missed her body. Missed *her*. Although he reasoned that that was just a case of missing a habit. Yes, he had hurled himself back into work, had even made the effort to take Michelle out—a woman he had spoken to for half an hour at a cocktail party the week before and who had emitted all the right signals of being interested. This was his second date with her and she left him cold.

Unlike the small, curvaceous woman now reluctantly dancing with him. He could feel her desire to get away in palpable waves, and wondered whether she was sleeping with the date wilting on his own at her table.

The thought made his teeth snap together in fury.

'So…how are you?' he asked, lowering his voice, perversely desperate to know that she still wanted him.

'You asked me that already.'

'I'm asking you again,' he said irritably.

'Fine. I told you. I'm fine.'

'What have you been up to?' The question emerged in an aggressive, demanding undertone that made her even more tense. He felt it in the way she stiffened in his arms. 'Am I making you nervous?' he asked softly.

Just the sort of sexy voice that had had her head spinning in the past. Did he even *know* that he was doing that? Heather thought of his new conquest, probably seething at the sight of him parading on the dance floor in close proximity with another woman, and a self-protective layer of cold settled over her. She'd never thought that she had it in her to be frosty, but she was fast discovering that she had.

'Don't be ridiculous. Why should you be?'

'You've changed,' Theo said grimly.

'People do.' She shrugged as he spun her around to the melodic tunes of some stupid love song.

'You never used to be so hard,' he said accusingly.

'If by *hard* you mean that I no longer turn to mush whenever you're around, then I'll take that as a compliment.'

'You used to *turn to mush* whenever I was around?' Theo mused with considerable interest. 'I never knew that. For how long?'

'I *meant* that I actually used to…used to…'

'Yes? Carry on. Were you turning to mush before we had a sexual relationship?'

'I'd prefer to forget that!'

'Why would you want to forget something you so obviously enjoyed?'

'This is a ridiculous conversation and I'm not going to carry on with it any more.'

Theo swung her round into a dip that had a few of the other

people on the dance floor chuckling with delight, and their eyes locked for a few heart-stopping seconds.

'Why not?' he murmured lazily into her ear, swinging her back into an upright position with an easy flourish. His ego felt gloriously boosted at the thought of the effect he had had on her…for a satisfyingly long time, from the sounds of it. The evening, which had been plodding along, had taken on a wonderful shine.

When the music stopped and she tried to wriggle her way out of his arms he held her tighter.

'I'm sure Stephen—'

'His name's *Scott*!'

'Whatever. I'm sure he won't mind if we have another dance. He doesn't strike me as the sort of fellow to kick up a fuss over something as innocuous as that. Of course he might if he knew our history…'

Heather recognised when she was being played with. She struggled to maintain her composure, and to remember how he had discarded her without a backward glance. He hadn't even bothered to try and get in touch, although he could have. She had told him about the flat opportunity Beth had offered, and he was clever enough to have put two and two together and worked out that she would now be living there. But he hadn't got in touch because he hadn't wanted to. He had picked up the threads of his normal hectic life and hadn't given her a second thought. So much for the sincerity of his well-meaning questions about what she had been up to and how she was! She could be lying under a slab of granite for all he cared!

'We don't *have a history*,' Heather retorted, gaining strength from her thoughts. 'We had a make-believe relationship that lasted a few weeks!' With a little flush of guilt she carried on gently, 'How is your mother anyway? I'm sorry I haven't asked earlier…'

'Getting better and stronger by the day.'

'Have you told her about us?'

'No need to.'

'I did think of her a lot after…after I left, and wondered how she was getting on. She's an amazing woman…so full of enthusiasm and so sharp…sharper than lots of people half her age…'

Theo had no interest in discussing his mother.

'Of course we have a history.' He sidestepped the issue smoothly. 'We didn't just sleep together. We shared a house for well over a year…and I just want to say right now that I apologise for accusing you of targeting me willfully. Like I said, a rich man looks for the hidden agenda when it comes to the fair sex. I had no idea that you wanted me long before we actually ended up in bed together.'

Heather ducked her head. She could feel herself burning up—every part of her. If Scott glanced across at them now he would have to be blind not to realise that this was the man who had made her cautious about the dating scene. Awareness and confusion would be written in blazing symbols on her crimson face.

'Well?' Theo prompted.

'Isn't your girlfriend going to be angry with you for dancing with me?'

'And jealous,' he confirmed, leaning into her so that his mouth was brushing her ear. 'Especially if she knew what thoughts were going through my head right at this instant. You know, don't you? You can feel what I'm thinking…literally.'

Heather had been so wrapped up in the disastrous twists and turns of their conversation that she had been oblivious to what was now magnificently evident. Theo was in a state of unashamed arousal. She felt immediately faint at the pressure of his hard manhood stirring against her. Her mind, which she had successfully managed to keep under control, sprinted off at a pace and presented her with a graphic, uninvited parade of memories of them in bed together, making love, his big body thrashing above hers. She closed her eyes and had a sickening sense of falling.

'Are *you* jealous?' he whispered into her ear.

'No, of course I'm not,' Heather lied. 'Why should I be? We haven't seen each other for weeks. It's over between us and I'm getting on with life. I have a new flat, a new job and a new boyfriend.' Two out of three wasn't bad—and anyway, technically Scott *was* a boyfriend, if you categorised the term as a friend who happened to be of the male sex.

'How long have you been seeing this Stephen guy?'

'Scott.'

'All of three weeks?'

'That's none of your business, Theo.' Having spent so long sharing her thoughts with him, Heather heard the words leave her mouth and felt a little sense of victory and empowerment.

He might be rampantly turned on by her, but that made him no less of a commitment-phobe than he had been when he had told her to leave. Did he think that he could say whatever he wanted because he thought that she was still the silly fool who had been enraptured by him? Did he think that she hadn't moved on at all?

'I don't think so,' he mused to himself. 'It's not like you to go out hunting for my replacement the day after you leave my apartment.'

You did, she was tempted to retort, but she refused to allow him any insight into how much she was still affected by what had happened. Anyway, concentrating was proving difficult just at the moment.

'So that must mean that he's fresh on the scene. Am I right?' Theo liked the idea of that, because it meant that she wouldn't have slept with the man. Heather just wasn't the type. Heather was… He glanced down at the tight black dress and frowned. Not the sort to wear a dress that managed to cover up all the bits and yet still look provocative at the same time. And not the sort to be coldly giving him the brush-off.

'Have you slept with him?' he asked huskily, and she laughed. *Laughed*! Laughed and refused to answer! 'Answer me!' he growled.

'Why should I answer you? You're no longer a part of my life.' Heather didn't quite know where her strength was coming from. She still loved him, and always would, but those times of mindlessly allowing him to dictate her behaviour were over—because they had to be. They had slept together and he had still walked away the minute he felt threatened by the possibility of having to give more of himself than he wanted. He hadn't even bothered to try, and she had taken her cue from him.

The jazz number came to a mournful end and they separated. Heather breathed a sigh of relief, because being strong took a lot of energy even if she believed in herself, and Theo breathed hard, disturbed by the gut-wrenching premonition of something slipping away.

'Thanks for the dance,' she said coolly, turning around in mid-sentence to check on Scott, who gave her a little wave which she returned. 'I think you ought to go back to your date now. I can just about see her from here, and she doesn't look very happy.'

Nor did he, come to that. She felt a spurt of female satisfaction. Had he thought that he would run into her accidentally and turn her on with his charm *just because he could*? Did he get turned on by the fact that he felt he could still have her if he wanted, even though there was another woman waiting in the wings? That poor, besotted Heather, who had run around behind him in her dowdy clothes, with her open and trusting nature, was still the same gullible woman he had been forced to turn away because he could smell her becoming a tad too demanding for her own good?

'And yours looks fine,' Theo muttered savagely. 'Wonder what that says?'

'Do you?' She smiled politely at the man who could still make her heart flip, before turning around and walking away, leaving him with her indifference.

Theo quietly seethed for the remainder of the evening. His date was everything a red-blooded male could wish for. Drop-dead gorgeous, attentive, showing green light signals and intellectually unchallenging. No chance of being distracted by serious conversation. Yet he was hugely irritated by her and more irritated by himself as he found his eyes wandering over to where Heather and her bland, blond-haired date seemed to be having a whale of a time. Lots of laughter and body language was speaking volumes.

The minute he saw them rise to leave, he turned to Michelle, cutting her off in mid-sentence.

'We're going.'

She recovered quickly and gave a throaty laugh. 'My place or yours?'

'Yours.' He must really be losing it if he couldn't get worked up about sleeping with this very beddable woman batting her eyelashes at him. 'But sorry, darling. No sex tonight.'

He needed to get back to his apartment and clear his head.

Having never suffered the power of jealousy, Theo did not recognise it for what it was. Instead, he directed its force towards himself, ferociously regretting the time he had wasted with that damned woman on his mind. He had had the generosity of nature to actually give her a moment's thought, to wonder what she was up to, when in fact she had being doing very well, thank you very much.

He half heard Michelle's protests as he drove swiftly through the deserted streets of London to drop her off. With his vast experience of women behind him he had no difficulty in recognising the variations in her tone, from understanding to plaintive and finally to apologizing, in case she had done anything to upset the apple cart.

'I'll be in touch,' was all he said when he finally pulled up outside her townhouse. He reached past her to open her door and gritted his teeth when her long fingers gently stroked his forearm.

He was behaving like a cad. That much he knew. He had barely spoken to her for the entire evening, and when he had it had been with a blatant lack of interest.

'I'm sorry, Michelle,' he said, tempering his voice guiltily. 'I haven't been myself tonight. Work, you know.' He let that sweeping generalisation cover over all the cracks and watched her disappointment become tinged with a glimmer of hope. 'And a ton of it to come over the next few weeks,' he added, squashing any temptation she might have to arrange a further meeting. What he needed was a break from the opposite sex. They were trouble.

It was what he continued to tell himself over the next few days as he thundered through his offices, barely aware of his employees scattering like ninepins from his path. Even his secretaries ducked low in an attempt to ride the storm, baffled as to the cause of its eruption.

Finding out Heather's address went some way to defusing Theo's foul temper, but only because he told himself that, whatever lifestyle she had decided to adopt, he was still concerned about her welfare.

Well, he thought, fingering the piece of paper and staring broodingly out of his office window, what reasonable human being wouldn't be?

For all she might be pinning a semblance of sophistication on her shoulders now, Heather was essentially green round the ears—a vulnerable innocent, ripe for being preyed on by anyone with half a brain and an urge to grab what seemed to be on offer. If she had decided to chuck out all her old clothes—*in accordance with the new flat, the new job and the new boyfriend*—and dress with maximum provocation in mind, then God only knew what trouble she was headed for.

He thought of those lush breasts being paraded around London while every man with two eyes stared, and of what Heather, who would naturally be immune to the effect she was having, would do if one of those leering men decided that looking wasn't going to be enough. Scare him off with her streetwise attitude? Hah!

Realising what he had to do was like the parting of dark clouds by a single shot of sunlight.

Four hours later he had pulled up outside the block of apartments. He killed the engine of his car and took a few moments to think.

For fleeting seconds he wondered what the hell he was doing here, especially as it was later than he had planned—after nine. Then he reminded himself where his duty lay. It lay with giving some sensible advice to a woman he knew—had known intimately. Any relationship they had had was now dead and buried, but as a responsible human being he still felt obliged to offer some advice. He was a man of the world—the sort of man, he reflected, proud of his ability to be truthful to himself, who would be one of those drawn to her if he saw her waltzing along the High Street swinging her hips and wearing a top that left little to the imagination.

With a sigh of self-righteousness, he slipped out of the car and bounded up to the front door, pressing the pad with her number.

The apartment block was very modern, but not unattractive. Attempts had been made to introduce some greenery around the façade, and he could glimpse shadowy clumps of shrubs and immature trees to one side.

Inside the apartment, Heather heard the buzz of the front doorbell and wondered who on earth it could be. Big advantage to apartment living. There were never any unannounced visitors. She briefly thought of the last unannounced visitor to an apartment, Theo's mother, and squeezed her eyes tightly shut to block out the image.

'Yes?'

'Heather?'

The deep drawl of Theo's voice slammed into Heather like a shock from a live wire. She still hadn't recovered from bumping into him at that club. She felt as though the air had been sucked out of her lungs and she flopped down on the chair.

'Yes?' Her voice was breathless.

'We need to talk.'

'What about?'

'Nothing that can be said down the end of an intercom. Buzz me in.'

She did. Her mind was awash with a thousand things. He had come to see her. She hadn't thought he would, but he had, and it could only mean that meeting her in that club had reminded him of what he had lost. Hadn't he spent ages dancing with her?

Willing to leave his date wilting in a distant corner while he whispered into her ear that he was aroused by *her*?

Her fragile mantle of cool, composed self-assurance fell away in a blink.

She heard the knock on her door and her heart sang. When she opened it, she was smiling.

CHAPTER EIGHT

'Hi. What brings you here?' Heather stood aside to let him in. He had come straight from work, but typically he had already loosened his tie and unbuttoned the top button of his white shirt. It was one of his habits, as though the restraints of a suit were unbearable once he had left his office surroundings.

'So this is the new flat,' Theo remarked, positioning himself squarely in the middle of the room and looking around him.

'Do you like it? It's quite small.'

But it was in a good area, and she had worked out that she would just about be able to cover the rent. Decent places were hard to come by in London, and even though it was really more than she could reasonably afford if she were to actually want a life of any sort, Heather had been grateful to Beth for securing it for her and hanging on to it even though the landlord had had innumerable queries.

'I haven't had much chance to do anything with it as yet,' she continued, edging towards him. 'I've hung a couple of my sketches.'

'I recognise them.' They had come off his wall, leaving oblong spaces which got on his nerves more than he might have expected. He had obviously become accustomed to seeing them there—which only proved yet again how danger-ous habit could be.

He strode through to the bedroom, peering in, then the bathroom, and finally the kitchen—which was small, but big enough to fit a tiny square table with four chairs pressed into it. There were no signs of male occupation, but then whatev-er-his-name-was probably hadn't had time to make his presence felt as yet. If, indeed, he intended to. Heather might fancy *him* as commitment-shy, but she was in for a brutal shock if she imagined that he was so different from half the eligible men roaming the streets of London, willing to sleep with any halfway attractive woman who didn't have the ability to say no. Or, in the case of Heather, the ability to spot a cad from a mile off.

He finally concluded his inspection and returned to where Heather was standing by the two-seater sofa. Just as he had thought, her uniform of shapeless tracksuits had been discarded and she was wearing a pair of faded jeans and a small top which couldn't help but draw his eye to her bounteous breasts.

Thank God he was being magnanimous enough to consider helping her, telling her—as the friend he still was, whatever had happened between them—of the dangers of the opposite sex. He felt a zing of pure satisfaction—and why not when he was being as unselfish as was humanly possible?

'Not bad,' Theo conceded, tearing his eyes away from her and focusing instead on the kitchen to the left of her. 'Small, but not the usual dump most single people get shovelled into.'

'I wouldn't stay in a dump,' Heather protested. She thought of the place she had been renting before she had moved in with Theo and flushed. That hadn't been the height of elegance, that was for sure, but time spent in one of the plushest of pent-house apartments had considerably elevated her expectations of living accommodation. 'Well, not now, anyway,' she amended truthfully. 'Would you like something to drink? Tea? Coffee? I don't have any of the fresh stuff, I'm afraid.'

'Have you got anything stronger? Some whisky would be good.'

'You know I don't drink whisky, Theo. Why would I stock it?' He wasn't throwing himself in her arms, declaring himself a fool for not having realised earlier how much he needed her, and she began to have a few healthy doubts about the reason for his presence in her flat. These, though, she decided to keep to herself. Theo was not a man who could be pushed into saying anything he didn't want to say. He obviously had *something* to say—or else why would he be standing in her flat right now?—but he would say whatever it was in good time. Anyway, once she'd removed the burgeoning little worries beginning to niggle, the anticipation of taking up their relationship once more would be worth the wait.

'What about some wine?'

'I think I could do wine. I had a glass yesterday, and the rest is in the fridge.'

She began walking towards the kitchen, leaving Theo to wonder who she had been sharing the wine with. Heather was not the sort of woman who enjoyed drinking by herself. Which meant that she would have been drinking with someone, and the only person who sprang to his suspicious mind was the opportunist date of a few evenings before. He felt his mouth tighten in an instant, glowering hostility, but soothed his distaste by quickly reminding himself of his generous mission tonight.

'Have you eaten?' Heather asked, stretching up to fetch down a couple of wine glasses and looking at him over her shoulder.

'There's no need to put yourself out on my behalf,' Theo said, 'but, no, I haven't. In fact, I've come straight from work.'

'I haven't eaten either.' She smiled, guiltily aware that she shouldn't really be enjoying his company, having him in her flat. Beth would have a thousand fits if she knew. 'Actually, I've spent the day getting my portfolio together in preparation for my new job. They had a look at the interview but I'm going to take it in anyway when I start—just so that my immediate boss knows what I'm capable of. Beth said that's the only thing to do—make them know from the start that I have the potential to get into the area I want. People don't know what you're capable of unless you blow your own trumpet.' She handed him a glass of wine, noticing how he seemed to dwarf the small kitchen even though he had sat down and pushed the chair back as far as he could, so that he could stretch out his long legs.

This gave Theo the leeway he needed to get across his point, but ramming it home wasn't going to do. Heather was obviously very excited about her brand-new life, and slamming into her about its pitfalls would simply get her back up. He decided to let the evening unwind and drop sufficient casual hints that would build up into an insurmountable wall of unavoidable fact. He sipped the wine, watching her as she smiled at him, cheeks attractively pink.

'This Beth character has too much influence over you,' he contented himself by pointing out. 'If you are going to be cooking something for yourself, then I might share it with you. I'm in no rush this evening.'

Heather was dying to ask what had happened to Michelle. Surely if they were an item she would be around on any evening Theo had free?

'Just some pasta actually.'

'Tell me about this job.'

'Do you want some pasta?' It was on the tip of her tongue

to offer to cook him something else instead, but good sense held her back from saying it. Yes, he had come to see her, and she was quietly stunned and overjoyed, but it wasn't quite enough to make her forget what a push-over she had been in the past, putting herself out to do whatever he wanted, even if it was a meal at some ungodly hour of the evening after he had worked his usual mammoth hours and still had more to do.

'Why not?'

'Don't let me push you into having it,' Heather said, with an uncustomary surge of rebellion. 'The sauce is just from a tin, and I know you don't like anything from tins.'

Theo frowned. 'Simply because home cooking is a damn sight healthier, not to mention tastier, than anything you can get from a can. Canned foods are loaded with preservatives.'

'And, of course, you've always had the luxury of never having to take the quick and easy way out…' Before she had come along Theo had had the chef from his favourite restaurant prepare food for him which he could freeze and pull out for instant healthy home-cooked food whenever it happened to suit him.

'I didn't come here to have a pointless argument with you over the advantages and disadvantages of processed food,' Theo grated. 'You were going to tell me about your job…?' He stood up to fetch himself another glass of wine and brushed past her, sending little electric currents whizzing through her body.

Distracted by that fleeting physical contact, Heather forgot the question that had risen to her lips—which had concerned his reasons for coming to see her, now that he mentioned it—and found herself chatting to him about the whole nerve-racking interview through to its happy conclusion.

As she chatted she chopped tomatoes, making a small concession to his distaste of anything pre-prepared, which she added to the concoction from the tin. She also shredded and tossed in a few basil leaves from the little plant she had growing on the counter, and crushed some fresh garlic to give it a bit of extra bite.

The end result looked mouthwateringly home-made, and she ladled good amounts for both of them onto some steaming tagliatelle.

'Very healthy,' Theo announced, eyeing her appraisingly. 'Is this a new diet to go with your new life? You've lost weight.'

Heather was proud of the achievement. There was no way she was going to let on that sheer unhappiness had curbed her healthy appetite, and that in the process something weird but wonderful had happened. She had lost some of her cravings for sweet things. Instead, she nodded, and looked at him over the rim of her glass as she swallowed a mouthful of wine.

'I didn't think you'd noticed,' she said, pleased that he had. In those few glorious, heady weeks when they had been together as a couple he had commented often on how much he adored her body, its fullness. 'But I'll never be a stick insect,' she continued. 'I mean, aside from my waist and stomach, everything's pretty much the same as it was before.'

'I'd noticed that as well. Your breasts are still as luscious as ever.'

Heather blushed and told herself not to get her hopes up, not to imagine that the passing compliment was an indication of things to come. But hope sprang inside her like an unchecked river breaking its banks, and it was all she could do not to tremble.

'You don't have to pay me compliments because I've

cooked you a meal, Theo. Anyway, you have a girlfriend, and I'm pretty sure she wouldn't be overjoyed to know that you're sitting in my kitchen making flattering noises about my figure.'

'I wouldn't call Michelle a *girlfriend*. She's a woman I took out on a couple of dates and is no more, as a matter of fact.'

'Oh, dear. Did she get a little too possessive for her own good?'

'At the moment I have just a little too much work to devote time and attention to courting a woman,' Theo said smoothly. Dwelling on his love life wasn't part of his agenda, and particularly not when it came close to discussing their relationship or the demise of it. Post-mortems had never been his thing.

Heather shook her head in admonishment. Actually, she found that hard to believe. From what she had seen of Theo over time, pressure of work played almost no part in his ability to wine, dine and bed the fairer sex. It seemed that oodles of charm, looks and money went a long way to success, with or without the availability of free time.

'All work and no play…'

Theo felt his hackles rise, and with his usual rapid leap of logic worked out why. In all the time she had been living with him, dutifully listening and obeying, she had never questioned him in that tone of voice. He was fast realising that she had broken out of the cocoon to which he had become lazily accustomed and was expressing opinions which went way beyond the point of acceptability.

He ignored the flagrant breach of his boundaries and gave her a slow, curious smile.

'More advice from the house of Beth?' he asked mildly, and, as he'd predicted, she went bright red. The cynical words might be there, but the lack of accompanying polish told their own story. He had never met her friend, although he had heard her mentioned frequently in the past—usually in connection with some ridiculous piece of rampant feminism. Now he could clearly see what was happening. Heather was being swept along on a tide of Girl Power that was essentially not her at all.

But swept along she was. Which just proved how gullible she was. It only stiffened his resolve to steer her away from all possible dangers lurking in her path. Who else was going to do it for her? Certainly not her free-thinking friend, who was quite possibly a man-hater.

'She has a lot of experience,' Heather said defensively. 'She comes into contact with all manner of people in the courts of law, and she's naturally developed a hard shell. Basically, she doesn't get taken for a ride.'

'Which is what happened to you?' His annoyance with this absent but influential friend was increasing at a rate of knots.

Heather maintained a stubborn but pointed silence and his face hardened into implacable lines.

'I don't believe anyone held a gun to your head, forcing you to work for me,' he pointed out. '*In fact*, I don't believe there was any necessity for me to offer you that job in the first place. And, having been offered the job—which, incidentally, was quite a generous package…free accommodation in fairly luxurious surroundings…a good pay cheque at the end of the month…a light enough workload to enable you to carry on with your course, unhampered by concerns over time or money—having been offered all that, you always had the right to turn it down.'

If there was one thing Theo knew how to do, it was to win an argument. Before she could defend herself Heather could see the pitfalls of any point of view she might come up with—because the conciseness and clarity of what he was saying was inescapable. She *had* taken up his offer, and chosen to feed her infatuation with him at her own peril.

Just in case she failed to get the message, and infuriated that she might be trying to pin him down as the big, bad wolf in her head—*especially when he had come to see for her own good*—Theo decided to drive home his point.

'When my mother paid us that unexpected visit and jumped to all the wrong conclusions about our perfectly platonic relationship, yes, I admit I asked you to do me the favour of going along with the pretence for the sake of her health. But I didn't force you to climb into bed with me. I never used you, and you were never taken for a ride. We enjoyed what we had and you always knew that I was not the kind of man who wanted to settle down.'

His words drove into her fragile hopes like a hammer obliterating a cardboard box.

'Look, I didn't come here to argue with you.'

Heather stood up abruptly and began clearing the table, waving down his perfunctory offer to help. In a minute she would be able to speak, but right now her mouth felt as though it was stuffed with cotton wool, and there was the sharp, painful pricking of tears behind her eyelids.

She could feel his eyes narrowed on her as she bustled about, with barely enough room to move. Eventually she turned around, propping herself against the sink, and folded her arms.

'No, of course not. And I don't want to argue with you either. It seems a waste of time when we've known each other…well…for a while…' Civilised and mature was how she sounded, which was the only thing Theo could deal with. He certainly wouldn't want her to freak out because she had expected more from this visit than was being extended. Yet again she had misread the circumstances. When was she ever going to learn? Were there courses for people like her? People who allowed their hearts to be eaten up and then dumped all the good advice their friends and their heads gave them so that they could walk right back into the same trap and end up being eaten up all over again?

He still hadn't told her why he *had* come, but she was beginning to think that it was to do with something horribly simple. Like a request for her to come and collect some piece of nonsense she had forgotten at his apartment in her rush to leave.

'Would you like some coffee? I'm afraid I'm going to have to rush you away pretty soon. I'm exhausted.'

'Painting the town red?'

Heather could detect some amusement in his voice, and she pinned a bright smile on.

'Amongst other things,' she said vaguely, stretching the truth like a piece of elastic. 'Now that I've got my own place, I don't see the point of sitting around.'

'More advice from your wise friend?'

'It's very unkind of you to pick holes in Beth when you've never even met her,' Heather felt constrained to point out. She glanced at her watch, then at him.

'Forgot. Exhaustion's kicking in.' He stood up and flexed his muscles. 'Okay. A cup of coffee. I still need to talk to you, and somehow we haven't managed to get around to it.'

'If you want to go and sit down I'll bring you the coffee.' Knowing that he was in the kitchen, watching her, put her on edge, and right this minute she needed to get her bearings. She needed him out.

She made sure not to make herself any coffee—another hint for him to leave. An image of Beth kept popping into her head, telling her what a good idea it had been to take charge of her life and move out.

She found him sitting on the sofa, leafing through one of her art books, which he proceeded to dump the minute she walked in.

'If you had something to tell me, you could have phoned.' Heather handed him his coffee and retreated to the chair facing him.

She tried to think of him as just an ordinary chap she was no longer involved with. She tried not to absorb the slashing cheek-bones, the piercing eyes, the extravagantly handsome features.

'The number here is ex-directory.'

'Oh. Yes.'

'And I couldn't get through on your mobile phone.'

'It broke. I've been meaning to get another one, but I haven't got around to it.'

Theo clicked his tongue in irritation. In this day and age of fast technology Heather was the only person he knew who could blissfully live life without a mobile phone. When she *had* had one, it had generally been left in the house when she was out, or switched off when it was in her bag because she was convinced that it was permanently on the verge of running out of charge. Arguments about the need to have it fully charged and on her person at all times fell on deaf ears, because she was of the opinion that if the world had survived for centuries without its invention, then why should it suddenly be a necessity?

'Please don't lecture me on why I need to go out and buy one tomorrow. I'm quite happy not to have one.'

'What if someone needs to get in touch with you?'

Heather shrugged. 'So why have you come?'

Theo recognised a no-win situation when he heard one, and promptly dropped the contentious matter of the non-existent mobile phone.

'I've come—and I'm not sure how to phrase this—because seeing you in that nightclub with that Sam character…'

'Scott.'

He ignored the interruption. Actually, blessed with almost perfect recall, Theo was well aware of the man's name, but no way was he going to be accurate on the subject and give her any notion that he had been thinking about her and the man in anything more than vague paternalistic terms.

'…made me realise how incurably green around the ears you are.'

'I beg your pardon?' Bewildered, Heather ran her pink tongue over her lips, and Theo's eyes narrowed broodingly.

That, he thought, was a perfect example of what he was talking about. Most women with any nous would know that to be a gesture of pure provocation—but did Heather? Absolutely not. His eyes, which he had obediently kept plastered to her face, now drifted to her breasts, and to the cleavage he couldn't fail to see as she leant forward, all ears.

He felt himself turn on, and lowered his eyes with considerable will-power.

'Look at the way you're sitting.'

More bemused by the second, Heather frowned. It occurred to her to ask whether he had been drinking before he came to visit her, because he wasn't making any sense. Then again, she thought, bringing herself up short, she could hardly trust her own keen sense of deduction, could she?

'How am I sitting? What are you talking about? You haven't come here to talk to me about my posture, have you?' Theo rarely uttered anything that wasn't relevant to what he wanted to say, but she was at a complete loss as to where he was heading with this line of conversation. 'I know I slump,' she said nervously, 'and I'm going to correct that just as soon as I buy my mobile phone.'

He failed to see the limp stab at humour. 'When you lean forward like that, pretty much everything is on display.'

Slow colour mounted in Heather's cheeks, and she pushed herself back and fiddled with the neckline of her top. Changing her drab wardrobe in favour of clothes that were younger and fresher had not taken much encouragement on Beth's part. Pleased with her new figure, which for her was probably the slimmest she had been in a very long time, she had enthusiastically taken to the shops and bought herself a range of things that *showed off her assets,* as one of the sales assistants had confidently assured her.

Guilt and a lifetime of circumspection washed over her in a burning tide of embarrassment.

'You don't have to look,' Heather countered belatedly.

'It would be impossible not to.' Theo sat back and linked his fingers on his lap. 'Either you really and truly are not aware of the signals you give off by something as simple as that, or else you are showing me what's on offer deliberately…'

Heather reeled from the humiliating assumption. Theo's ego was big, but she had never known just how big until now. *Did he really think that she was trying to turn him on? That she was desperate enough to do anything to win him back, even after he had reiterated his views to her only minutes earlier?*

Of course he did, she thought in frank, shameful honesty. She had opened that door to him willing to forgive every cutting remark on the simple thread of hope that he had come back with reconciliation in mind. How pathetic was that? Even if he couldn't read her mind, he was astute enough to sense her need, and naturally he would assume, with that splendid arrogance of his, that she would do anything to tempt him back. Including revealing her body.

For a few taut seconds she couldn't think of anything to say, and then she felt a slow rush of anger to her head.

'You really think that I'm sitting here trying to get a response out of you?' she asked, her voice shaking. '*That* is the most arrogant…conceited…*ridiculous* assumption you could *ever* make…'

Theo inclined his head, hearing her out but unmoved by her heated response, and then he shrugged in an exquisitely dismissive gesture.

'That being the case, then you clearly have no idea how to survive in a world that is full of predatory males…'

'Predatory males?' Heather's thoughts stopped on those two simple words and she stared at him, dumbfounded. '*Predatory males*? The world isn't full of predatory males, Theo. Not everyone is built along *your* lines!'

'I am very far from being a predator,' he pointed out with insufferable calm. 'Predators are driven by a need to find and catch their prey. Actually, I have never felt any such need. In fact, I would say that I am more the prey than the predator…'

Heather gasped in disbelief at this wild distortion of fact. 'Are you trying to tell me that you're as innocent as the driven snow?'

'Incorrect analogy. I'm saying no such thing. Merely that women chase *me* more often than not.'

He was probably right too. But that didn't stop him from being an all-time predator of the highest order. Sensing yet another argument she would be in danger of losing, Heather contented herself by fulminating at his high-handed smugness.

'Which brings me to the boyfriend…'

She opened her mouth to refute the label, and closed it as quickly as she had opened it. Scott, actually, had been the sweetest of dates, in so far as they had talked until the early hours of the morning over coffee at her flat. She had listened to him pour his heart out about his ex-girlfriend, on whom he was obviously still hung up, and they had parted company promising to keep in touch.

'Scott isn't a *predator*.' The unlikely thought of that brought a smile to her lips, and seeing it filled Theo with an uncustomary surge of belligerence which he put down to his unsurprising frustration at her naïveté.

'How would you know? The way you were dressed at that nightclub was a green light to any unattached male. I'm telling you this for your own good, Heather.'

'You came here to *preach to me*? Because you don't think that I'm sensible enough or adult enough to take care of myself?' She stood up, hand outstretched for his cup. 'I think it's time you left, Theo. You should never have come in the first place! What gives you the right to come into my flat and start treating me like a kid?'

'Calm down. You're beginning to sound hysterical.'

Heather laughed hysterically and snatched the coffee from his hands, spilling some on his trousers in the process. Her only regret was that the stuff had gone tepid, although he automatically flinched back and sprang to his feet to brush himself down.

'And I won't be offering to launder them for you!' she shrieked. 'You deserved that!'

Theo, although he didn't show it, was taken aback by this display of temper. The calm, obliging, sunny-tempered girl... where had she gone?

'For what? For being decent enough to show concern about protecting you?'

Through the red mist of her anger Heather resisted yelling

at him that the only person she needed protecting from was *him*—and only because she had been idiotic enough to fall in love with him.

Thinking it managed to bring a few seconds of calm to her shattered thoughts, and she took some deep breaths. When in a crisis, breathe deeply and don't panic. One rule for all situations.

'That's very kind of you,' she managed to say frozenly. 'I do apologise for spilling the coffee on you, but I won't be paying the laundry bill.'

'To hell with the damned trousers!' Theo exploded. He paced the room, finally leaning against the wall and folding his arms. 'I don't care if I have to throw them out! You shriek at me like a *fisherwoman* when *I* am the one who should be aggrieved. You have thrown my good intentions back in my face!'

Heather took a few more deep breaths. So this was what love did to a person. Turned her from an even-tempered, cheerful sort into a screaming banshee. Her days of mute adoration seemed a lifetime ago—as did tranquillity and peace of mind.

'I can take care of myself.' She folded her arms protectively over her breasts and felt a heady, disturbing rush of awareness as his eyes stripped her of her modest gesture.

'Tip: watch what you wear, and make sure you don't flaunt yourself the way you were doing with me a few moments ago…'

'I'll remember that. Thank you.'

Her sudden compliance got on his nerves and he stared at her narrowly. Maybe—and it wasn't a nice thought—he was trying to lock the gate after the horse had bolted. He suddenly had a driving, obliterating need to find out whether she had slept with her date or not, and there was no way he could reasonably put *that* down to anything caring, concerned or paternalistic.

He walked slowly towards where she was now cringing back into her chair, as if willing the inanimate object to swallow her up, and he leant over her, bracing himself with his hands on either side of her.

Every nerve in her body jumped in wild, searing alarm, and she was aware of her breath coming and going in short, painful bursts.

She kept repeating the mantra about taking deep breaths, but with his face only inches away from hers the exercise was singularly failing to work.

'And did you remember that when you were with your date? Or did you innocently imagine that he was talking to you and not your breasts?'

'Don't you dare insult me like that, Theo.' Her voice lacked conviction, however. She was sickeningly mesmerised by the dark, burning depths of those magnificent eyes.

It *was* an insult, but Theo brazenly outstared her. 'Are you telling me that he didn't manage to get his paws on you?'

'I'm telling you that it's none of your business. Actually, Scott is a really nice guy. He *respects* me—which is more than I can say for you!'

Theo made a sneering sound under his breath and Heather glared at him coldly.

'Scott would never *talk to my breasts*—which is a disgusting expression. I suppose you think that he's wimp, but he isn't. And he would never sneer at me either!'

Thinking back on it, Scott, in an ideal world, would have been the perfect partner. Her eyes misted over at the sheer unfairness of life, and as he watched her expression change some new emotion was added to the boiling pot in Theo's head. He couldn't put his finger on what it was, but he didn't like it.

He was deeply regretting his generous urge to pay her a surprise visit. He should, he told himself fiercely, have let her loose on the London scene and then just waited until she came crawling back to him. Naturally she wouldn't have found him, but she certainly would have learnt her lesson, and sometimes lessons had to be learnt the hard way.

She was still looking at him in that defensive, wary, but ultimately mulish way, and with a soft groan Theo dipped his head and covered her mouth with his. No gentle kiss, this. Urgency and something powerfully elemental pushed her back into the chair.

For a few breathtaking seconds, caught off guard, Heather gave in to the rapturous pleasure only his mouth could give her. She twisted under the pressure of his hot embrace, and as his hand brushed against her breast she felt her nipples harden in response, straining to be touched and caressed. Imagination filled in all the gaps with remorseless speed, reminding her of how exquisitely his hands would move over her body, and how completely his mouth would seductively follow the path, until her whole body was on the brink of orgasm, waiting only for his hard thrusts to bring her to a state of mindless climax.

But hot on the heels of surrender came reality, and she pushed him back with one sharp jolt.

Theo stood up immediately. His erection was like steel. Painful.

'Were you trying to show me first hand what kind of man I should watch out for?' Heather asked shakily. She felt assaulted—and horribly, horribly turned on. How could her body betray her like that? She couldn't meet his eyes. Not when he might see things there that were shameful. Instead, she twined her fingers convulsively together and held her breath.

'Maybe,' he said, turning away, 'I was trying to show you that settling for second best on the rebound from me isn't such a good idea.'

'Maybe,' Heather burst out tremulously, '*I* don't want to be the one who's *second best*! Maybe I want to be number one with someone—and why not? What's so odd about that?'

For once she entertained the unusual sight of Theo lost for words. Then, without saying a word, he walked away. Out of the room and out of her life for the second time.

It was only when the door slammed shut behind him that Heather finally gave in to the jag of sobbing that had been threatening to come.

CHAPTER NINE

HEATHER was asleep when her telephone rang. It was a rude awakening from the dream she had been having. In her dream she had risen to glittering heights of success with a job that seemed to be unrelated to the one she was taking but which paid bucketloads of money. And there was Theo, present at a sparkling social event which she knew was for her—even though in the dream she was standing on the sidelines, watching. He was looking at her in a different way, in a way that signified respect, and she was basking in the glow of appreciation.

She ignored the phone, wanting the dream to go on and on for ever, but she could feel it disappearing like mist in the sun as the phone shrilled next to her on the bedside table.

'It's me,' Theo said flatly, stating the obvious. Heather would have recognised his voice if he had been wearing a handkerchief over his mouth.

Disoriented, she sat up and looked at the illuminated hands of the clock on her dressing table. A little after eleven-thirty. He had only been gone for a matter of an hour and a half! Struggling with the shock of hearing his voice, it took her several minutes before she gathered herself together sufficiently to realise that he was saying something to her down the phone.

'How did you get my telephone number?'

'Have you heard a word I just said?' Theo imagined her in a state of drowsiness, hair everywhere, cheeks pink. He looked across the room and grimaced, then turned away from the person who had made herself at home and was staring with great interest around her. 'Look, the telephone number was scrawled next to the telephone on a jotting pad. I made a note of it—and just as well, as it turns out.'

'Do you know what time it is?'

Theo stifled a groan. He had driven back from her flat in the minimum amount of time, only resisting the temptation of heading for the local pub because there had been no convenient parking on the street outside, and had arrived at his apartment in a foul mood which not even the challenges of his latest deal could alleviate. In what had become a disturbingly familiar pattern, he had stared at the columns of information blinking at him and had had to concentrate very hard to bring it all into meaningful focus.

Having lived his whole life at the control panel—a place of pleasing superiority from where he could orchestrate events and determine the ebb and flow of his life, both public and private—Theo had found it nigh on impossible to cope with the lack of control he had felt ever since Heather had walked out of his apartment.

He had spent a good while telling himself that it had been for the best, that Heather's believing the fantasy of their fictitious relationship had been the inevitable start of the whole thing unravelling. The speed at which it had unravelled had taken him by surprise, but he had had no choice but to do what he'd had to do.

That done, he had assumed that his life would effortlessly continue the way it always had, although he had naturally suspected that she might cross his mind off and on.

When he had found himself thinking of her more than he had anticipated, he had told himself that it was because she had been more than his usual fling. After all, hadn't she worked for him, shared his space, for well over a year?

He would, he'd reasoned to himself, have been inhuman to imagine that they could part company without the occasional lingering aftermath.

He had consoled himself with the thought that he was anything but inhuman.

Seeing her with another man had catapulted all reason out of the window. He had reacted with a fury that had left him shaken.

On the drive back from her flat earlier, he had looked at the situation with honesty and had been forced to admit to himself that his pretence of going over to see her so that he could *give a bit of friendly advice because he was such a good person at heart* had been a load of hogwash. He had driven over to see her because he had been jealous—had been driven by some pressing need to discover whether she and the man were serious.

And, judging from the soft expression on her face when his name was mentioned, he had been forced to concede that they were. Or at least had the potential to be.

Her parting shot about not wanting to be *second best* had seemed to him singularly unfair.

When, he had thought with self-righteous fury, had he *ever* treated her as second best?

Just the opposite! He had given more of himself to her than he ever had to any woman before.

He had spent weeks regulating his work life to be around her more. True, the presence of his mother had kind of necessitated that, but the fact remained that he had striven to arrive home early, and had even accompanied her several times to the supermarket—which was virtually unheard of.

How she could then turn the tables on him and try to make him feel bad about himself was sheer female contrariness.

But going through the unblemished fairness of his attitude still hadn't made him feel any better about walking out on her.

The simple truth of the matter was that he missed her. The apartment suddenly seemed empty and forlorn without her presence.

Having arrived at this conclusion, which had taken him down mental highways and byways he had never travelled before, he had finally abandoned his work, stretched, and approached the situation from an utterly pragmatic point of view.

She might be going out with a non-starter of a man—might actually think that that brought certain advantages—but as far as he was concerned that fledgling relationship was simply a technical hitch.

He wanted her back and he would get her back. Simple as that.

Considerably restored by an active workable plan, he had been on the point of going to bed when the doorbell had rung…

Theo brought his attention back to the reason for his phone call.

'I realise it's an unusual time to call, but you have to get over here. Right now.'

'Why? What's the matter?' Suddenly scared by the tension she could detect in his voice, Heather sat up properly and switched on the bedside light, thereby dispelling all possibility of going back to sleep.

'Nothing that can be discussed over the telephone.'

Questions were zooming through her head in their thousands. Theo was not, generally, an unpredictable man. His visit to her earlier in the evening had been unpredictable enough, but this telephone call out of the blue filled her head with all sorts of unpleasant possibilities—including the overriding one that he had somehow had an accident and was possibly in a bad way. Maybe he had already called an ambulance but needed her there for support. Or at least, she thought, checking herself, to look after the apartment while he was in hospital.

She had images of him lying on the ground, his strong body weakened and broken, and she leapt out of bed, clutching the phone to her ear while she flew around the room, yanking open drawers and pulling out clothes.

'Do I need to bring anything?' she asked anxiously.

'Anything like what?'

'I don't know!' She tried to imagine what someone with broken bones might need, and could come up with nothing except an emergency trip to the nearest casualty department. 'There's a first aid kit in the kitchen. In that cupboard under the sink. It's tucked away behind the dishwasher tablets.' To the best of her knowledge he had never opened that particular cupboard.

Theo, taken aback and somewhat puzzled by this could only say mildly, 'Is there? Thanks. That's helpful to know. I'm going to hang up now. Just make sure you get here fast. In fact, get dressed, and while you're getting dressed I'll send my driver over. He'll be with you in twenty minutes. There's not much traffic on the roads at this time of the night.'

'Right.' Before she could ask any more questions she heard the flat dial tone and went into overdrive, flinging on jeans, tee shirt, jumper. No time for make-up or hair. Just sufficient time to wash her face and quickly brush her teeth.

She should really fly over to Beth's, just to let her know that she wouldn't be in her flat overnight, but the prospect of having to cope with the inevitable barrage of stern cross-examining put her off the prospect. She decided that she would phone her friend first thing in the morning.

Theo's driver arrived in under twenty minutes, as predicted. Knowing how much Theo respected his privacy, and taking the lead from the taciturn middle-aged man who politely ushered her into the back seat, Heather felt it best to maintain a discreet silence—although she was itching to ask questions, just in case…

She half expected to arrive and find an ambulance waiting outside, lights flashing, and men racing about with stretchers or whatever they raced about with when carting off someone with injuries. But the apartment block looked remarkably peaceful.

Having left her key behind, it felt odd for her to buzz on the intercom when she had been accustomed to coming and going as she pleased. Theo answered immediately, releasing the door from the phone inside the apartment.

The ride up in the lift took a mere few seconds which felt like years.

It was something of a shock when, after one knock, the door was opened by a Theo who looked remarkably fit and healthy.

Heather released a long sigh of relief and sagged against the doorframe. 'You haven't fallen and broken your bones,' she breathed.

'I beg your pardon?' Theo gave her a perplexed look from under his lashes. She had thrown some clothes on and clearly had no idea how sexy and ruffled she looked.

Having reached his momentous decision to win her back, he knew that he would have to approach her in a different manner. He recognised that he had taken her for granted—hence her unjustified remarks about being second best. It was something he intended to rectify, so he smiled warmly at her and stood aside.

'You're smiling,' Heather said suspiciously, not budging. She longed to fly inside his apartment, which she missed horribly, even though she had told herself a million times that it was far better having her own place, where she could do her own thing without restriction. 'Why are you smiling? I thought…'

'What…?'

She rapidly revised the truth that had been about to emerge. 'That you weren't in a very good mood when you left earlier. I didn't think you ever wanted to set eyes on me again.'

Theo flushed darkly. The way he had stormed out of her flat was not something he especially wanted to remember. It was distinctly un-cool. Fortunately, something else seemed to be playing on her mind and she rounded on him fiercely, stabbing one finger into his chest.

'And there's nothing *wrong* with you!' she couldn't help but hiss.

'Were you hoping that there would be?' Theo asked, frowning.

Released from her state of dread, Heather could feel herself ready to vent eloquently on the object of her misplaced worry.

She caught herself in the nick of time. She had already suffered one episode of misreading a situation and reacting like a fool. She wasn't about to let on to him now the extent to which she had been worried about him. He might suspect that the glorious life of unbridled freedom she was living was anything but. She inhaled deeply.

'I'm not coming inside until you tell me why you had to get me out of bed at an ungodly hour and come round here.'

'It's not the first time I've got you out of bed at an ungodly hour…' To work, yes, when she had been living with him in her role as general factotum, and later, when his mother had been in the apartment recuperating, to make love. His eyes darkened at the sudden memory and a smile of pure sexiness curved his mouth.

Heather steeled herself against the rampant heavy-lidded provocation of his gaze. 'And that was fine when it just involved a dressing gown and a few paces to the nearest computer.' She looked at him narrowly. 'Please don't tell me that you dragged me all the way here because you need some work doing.'

Much as Theo was enjoying the sight of her, pleasantly at peace with himself for the first time in weeks now that he had resolved to get her back, they could hardly stand at his door talking indefinitely.

'All will be explained once you're inside. In fact…' he paused to step aside and allow her to pass '…I won't actually have to say a word. It will be self-explanatory.'

Intrigued to death, but still suspicious after her foolish mistake in jumping to all the wrong conclusions earlier on, when he had sprung his visit on her, she scuttled past him, taking care not to come into contact with his body even in passing.

'Okay. So what exactly am I supposed to be doing now? It's late, and I'm not in the mood for games.' Heather folded her arms imperiously and stared around her, aware that he was heading towards the kitchen, cool as a cucumber.

'Wait a few minutes. Care for a drink?'

He didn't wait for her to answer. Instead, he poured her a glass of wine and brought it over to where she was still standing, bristling as much as it was possible to bristle without saying anything.

'Come and sit.' He urged her towards the black leather sofa. 'I really am sorry to have disturbed your sleep…' Theo attempted to look contrite, a sentiment that did not sit easily on his face. 'I myself was working when…'

'When…? When what…?'

He didn't answer, because he didn't have to. Heather followed the direction of his gaze, twisting around with her glass in one hand, and her mouth dropped open.

Standing there in all her natural glory was the sister Heather had not clapped eyes on for longer than she cared to remember. Claire had changed surprisingly little, although her hair seemed much blonder than it had years ago.

A smile of pure pleasure illuminated Heather's face, and after the initial shock she stood up, rested her glass gently on the nearest table, and went towards her sister with outstretched arms.

'Claire.' She hugged her, then stood back, then hugged her again. 'You never said you were coming!'

Claire allowed herself to be hugged and smiled sheepishly. 'Well, I didn't actually make my mind up until recently,' she said, clearing her throat. 'And then I thought I'd just pay you a surprise visit. You've changed.' This time it was she who stood back and surveyed her sister assessingly. 'You've lost weight or something. Remember what a little podge you used to be?'

All at once Heather was catapulted back through time, back to the days when their roles had been clearly defined, with beautiful Claire winning all the physical plaudits. She blushed and nodded.

'If you had given me some advance warning, I would have…made a bed up for you. I don't live here any more, you see. In fact, I now rent a flat of my own, not too far away.'

Claire had already installed herself on the sofa alongside Theo, and was checking out her surroundings with the same assessing eyes that she had used on her sister. 'Shame. This is an amazing place. As I told Theo when I got here.'

Heather blinked and the disturbing image settled into focus. Her stunning blonde sister, taller, thinner and prettier

than she could ever be in a thousand years of changed ward-
robes and weight shedding, sitting next to a man whose dark,
devilishly sexy good looks were a striking and yet harmoni-
ous contrast, if such a thing were possible.

She felt her cheeks grow pink. Jealousy was trying to
burrow its way into her, and it was a huge effort not to
succumb. As if to add fuel to the fire, Claire turned to Theo,
her face wreathed in smiles, and began an extravagant one-
woman monologue on the charms of his apartment.

When Claire bothered to make an effort with men, it was
always a sight worth seeing. As an adolescent, Heather had
looked on in awe whenever her sister had decided that some
boy or other was worth making a play for. Out would come
the sweetest of smiles, the liveliest of sidelong glances, the
most sincere of expressions, and of course Claire was not
stupid. She did not simper banalities like a bimbo. She might
not have seen the point of exercising her brain over-much, not
when her chosen field of work was acting or modelling, but
she could still yank it out of cold storage when it suited her.
And from the looks of it, it certainly suited her now.

Heather shuffled to a chair and found it hard to get a word
in edgewise. Matters weren't helped by the rapt attention
Theo seemed to be giving Claire. All ears, and probably eyes
too, Heather thought dazedly.

When she finally managed to make her presence felt,
Heather asked her why she had suddenly decided to return to
England. Was it a holiday? Was she back for good?

But Claire was now exhausted, it seemed. She yawned
delicately, covering her mouth with her hand, and then stood
up and stretched. It was very graceful. It made Heather think
of some kind of choreographed dance movement. The nasty
and uncharitable thought flashed through Heather's head that

it was contrived and designed to draw Theo's attention to the pert breasts, the slim waist, the flat brown stomach peeping out when she raised her arms.

She squashed the thought and stood up as well. 'Where are your bags?' Knowing her sister, there would be more than one. 'I'll fetch them. I'm sorry. You must be exhausted. We'll go straight back to my place, and of course you're welcome to stay with me for as long as you're over here.' She smiled, but the smile felt forced, and she didn't want to look at Theo just in case she found him staring at her sister. Men always did. It was a natural reaction they just couldn't help. 'It'll be great catching up in the morning, Claire.' There, that was better. Back into her usual appeasing role, always making life easier for her sister. 'You can tell me what you've been up to.'

'Dear Heather.' Claire gave Theo one of her most wide-eyed expressions of girlish camaraderie. 'She's always been such a *carer*. I know I've been horrid—' she turned to her sister with a rueful smile '—hardly ever getting in touch. But I knew you wouldn't mind. I had dreams…' The implication was that Heather was just a little too dull to have dreams.

Heather hoped guiltily that Claire's move home wasn't going to be a permanent one.

'I have dreams too, Claire.' Asserting herself was an uphill struggle. Having always played the same role in her relationship with her sister, it was woefully easy to slip back into it.

'Have you? Well…look, I've just brought a couple of bags, and to answer your question, yes, I'm planning on making my home in London.'

'That's super.'

'I shall need somewhere to stay until I get a place of my own…'

'You can stay with me as long as you like. Although it *is* a very small flat…'

'Oh, it'll be fun to share! Remember we used to at home, when we were kids?'

Heather remembered a shared room in which ninety per cent had been given over to her sister's possessions while she'd had to make do with compacting everything she owned into the minimum amount of space. She nearly groaned aloud at the prospect of that recurring.

'Unless,' Claire said, sliding her eyes mischievously over to Theo and lowering her voice huskily, 'some dishy chap comes along and rescues poor little me…'

Heather held her breath and waited for the inevitable offer. After all, wasn't there a vacancy for one housekeeper up for grabs? Housekeeper able and willing to offer services beyond the call of duty? And who could resist Claire's charms? She might not have the elongated stick-like beauty of his usual women, but she had a hell of a lot more vivaciousness. And she wouldn't be one to go harping on about commitment and relationships. She enjoyed her freedom as much as Theo did.

Theo couldn't fail to catch the meaningful glitter in Claire's eye. He stood up smoothly, making sure that he didn't reveal in his eyes the depth of distaste that he felt, and nodded in the direction of the bathroom.

'Your sister had a bath when she arrived,' he told Heather. 'You must have things there to collect…?' He spared Claire a glance, noticing the little pout that changed her face from appealing angel to sulky child.

'Heaps. Thanks for reminding me.' She flounced out.

Theo looked at the cute retreating rear thoughtfully, then walked over to Heather and stared down at her.

'I'm sorry Claire interrupted your evening. I didn't get

around to dropping her an e-mail to let her know my new address.' In truth, Heather's e-mails to her sister had become few and far between. Claire rarely replied to the ones she sent, and in the end Heather had confined herself to the occasional one, filling her in on superficial bits of information.

Now, of course, she felt horribly guilty. She had to remind herself that they were no longer kids. They were both adults, and Claire had as much responsibility for maintaining their relationship as she had. But lifelong programming had kicked in. Heather felt muddled. Suddenly she wanted her old self back. The big, sack-like clothes she could hide behind. The ungainly body which had never deserved to be put on display.

'Has she always been like that?' Theo asked quietly, wishing that Heather would at least look at him. But she stubbornly stared down at the ground and shrugged.

'Like what?'

He gently placed his finger under her chin and Heather grudgingly met his eyes.

'Asserting her superiority…putting you down…showing no interest in you or what you've been up to. I could go on. She had quite a little chat with me before you came here. Made sure to let me know in not so many words how poor little Heather had been such a sad thing growing up, such a *brick*…always there in the background helping out.'

Heather couldn't actually reply to this because her throat felt thick with tears of humiliation.

'You don't have to feel sorry for me,' she said in a fierce undertone.

'I don't. You feel sorry for yourself.'

Heather recoiled as if she had been struck. How dared he be so accurate in summing her up? Claire would have had loads of stories to tell and, yes, she could just imagine her sister cleverly putting her down. She wondered whether they had both chuckled over her. Had he told her about their brief fling? Had he confided his own amusement and irritation over the way he had managed to ambush her emotions? She hated herself for thinking like that, and in some part of her knew that Theo was not the type of man to behave in such a manner, but she couldn't think straight. She was fifteen again, fat and gauche and watching from the sidelines as her sister flaunted her good looks and tried to give her little pointers on improving her image.

'I do not!' she retorted feebly. 'Anyway, Claire can't help being the person that she is.'

'I saw my bathroom after she'd used it. How are you going to live with all that clutter in your small flat?'

'Is that your way of telling me that you'll do me a favour by letting her move in here with you?' Like a horse without reins, her imagination galloped along at a pace, disregarding the hurdles and bolting towards a conclusion that left her miserable and sickened. She just couldn't *bear* the thought of Theo and her sister…

Whatever answer he had been about to make was interrupted by Claire, who breezed back into the room gaily waving a larger than average holdall which, she informed Heather, was jam-packed with all her cosmetics. 'The bags are over there, in the corner. Would you be a darling and bring them for me? I'm so tired I could lie right down on this floor and fall asleep!'

Heather sighed under her breath. She would have to have a long chat with her sister about the impossibility of staying with her for long. There just wasn't going to be the room to house the mountain of things Claire seemed to have brought over with her—and who only knew what else was sailing its way across the Atlantic, destination one minuscule flat that could barely contain the possessions of its one frugal tenant?

'I'll get my driver to take you to your place. Leave the bags. He'll bring them down for you.'

'You have a driver?' Claire's eyes widened as she digested this further piece of information about Theo's financial status.

'He's very, very, *very* rich,' Heather said, with a lack of tact that shocked her—although when she glanced at Theo it was to find that he was smiling with dry amusement.

'Oh, three *verys* might be one too many,' he murmured, wickedly teasing.

Claire, catching an undertone that Heather seemed oblivious to, waded in quickly, making sure that attention was returned to her. 'One can never be too thin or too rich,' she piped up. 'To quote somebody or other.' She grinned flirtatiously at Theo while Heather ostentatiously avoided them both by planting herself firmly at the door, hand on knob, ready to go.

'So I've heard,' Theo said noncommittally. He reached into his pocket for his mobile and had a swift conversation, unnerved by Claire's china-blue eyes narrowly fixed on him. By the door, Heather was standing in a state of such rigid tension that he felt she might crack if he touched her.

'Thanks again,' Heather said as they congregated around her.

Theo deliberately positioned himself so that his back was to Claire and leant over Heather, resting his arm against the doorframe. 'Okay?' he murmured. Having lived his life on one manageable emotional plane, Theo was now resigned to the wild assortment of feelings the woman standing and glaring roused in him. Right now, the urge to protect her was like a physical need. The phoney, altruistic intentions he had piously claimed for warning her away from Scott now crystallised into a very real, pressing desire that she shouldn't be hurt or over-whelmed by her sister.

Unfortunately, he thought, she was hardly going to believe a word he said on the subject, given that he had already used up his ration of so-called concern for her welfare.

'I'll be seeing you,' he promised, and Heather shot him a jaded, disbelieving look.

'Well,' she muttered, 'if you do, it certainly won't be in your office on all fours, cleaning your floor.'

'Are we ready to leave?' Claire said plaintively, and Theo drew back, cursing under his breath.

'My car should be ready. I'll come down with you.'

'No need!' Heather said brightly. 'We sisters just want to catch up on our own now!'

Claire surrendered grudgingly to this suggestion, but rounded on her sister as soon as they were in the lift and heading down.

'God, Heather, you never told me he was drop-dead gorgeous!'

'If you like that sort of look…'

'Well, yes. I know you go for the more boring type, but he's definitely my kind of guy—and *if I'd had any idea what he looked like I'd have worn something a bit better*!'

Heather was still dwelling on the assumption that she could only ever be interested in boring men. Since when had she let her sister get away with thoughts like that? Had she always accepted Claire's sweeping assumptions that she was someone prepared to let life slip by her while she toiled away in the background, doing nothing in particular?

'Wait a minute,' she objected belatedly, as they stepped into the waiting car—Claire's *oohs* and *ahhs* leaving Heather in no doubt that Theo's already magnificent standing had now flown off the scale— 'since when did you think that I only *go for boring men*?' It took a lot of courage to stand up for herself, and she could feel her neck begin to prickle uncomfortably.

She waited for Claire's famous temper to become evident, and was surprised when her sister stared at her, red-faced and open-mouthed. 'I didn't mean that you just *go* for boring guys,' she stuttered. 'It's just that…you know…well…'

'That the only kind of men who would be attracted to me would be the boring type…?'

'You have to admit that dynamic, sexy men would never have given you a second glance in the old days!' Claire burst out, and Heather stared at the stranger sitting next to her coldly. With everything in her she wanted to tell Claire about her fling with Theo, wanted to throw it in her face as proof that she wasn't the eternal no-hoper her sister seemed to think she was. But that would have been a terrible breach of confidence, and since it was apparent that Theo hadn't said a word about it there was no way that she was about to.

'Not that you don't look fantastic now,' Claire conceded. 'In fact I was a little shocked.'

If that was an olive branch, then Heather decided there and then that she would take it. Claire was the only close family member left to her in the world—and anyway, what was the point of bearing a grudge? With her natural inclination to forgive, she told herself that, whatever impression Claire had of her, it had been gained with Heather's assistance. She had meekly lived down to her sister's sweeping generalisations. Even her e-mails had played down her plans for her career. No wonder Claire thought that she had no dreams.

'But getting back to Theo…'

'Must we?'

'Did anything happen between the two of you while you were living in that apartment and working for him?'

Heather frantically tried to come up with a lie that wouldn't be a lie. Eventually she said, with a little self-deprecating laugh, 'I'd be a fool if it had…'

'In which case you wouldn't have a problem if I got in touch with him? You know, just to say thanks for lending me the use of his shower and being so courteous when I showed up at his place out of the blue? Men can be such pigs. Honestly. Your hair would stand on end if I told you some of the things that have happened to me!'

'Well, no…'

Claire regarded her sister narrowly. 'Good. Because you're way out of his league—and I'm not saying that to be insulting, Heath. Okay, I admit I was out of order to pigeonhole you into the type that old dullards would be attracted to, but…face it… Theo's a sex god, and sex gods just don't look at…well, girls like you…'

'No. No, they don't. They look at girls like you.' And maybe Claire was right. After all, Theo hadn't wanted her in the end, had he? So she had grown in self-confidence. Reality was still a bucket of cold water she couldn't avoid. And, sure, Claire was blunt to the point of rude, but truth was truth, however nicely it was packaged.

For the duration of the trip back Heather was aware from a distance that she was mouthing the right answers as her sister rattled on speculatively about her chances with Theo.

America had taken Claire's arrogance and honed it into a lethal weapon. Heather had visions of Claire gradually dismantling all the confidence she had slowly gathered for herself over time and had to tell herself not to be over-imaginative. But she was finding it difficult to remember the reasons she had once admired her stunning sister, and to put her finger on the loyalty she had always shown to someone who now seemed shallow and just a little cruel.

CHAPTER TEN

HEATHER was standing in the middle of her small sitting area and surveying the sight that now greeted her with dismay.

They had arrived back at the flat the evening before, and after a quick cup of coffee she had retired to bed. That in itself had been a further cause for stress. Claire had objected to being planted on the sofa in the sitting room, claiming that she was so exhausted after her long haul flight that surely she could have the bed for *one night*.

The old Heather would have easily obliged. The new Heather had seen the start of a precedent from which it would be difficult to backtrack. In the complicated world of family dynamics Claire had always been allowed to get her own way, whatever the cost to everyone around her. The bed for 'one night' only would become a permanent state of affairs, and Heather was just not going to let that happen. So she had stuck to her guns and had even refused to make up the sofa, instead handing her disgruntled sister a bundle of linen and, as politely as she could, telling her to get on with it.

Obviously she had got on with more than just making up the sofa and going to sleep. Rudimentary unpacking had begun, and the effects of it were a glaring reminder of why she had to make sure her sister moved out as quickly as possible.

Clothes trailed out of unzipped cases. Some had been stacked on one of the chairs but the rest randomly covered the ground, seemingly in an attempt to stage a complete takeover of all available free space. The towel she had given her sister the night before had been dumped over the coffee table, and the clothes Claire had worn were a rumpled heap at the bottom of the sofa on which she now lay, sleeping like a baby.

Heather's first impulse was to scream. Then to begin tidying up. She did neither. Instead, she marched across to the sofa and gave her sister a brief but very firm shake.

'Come on, Claire. Time to get up.'

'Uh.' Covers were pulled up over her head as Claire squirmed into retreat from the intrusion.

Heather took a deep breath and did the unthinkable. She yanked the covers right off her sister and watched as the very scantily clad body writhed in protest and then Claire finally sat up and glared.

'It's nine,' Heather said calmly. 'And you can't carry on sleeping in here. This place needs to be tidied up, for a start.' She looked around her with irritation. 'I told you last night, Claire, my flat is very small, and I'm not going to live in a state of chaos, cleaning up behind you…'

'I never *asked* you to!'

'Because you assume that I will…!' A flood of unfortunate memories took a stranglehold and Heather had to calm herself by taking deep breaths. Then she perched on the edge of the sofa—the lovely pale sofa she had bought, after much indecision, only a few days previously. 'I'm not tidying up after you, Claire. And I'm not allowing you stay here indefinitely, doing whatever you want to do, bringing back whatever friends you decide to bring back, until such time as something better comes along. This is *my* flat, and you're not going to move in and wreak havoc with it.'

Claire was wide awake now and glaring. 'Mum would have a fit if she could hear you now!'

'That's as maybe…' Heather thought that their mother might have been quite proud. 'But I'm just laying down a few rules and regulations…'

'Oh, you and your rules and regulations!' Claire leapt out of her bed, lean brown body barely clothed in a clinging vest and a pair of stretch pyjama shorts.

Heather noted that her sister was positively bristling with anger, and worked out that for once in her life she was having to deal with the harsh reality of not being treated as special. Claire had done a great deal of bristling in the past, and had always succeeded in getting her own way. Heather thought with some regret of the extent to which she had aided and abetted her sister's selfishness by tiptoeing around her, backing off rather than facing an unpleasant confrontation.

Feeling very serene, she watched as Claire stormed out of the room. There was the sound of the tap being run and things being slammed down in the bathroom, then she was back, scooping up her clothes with the ill grace of a child who had thrown a temper tantrum but lost the battle.

'There,' she announced finally. 'Happy?'

'No. You'll have to clear the lot into your suitcases and then put the suitcases behind the sofa. It's no good piling them into bundles on the ground. There's not enough floor space and it looks horrible.'

While Claire continued to grumble, Heather went and made herself a cup of coffee and some toast for her breakfast. That was something else she wasn't about to start doing.

Cooking for her sister, who was faddy in her eating habits and inclined to complain.

No wonder Theo had felt sorry for her, Heather thought sadly. He had sussed Claire out from the word go and presumed that Heather was no match for her.

'You haven't made me any breakfast.' Claire materialised in the doorway of the kitchen and folded her arms. 'If you're going to be horrible to me, then I'll leave right now. I *thought* you might be happy to see me, but *obviously I was wrong.*'

'I *am* happy to see you, Claire, but I'm not so overjoyed that I'm going to hand over the keys to my flat…' *Not to mention my life.* 'Anyway, where would you go?' She sighed. 'I don't understand why you left America in the first place. I thought you were having a brilliant time there. I thought it was the sort of place *where anyone with ambition could strike out.* Not like England which was *too small and narrow-minded.*'

Claire looked uncomfortable, then she shrugged and strolled into the kitchen and began going through the contents of the fridge.

Even from an impersonal point of view, and feeling pretty strong at that moment, Heather could still reluctantly admire her sister's utter contentment with her body. She doubted she would ever get to that point in life, however mentally strong she became. Having always been conditioned to think of herself in elephantine terms, showing off her body would have been an alien concept.

Claire sat on one of the chairs, bread, butter and honey in front of her, and began preparing a sandwich without the benefit of a plate to catch any falling crumbs. Her silky flaxen hair fell around her face like a curtain, flicking up against her thin tanned shoulders. 'Anyway,' she said between mouthfuls, 'I could always go crawling to your pal Theo for a roof over my head.'

Her face adopted the expression of someone doing a few mental calculations. 'I mean, I figure he would let me stay, since he knows you and he'd be kind of doing you a favour…'

'You can't do that!' Heather said sharply, her colour rising, and Claire looked at her shrewdly. 'Ah. Why not? Would that be because you don't believe in asking for favours unless you're, like, best friends with someone? Or would it be because you might just be a *teensy-weensy bit jealous*?' She grinned and pretended to look innocently surprised at her own processes of deduction while Heather looked at her in silence. 'I knew it! I just got a *feeling*. I thought that you two might have had something going on, but of course that would have been ridiculous, which means that you must have had some kind of crush on him!'

Heather could feel her sense of power and control begin to seep away. In an effort to hold on to it, she stuck her chin out and said with bravado, 'Why do you assume that Theo and I *didn't* have *something going on,* as you put it?' Phrasing it as a question, Heather didn't feel so bad about revealing the possibility of the truth just to shut her sister up.

With determination, and a good following wind, Claire could strip her of all her defences just when she thought they were firmly in place. Winning the battle over the tidiness issue was one thing, but going back to that place where she had lacked the strength to believe in herself was quite another matter. Heather wasn't about to let that happen without a damn good fight.

'Because I don't. You wouldn't be able to keep that kind of thing to yourself, for a start.'

'I don't want to be having this conversation.' Heather stood up abruptly and turned her back on her sister's amused, taunting face. She felt hot and bothered. In a minute she would have to escape, go out, but she had a sinking feeling that the conversation would resume the minute she was back in her flat. A tide of frustration and anger clawed at her throat. Not only had Theo demolished her life, now here was Claire, picking over the wreckage.

In the midst of her miserable thoughts the doorbell rang, and never had she been more pleased to hear it peal through the flat. She briskly turned around and realised that Claire had similarly risen to her feet. Her privacy was beginning to look like a thing of the past. She didn't stop to question her sister's state of dress. She just felt mightily annoyed at the shadow trailing in her wake as she pulled open the door, expecting to find Beth.

Claire skidded to a halt behind her as Heather stared up at Theo. She was wearing a hunted, harassed expression, and in that fleeting instant Theo knew he had done the right thing. He held out the blood-red roses and stepped through the door, past a shell-shocked Heather, to be confronted by her sister, who seemed to be wearing very little and not be much ashamed of it, judging from the broad smile on her face.

'We were just talking about you,' Claire announced with satisfaction. She strolled across to the sofa and sat down, drawing her knees up. 'That's really sweet of you to bring us some flowers. I love roses. They're my favourite.'

Theo hid the distaste from his face. He couldn't imagine what nature of conversation Heather and her sister had been having, but Heather looked fairly distraught. She had managed to scuttle away, and he could glimpse her in the kitchen, doing something industrious with the roses.

Even with her back to him Theo felt as though he could read her mood, see it in the slump of her shoulders.

'Come sit by me.' Claire patted a space on the sofa next to her, which Theo ignored. 'I have a little favour to ask of you,' she carried on as Heather emerged from the kitchen, wiping her hands on her trousers and then hovering in the background. Claire obliged him with a hundred-watt smile. 'Heather's been having fits since I arrived here.' She pouted attractively. 'She can't bear the mess—even though I've tidied it all away.' She coiled one strand of that impossibly silky hair around her finger and wriggled her toes. 'So here's my request…is there *any chance* that I might kip down in your place for a couple of days…?' She inclined her head teasingly to one side and managed to give a very good impression of a beautiful lost little kitten in dire need of a kindly helping hand.

Heather gritted her teeth together and wondered what was going through Theo's head. She was only just recovering from the shock of seeing him, and was beginning to wonder about those red roses. He wasn't a flowers and chocolates kind of man. More the sort to get his secretary to purchase something impossibly expensive as a gift, or to arrange a flight to Paris for lunch for a woman. She had done enough gift-purchasing in her time to know that his gestures were expensive but entailed almost no effort on his behalf. She wondered, jealously, if her feisty self-willed sister had managed to strike some chord in him, and was chewing her lip and pondering the possibility when he turned to look at her.

'Somehow I don't think Heather would approve of that arrangement,' Theo drawled, moving behind Heather and resting his hands on her shoulders.

Heather's brain went into immediate shutdown. All she was aware of was the feel of his hands through her top, gently massaging her shoulders, and his warm breath against her hair. Her intention to pull away was brutally ambushed by leaden legs that suddenly couldn't function properly.

Claire's expression had gone from flirtatious helplessness to frank confusion.

'I don't see what Heather has to do with anything,' Claire eventually said, recovering her aplomb. 'Actually, you're wrong about that, anyway. Heather doesn't want me here.' Her lip wobbled. 'She practically told me to leave.'

'I can understand why, judging from the state of chaos in this place.'

'It looks worse than it is,' Claire stammered, backing away at speed from her damsel in distress routine in a scramble to reassure Theo that she would be a very tidy guest. 'I wouldn't make a scrap of mess in your apartment. In fact, I'm kind of looking for work at the moment. I could do whatever Heather did when she worked for you. And…' Claire smiled triumphantly at her sister, unnerved by the way Theo was draped around her protectively '…you wouldn't have to worry that *I* might embarrass you by developing an unhealthy crush…'

Heather wanted the ground to open up and swallow her. Her face had gone bright red. She knew that without the benefit of any mirror. Telling Theo what she had worked out for herself had been a low trick on her sister's part—but then Claire had always been full of low tricks, to which she happily resorted if she thought they would help her get what she wanted. Right now she wanted Theo—and his apartment.

Heather felt movement return to her stricken limbs as Theo moved away from her to stand by the window, obliging Claire to twist around to look at him.

'I don't think you're getting the message, Claire,' he said, his voice dripping cold disdain. 'You won't be staying in my apartment.'

Claire's mouth sagged open in shock, and Heather could see her sister regrouping her ammunition. She almost felt sorry for her. Almost, in fact, waded in with a soothing confirmation of her own offer of free lodging. In the nick of time she bit back the instinctive sympathetic response.

'You haven't told her, have you, darling?'

'Told me *what*?' Claire demanded.

At the same time Heather said, gaping, 'Told her *what*?'

'About us…' Theo felt a powerful kick of sweet satisfaction as he strolled towards Heather. Claire looked as though she had been whacked on the head by a sledgehammer. Her mouth had formed a perfect circle of pure astonishment.

He slung his arm around Heather's shoulder and pulled her against him, expecting some resistance but encountering none. He didn't know why, but his heart was soaring. He could feel her tremble slightly, and he wanted to tip her face up to his and kiss her.

'About *you*?' Claire looked between them in bewilderment. 'What about you?'

'That we're engaged…'

Heather was appalled by the lie, but just for a few precious moments she savoured the unique sight of her sister looking utterly flabbergasted. The colour had left her face and her attempts to speak emerged as strangled gasps.

Through the fog of her muddled thoughts she was aware of Theo talking, expressing surprise that the little confidence hadn't been shared between sisters—but then they weren't exactly close, were they?

In the middle of his coolly confident revelation Claire leapt to her feet and shot off to the bathroom with a handful of clothes, to re-emerge seconds later, upon which she slammed out of the flat without so much as a goodbye.

Heather felt inclined to say a big thank you to Theo for providing that moment of uncharitable satisfaction—which was wrong, she knew, but she *was* only human after all, and it would do Claire no harm at all to discover that her sister wasn't the complete nitwit she seemed to think she was.

Instead, she wriggled away from Theo and turned to face him, chin up, arms folded.

'What possessed you to say *that*?'

'Are you going to tell me that you didn't get a kick when you saw her face?' In truth, Theo didn't know what had possessed him. Why had he said that? And why did he feel disinclined to *un*say it?

'That's beside the point,' Heather stormed. 'What gives you the right to come here on a *rescue mission*? No, don't interrupt!' She flung herself onto the sofa and hugged one of the cushions to her. Tears squeezed themselves out of the corners of her eyes. 'You felt sorry for me. Am I right? Poor Heather can't look after herself when it comes to the big, wide world. And she can't look after herself when it comes to tackling her sister.'

Theo walked towards her and sat at one end of the sofa, keeping his distance with difficulty.

When there was no reply to her self-pitying outburst she finally looked at him, and looked away just as quickly. Something in his eyes seemed to suck the breath out of her body.

Heather no longer trusted her responses to this man. She reminded herself that in his presence she was continually walking on quicksand. She had given herself wholly to him, and in her naïveté had been pushed away. She wasn't going to repeat the same mistake twice. Although his expression was tearing down her defences and making her want to rush into his arms.

'I can't believe you would enter into this stupid charade all over again,' she said in an unsteady voice.

'That *would* be crazy,' Theo agreed in a low voice.

'Claire isn't going to just disappear conveniently, like your mother did, leaving you the chance to fabricate some story about us drifting apart. She's going to be around, and she's going to be asking loads of questions that I won't be able to answer.'

'I expect she will be.'

Heather looked at him in angry frustration. It was okay for him to sit there, staring at her and agreeing with everything she said, but he wasn't going to have to pick up the pieces. Claire might have been stunned by his revelation, but admitting the truth to her would be equally dramatic. Heather shuddered when she thought about it.

'You have no right to barge into my life and turn it upside down,' she muttered, with heartfelt honesty, and Theo gave her the strangest of looks.

'I might say the same thing about you,' he murmured, flushing darkly.

'I made your life easier.' Heather glared at him over the cushion. 'I was always there, making sure your fridge was stocked and your apartment was clean, buying things for people you didn't have time to buy for, and never complaining when you pointed me in the direction of your computer at ridiculous hours of the night because you had some e-mail or other that just couldn't wait.' She could hear the wobble in her voice as she lashed out at him, but she couldn't seem to help herself any more. Life, recently, had been careering off its tracks, and the arrival of her sister had catapulted it straight off the road.

'You did.'

'And you can stop agreeing with me!' she fumed. 'If you think I'm going to tell you that it was okay for you to concoct a lie about us because Claire was being obnoxious, then you're wrong! *I don't need you to save me!*'

'No, you don't. But maybe I need *you* to save *me.*'

Heather looked at him in sudden confusion. Was this some

ploy? Some other remark that she would stupidly proceed to misinterpret, only to repent her mistake afterwards? But his face, as he leaned towards her, was filling her head with a thousand forbidden thoughts and hopes, and her heart was fluttering wildly inside her.

'Don't,' she said abruptly, slipping off the sofa and retreating to the window, where she stood and watched him guardedly from a safe distance.

'Don't what?'

'Trick me with words.'

In mesmerised fascination she watched as he proceeded to follow her, until he was standing right in front of her, then he leant against the wall and stared down at her. 'Tricking you is the one thing I never intended to do,' he murmured roughly. 'If you think that's what I did, then I apologise.'

'You *apologise*?' She looked at him in confusion. 'You never apologise, Theo.'

'The fact is,' he said heavily, 'the only person I managed to trick was myself.' He couldn't help his hand reaching into her hair, smoothing it away from her face, or his thumb caressing her temple. 'We shared the same space, and I kidded myself that the reason I started looking forward to returning to my apartment had nothing to do with the fact that I would find you there. Then we slept together, and I told myself that it was just sex, that there was nothing more involved. When you left I did my damnedest to accept the obvious truth, which was that that was the way it should be because my life had no room for anything more than passing relationships that wouldn't interrupt the big picture. What I didn't realise was that the big picture was all about *you*.'

'What are you saying?' Heather did her best to choke back

the flood of hope. She closed her eyes briefly, wishing for this moment to never end.

'You know what I'm saying. I came here to win you back. But I want more than that. I don't just want you back in my apartment, or back in my bed on a temporary basis. I want you in my life for ever.'

'*For ever*?'

'Isn't that what you want too?' He smiled slowly at her, and Heather felt happiness swirl through her from the tips of her toes to the top of her head.

'Yes, I love you. I've always known that.'

'And I love you too. But, fool that I am, I've only just realised it.'

Heather's eyes rounded.

'I hadn't planned on telling your sister that we were engaged, but the minute I said it, it was like *wham*! Everything slotted into place. And I knew that being engaged to you, being married to you, spending the rest of my life with you, was exactly what I wanted. And you *love* me.' He murmured that with considerable masculine satisfaction. 'So will you marry me…?'

Theo did not waste any time. Within four weeks—the most joyful four weeks Heather could ever have envisaged—arrangements were made and they were married in Greece, surrounded by family and friends and fussed over by his mother.

Claire was invited, and she attended. Reversing the power balance within their relationship was going to take time, but they were already on the way. Claire had poured her heart out to Heather, had admitted that America had been a big mistake and that she had become involved with a married man who had damaged her emotionally, leaving her badly equipped to discover a sister who was not only going somewhere with her career but in love with a man who adored her back.

Now she rented the flat that had been Heather's, as Heather and Theo had moved to his country house—the perfect place, Theo said, grinning, in which to bring up the children they would have together.

In the silence of the bedroom, after a blissful marathon of lovemaking, Heather gazed adoringly at Theo as he slept, his ridiculously long lashes drooping against his cheekbones. His hand rested possessively across her and she sighed with pure pleasure, adjusting her body so that long brown fingers slipped across her breast and lay there. He opened his eyes and smiled at her.

'You wanton woman,' he murmured in a low, sexy voice. He marvelled at how, every time he looked at her, he felt his heart swell with pure adoration.

'Well…' she gazed at him with a smile '…we have to get a move on if we're to fill some of these bedrooms with the pitter-patter of tiny feet…'

THE GREEK'S
BRIDAL PURCHASE

BY
SUSAN STEPHENS

Susan Stephens was a professional singer before meeting her husband on the tiny Mediterranean island of Malta. In true Modern™ style they met on Monday, became engaged on Friday and were married three months later. Almost thirty years and three children later they are still in love.

Susan loves her family, her pets, her friends and her writing. She enjoys entertaining, travel and going to the theatre. She reads, cooks and plays the piano to relax, and can occasionally be found throwing herself off mountains on a pair of skis or galloping through the countryside.

Visit Susan's website: www.susanstephens.net. She loves to hear from her readers all around the world!

Don't miss Susan Stephens's exciting new novel, *Italian Boss, Proud Miss Prim*, available this month from Mills & Boon® Modern™.

PROLOGUE

'IT's time you found a wife, Theo. You have responsibilities. If you agree, I will transfer my controlling interest of the Savakis shipping line to you upon my death. If you refuse, I sign this.'

'This' was a document that would consign the company to the greed of the old man's remaining cronies on the board, Theo Savakis realised, holding the stare of his grandfather, Dimitri.

Dimitri had been a chairman in the old style, squandering his wealth and caring little for the welfare of his people. Was Theo to lose everything he had built up during his tenure as acting chairman at the whim of such a man? Should he stand back and see the company slump back into ruin, the people he cared about thrown out of work? Or should he do as Dimitri wanted: marry a virgin and breed from her?

'You leave me no choice.'

'Don't sound so bitter, Theo. What am I asking of you— that you should go find a young girl? Is that so much?'

His grandfather's gesture made Theo's stomach clench with disgust. The wheedling he was accustomed to, but the cynical use of women as breeding stock, the dynastic marriages that so often failed between prominent Greek families?

Those he would never embrace. '*Theos*, Dimitri! This is the twenty-first century—'

'Exactly.' The old schemer cut across him. 'Where would you get such a bargain today? All I'm asking for is your signature, Theo. And for that you get your own shipping line, with a woman thrown in.'

His grandfather's domineering personality had broken his father's spirit, driving Acteon Savakis into a life of self-indulgence. That would never happen to him, Theo had vowed silently. After his parents had been killed in a tragic accident he had seized the helm of the Savakis shipping line and devoted his working life to rebuilding the company into a world-class business. His grandfather had retained a controlling interest, and if Theo was to realise his vision for the future he had to inherit those golden shares. To achieve this it appeared he must commit to a marriage before he had even identified a bride.

'I want my name to live on, Theo,' Dimitri wheedled. 'Is that so hard for you to understand?'

Hard to understand? No. Dimitri's life had been entirely self-focused. But it was Theo's family name too, and he was damned if he would allow the Savakis shipping line to fall into the hands of his grandfather's sycophants. 'I will sign,' he agreed. 'On one condition. *I* choose the mother of my child, Dimitri. *I* choose my bride.'

'No.' The old man shook his head. 'I have already found you a woman.'

'A virgin?'

'Cut the cynicism, Theo. Lexis Chandris is the daughter of my closest friend.'

As good a reason as any to refuse, Theo mused as his grandfather opened his arms wide.

'At least give her a trial…'

'A trial?'

'Don't play the innocent with me, Theo. Take her to bed, and—'

'Yes—thank you.' He silenced Dimitri with a glance.

'Her father has already sent her to Kalmos—'

'He's *what*?'

'I told him you were intending to take the yacht there, and that it would be a good opportunity for you to take another look at her. Surely you can see the advantage of making such a marriage? I'm talking about the daughter of another shipping family. Together the two companies will form an impregnable empire. You can't avoid your fate, Theo. This is your destiny!'

'No, Dimitri. I make my own path through life.'

Theo held his grandfather's stare until it faltered, and Dimitri shrugged. 'Well… But if you want me to sign over my shares you must settle on a woman before I die.'

'That may not be possible.'

'Not good enough, Theo.'

The fate of the Savakis shipping line was hanging in the balance. 'Very well. I give you my word.'

'Excellent. Lexis won't be wasted. I hear she's beautiful, but if she's not to your taste just use her and send her back.'

Theo stared at his grandfather in disbelief. Each time he thought Dimitri had plumbed the depths, he managed to surprise him. 'Is this how you treat the children of your friends?'

'You're too soft, Theo.'

'Really?' Theo wondered how well Dimitri knew him. He might have been brought up beneath his grandfather's roof after the death of his parents, but they were still strangers to each other.

'Remember,' Dimitri cautioned, 'if you shun this girl you must find another before I die. But stay away from trouble.

No artistic types, no Cinderellas, and no worthy causes. I see you looking at me with distaste, Theo, but you and I are from the same mould—destined for greater things than hearth and home. Some women understand that—my friend's daughter would understand that. Other women look for something more, something we can never give them.'

'And what's that?'

'Love, Theo. Now, will you sign?' Dimitri Savakis pushed the relevant document across the desk.

Uncapping his fountain pen, Theo signed below his grandfather's signature, adding the date, and then, for the last time, he shook Dimitri's hand.

CHAPTER ONE

KALMOS. A tiny island, set like a gem in the Aegean. Perfect.

Miranda leaned over the rail as the ferry reversed its engines and drifted slowly into port. It had taken an age, but, however slow and primitive the inter-island ferry might be, it was better than trusting her life to the small turbo-prop aircraft that made the same journey. Her knees were still knocking after the flight to Athens.

She was in a crowd of maybe twenty people waiting to disembark, the only pale and silent stranger in a cheery mob of smiling faces. The sun gave you licence to raise your voice, to laugh out loud, to catch someone's eye and greet them like a friend...

'Oh, no, thank you, I can manage!' She dragged her roll-along suitcase a little closer as an elderly man tried to help her with it. He took it anyway.

She waited for the familiar anger to surge up inside her, and then realised she wasn't angry. Well, that was a start. Anger was such a destructive emotion. If she couldn't lose the anger she would never heal inside, and those wounds were far more serious than the damage to her arm.

Thinking she was behind him, the man had already lifted her bag and walked away. She caught up with him onshore.

'*Efharisto*. Thank you.' She smiled, practising one of the essentials she had picked up in her phrasebook.

'*Parakolo*.'

Still beaming, he turned back to his group after returning her courtesy.

He was intent on his family, she noticed, and suffused with the type of joy that made her feel wistful. She had cut herself off from her own family. She had lied to them. She had said she would teach for a short while—just until she regained full use of her arm.

'*Adio*,' he called, waving as she walked away.

'*Adio*,' Miranda called back. It was such a thrill not to be stared at, or to be treated any differently.

Miranda Weston, world-class violinist. She had led a charmed life up to the accident. Afterwards she had become an embarrassment, usually discussed in the third person, as if her hearing had gone along with her ability to make music.

She had never been weak; she couldn't afford to be. You couldn't show a tender underbelly in the world of classical musicians—not unless you wanted it ripped out. But the accident had stripped all her confidence away. She'd lost so much. She had been faced with two options: to stay in London, where everyone knew her, or to leave the country and start again, one building block at a time.

The irony was that what had allowed her to make this trip were the royalties for her one and only CD, which had landed on the doormat at just the right moment. She had been hugging herself in a huddle of misery at her apartment, curtains still drawn against another unwelcome day. But when she'd read the cheque she had been forced to count the noughts three times. *How* many copies had she sold?

That had been the turning point, when she had decided to get away—partly to avoid telling a family that had sacrificed so much for her about the latest prognosis on her ruined arm, but more in an attempt to redefine herself and find new purpose and direction for her life. Perhaps she couldn't be an international violinist, but she had to be *someone*. She couldn't just step off the bandwagon altogether.

The tiny Greek island of Kalmos was far enough away for people not to know who she was or who she had been. And she was attracted to the sunshine, the sea and the swimming—something she could still do, and *had* to do if she wanted to improve the movement in her arm.

As people started to drift away from the quay Miranda gave a happy sigh and turned her face up to the sun, revelling in the knowledge that at last she was free. Free from the past and free from those who wanted to manipulate her. She was still stinging from memories of her own Svengali figure, the manager who had directed her career only to try and turn her into a sob-story for the tabloids when she was no longer any use to him. And she was still suffering from nightmares after the accident that had destroyed a lot more than a career.

But she would not sit back and let others cast her in the role of victim. She would rebuild her life, but on her own terms. And one very good way to make a start was to locate her apartment, unpack, and find a job. That was her target for today.

Tomorrow, the world…

This was as close to perfect as it got. She had a sea-front balcony, and the sea was an improbable shade of blue. The sky was even bluer, if that was possible; in fact all the colours seemed a little brighter here on the island.

She had chosen Kalmos because the girl at the travel agent had said it was the most picturesque and least commercialised of all the Greek islands. Well, it was certainly beautiful, and her simple apartment was in a prime location. Set in a small block, it was in the centre of a long sugar-sand beach. And, just as she'd hoped, there was a taverna within walking distance.

She'd travelled light, knowing she wouldn't need much in a hot climate, but she had brought a couple of special outfits just in case she found some singing work. When she had been a student at the music *conservatoire* she had brought in extra money by singing with a band. It hadn't paid too well, but she'd usually got a free meal as part of the deal.

And if she couldn't get work as a singer she would take any job. She felt sure that whatever happened would give her a whole new view on life. It wasn't everyone who got the chance to start over with a clean sheet.

Miranda's optimism took flight. Her twin, Emily, had met her prince the night a dose of flu had kept Miranda in bed, putting Emily on stage in her place. One night was all it took...

Yes, but get real, Miranda, she told herself. *Lightning never strikes twice in the same place. And even if it does, it's life, and it's up to me to sort it out.* Even Prince Charming waiting in the wings couldn't change her mind about that.

Quickly twisting her long black hair into a respectable coil, she pulled on a jade green T-shirt the same colour as her eyes. Satisfied that she was ready for her first job interview, she added a slick of lipgloss and grabbed her bag.

The golden sunlight embraced her the moment she stepped outside. Miranda could feel all her tension easing away as she slipped sunglasses onto her nose and shifted the strap of her bag containing music and all the other paraphernalia associated with auditions. She had no idea what to expect, and it wasn't easy to strike a balance between, *Yes, I would love to sing for you,* and, *Yes, washing up sounds perfect,* when it came to achieving the right look.

She had gone for understated, wearing what she imagined

would become her daytime uniform: plain top, cropped pants and flip-flops. Flip-flops because she had to walk across the sand to her first job interview. Who wouldn't be smiling?

It didn't take Miranda long to discover that a nut-brown friendly individual named Spiros owned the taverna.

'And this is my wife, Agalia.'

'Miranda.' Miranda smiled back at Agalia, who was just as round and sunny as her husband. She had a feeling everything was going to be all right. The couple's welcome was so warm, and it wasn't long before Spiros was offering her a job. Waiting on tables, singing, working behind the bar—anything, as and when required, he said.

Concerned about letting him down, Miranda quickly explained that she might not be quite as dextrous as the rest of his staff and might be better off in the kitchen. Spiros only made a dismissive gesture, barely glancing at her hand. The pay was minimal, but the clientele was rarely demanding, he reassured her, and, above all, she was their friend and a welcome guest to the island.

She needed this like oxygen, Miranda realised. Real people—people without an agenda, people who didn't know the celebrity she had briefly been. Out here on Kalmos she was just someone else on the brink of life, testing what the world had to offer before the weight of responsibility tied her down. It was all the therapy she needed. She could feel the tension easing from her shoulders, and smiled happily when Spiros and Agalia suggested she should join them for lunch.

'I can't think of anything I'd like more,' she said eagerly.

'You must be tired after your journey?' Agalia suggested, passing a dish of plump green olives and a basket of freshly baked bread.

'No, not at all.' It was true, Miranda discovered. She was infused with life already, as if friendship and sunshine had washed warmth through her veins. 'I haven't felt so good for such a long time.' She blushed, noticing her blunt admission had cast a shadow over the faces of her hosts. 'To Kalmos,' she added brightly, determined to restore the mood again as she raised her glass in a toast.

'To you, Miranda,' Spiros and Agalia chorused warmly, exchanging the briefest of glances before chinking glasses with her.

The moment she woke the next morning Miranda was overwhelmed by disappointment and frustration. The nightmare had come back. She had hoped the change of scene would help, but here she was, tense and trembling, because of the deep-laid guilt that was her constant shadow. Maybe she would never escape…

But if that were the case she had to learn to live with it and get on with her life, or the guilt would destroy her.

Swimming. Yawning, she stretched. That was what she would do. She would fight the mental demons with exercise. She loved swimming, she was good at it, and it was essential if her arm was to improve at all.

She had been swimming every day back home, to try and strengthen it, and here she had the chance to ease the tight muscles of her hand in the healing waters of the sea. The ugly red scars had faded a little since the accident, but her fingers were still awkwardly bent, and her arm hadn't straightened properly either. It was always a little stiff to start with, but if she had to undergo physiotherapy anywhere, Kalmos was the place.

Heading for the water, Miranda tested the temperature with her toes and found it warm. She had always been a good swimmer, confident too, and this was one thing she had really been looking forward to.

She hit the current when she was about a hundred yards

out from the shore. There was no tell-tale sign, no gradual tug on her legs—nothing to alert her at all. It came fast, like so many watery hands, pulling her out to sea. For a few seconds she panicked, and started flailing around, but then she relaxed into the drag, keeping her head above water to try and work out how to steer herself to safety, or find something to grab on to—a rock, an anchor chain, anything…

Then, just as suddenly, the current spewed her out into calmer waters. She picked a course back with greater care, taking a route that would take her closer to the moored boats. She had learned a valuable lesson, and would show the unpredictable current more respect in future.

When she first heard the whine of a high-powered engine she had no idea that the speedboat was heading straight for her. The moment she realised, she shot up an arm to warn of her presence in the water. She caught a glimpse of a man standing up in the bow, and then he slewed the boat around, swamping her in the wash. The next thing she knew he was dragging her on board, and she was coughing up seawater on his deck.

'There are dangerous currents between these two islands. What did you think you were you doing?'

The deep and very masculine voice was like a rasp on metal, and about as welcome as a curse. She couldn't talk and choke at the same time, which held her back from stating the obvious. She put out her good hand to shut him up.

'*Vlakas!*'

'I beg your pardon?' She hadn't a clue what he had said, but knew it wasn't nice. Rather than showing remorse after swearing at her, the man gave another, equally scathing sound of contempt as he tossed a heavy towel across her shoulders.

Miranda dragged it around her shoulders, taking a moment to recover from the shock. Then, shading her eyes, she gazed up. The man drew himself a little taller.

'You people stop at nothing, do you?'

He sounded so hostile. 'Do we know each other?' she enquired coldly.

'I expect you know me from a newscast, or from some journal.'

'Oh, really?' She pressed her lips together, trying not to smile. The situation was suddenly very funny. The man must be someone famous—but who was he? She didn't have a clue. It appeared they both feared the consequences of fame, and were both mistaken in imagining their celebrity had found a worldwide audience. It made her feel better. In fact, it made her feel great.

'So what is this?' He glanced around suspiciously. 'A set-up?'

'A set-up?' She struggled into a sitting position. 'What are you talking about?'

'The rescue…was it a device to get a good photograph?' He scanned the shore. 'Where's your cameraman?'

'Are you insane?' She choked back a laugh.

'So this is just a coincidence?' he asked sarcastically.

He was really quite stunning, she saw now, but that was no excuse for his behaviour. 'A coincidence?' she repeated. 'What do you mean?'

'*Vlakas!*' he muttered again, apparently on the edge of fury.

She cooled rapidly at his tone. 'Right. First of all, I didn't need rescuing. And secondly—'

'What?'

'Secondly, don't bark at me!' That wasn't what she had intended to say, but she didn't like his tone of voice; she didn't like the arrogant way his feet were planted on the deck; she didn't like the way he was towering over her.

'You're lucky I was around to bark at you. I might have been dragging your lifeless body off my anchor chain instead.'

And then, before she could answer him, he added, 'How long have you been watching me?'

'Watching you? I had no idea you were so fascinating.'

'Oh, so you didn't notice my yacht?' His turn for sarcasm.

Following the pointing finger, Miranda blenched. There it was, a huge white monstrosity, sleekly sensational and totally unmissable, though from her apartment she might not have seen it. 'I didn't see it—and anyway, how would I have known it was yours?'

'The same way you recognised me, I imagine...from some tawdry magazine.'

Anger shot her to her knees, then to her feet, and at the sudden movement the small craft rocked perilously beneath her, throwing her against him, flesh on flesh, brief, warm, frightening. She pulled away fast.

'You'll have us both in the sea!' He roared the words, planting his legs apart like some rampaging pirate, straddling the deck to steady the boat with sheer brute strength.

'You're yelling at me? When you almost drowned me?' She planted her hands on her hips. 'What the hell did you think you were doing, turning your boat around in the water so quickly like that?'

'Trying to save you! You nearly drowned through your own stupidity. I had to act quickly before you were dragged under again. Didn't you think to ask about the currents before you went into the sea?'

'*Excuse* me?' She was ready for battle, but it wasn't easy doing battle with a bronzed opponent wearing nothing but clingy black swimming shorts and a diver's watch.

'Idiot!' He glared down at her.

The distraction wore off fast. She suspected he was translating, in case she hadn't got the message that he'd been insulting her before. 'So, who the hell are you?'

'Theo Savakis,' he said, with a gust of disdain. 'As if you didn't know.'

'Well, I didn't know. But now that I do—is *idiot* your favourite word, Mr Savakis? Or is it just that your vocabulary's rather limited?'

That stalled him.

'And now, if you've quite finished, I'd like you to take me back,' she added, gesturing towards the shore.

To her surprise, his lips quirked at one corner—as if he wanted to laugh, as if it was the first time anyone had ever spoken to him that way. But he quickly got over it and hardened his expression.

'Now would be good.' She drummed her fingers on the side.

'Before we do that you might want to…' He dipped his head rather than elaborating, and then she discovered that one of her breasts had parted company with the top half of her bikini. Tilting her chin a little higher, to stare him in the eyes, she made the necessary adjustment. But holding his gaze was a mistake. She hadn't expected such humour. And he did have very beautiful eyes: grey, with extremely white whites, and the pewter-grey iris was rimmed in pitch-black, like his hair…

'The shore?' she reminded him, but unfortunately her voice came out as more of a squeak than at the volume she had intended.

'When I'm ready…'

A flutter of alarm spread outwards from Miranda's heart as Theo Savakis continued to stare at her. Firm mouth, uncompromising bearing, and showing not the slightest intention of allowing her to stare him down. He didn't have a melting point anywhere. And, in spite of not liking him, she liked that.

'That arm looks sore. Have you seen a doctor?'

Now she was completely thrown. No one talked about her injury. Most people turned away, too embarrassed even to admit its existence.

'Several. Can we go now?' Instinctively she moved her shoulder back, hiding the worst of the damaged area by angling her body—something she'd become rather good at.

He seemed lost in thought as he narrowed his eyes. 'Like I said, when I'm ready.'

Was he trying to place her? Not a chance, Miranda realised thankfully. No one knew her here in Kalmos. The chance of this brute remembering her fleeting appearance on the world stage was as unlikely as slicing a loaf of bread with a banana. As far as he was concerned she was just one more tourist, lowering the tone of his precious island. He would soon forget this incident, and file her away with the rest of the trash.

'I know you…'

Her look of blank disbelief was greeted by an infuriatingly confident smile. And as colour raged into her cheeks he rasped a thumb across some early-morning stubble.

'All right, I forgive you. I guess you weren't looking for a scoop. But I must admit I'm a little confused as to what you're doing here on Kalmos.'

'Only a little?' Miranda drew herself up. He was mistaken. He couldn't possibly know who she was.

'Aren't you the violinist Miranda Weston?'

CHAPTER TWO

'I WAS the violinist Miranda Weston.'

'Of course. Your arm…'

And then he didn't just glance at it and look away. He gave it a good long stare, as if assessing the level of damage. 'I seem to remember reading something. It must have been a serious accident?'

His words echoed through her, bringing all the horrors of the nightmare back. His blatant disregard for convention was hard to believe. No one discussed a serious injury with a stranger. Theo Savakis should have known that. He had no right to be so blunt. He should have shown more control, more consideration for her feelings, more sensitivity—

'What are you doing here in Kalmos, Miranda? Recuperating?'

She made a noncommittal sound. She wanted to be out of the spotlight. She didn't want to answer his questions. She didn't want to be drawn into conversation by someone whose very wholeness and vigour was like a distorting mirror at a fairground, that reflected her disfigurement and made it seem more pronounced.

'You couldn't have chosen anywhere better to recuperate than Kalmos—'

'I'm getting cold.' She spoke churlishly, not caring what he thought of her manner.

Turning away to the controls, he put his hand on a lever and moved it out of neutral. He opened up the throttle, and pointed the slim fast craft towards the shore.

She didn't speak on the ride back. It would have been impossible anyway against the noise of the engine. She waded in the last few yards to shore, after he'd helped her over the side of the boat, feeling horribly exposed in her skimpy bikini, and almost brandishing her injuries under his nose like a warning to leave her alone. She didn't think she had much to worry about, though. His type avoided imperfections as though they were catching.

But on the walk back to her apartment Miranda felt an ache growing inside her. Theo Savakis hadn't looked at her in the way a man looked at a woman when he wanted her in his bed. But why would he want her, when she was angry and touchy—damaged inside as well as out?

And now she was feeling sorry for herself again, which was everything she had vowed to leave behind.

It was absurd to feel like that! Theo Savakis was possibly the most obnoxious individual on the planet. And yet, in spite of that, she did feel something for him…a tingle? More like a full-throated roar! Under the circumstances, that was nothing short of amazing—because she hated sex. She'd only tried it once, and that had been a disaster. It had hurt, and had made her feel like an object. She had stared at the wall until it was over. She could still remember the peeling paint in the student bedsit…

Theo's touch had been firm and warm. Safe? She couldn't say, but at least it had been completely impersonal.

When Miranda closed the door of the apartment behind her she sighed with relief. So much had happened, and it was good to be alone. She had thought her time on Kalmos would allow for a slow healing process, conducted to the sound of seagulls and lapping waves. She had not expected to be thrown into a full-scale drama with a man like Theo Savakis.

But at least the incident had proved one thing. She was daring to tap into emotion again.

Miranda threw all her energies into preparing for her first day's work at the taverna. She showered and dressed quickly, tying back her hair and not bothering with make-up, telling herself she was going to forget Theo Savakis. She was going to love working at the taverna. She could feel it in her bones. And no one was going to spoil it for her.

'*Oy!* Miranda! It's great to see you!'

Spiros looked up as she approached the wooden jetty where he was washing down tables.

'Would you like me to do that for you?' she said, running up the steps.

'You can help me if you like.' Dipping into his bucket, he squeezed out a second cloth and handed it to her. They started working companionably in the same easy rhythm.

'We're having a party tonight,' Spiros told her when they had finished. 'I know it's short notice, but would you sing for us, Miranda?'

She had offered to sing, she had even come to Kalmos hoping to sing, but all Miranda could think now was that she hadn't been in the spotlight since the accident. She hadn't sung in public since her student days, which in fairness weren't so very far behind her—eighteen months, two years, perhaps. Her professional career had been so short...

'If you'd rather not, I understand. We have a *bouzouki* band, so there will be music during the evening. It's up to you, Miranda.' Cocking his head to one side, Spiros waited for her answer.

'Of course I'll sing for you.' How could she possibly let him down? And she had no intention of hiding away for the rest of her life either. 'I brought some backing tapes with me, and a dress. I'd love to sing for you, Spiros.'

'That's settled, then.'

'And I'll come over early tonight, so that I can help you in the kitchen, too.'

'You're like a member of my family already,' Spiros declared happily. 'And tonight you'll meet some more of my relatives. It will be like one big, happy family.' He beamed at her. 'Why don't we go and see what Agalia has prepared for our breakfast?'

She dressed simply that evening, in clean Capri pants with a loose white shirt over the top. She wanted to be comfortable, and Spiros had told her that none of the staff at the taverna wore a uniform. Most of them were relatives, she understood, marvelling at the size of Spiros's family. She packed a dress as well, something she could wear for singing, as well as some decent shoes, and put everything, including her backing tapes, into a large soft bag.

Standing on the balcony before she left, she felt a rush of excitement. She could hear the taverna springing to life; she could hear rolling waves mingling with the conversation. Gathering her long hair into a loose ponytail at the nape of her neck, she smiled with anticipation.

Once she was outside, she slipped off her sandals and picked her way across the cool, damp sand. It was a romantic way to go to work, and there was even a full moon, Miranda noticed, gazing skywards. Anyone on earth would have envied her at that moment. And she was lucky. People got killed in car accidents like the one she'd had, but she had been given a second chance—and she wasn't going to waste it.

But when she drew closer Miranda's mouth dried as she saw how many people were piling into the taverna. Was this Spiros's idea of a family reunion? But then he *did* have a rather large family, she remembered wryly. Even so, she had been expecting a party, not a stadium event! She had envisaged a low-key gathering, which would have given her the opportunity, after so long an absence, to mount the stage and sing a few songs without any pressure.

How wrong could you be? There were dozens of cars in the car park, and headlights were still streaming in procession down the hill!

Keeping to the shadows beneath the jetty, she took her time brushing sand off her feet. Anything to put off the moment when she had to walk into the light and be noticed...

'Miranda—there you are! Come and join us!'

As Spiros hurried down the steps to greet her Miranda came out of the shadows, feeling ashamed that she had been hiding.

Spiros kissed her continental fashion, on both cheeks, and then put his arm around her shoulders, reaching for her heavy bag at the same time. 'You don't know how much we appreciate this, Miranda.' Drawing her with him, he steered her through the crowds already massing in the main body of the taverna. 'Isn't this wonderful!'

As Spiros turned to her, Miranda's tension relaxed into a laugh. If chaos was wonderful, then this was superb!

'How could you fail to feel on top of the world with people like these around you?' Spiros demanded, enthusiastically shouldering open the door into the kitchen. 'This is a very special night for us, Miranda.'

As people glanced up from their tasks to smile, Miranda knew Spiros was right. This wasn't a big city, and she wasn't about to face some critical gathering of classical groupies; this was Kalmos, where life was simple and good.

And yet she was still feeling apprehensive. Which was ridiculous, she told herself firmly. What on earth did she have to be apprehensive about?

It was hot working behind the scenes at the taverna; hot, but good-humoured, and ear-shatteringly noisy. Each time the swing door flipped open for a moment Miranda saw that every age group was represented outside, from the oldest folk in the village to babes in arms. Children were allowed to run free, dodging under the tables and weaving in and out of tightly packed groups, causing even more disruption. But no one seemed to mind, and no one called out rudely to any of the waiting staff. In fact people were just as likely to follow them into the kitchen, choose something to eat, and then help the waiters carry the plates of food back to their table.

'Come and meet my family,' Spiros insisted, shepherding her outside during a brief lull in the proceedings. Resplendent in a crisp white shirt and a bright red waistcoat, heavily embroidered with gold, he looked every bit the proud and successful restaurateur. Agalia, Miranda had learned, preferred her position as kitchen general. Nothing went through the doors without her say-so.

'*Ya-ya!*' Spiros exclaimed, tugging Miranda along with him. 'Meet my young friend, Miranda. He bent to kiss an elderly woman on the cheek, and then straightened up, turning to Miranda. 'This is my grandmother,' he explained with obvious pride, 'and next to her Petros, my youngest son, with his wife and children…'

And so it went on, down the long table, and while Miranda smiled she couldn't help remembering her own family, and the wedge she had driven between herself and them.

'This is what happens when my family comes together,' Spiros explained expansively, extending his arms wide to encompass Miranda. 'Everyone enjoys themselves. And now you are a member of my family.' He struck his chest for emphasis. 'I insist you meet everyone. Come with me.' He tugged her along by the hand. 'I'm going to introduce you to one of my closest friends.'

There was no arguing with Spiros when he was in this mood. Miranda followed happily, and then her smile quickly died.

'Theo, meet Miranda. Miranda, I'd like you to meet Theo Savakis.'

'We've already met.' Theo spoke coolly as he rose from his seat to greet her.

'You two know each other?' Spiros hardly missed a beat. 'That's wonderful! Well, if you will excuse me, I must be getting back to the kitchen...'

Was Spiros's voice coming down a long dark tunnel, or was she going mad? It hardly mattered, because Spiros had vanished, and now there was just Theo Savakis standing in front of her. She couldn't see past him; she couldn't see round him; she couldn't see anything but him. She felt stranded and alone, and very angry with herself for the rush of confusion that had left her speechless. Her first impulse was to follow Spiros back to the kitchen. But why should she do that? Why not stay and make polite conversation for a few moments? Was she frightened of Theo Savakis?

He was waiting for her to say something, with that confident, somewhat amused expression tugging at his lips. Well, she wasn't going to make a fool of herself for his entertainment.

To give herself a chance to regroup, Miranda focussed on a button on Theo's shirt. The button was white, pearly white, and his shirt was very white too—unlike the sliver of toned flesh just visible beneath the placket. And what a wonderful warm, spicy scent...

'Won't you join us, Miranda?'

She jerked back to attention on hearing his voice, and was furious to feel her face reddening beneath his gaze.

'Lexis, make room for Miranda to sit down, will you?'

There were businessmen seated at the long table, several of them still dressed for the office, though they had shed their jackets and dispensed with their ties. Theo appeared to be freshly showered, and was wearing dark trousers with his crisp shirt, and Miranda noticed how waves of his thick, damp black hair caressed his neck. It made her heart lurch unexpectedly.

There was only one other woman at the table—the woman he had called Lexis. She was staring up at Miranda now, brows raised and contempt brewing in her luminous sapphire eyes. She didn't want to move along the bench, not for another woman, and certainly not for one whose face was crimson and whose clothes were spattered with grease stains.

'Don't worry, I wasn't going to stay,' Miranda explained. 'I have to go and help Spiros in the kitchen.'

It was a great excuse, but she hated herself for being such a coward. The look she was getting from Lexis didn't help. She schooled her face to make it expressionless. Lexis was slim, and blonde, and very beautiful. In fact, Lexis was about as close to perfection as it got…

'Lexis! Move!'

Miranda's eyes widened into golf balls. Was that how Theo Savakis spoke to his women? She was equally amazed to see how quickly Lexis got her rear end into gear.

'Miranda?'

Theo indicated that she should sit down in the space that had been made for her, but she didn't feel like joining his harem. 'Thank you, but I'm too busy to sit down.'

'Not too busy to share one drink with me, I hope?'

He made it sound as if it would be rude to refuse, and she was conscious of the other men watching the mini-drama unfold. She didn't want the responsibility of bringing the Savakis universe crashing down, thanks to some mistimed feminist stand. 'All right, but just one.'

As he gave her a mocking bow she took her place on the bench, sliding in beside Lexis, which was like sitting next to a wall of ice. Theo appeared not to notice. He appeared to be completely, infuriatingly relaxed.

'Spiros tells me you're going to sing for us tonight.'

He leaned towards her as he spoke, so that she had no place to look but into his eyes.

'That's right.' She felt as if she was being sucked down into some very complex shadows.

'Chef and cabaret singer? We had no idea your friend was so talented, Theo.'

Lexis's scorn-filled voice made Miranda's back stiffen, but she was careful not to show her feelings.

'How did you say you two met, Theo?' Lexis pressed.

'I didn't.'

If he had given an hour's explanation he couldn't have generated more interest around the table. And was that amusement tugging at his lips? Miranda looked away quickly as he straightened up.

'Gentlemen—and lady,' he announced with some ceremony, 'allow me to present Miranda—'

Miranda tensed, waiting for Theo to announce her full name, waiting for the questions that would inevitably follow—questions she didn't want to answer.

'I had the opportunity to see Miranda briefly in London once,' he said, with barely a pause, 'and then, by some incredible coincidence we met again on the beach this morning.'

'Incredible,' Lexis murmured. But her voice was lost in the

general buzz of interest. Lost to everyone, that was, except Miranda.

Miranda stared at Theo. Why had he lied about seeing her in London when they had never met before this morning? He held her gaze, as if willing her to say nothing, and she dipped her head minutely in gratitude at the way he had handled the situation.

'And now Miranda's here on Kalmos, working as a Jack-of-all-trades for your good friend Spiros?' Lexis observed. 'How convenient for you.'

Did Lexis think she was Theo's mistress? No, out of the question. So was *Lexis* Theo's mistress? Miranda was surprised at the force of her rejection of this thought. Why the hell should she care a fig for his domestic arrangements?

Raising the glass of wine Theo had poured for her, she tipped it in a toast.

'*Ya sou sas*, Miranda,' Theo responded, with a faintly curving smile. Everyone at the table but Lexis echoed his words.

'So, is this how you make your living?' Lexis said, opening her eyes a little wider.

This was no innocent enquiry, Miranda realised. Lexis's eyes were as bright as if she had a fever. The fever to stifle competition? 'If you mean do I work for a living,' she replied pleasantly, 'the answer is, yes, I do.'

'You're a busy woman, aren't you, Miranda?' Theo spoke in a relaxed manner, to dispel the tension that had brought a sudden hush to the table.

Was that barely perceptible sound—something like a cat snore—Lexis sniggering? Miranda wondered. She was still burning from her innuendoes.

'*Mezedes?*'

She collected herself as Theo offered her a plate loaded with delicacies.

'Thank you, Theo.' She was determined to stay now, determined to face it out, determined to keep her voice neutral. She was not going to let Lexis insinuate that she was a rich man's tart and get away with it.

Agalia's snacks lightened everyone spirits; they were delicious crispy filo pastry parcels filled with spinach and a soft, tangy cheese. But after a few moments Lexis said, 'Doesn't *that* make life hard for you?'

Miranda paused mid-munch. 'I'm sorry? What are you talking about?' And then she saw the curl of distaste on the other girl's lips as Lexis stared at her injuries. And now the men were looking too—except for Theo.

Perhaps because he wanted to distract everyone from Lexis's deliberate jibe, one of the older men said in an overly loud voice, 'I have a complaint to lodge with you, Theo.'

'Which is?' Theo demanded good-naturedly.

Miranda noticed how easily he smiled, even when he sensed a joke at his own expense coming along. The smile lit up his face…

'You always have the most beautiful women seated next to *you*.'

There was a chorus of agreement as the tension drained away, and Miranda suspected Lexis must be preening, flashing her perfect white smile.

'Well, you know what they say, Costas…'

Miranda held her breath, wondering what Theo was about to reveal.

'A beautiful woman is like a painting. Having one doesn't stop you wanting another.'

She almost choked on her pastry. Everyone else was laughing now, including Lexis. And Theo was staring at her with that same mocking challenge in his eyes. How had she ever thought him attractive? How had she ever come to relax her guard? She should have known Greek tycoons were hardly standard bearers for equality, but did this one have to be the worst type of alpha male?

Her cheeks were blazing. She couldn't bear to have complete strangers evaluating her—though Lexis seemed to take it in her stride, as if they were both on the open market.

She stood up abruptly.

'Miranda? Where are you going?'

She looked down coldly at Theo's hand, resting on her arm. 'Will you let me go, please? I've got work to do.' Why would he possibly want to keep her at the table—to humiliate her some more?

He stood too, shielding her from the rest of the table. 'Won't you stay a little longer?'

'No, thank you.'

'You don't appreciate my sense of humour?'

Her eyes were cold. 'I love it.' Moving past him, she smiled at the other men. 'I enjoyed meeting all of you.' Turning back to him, she said crisply, 'Thank you very much for the drink.'

'Must you go?' Lexis's query was loaded with sarcasm.

'I'd love to stay and chat with you, but as you know I have to sing.'

'Oh, yes.' Lexis sighed. 'We're *so* looking forward to that—aren't we, Theo?'

Theo didn't answer. In fact, he barely shrugged. His eyes were shuttered, and Miranda guessed he wasn't used to women walking out on him without permission.

Tough.

He might be gorgeous, but as far as she was concerned he was a patronising misogynist. Any man who collected women like so many works of art was an idiot. But as she went to move past he caught hold of her arm and swung her round.

'Do you do requests?'

'No, Theo, I don't. And this isn't a bell chain,' she added, glancing at her arm. 'If you want to ask me something, you don't have to jerk on my arm for attention. You only have to ask.'

'I may have to take you up on that.'

'Please don't,' she snapped.

'I've not made a great start, have I?' he said.

'A start to what?'

Slanting a gaze at her, he put his hand in front of his mouth and blew on his fingers as though they'd been burned. 'Angry lady.'

'Well, you've got something right tonight. Now, can I go?'

With an ironic wave of his arm, he moved aside to let her pass.

It had been hard, wriggling out of her casual clothes in the confined space Agalia had found for her with only one hand working properly, but somehow Miranda had shoehorned her way into the gown. It was a little bit of glamour: a ruby-red sheath, floor-length and fitted. And it was suitcase-friendly, in a crush-free fabric.

Freeing her hair, she combed it through with her fingers. Her face looked deathly white in the mirror Spiros had propped up for her on a shelf, and her eyes were huge and very green. When she shivered now it wasn't with cold—she was petrified. She didn't have an entourage to guard her back, as she'd had in the old days; tonight she was on her own.

Peeping through the curtain, she saw Theo had turned his chair around to face the improvised stage. Lexis was sitting beside him.

Forget Lexis. Did Theo Savakis have to have the sexiest mouth she had ever seen?

Okay, forget that too. Taking a deep breath, she walked into the spotlight.

CHAPTER THREE

THE first song went without a hitch and received enthusiastic applause. Perched on a barstool, Miranda found she was growing in confidence. She launched into a favourite late-night ballad in her trademark smoky voice.

The third song involved walking around the tables. Normally this wouldn't have concerned her, but she had underestimated the difficulty of removing the microphone from the stand with one hand out of action. By the time she freed the microphone she was uncharacteristically flustered, and with a clumsiness born of nerves she caught the heel of her shoe in her gown. As she stumbled, she heard a collective gasp, but the next thing she knew she was being held up by a pair of strong hands.

'This just isn't your night, is it?'

Theo had saved her from falling on her arm and almost certainly aggravating the injury, but close up he looked a lot more dangerous than he ever had before.

'Are you sure you're all right?'

The murmur reassured her; the private smile they exchanged she wasn't so sure about. 'No damage done,' she confirmed discreetly as he steadied her back on her feet.

She made a joke of it with the audience while Theo returned

to his seat, and soon had the good-natured crowd on her side. Only Lexis stared coldly at her, as if she would have much preferred her to stay down for the count. Lexis in her low-cut dress, with half a ton of diamonds weighing her down...

Let's face it, Theo would always have a beautiful woman on his arm. And Miranda had never felt the urge to be part of a crowd...

What was she thinking? Miranda averted her glance from Theo as he sat down. He was nothing to her. So why was her heart beating like a piston?

Closing her mind to everything but the music, she made sure that the rest of the set went without a hitch. But when Theo stood up to leave she was thrown again. She watched him drape a pashmina around Lexis's shoulders and had to force herself to concentrate as he ushered her out of the taverna.

Pausing by the door, Theo wondered if Miranda would notice he was leaving. But she was too absorbed in the music, denying him the chance to take another look into those incredible emerald eyes. She intrigued him and irritated him in equal part. He had never met a woman who was so vulnerable and yet so aggressive. And she was a great-looking woman too, with that fantastic night-dark hair and peachy skin.

Because he had known her in her former incarnation as a violinist he hadn't expected her to be such a good singer. Maybe she wasn't great in the true sense of the word, but she was certainly special: that husky voice and soulful delivery touched him somewhere deep. And that was a talent in itself. No one touched him. Ever.

No one, Theo reflected ironically as he helped Lexis into the car—and especially not his grandfather's choice of bride for him. Lexis was so far short of the mark it was a joke. Whatever Dimitri might have thought, Lexis was a wild child, the

Greek equivalent of an It Girl. She was already pining for the bubblegum generation. There wasn't enough excitement for Lexis in Kalmos—no clubs where she might get herself noticed, no paparazzi hanging round the door, no crazy surfers cosying up to her in need of a loan. He was going to do as she had asked and get her on the first flight home.

It jeopardised the agreement he had signed with Dimitri, of course. But maybe fate was smiling on him. Of course it made no sense in many ways—Miranda Weston was everything his grandfather had warned him against—but that in itself made her interesting.

The business could do without him for a while. Miranda Weston wasn't the only one who needed a holiday…

'We've put a sunbed and a parasol on the beach for you.'

'Spiros?' Pulling the receiver away from her mouth as she subdued a yawn, Miranda glanced at the clock. She had slept right through her alarm! 'I'm sorry, I must have overslept.'

Spiros's reaction was not the reaction of the average employer. His robust laugh forced Miranda to pull the receiver away from her ear again.

'You deserve to sleep in! This is just a little thank-you from Agalia and me for your wonderful performance last night. We want you to enjoy your stay while you're with us on Kalmos. It can't be all work, you know.'

'So you put a sunbed on the beach for me?' Slipping out of bed, Miranda padded across the cool tiled floor to take a look. 'Just a minute while I open the shutters… Oh, I see it!'

She sounded childlike; excited. Perhaps for once she would relax, and he could get to know her a little better, Theo mused, standing at his good friend's shoulder.

'Thank you, Spiros,' he said, clapping the older man on the shoulder. 'I'll see you later.'

Spiros gave him a shrewd stare. 'Something tells me we are going to be seeing a lot of you this visit, Theo.'

Pausing to smile, Theo slipped on his sunglasses again, and kept his thoughts to himself.

Miranda had no sooner settled into the comfortable cushions than she shot up again. The roar of the outboard engine was tuned to a certain key, like a song. Like a warning!

Her heart was thundering as she scanned the glittering surface of the sea, and when the boat came into view she quickly grabbed her wrap and started gathering all her clutter together.

'You're not running away from me, are you?'

She might have known Theo would beat the world record in transfers from boat to shore. 'No, I'm not running away from you,' she managed coolly, but it was a fight to keep her voice steady.

'Is this a private area?' He scanned the deserted beach. 'Or can anyone sit here?'

'Be my guest. I can't stop you.'

'How can I refuse such a charming invitation?'

At least he was wearing more clothes than the last time she had seen him on a boat, Miranda noticed with relief: frayed denim shorts, bleached almost white by the sun, with an old vest top. *Haute couture* for billionaires? She didn't think so. These were the genuine article, not some fancy make that had been treated to a fake distressed finish. He looked like a deckhand, rugged and toned, with wayward hair and a wicked line in smiles.

Lolling back with as much grace as she could muster, she slipped her dark glasses from their perch on top of her head and slowly lowered them onto her nose. 'Why are you here, Theo?'

'Why? To see you, of course.'

Theo hunkered down so their faces were on a level. She

turned her head to look at him and he could see the pulse beating in her neck—her *racing* pulse, fluttering in her neck. He had to govern every one of his reactions, using every trick in the book to keep her from suspecting the effect that was having on him. 'Did I hurt you when I grabbed your arm last night?'

'Only my pride.'

'Well, I'm sorry. I hope you accept my apology?' He was relieved when she inclined her head a fraction. 'I forgot. About your arm, I mean.'

She didn't look convinced. And now she looked uncomfortable. Maybe she thought he shouldn't have broached the topic, but someone had to. 'I don't see you that way, Miranda,' he said quietly.

'What do you mean?'

She had tensed visibly. 'I don't see you in terms of your injury,' he explained. 'That's why I forgot about it.'

'So you weren't just careless?'

'I wanted to speak to you, not your arm.'

Better. She almost smiled. He could see her fighting to hold it in. 'I was at your first concert at the Royal Albert Hall in London. I heard you perform.'

'Oh! Oh, I see.'

'You thought I was lying about seeing you in London?'

'Well, I…'

Of course she had. She made a dismissive gesture, but he could see he had surprised her.

'You must have seen me on my first and last concert tour.'

And now she was off in her own world somewhere. 'So the accident happened while you were in London?'

As he asked the question her desperation for him to change the subject lit up in neon lights. He could never have anticipated that it would have such a bad effect on her. After all, how long had it been—months now, surely? What was she hiding? She wasn't going to tell him now.

He looked at the sky, seeking distraction in the weather. 'The sun gets to everyone in the end. I can see you're in no mood for talking.'

'I am,' she disagreed. And then after a moment she added, 'You still haven't told me why you wanted to see me.'

'I've come to ask you to a party on my yacht tonight.'

He reeled back as she jerked into a sitting position.

'What? As your performing monkey? Or are you short of waitresses, Theo?'

'Neither.' He stood up to put some distance between them. 'I'm inviting you to the party as my guest.'

Slipping her sunglasses down her nose, she gave him a long, considering look—as if she was weighing him up to see whether or not he could be trusted.

'As your guest?'

'That's what I said.'

He watched her drop her sunglasses again and gaze out across the bay at the sleek white colossus he had always thought of as a toy…a toy to entice, as well as a toy for his own enjoyment. He could usually detect a flare behind the eyes when he issued an invitation like this—of anticipation, of excitement. But Miranda wasn't so easy to fathom. After her meteoric rise to the very zenith of her profession she had experienced so many things. Would a party on board a luxury yacht only serve as a reminder to her of everything she had lost?

Lowering her sunglasses to the tip of her nose, she answered his question.

'Thank you, Theo. I'd like that.'

He should have known she would show more character. And there were no fireworks, no acquisitive gleam in her eyes. The only fireworks going off were inside him. 'Good. Why don't you come along with Spiros and Agalia?'

'They're coming?'

As he'd hoped, that relaxed her completely. He wanted to be sure she felt comfortable from the moment she arrived. 'They're invited.' He gave a shrug, as casual as he could make it. 'I'll send a boat for you.'

'See you tonight, then,' she said.

She didn't turn her head towards him as she spoke. He liked that. She was as cool as he was, which had the effect of making him doubly hot for her.

Miranda's outfit was a compromise. She told herself it was simple, but effective.

Amazing how you could convince yourself of anything when you wanted to, Miranda mused as she stared at herself in the full-length mirror in her bedroom at the apartment. She was wearing cropped black pants with plain black sandals—no one would be wearing high heels on an expensive teak deck. So far, so good. She had teamed these with a white strappy top to show off the first hint of a suntan, and had left her hair loose because it made her feel sexy that way. And, yes, okay, because she did want Theo to notice her. And then, because she was still conscious of her scars, no matter how many times she reminded herself that Theo had said they were irrelevant, she added her one and only shawl to the mix, draping it around her shoulders so that it covered her injuries.

Spiros and Agalia were right on time, but Agalia seemed agitated, and Miranda soon discovered why.

'Theo sent a powerboat for us, but Spiros sent it away. He insists on rowing us out to the yacht,' Agalia explained, plucking at a button on the front of her dress.

'It will be lovely out on the water tonight,' Spiros said, looking to Miranda for support.

'Yes, but we want to arrive before the party is over, Spiros,' Agalia pointed out.

'I'm happy whatever we do,' Miranda said, smiling at both of them. 'Really, Agalia, don't worry—this is fine by me.'

But it wasn't fine. In fact it was extremely wet. Within yards of the shore the wind kicked up, and all of them were drenched.

Miranda and Agalia clung onto the sides as Spiros flung his back into his rowing in an attempt to beat the waves threatening to swamp the small boat. Progress was painfully slow, but finally Spiros brought them under the lee of Theo's yacht.

Shielded from the worst of the wind, it was still a tricky manoeuvre to keep the rowing boat in place while they climbed on board. Fortunately, some crew had been watching their progress with concern, and quickly came down the steel ladder to lash the small craft to the stern.

As they threw a blanket round her shoulders, Miranda could see the strings of lights criss-crossing the prow and midships, where the party was being held. A live band was playing, and it was clear the short-lived squall hadn't dampened anyone's enthusiasm. From the sound of it, she gathered it was a large party. She felt reassured, knowing she wouldn't be subjected to scrutiny when she finally made an appearance. She could always lose herself in a crowd.

Thanks to the party being in full swing their arrival had largely gone unnoticed, which was a bonus. At least there would be chance to dry off and recover before she had to face Theo. But Miranda could see that Agalia was angry, and that Spiros's pride had been badly dented. She hurried to reassure them and make a joke of their drenching. Far from being sophisticated guests at a glamorous party, they looked more like three drowned rats.

At last Agalia's face cracked and she saw the funny side of it, and by the time a crew member rushed up to escort them below decks, where they could take a shower and recover, all three of them were laughing helplessly.

'This is not quite the arrival I had planned for you,' Spiros admitted anxiously, chewing the tip of his moustache.

'No harm done, and we'll soon dry off,' Miranda assured him.

They were assigned staterooms where they could relax in comfortable robes after their showers while their clothes were being cleaned and dried for them. They agreed to wait for each other, and to make their appearance as a united team.

'Shipmates?' Miranda suggested.

'Lunatics,' Agalia argued, whacking Spiros affectionately over the head with her wet shawl.

CHAPTER FOUR

By the time the knock came on the cabin door Miranda's eyes had been opened to what it meant to live a life where expense was no object. Banks of snowy white towels stretched to the ceiling in the bathroom, which was of course lined in marble, with all the latest in high-tech fittings. There was even a flatscreen TV on the wall for those idle moments in the bath, not to mention an invisible sound system. In the stateroom itself there were priceless *objets d'art* from right across the globe, and the type of sumptuous fabrics to which the damning label 'manmade' could never be attached. In fact, everywhere she looked everything was of the best.

'I could get used to this very quickly,' she said to herself, padding across to answer the door in a warm, plush robe. 'In fact, I feel like a princess.' She opened the door and smiled at the uniformed steward who stood there.

'Here's your uniform. Hurry up, they're waiting for you in the galley. And don't forget to tie your hair back.'

Miranda's jaw dropped. Her reign as a princess had been somewhat short-lived! Her mouth was still open when the steward had disappeared down the corridor. Flattening her lips, she pressed them together angrily. She should have known. Why had she fallen for it? Had she thought a leopard like Theo Savakis could change his spots in the space of a day?

When Miranda finally emerged from the stateroom Spiros and Agalia were waiting for her outside their own room.

'What on earth are you wearing, Miranda?' Agalia said, staring at the smart black dress and white apron. 'What happened to your clothes?'

'They were taken away, I suppose. These were just delivered.'

'But you can't go up on deck dressed like that. Someone will ask you to get them a drink!'

Spiros's eyes were twinkling, but Agalia soon put him right with a hissing sound and a firm hand on his arm. 'This isn't funny, Spiros.'

'Oh, I see... No, I suppose not,' he said, realising his mistake. 'So what will you wear, Miranda?'

'Why, this of course.' There was steel in Miranda's voice, and the glint of battle in her eyes. If this was someone's idea of a joke, she was about to call their bluff.

'You're not serious?' Agalia was quite clearly horrorstruck.

'Oh, but I am,' Miranda said evenly. 'Don't worry about me. I'm a big girl now. Really,' she added, seeing her two friends exchange a glance, 'I'll be fine.'

Miranda felt Theo's presence on deck before she could see him. And then she spotted him, standing in the centre of an admiring throng with Lexis hovering just on periphery of the group. She felt sure Lexis was in on it, because she kept spearing glances at the companionway leading to the guest suites.

Lexis knew what to expect, all right—but had Theo put her up to it?

With aplomb, Miranda removed a tray from the hands of a passing waiter. 'Don't worry,' she reassured him. 'The weather delayed me, but when I arrived they told me to take care of the drinks.'

He looked at her uncertainly for a moment, and then backed off. Fully armed, she made straight for his boss.

Theo turned immediately. 'Miranda! They told me you had arrived. Thank goodness you're all right! Did they look after you properly? I would have come to see you myself, but there were so many guests…'

'Don't worry, Theo, I can imagine how busy you must have been.'

'Miranda?' Her sarcasm stalled him, and for the first time he looked her over properly. 'What are you wearing? This isn't a fancy dress party, you know.'

'Yes, I do know that, Theo. These are the clothes that were sent to the stateroom for me to wear.'

'Don't be ridiculous.'

'I don't think *I'm* the one being foolish here, Theo.'

Without breaking his stare, he barely had to crook his little finger for the same waiter she had swiped the tray from to reappear.

'Take this tray from Miss Weston, will you? And have someone find Miss Weston's clothes. I believe they're being cleaned and dried out, so you might start in the laundry room.'

'The laundry room? I'm impressed,' she said stonily.

'Then you impress far too easily.' There was a glint in Theo's eyes.

'So you're not responsible for sending this uniform to my stateroom?'

'What do you think, Miranda? I'll be in my suite,' he added to the steward.

'What do you think you're doing?' Miranda could feel Lexis's gaze boring into her back as Theo took a firm hold of her arm and steered her towards another flight of steps.

'We'll talk when we get there.'

'No, we'll talk now.' Stopping dead at the top of them,

Miranda firmed her jaw. 'As far as I know, I'm not hanging on your wall just yet.'

'Meaning?'

'Remember those paintings you were bragging about, Theo? Well, I'm not one of them. And I'm not going anywhere with you until you tell me what all this is about.'

'All what?'

She pointed to her outfit. 'Will there be another set of clothes delivered to my stateroom later on, for when I have to sing to your guests?'

'I'm disappointed in you, Miranda, if that's what you think of me.'

She drew an angry breath and mulled it over for a moment. Truthfully, she couldn't picture Theo wasting his time on such a clumsy put-down. 'You didn't pull this stunt, did you?'

Theo levelled a stare on her face, brow raised, eyes amused.

'So, who did, then?' Miranda tried to ignore the fact that her heart was thundering.

'I think we both know the answer to that.' Theo gazed down the deck to where Lexis was dirty-dancing in the shadows with another young guest.

'But I thought you and—'

'Me and Lexis?' Theo cut across her. 'Not this side of sanity, Miranda, I can assure you.'

'But you both seem…'

'To know each other? We do. Lexis is the daughter of another shipping family.'

'Oh. I see.'

Switching the clothes must have been Lexis's infantile idea of a joke, Theo guessed. He wanted to reassure Miranda that the other girl held no appeal for him, and was relieved when he saw a faint smile on her lips.

'I found it hard to believe that it was you,' she admitted.

He smiled, easing his shoulders in a shrug. 'Please accept my apologies anyway.'

'I do.'

'But why would Lexis do a thing like that? Why feel the need to be so unpleasant?'

'Because she knows I don't want her, and she sees you as competition.'

'Me?' She looked incredulous. 'Oh, come on.'

He had to be careful what he said. Miranda didn't see herself as beautiful…which said *what* about his feelings towards her? It might be an idea to find out. 'Can I offer you a drink while we wait for your clothes to arrive?' When she looked back towards the party he found himself adding, 'In my stateroom. I'll make sure they call me there.'

Theo's lips were curving in a way Miranda wished she didn't find quite so attractive, and his eyes were clear and frank. 'Well, I…' But then she remembered that he wasn't always quite so uncomplicated. 'I'm not sure I should.'

'And why is that?'

'Should I go to a man's stateroom when he admits that he views women as so many works of art? I'm not sure I want to be considered as a possible collectable.'

It surprised him to feel a rush of satisfaction seeing her confidence had returned to the point where she would challenge him. 'You're right to be cautious. But I should tell you that my collection is priceless.'

Women or paintings? Miranda wondered. And then she realised that she was dangerously close to flirting with him, and cooled her expression.

'Are you coming or not?' Theo pressed. 'I thought you wanted to get out of those clothes?'

'I do.'

'Then come with me. I can assure you my crew will find yours and bring them to us there.'

He gestured towards the shadows pooling at the bottom of the companionway, but as he sought to reassure her Miranda's mind was racing. Why wouldn't Theo remain on deck to mingle with his guests? Why couldn't one of the stewards tell her when her clothes had been found? But of course as a considerate host it was his duty to make sure everything turned out all right after the way she had been treated...

'Although that *is* a very fetching outfit,' he observed, reclaiming her attention. 'The Peter Pan collar is a particularly nice touch.'

'Well, I feel ridiculous!'

'I can assure you that you don't look the least bit ridiculous to me.' And now he'd said too much. He stepped back, putting some distance between them. She was still uncertain, and the last thing he wanted was to move too fast.

'What if they can't be found?'

As she turned her face up to him he felt his heart thud heavily in his chest. This was extraordinary, this feeling inside him...but not unpleasant. 'If the worst happens I'm sure we'll find you something else to wear.'

'A negligee? A French maid's outfit?'

She wasn't ready for this, Miranda realised as he smiled devastatingly. Flirting with Theo Savakis was out of her league. But then she saw Agalia and Spiros and they were giving her an encouraging nod. They had been on their way over to talk to her and had halted mid-step, realising who she was talking to. Surely they wouldn't send her below decks with a man they considered dangerous? And, as Theo had pointed out earlier, she couldn't stay at the party wearing fancy dress. 'All right,' she agreed finally.

* * *

Miranda's pulse gathered speed as she gazed around Theo's fabulous stateroom. It was about three times the size of the one she had been allocated. But she had to ask herself—what was she doing alone with him?

'I'm going to call and see what progress has been made,' he said. 'And in the meantime…' He gazed at her as he punched in some numbers on the phone. 'I can only apologise for the inconvenience you have experienced so far this evening.'

'Thank you. You're a very considerate host.'

'And you're too kind.' He pulled a wry smile, and then turned to fire off some words in Greek. 'Now we wait. Don't look so worried. I can assure you I don't bite. Won't you sit down?'

She headed for a straight-backed chair, stiff and uncomfortable.

'You'd be better on the sofa.'

'I'm fine here,' she assured him, perching on the edge of her seat.

'We didn't get off to the best of starts,' he commented ruefully. 'I had hoped that this evening would make up for it.'

'Don't worry, it can only get better.' Now, why had she felt the need to reassure him?

They both turned at a knock on the door. But rather than her clothes it was a waiter, with a tray of champagne and some scrumptious-looking canapés.

'The evening hasn't been much fun for you up to now,' Theo explained, 'and I didn't see why you should have to miss the party. Champagne?'

She hesitated, wondering if he had planned it this way. 'How long do you think my clothes will take?'

'As long as it takes you to drink one glass of champagne.'

His smile was infectious. 'And if I drink quickly?'

'Two.'

Theo was looking at her in a way that made it impossible to think the worst of him. 'Okay, I'd love a glass.'

'Feel free to remove your apron.'

'What? Oh!' She laughed easily for the first time. Life looked so much better through a cloud of champagne bubbles.

'Another glass?' Theo suggested, before she got round to the apron.

Why not? She wasn't used to drinking, and was still a bit edgy. Time was ticking by with no sign of her clothes. She had downed the first glass of champagne in a thirsty gulp, and the second slipped down just as easily. She was a little unsteady on her feet by the time she stood up to sort out the ties at her back. 'Is this boat moving?'

Theo was at her side in an instant, with a steadying hand beneath her arm. 'I'll order some orange juice,' he said, deftly freeing the knot at the back of her waist.

'Perhaps black coffee would be better...' Theo's face seemed very close as she stared up at him. 'Lots of it, and strong.' She wasn't prepared for him capturing a tendril of her hair to wind around his finger. 'Theo...'

'Miranda...'

He said her name in a teasing way, and she wasn't sure if Theo drew her closer or if she swayed towards him. She only knew that their mouths were almost touching, and that her lips were tingling, and that she was happy to drown in the scent of sandalwood and clean warm man. 'What's happening to me?'

'I would have thought that was obvious...'

She frowned and pulled back a step. 'Why are you whispering? Why am I?' She shook her head. 'And why am I flirting with you?'

'I don't know, but you're very good at it. Shall I kiss you, Miranda? Would you like that?'

Her body certainly seemed to think he should.

'Let me put it another way—would you rather I didn't?'

'Oh, no, no—that would be fine.' She closed her eyes and waited.

Nothing.

She opened her eyes again indignantly. 'Do you enjoy teasing me?' she demanded, firming her mouth as far as her traitorous lips would allow.

'Very much,' he admitted softly.

'Did you plan this?'

'Hand on my heart, no.' Just a fortunate coincidence, Theo reflected, trying to remember the last time he had owed any thanks to a short-lived storm.

'All right, I forgive you.' Miranda's jade-green gaze flicked up.

Theo drew her into his arms and kissed her chastely on the lips.

Chastely, yes, but he knew exactly what he was doing, Miranda realised as her body yearned towards him.

'Better?' he murmured.

She heard the humour in his voice and ignored it. 'Absolutely not.'

Had she really believed the accident had drained all the passion from her life? Nothing had ever fired her like her lost talent for making music—nothing until just now, when Theo had kissed her. So was this wild frenzy in her mind, this all-pervading sense of rightness, of love? Or was she going crazy? Her body was melting, craving, aching. Had she really put all thoughts of sex out of her life after one failed attempt? Right now she could think of nothing else...

When Theo kissed her again he made it slow, seductively slipping his tongue between her teeth to taste her and then pulling back the moment she softened against him.

Nipping the full swell of her bottom lip, he smiled against her mouth.

'Is this what you want, Miranda?' he murmured, rasping the stubble on his chin against the most sensitive part of her neck.

'No, I don't…' But her sigh told him otherwise, and as she gazed into his eyes—such dark, beautiful eyes—she wanted nothing more than for Theo to hold her.

'Well, this is exactly what I want,' he said.

And then she could only quiver beneath his touch as he feathered strokes down her spine. But when she tried to move closer he pulled back.

'No, Miranda.'

'No?' Miranda's face reddened as she stared up. She couldn't even catch her breath, but Theo was perfectly calm.

'I'm not going to make love to you here, while we're waiting for a steward to arrive with your clothes.'

'Too right,' she snapped, caught in a maelstrom of emotion and desire, and she swung away. Teasing was one thing, but this had gone too far.

Theo caught up with her at the door and gently pulled her back into his arms, holding her until she cautiously relaxed, and when she did it was the most wonderful and overwhelming feeling.

The idea had been growing on him steadily, and now he was sure. He had found his bride. He still had to convince her to marry him, of course.

It was an incredible stroke of good fortune that had brought Miranda to Kalmos. He needed a wife, but feeling as he did about her was a bonus he hadn't expected. Her obvious inexperience made him feel fiercely protective; he looked at her and felt…

The emotions he felt were new to him, and he didn't quite trust them. Therefore he used his business brain to analyse the positives and negatives. She was talented, she was beautiful, and from what he remembered her sister had married a prince. She didn't hesitate to stand up to him, which meant she was likely to keep his interest long-term. Genetically she was clearly sound, and any children they had would benefit from both gene pools. They wanted each other; that much was glaringly obvious. It was blindingly simple, really: this just felt right.

Slowly and carefully he relaxed his grip and let her go. 'You're very special, Miranda, and I want to see you again.'

It pleased him to exercise self-control, but if Miranda agreed to be his bride they would have to be married quickly—and not just for the sake of Dimitri's failing health. He had never found himself in this position before, knowing that no amount of mental control would be enough to subdue the physical desire raging through him. But then, for reasons that completely eluded him, he had never before wanted a woman as he wanted Miranda Weston.

He moved away from the door so that she could see all she had to do was walk past him and leave if she wanted to. She was still quite wary after what had happened between them, still not quite sure of him.

'Go up on deck to get a breath of fresh air if you want to, Miranda. I'll make sure someone comes to tell you the moment your clothes have been found.'

'No,' she said, as if she had come to a decision. 'I'll stay here.'

He felt a rush of triumph as she walked back into the room, and another when she chose the sofa. But as she turned to look at him he briefly felt a twinge of guilt. She'd had a lot to deal with since the accident—it had wrecked her life and she must still be haunted by it. Was it fair to marry a woman like Miranda when he didn't even know if he was capable of love? He didn't have any shining examples of happy family life to draw upon—and didn't she have enough baggage to carry around without him piling more regrets on top of those she had already accumulated?

Dimitri said that when you shut out emotion your journey through life was easy. He had grown up believing Dimitri was right. Even as a child love had seemed to him like an unattainable goal, secretly desired but always denied. As an adult he had learned not to expect it. Letting down the barricades only led to disappointment.

Theo pulled himself together, rejoicing in the fact that, as it always did, logic had saved him. He needed a bride; Miranda needed a protector to care for her while she recovered from her injuries and forged a new life. If she agreed to marry him he would give her the world. In return for the bargain they would forge he would protect her. And love would come from the children they had together.

CHAPTER FIVE

'I ATTENDED one of your concerts, Miranda, and you had me hooked,' Theo remarked, deliberately changing the mood.

'Do you have my CD?'

'Of the Brahms? No, I don't.'

Her frankness had thrown him for a moment, but he wasn't going to lie to her. That was Miranda, he was fast discovering. Always to the point. The type of woman he was used to would have covered for him. Not Miranda. She cut right through the bull, exposing any tiny bit of flattery for what it was: a means to an end. Every flatterer had something to gain. Her career might have been short, but she had learned that lesson. He toned it down. 'I'm not even that keen on violin concertos, but hearing you play—'

'Can we talk about something else, please, Theo?' She cut across him, clearly unimpressed. 'Surely we can find some other common ground?'

'Of course we can.' He searched for something else to discuss, and for once in his life nothing came to him. It was a first. Whether in business or at a social function he was always sure-footed, always confident. He'd have to come up with some new rules of conduct for courting a prospective wife—and fast.

'What's in it for you, Theo?'

He sharpened his focus. 'What are you talking about?' he said carefully.

'Being so nice to me.'

What could he say? He had wanted to make love to her and had then decided that he had more to gain from marrying her? He could hardly tell her what lay behind his interest.

He let out his breath slowly. 'Does there have to be something in it for me?' Tipping his head, he viewed her keenly, and got a direct stare right back. 'Okay.' He held up his hands in mock surrender. 'You're right. I'm usually a better host than this. I let you down tonight and I'm trying to make up for it.'

There was a knock on the door, and when he called out a maid entered with Miranda's neatly pressed clothes in her arms. Although it had been a prolonged wait, rather than complaining he felt like falling on his knees and praising his staff for giving him space. 'Thank you.' Taking them from the maid, he closed the door and turned to Miranda. 'Use my bedroom—or the bathroom, if you prefer.'

Holding the outfit up, she exclaimed, 'They're as good as new. I'm impressed!'

At last, a result! And then he discovered that it pleased him to please her. It pleased him even more to see her smiling and relaxed, because that meant he was one step further forward and they could both relax.

'You're a very lucky man, Theo.'

Wisely, he said nothing.

'I won't be long.' With a fleeting smile, she made for one of the doors he had indicated.

She was almost as good as her word. He only had time to pace round the salon three times before she returned.

'You look lovely,' he murmured. Major understatement.

With her hair loose, the understated outfit, and no adornment other than her sun-kissed skin, she looked sensational.

'Are you ready for the party?' He offered to link arms.

She hesitated for a moment. It was the longest moment of his life.

'Okay.' She flashed him a smile and walked forward to take his arm. 'Let's do it.'

Briefly her trust brought on the guilt again. Why did he have to trap someone so pure and lovely in a web of business strategy? But the business had to be saved. Fortunately for him Miranda was an intelligent woman, and he was confident that she would soon come to see the long-term benefits of his plan. The red-hot attraction between them would make it easier for both of them.

She hadn't known it was possible to have so much fun with a man. When he relaxed, Theo was the best of company. By the end of the evening Miranda was beginning to conclude that she had misjudged him. She had certainly been a little harsh. Even Lexis didn't seem to mind that she was dancing with him. But then Lexis was enjoying herself with a high-spirited group much closer to her own age.

Theo made a point of introducing her to his friends— charming people, some of whom even remembered her starburst career but were sensitive enough not to probe. She could get used to this, Miranda realised, smiling happily, but she also had to remember she was going home soon, and to a very different life.

'Is this a Greek thing?' she found a chance to ask him during a lull in the conversation.

'A Greek thing?' Theo frowned as he leaned closer to hear her over the music and chatter.

Only Theo could smile and frown at the same time, Miranda

thought, feeling her senses stir as she looked at him. 'I mean all the *bonhomie*. It cuts right across every barrier—'

'*Bonhomie?*' He smiled down at her. 'I thought that was a French thing?'

When he teased her in that confidential tone, and leaned close enough for her to feel the sweep of his warm, minty breath, it was impossible to concentrate. 'You know what I'm talking about, Theo,' she chastised him gently. 'Everyone mixes so easily here in Greece.'

'Everyone?' Pulling back, he gazed around. 'We're all the same at heart—surely that's the only thing that matters?'

'Well, I love being part of it.'

'You do?'

She had been too frank—but what the hell? 'Yes, I do.'

'In that case, I've got another suggestion for you.' Taking her arm, he led her to the bow rail, where it was quieter and they could have a little privacy. 'Come swimming with me tomorrow.' He drew her in front of him. 'No strings, no company. Just you, me, and a very private beach…'

'Just you and me?'

He saw the flicker of concern in her eyes and knew he should reassure her, even if he did have rather more style than she seemed to imagine—grinding skin against sand had never been his sexual position of choice. 'You, me…and Agalia as chaperone.'

'Really?'

His suggestion was working. She gave him what he thought of as her funny stare: half-grin, but deadly serious behind the eyes. 'Yes, really.' He pressed his lips down in a wry smile. 'Why shouldn't we invite Agalia? It will be fun for her too.' That swung it. He didn't even wait for Miranda to say she agreed to his idea. 'Great. I'll pick you up at the apartment tomorrow morning at ten.'

'I'll look forward to it.'

He felt like punching the air when she smiled back at him. He had never felt like this before, not even when he'd signed his biggest deal…except, of course, that *this* was the biggest deal. 'That's great, Miranda,' he said, and kept his voice cool.

Agalia took her job as official chaperone so seriously that she arrived at Miranda's apartment shortly after nine to supervise her charge's preparations.

'You will take a shirt to cover up all that nakedness,' she insisted sternly.

Miranda had chosen the most modest costume in her small collection, but she suspected Agalia would have preferred her to don a Victorian bathing suit with matching mob cap. There was only one thing to do. She plundered the sparsely filled rail inside the simple wooden wardrobe, plucking out her comfiest shirt. It was a cover-all, with no sex appeal whatever: a brushed cotton faded plum number about ten sizes too large.

Agalia's face lit up when she saw it. 'Perfect. And you will need this too.'

'A book?' Miranda stared at the heavy, worthy-looking tome Agalia was holding out to her.

'It wasn't easy to find one in English,' Agalia told her, her mouth firming into a 'no surrender' line. 'It is just what you will need when you are sitting quietly in the shade. I have my own collection of books…' Opening her straw basket, she let Miranda peer inside to see a number of well-thumbed paperbacks.

'It's very good of you to go to all this trouble for me, Agalia.'

'Nonsense. How can you go out alone with a man on his boat unless I am with you? And what will you do when you reach the shore if you do not have a book to read?'

Miranda smothered her smile. When two worlds collided

it was better to respect the mores of the host country. Kalmos was tiny, and little changed, she suspected, for centuries. And far from resenting Agalia's attention, she felt as if the elderly Greek woman was standing in for her own mother.

It wasn't that she was a child again, but since the accident she hadn't been so sure of her own judgement...

Theo glanced at his wristwatch again. He was growing impatient. He'd arrived early, and the boat had been moored at the quayside for almost half an hour.

This was the most bizarre situation in which he had ever found himself. Having broken free from all those traditions that irked him, courting a woman in the old-fashioned way was hardly his area of expertise. But if that was what it took...

Here she was, and her eyes were fixed on what he held out to her.

'Flowers?' she exclaimed.

He watched Miranda gaze at the bouquet in his outstretched hand. They looked as if they had come from someone's garden and been carefully arranged before being simply tied at the base with a pale raffia band.

'Oh, Theo! They're absolutely beautiful...'

As she looked up at him her incredible jade-green eyes told him all he needed to know. Their expression was eloquent with surprise and delight.

'Thank you,' she said, taking them from him carefully.

'My pleasure.' He breathed a sigh of relief. Having simple flowers like this flown in from Athens was possibly the most extravagant gesture he had ever made.

'I'll just put them in water.'

She was still smiling when she turned away. It gave him quite a rush. He would normally have been feeling pretty pleased with himself, though for very different reasons. The flowers would have been a single step in a process both participants understood: a process conducted at a pace of his choosing that would lead to the inevitable conclusion in bed. But he had to remember that Miranda was inexperienced, and would therefore be unaware of such devices. Wooing the woman he intended to make his wife was very different from the norm; it required a lot more finesse. Hence the presence of Agalia, and his neatly groomed hair, the white polo shirt and respectable fawn Bermudas. He looked smooth and collected, but underneath he was humming with testosterone. He couldn't help it; that was just the way he was.

'Do you have things for me to carry?' The need to inhale Miranda's fresh, clean scent was starting to get to him.

He was right behind her. She could feel his gaze shimmering down her spine. 'Yes, all my things are over there…' She pointed vaguely. She didn't want to risk looking into his eyes, because there was something so seductive in his smile she didn't know if she could hide her feelings. 'And…' Her mouth dried as at last they locked glances.

'And?' Theo prompted her softly.

'There's Agalia's basket to carry,' she managed faintly.

Theo's 'boat' was a forty-foot sun-seeker's delight.

'I'm using this because one person can handle it and because it has a shallow draft,' he explained. 'The beach I'm taking you to is so secluded it can only be accessed from the sea. The sea at that point is very shallow, so—'

'You dipped into your lucky-bag of boats and came up with this one?' Miranda suggested dryly, coming to sit alongside him in the cockpit.

'Something like that.'

As Theo turned to gaze at her Miranda felt her breath catch in her throat. She quickly looked away, pretending interest in the scenery instead, which was beautiful. But she wasn't fooling anyone—even her earlobes were tingling.

Theo and Miranda waded ashore with the picnic, and then Theo returned to the boat to carry Agalia—as if she were thistledown, Miranda noticed, watching from the shade of a rustling tamarisk tree.

The tremor of alarm she felt at this practical demonstration of Theo's strength made an uncomfortable bedfellow for the frisson of arousal it provoked. All she could remember of sex was that it had hurt and left her feeling violated, and though she wanted Theo she found it impossible to shake off that first painful memory. But, watching Agalia laughing in his arms as he carried her so carefully, she did have to concede Theo had more control over his power than most men, and by the time he had reached the shallows her panic had subsided.

Agalia remained in the shade, lost in her novel, while Miranda and Theo lay at the edge of the surf chatting easily. When the sun grew too hot they retreated to a rockpool in the shade.

'The Greek islands provide sanctuary for more than one hundred species of orchid, thanks to the land having escaped the ravages of chemical fertilisers…'

Theo could have been telling her anything, Miranda thought as she struggled to concentrate. As a musician she had always been fascinated by beautiful sounds, and Theo's rich baritone voice was extremely beautiful…

'So, although the land is poor, there are undoubted benefits—' He broke off. 'You'll have to forgive me, Miranda, but conservation is one of my passions.'

Miranda was jolted back to attention. 'No, go on—I'm absolutely fascinated.' She wanted him to continue talking so that she had an excuse to stare at him. And the fact that he cared so deeply for such things was a both a revelation and a delight. He was full of surprises, and the more she found out about him, the more she wanted to find out about him.

They ate their picnic sitting together on a plaid blanket. The tartan seemed incongruous until Agalia pointed out that the Highlands of Scotland were just one of Theo's favourite haunts. The day had given her the opportunity to find out so much about him, Miranda realised, and she liked everything she had learned. Liking someone added a very powerful dimension to physical attraction. And how could she not be physically attracted to Theo?

She was the very model of reserve, in deference to Agalia, but the truth behind old-fashioned courtship was more startling than Miranda had realised. The sexual tension was extraordinary. The briefest glance, the faintest smile, the smallest gesture—each of them took on enormous significance. She wondered if Theo felt it too. And when Agalia fell asleep in the shade that question was answered.

As Agalia's breathing took on the rhythm of the surf Miranda turned her face to the sky. Closing her eyes, she leaned back on her hands, sighing with contentment. At first she wondered if she was dreaming, or if Theo's fingertips really were touching her own. It was only the lightest touch, but surely it was the most sensuous contact possible? When he trailed his fingertips across the back of her hand she gasped as a pulse of arousal took her by surprise.

Opening her eyes, she stared at him. Putting a finger over his lips, he tilted his head, indicating that she should follow him. Soundlessly, she got up and walked in his wake across the sand.

At one side of the cove the sea frothed and bubbled across some low-lying rocks. They were flat and slippery, and she was relieved when Theo reached out his hand to help her across them. He kept hold of her hand as they walked on around the curving cliff base. This led to a sandy inlet Miranda guessed must have been formed by centuries of waves stealing slivers from the shore.

They didn't speak, but she had never felt closer to anyone in her life. And when he came to a halt and drew her into his arms she didn't resist.

Kissing Theo was like sinking into someone and becoming them, becoming one, and when he finally pulled away to rest his forehead against her brow she saw that he was smiling too, as if they had both shared the same soaring emotion.

'I'm not going to let you go,' he whispered.

'I'm glad.'

'I don't think you understand me.'

'Oh?' Tilting up her chin, she stared at him, waiting for an explanation.

'I can't let you leave Kalmos until I'm sure you'll come back to me.'

'But I'm here for another week—'

'I'm not talking in terms of weeks, Miranda.'

'Then what do you mean?' She could hardly breathe, her heart was beating so rapidly. This was crazy. Surely he wasn't going to ask her to stay?

Taking hold of her hands very gently in his, he kissed each of her fingertips in turn, damaged and undamaged alike, and then the palm of each hand. 'We've known each other such a short time, and yet I feel I've known you for ever, Miranda. I don't want to lose you. I *won't* lose you.'

She could see he was engaged in some inner struggle that didn't allow him to meet her gaze. 'Lose me, Theo? I'm not going anywhere just yet—'

'Ever.'

'Ever?' She stared at him questioningly.

'Will you marry me, Miranda?'

'What?' she breathed incredulously.

'I said, will you marry me?'

Shaking her head, she tried in vain to form some sort of response, but she could only manage, 'But we hardly know each other.'

'We have a lifetime in front of us.'

'But we've only just met! You can't possibly know that you want to marry me!'

But he did. And there wasn't time for a long-drawn-out courtship. 'You'll be leaving Kalmos in a few short days, and I know what I want. I know what I've been waiting for. The only question is how do you feel, Miranda? Do you feel the same?'

'Shouldn't we talk about it first, at least?'

Allow her to ask questions he might have to refuse to answer? 'Yes—or no?' he said flatly, wishing it could be different when he saw the longing in her eyes. He consciously softened his expression, intensely aware of how many people depended on him getting this right.

Miranda saw something in Theo's eyes—a tiny flame. Fanned into life by love? Had they both been struck by the same thunderbolt?

The thought filled her with happiness. 'If you put it like that, then my answer has to be…yes.'

'Yes?' Catching hold of her hands, Theo raised them passionately to his lips. 'You have just made me the happiest man in the world, Miranda.'

CHAPTER SIX

'MIRANDA has agreed to marry me.'

Six words that had changed her life the moment they were spoken; six words that travelled around Kalmos like wildfire and were in the public domain almost immediately after that.

Miranda watched horrorstruck as the news broke on satellite TV. She should have known. She should have thought things through and understood the implications. But here she was in Agalia's snug home, on a remote Greek island, with a mobile phone that refused to work and a landline that was for ever engaged. Her parents, her twin sister Emily—everyone she cared about back home—were about to hear the news that she should have told them face to face. And if they hadn't picked it up on television they would hardly miss the announcement in the papers the next day. If the television anchorman's excitement was anything to go by, the news would make headlines across the world. It wasn't every day that the Greek billionaire heir to a shipping dynasty chose a bride. The fact that Theo Savakis was to marry the musician Miranda Weston had only added fuel to an already raging fire—and she could only sit there raging with frustration.

She had moved into the taverna as Theo had asked, to keep her safe from the paparazzi until their wedding. She hadn't given a thought to legitimate news hounds, let alone the paparazzi! She hated matters moving so swiftly out of her control. What had seemed the only right thing to do was already beginning to feel like a monumental mistake, and she couldn't bear to think that she might have made a second serious error of judgement. The last time she had placed her trust in a man there had been terrible consequences.

The phone calls to her family were the hardest she had ever had to make. They had always been close, but hearing her father's throat tighten when he spoke told her that he thought she had become a stranger whose behaviour he could no longer predict. Her mother had enthused, and had hardly seemed to care that a neighbour had told her first. The only thing that mattered, she said, was that Miranda was safely and splendidly 'set up in life'.

She couldn't blame her mother for enjoying the moment. From humble beginnings, on a modest housing estate, one daughter had won the heart of a prince while the other was on her way to marrying a Greek tycoon. But still Miranda yearned for her father's down-to-earth take on life. His common sense and inward satisfaction with even her smallest achievement was worth more than all the fanfares in the world. He had never asked her to be a world-class musician, he had only wanted her to make a difference. Would she be able to do that when the doors of the Savakis citadel had closed behind her?

She could picture her father trying to calm her mother's triumphant glee as he pointed out that their daughter would be facing the same pressures as any bride, and that marriage to a man like Theo Savakis would be fraught with its own problems. Having delivered such a momentous piece of news, she could hardly ring them back and say she'd changed her mind. And, on the positive side, at least her mother had something to focus on, so that when she discovered the truth about the repercussions from the accident it wouldn't come as such a blow.

The call to her twin sister Emily left her feeling particularly low, because she sensed it had made the rift between them deeper. Emily was still hurt from the way Miranda had pushed her away after the accident, and all she said was, 'But why, Miranda?' She must have repeated that phrase a dozen times. They had never kept things from each other before the accident. What would have been the point when each of them knew what the other was thinking?

The difference between her own family and Theo's was marked. The little she knew of his background sounded so sterile she doubted he had ever experienced emotion until the business world had claimed him. She could understand the attraction. Business gave him something tangible to grab hold of, balance sheets, reports, his own huge and sustained success; all of those cogs in a very visible wheel. Love was different. Love defied analysis. And its path could not be predicted in a neatly bound five-year plan.

So why had she got herself into this situation? Why had she agreed to marry Theo Savakis, a man she hardly knew? Was love enough?

Except, considering it, Miranda realised that life without Theo was already unthinkable. So that was her answer.

'Theo!' Her face lit up as he walked into the room. 'I've finished my calls.'

'Was everyone all right with our news?'

'Well, it came a bit of a shock.'

'That's only to be expected,' he pointed out.

'My mother took it well.'

'That must reassure you.'

No, Miranda realised, it hadn't. Her father was a tender, trusting soul, and she had bulldozed his concerns with a false bravado he had picked up on right away. And she still felt bad about Emily.

'Well, Agalia's excited too.' Theo placed his hands lightly on her shoulders as he spoke. 'Spiros tells me that she's already planning the wedding…'

'The wedding?' Since the accident she had often sought escape in a dream world where everything was lovely and nothing difficult or bad or dramatic ever happened. She had to snap out of it. This wedding was going to happen.

'You look surprised.' Theo frowned. 'There's no reason for delay, is there?'

'Well… Obviously I'd like my family to attend…'

His face relaxed. 'Is that all? I'll bring them over in the jet.'

Miranda felt panicked for a moment. This was a world she didn't understand, a world where anything was possible—for Theo. 'Of course. I hadn't thought of that.'

'Don't worry, it's going to be wonderful.' Coming to kneel at her feet, he took her hands and kissed her damaged fingers one by one. 'And we're going to sort this out too…'

She gritted her teeth. He meant so well, but she just wanted the moment to be over.

'And this isn't the only part of you I want to heal,' he added, seeing her expression. 'There's here, too.' Lightly touching her chest above her heart, he smiled reassuringly.

Miranda smiled back. She felt she should.

Weddings in Greece required a certain amount of red tape, but for men like Theo Savakis, Miranda soon discovered, the rules everyone else was obliged to follow did not apply.

She was racing pell-mell into the unknown, she realised anxiously as they discussed possible dates for their wedding over dinner that night at the taverna.

'I don't want to rush you,' he'd said.

But he did, she sensed, wondering why. Remembering Agalia's excitement, she put her doubts aside. 'Agalia has arranged for my wedding dress to be made here on the island—'

'Here on Kalmos? But I was going to take you to Paris.'

'You don't have to take me to Paris, Theo.' She touched his hand to console him, because he looked so disappointed. 'I couldn't possibly let Agalia down by insisting on some other dressmaker.' She could see Theo was battling to control the impulse to disagree with her. He was accustomed to having everything his own way, but that would have to change. She had no intention of spending her married life following orders.

'All right,' he agreed eventually. 'If you're sure that's what you want. I suppose a simple wedding dress will be more appropriate for such a low-key wedding—'

It was a strange use of words. What was he saying? Suddenly the paranoia from her former life and the suspicions she'd had about Theo flooded back. 'Why? Do you mean it will look good, Theo? Show you in a better light to the rest of the world? The Greek tycoon who appreciates the simple things in life and so marries a damaged woman in order to prove it?'

'What?' He stared at her, aghast. 'Is that what you think of me?'

'I don't know, Theo. I don't know what to think! Why are you marrying me in such a rush?'

'You know why! Because I love you, and some things can't wait.'

Something still bothered her, but she had nothing to go on. Why was a man like Theo Savakis getting married to someone he hardly knew on a tiny island in the middle of nowhere in such a rush? And why was she going along with it so complacently? Was it because this was the easiest way out for her? Was this a head-in-the-sand escape to a handsome, wealthy man who could provide her with all the distraction she needed to forget the nightmares, to forget what had happened to her arm?

'I don't give a damn what our marriage looks like in the eyes of the world,' he insisted, reclaiming her attention. 'The only people who matter are you and me, and after that all the people we care about. I'm surprised it even crossed your mind to doubt my motives. Don't you know me at all?'

'No, Theo, that's the trouble. I really don't.'

Instead of retaliating, as she had expected, he went quite still—as if he had his own doubts to subdue. But then gradually she saw all the old confidence and humour returning to his face.

'Are we having our first argument?' He slanted her a grin.

How could she remain angry with Theo when he looked at her like that? She was suffering from a bad case of pre-wedding nerves, and that was all. She took a deep, steadying breath and told him as much.

'Are you worried about the wedding night?' He had meant it as a joke, and was surprised to see all the blood drain from her face. She looked so young sometimes, so vulnerable…

'No, of course not.'

Her denial sounded hollow, and that worried him. In fact he'd been worried ever since she had made her phone calls home. She had become like a tyre running flat; all the pep had gone out of her. He could understand her family's concern. They knew what it was like for her to be in the public eye—they had lived through it once before.

'I understand your unease after speaking to your family, Miranda,' he assured her. 'They know what you're taking on. But remember I'll be at your side every step of the way. I won't let anything or anyone harm you. And as for our wedding night—' *Theos*, her eyes were wide and troubled; she made him feel like Bluebeard. Reaching across the table, he took her hand. 'I love you. What more can I say?'

Desire might be eating away at him, but he could and he would control it. He had a lot to gain from the marriage, and he wanted to make sure it was successful. He wanted Miranda to be happy, and awakening her to the pleasures of the marriage bed was just one way he could ensure that she was.

'Have I reassured you?' He held her gaze until *he* was reassured, and then turned to lighter things to distract her. 'So, the wedding dress and honeymoon are taken care of…' He ticked them off on his fingers.

'Honeymoon?'

'At least we won't have to travel far…'

'Of course—we're already here,' she guessed, and this time the smile slowly made its way up to her eyes.

She was like a child who wanted to be happy again but who didn't dare believe that she could be, he realised. It made him want to make everything perfect for her. 'There's nowhere on earth more beautiful than Kalmos.' He hoped his eyes reflected all the love he felt for his island, and for Miranda, and that it would shore up her fragile faith in him. 'I hope you're not too disappointed?'

'Disappointed? No, of course I'm not disappointed. Kalmos is the perfect place for a honeymoon…and an idyllic setting for a wedding.'

Her declaration prompted him to say, 'I know we're still building trust in each other, Miranda, and I can see how you must think it strange for me to want to get married with so little fuss. But the truth is Kalmos is my favourite place on earth, and I want to share it with you.'

'What are you doing?' she asked as he dug into the pocket of his shirt.

He had been longing to give her something, and now seeing her face wary but excited was everything he'd hoped for. 'This is for you.' He held it out to her. 'Would you like to try it on and see if it fits?'

'This can't be for me!'

She sounded amazed, and it touched him. She stared spellbound as he eased the wide gold band studded with diamonds onto her wedding finger.

'You don't need to give me a gift like this. It must be very valuable.'

'I want to give it to you. It's a family heirloom. Don't you like it?'

'Of course I do. It's fabulous.' Even as she admired the jewels, Miranda shrank a little inside. She felt as if Theo's high expectations of a wife were encapsulated in his gift of the priceless ring.

'The stones are flawless,' he pointed out.

For a flawed bride? Her disability had never weighed more heavily than it did in that moment. But then Theo drew her to her feet and, raising her hands to his lips, kissed each of her fingers very gently. The intensity of feeling she felt for him was frightening. Theo Savakis could have any woman in the world. He was always so tender with her…but what if he woke up one morning and saw her as damaged goods?

The next day Theo persuaded Miranda to come out on his yacht. He had business to do, he said, and couldn't bear for them to be apart. Agalia was resigned to the plan because Theo's yacht was like a bustling city; the chance of them being alone on a working day was remote.

During the morning Miranda was alarmed to overhear snatches of Theo's conversation while he was talking on the satellite phone. He had left her side and walked a few steps away to ensure his privacy, but one of the less admirable traits of being a musician was the enhanced hearing that allowed her to eavesdrop. An elderly aunt had once accused her of having 'ears on stalks', because she possessed more than the ability to distinguish fine differences in pitch and volume—she could also detect the softest note, the faintest sound.

What she heard was Theo discussing the date of their wedding. 'It can be changed if necessary,' he snapped.

Who was he talking to? And why would he change the date of their wedding without talking to her first? Was this how life was going to be from now on? Ordered at Theo's whim? Blind obedience had never been part of their agreement!

The moment he finished the call she asked him if something was wrong. Before Theo had a chance to answer a member of crew approached with another message for him. She had expected him to be busy, and had brought books to amuse herself, but she sensed that something out of the ordinary was unfolding. Because of it, she curbed her impatience and waited to see what he would say.

Eventually he slipped back into the seat at her side. 'I've been neglecting you. I apologise.'

She waited. She could hardly challenge him and admit to being an eavesdropper. 'Don't worry, I've got everything I need.'

As Theo hummed distractedly she gathered his mind was on anything other than whether she had a cool drink to hand, or enough sun lotion.

So what was happening? She had learned that Kalmos was the island of his birth, and he had talked of moving back into his ancestral home on the far side of the island. She had no idea who lived there now, or what the house might be like; Theo was sparing with adjectives, and 'big' told her nothing. Maybe a problem connected with the property had occurred? Perhaps it wouldn't be ready to move in to by the time they were married and the wedding might have to be postponed?

A prescient shiver coursed down Miranda's spine, telling her it wasn't that.

'Are you cold?'

'No… I was worried when I saw your face, that's all. The phone call?' she prompted.

'It was business.' He shrugged dismissively.

'Business?' She saw a muscle working in his jaw. 'Well, as long as it's nothing that can interfere with our wedding…'

'What makes you say that?'

She shook her head. 'An over-active imagination, I hope.'

Leaning towards her, he took her hand. 'I promise it was just a business call. Nothing is going to get in the way of our wedding.'

'Not even business, Theo?' She said it lightly, but she sensed that he didn't appreciate the interrogation.

'What do I have to say to convince you?'

'Tell me that you love me,' she said honestly, laying her soul bare for him. 'Tell me that you won't let anything come between us…'

He smiled. 'That's far too easy.'

As his lips tugged up and the warmth flooded back into his eyes she had to believe him.

Holding her gaze, Theo took her hand and kissed it gently. 'And as for loving you…I can't believe you still need my reassurance. Of course I love you, Miranda. I've promised to look after you for the rest of your life, haven't I?'

A hollow opened up inside her at his words. Was that it? She felt like a worthy cause he had taken under his wing.

Theo hated lying to her. He had never lied to anyone in his life before. He had never needed to. And now, even though it wasn't strictly a lie, he was deceiving her. The call *had* been about business—about everything he had devoted his adult life to building up. And in a way he had told her the truth too: the wedding wouldn't be spoiled or cancelled. If anything, it would be brought forward. He would have to wait for the doctor's report before he could make a final decision.

He had been warned that the old guard were hovering like vultures round a wounded beast. When Dimitri died it was imperative that the Savakis shipping line remained under his control, and if that meant marrying Miranda rather sooner than either of them had anticipated, then that was what he would do. He could not sacrifice the livelihoods of thousands of families for the sake of decorum and a few hours' delay. If Dimitri's illness was as serious as rumour said, they would marry at once.

'No, Theo! Absolutely not!'

Miranda couldn't even pretend to hide her shock.

Closing the door of the small office at the taverna to give them some privacy, Theo leaned back against it. 'I know this must have come as a surprise to you, and so I'm giving you time to think about it before you give me your final answer—'

'How long, Theo? Five minutes?'

He tipped his head, suggesting *maybe*, and said nothing.

'And if I disagree with your request to bring our marriage forward?'

He remained silent, telling her everything she needed to know.

'Marrying tomorrow is out of the question. I don't know how you can even ask me to do that. What's got into you? Have you forgotten my family? What about the wonderful day we had planned? Or are we just going to rush through our wedding as if you are ashamed of me, as if pledging our lives to each other counts for nothing?'

'Ashamed of you?' The words leapt out at him. How could she possibly think that? But then, seeing her unconsciously nursing her arm, he understood.

Leaning over the desk, he planted his fists so he could stare straight into her eyes. 'You're beautiful, Miranda. Every part of you is beautiful. And I'm proud that you have agreed to be my bride. It's more than I deserve.'

And now he was ashamed of himself. Seeing tears well up in Miranda's eyes told him she was reassured, but saying she was more than he deserved was too close to the truth. He had so much to gain from this marriage, and for the first time since all the pieces of the jigsaw had fallen so logically into place he found himself staring at the picture he had made and hating what he saw.

'Will you hear me out?' he asked her gently. He was confident he had left nothing to chance. The wedding would go ahead the next day—it had to. The latest bulletin said Dimitri was failing fast but had rallied sufficiently to demand proof that their contract would be honoured. Success or failure rested on Miranda. Theo must gain her agreement to the hasty wedding, but above all he wanted her to do so willingly.

'Don't worry about your family.' Going round the desk, he took hold of her hands. 'I have a plan.' Cupping her chin, he made her look at him. 'Don't ask me to wait, Miranda...' And when she started to protest he silenced her with a kiss.

'Okay,' she said reluctantly. 'What's your plan?'

Her eyes were wounded and she was still suspicious. He had to look away when she searched his eyes. 'We will have the civil ceremony tomorrow, and then a few days later we will have a public celebration—a blessing on our marriage with all your family present—'

'A blessing here on the island?'

'Yes. I'll fly everyone over.' It was a nice touch, and he was pleased that he had thought of it. 'I think your family would like that.' He waited tensely to see what she would say.

'We'd have to make sure the date was convenient for everyone.'

Relief flooded over him. 'Of course. I'm sure we'll find a suitable date—and don't worry about the ceremony tomorrow. It won't go unmarked. Agalia has already started the preparations—'

Her mouth fell open. 'You told Agalia before you told me?'

He had to harden his heart and take whatever she threw at him. 'Only so she could start getting everything ready…' But his excuse fell on stony ground.

'This is a *fait accompli*, isn't it, Theo? I have no say in it at all!'

Everyone thought business was hard at his level, but they were wrong. *This* was hard. 'You know how much I want you, Miranda. Don't make this difficult for me…' Instead of softening, her gaze hardened, and she pulled back when he tried to embrace her.

'I don't understand why we must change our plans and bring the wedding forward—and why go to the trouble of a second ceremony? Why not wait for my family to arrive, as we agreed, and have all the celebrations on the same day?' Getting to her feet, she went to stare out of the window with her back turned to him.

'Why all the questions, Miranda? It seems perfectly obvious to me.'

She turned. 'Then perhaps you'd care to explain your reasoning?'

That he couldn't do. 'I can't believe you aren't excited.' He was growing impatient, and in fact he felt quite wounded. Surely any bride should be delighted at the prospect of an eager husband? And his commitments to the business wouldn't wait.

She looked startled at his tone, then visibly made an effort to speak calmly. 'So your suggestion is that we marry tomorrow, quietly, with just a couple of witnesses?'

'Agalia and Spiros. Perfect, yes?' He was smiling, relieved that she had seen the sense of it. Dimitri might be a warhorse, but even Dimitri couldn't hold back the tide of mortality. It was crucial that he moved fast.

Miranda shook her head. 'There's more to this than you're telling me, Theo.'

'Are you calling me a liar?'

She didn't speak for a moment, letting him draw his own conclusions, and then she said, 'You tell me that you love me, and that you want to court me properly and respectfully, in the old-fashioned way—'

'I do!' He bit back the other things he wanted to say to defend his position. He did love her—if love meant wanting a woman in your bed, wanting her and no other to bear your children, wanting her soothing and reliable presence waiting for you when you'd had a stressful day's work...

'And yet a man in your position wants to rush everything through on this tiny remote island?'

'I love you, and I want you with me always, Miranda. *Theos!* I've given you my reasons—'

And then the penny dropped. Of course. Miranda's twin had married a prince at the cathedral in Ferara. He took a moment to calm down.

'I'm not trying to rush things through or hide you away. I'm sure that if you asked your brother-in-law Alessandro whether he would have preferred to take Emily away and marry her quietly rather than share such a precious moment with hordes of strangers, you would find Alessandro would envy us...' He saw with relief that at last he had said something she could agree with.

Miranda couldn't work him out. Did she know Theo at all?

Or was she back in that half-world where reality could conveniently be put on hold? Kalmos was supposed to have been the setting for her climb back, her fight back—but how far was she going to get when she couldn't even trust the man she loved?

And why was she feeling so heated, so uncertain? Theo's promise of a formal blessing on their marriage with all her family present was such a romantic idea. And a village wedding too—what could be lovelier?

And he was right. Hadn't Emily been almost unbearably tense on her wedding day, fully aware that the eyes of the world were on her? Theo was sparing her all that, and she was shouting at him.

'I'm sorry, Theo. I'm overreacting… I must be suffering from pre-wedding nerves.'

He softened immediately. 'You don't have to apologise, Miranda. It's my fault for being so impatient.' Taking her hands, he raised them to his lips and kissed them reverently. 'Do you agree to my plan?'

They would be the centre of media attention soon enough. One day of privacy in which to make their solemn vows was the most precious gift Theo could have given her. 'I agree,' she said softly.

'You've made the right decision,' he assured her, and she felt the tension in him relax.

'It's wonderful!' Agalia exclaimed when Miranda told her the news after lunch. 'It's so romantic! I knew the moment Theo told me he wanted to marry you that it would have to be soon. And now he is bringing the wedding forward! Don't worry— it's no trouble to me. The dress can be finished quickly, the feast prepared in an instant, and Spiros already has a new waistcoat…'

How could she give voice to all her worries about the future in the face of such enthusiasm? Miranda forced her concerns back behind a smile. As far as Agalia and Spiros were concerned Theo was the most wonderful man on earth. She was on her own when it came to doubting his motives for bringing the wedding forward.

'Tomorrow! Just think of it!' Agalia enthused, breaking into her thoughts.

'Tomorrow…' Miranda heard a faint note of alarm in her own voice.

'Don't tell me you had forgotten the day of our wedding, Miranda?'

'Theo!' Miranda turned and smiled at him. 'I didn't see you there.'

'You're a very lucky man, Theo!' Agalia embraced him.

'You think I don't know that?' As he gently disentangled himself Theo saw that at the sight of him Miranda's face might have been lit from the inside. For all her concerns about the hasty wedding she was resilient and adaptable; she was a woman he would be proud to call his wife. He produced the bouquet of flowers he was holding behind his back with a flourish.

'You spoil me,' she said, smiling up at him.

'I haven't even started to do that yet,' he murmured, holding her gaze.

'I'll leave you two alone,' Agalia said happily. 'But I'll be just inside my room, Theo, and I think I'd better keep my door open.'

'Quite right,' he agreed. 'You can't be too careful when there are ardent suitors on the premises.'

'You think I don't know that?' She slapped his arm playfully on her way past.

'I thought you would be too busy to come and see me this afternoon, Theo.' She looked up—but Miranda never just looked at him: she plumbed his soul. 'What's wrong?' she asked.

He tensed. She could read him like a book. Some of his advisors thought it would be better for the wedding to be held immediately—in the dark, if necessary! He had disagreed. There were only so many times he could manipulate the woman he intended to marry. 'Nothing's wrong,' he said evenly, 'other than my impatience to hold you in my arms.'

'Well, you'd better control yourself with Agalia outside the door.'

Miranda's humour was back, and with it her confidence. He thanked God for it. But how long would he be able to keep the truth about their marriage a secret? For ever, he hoped. But Miranda was bright and quick, and if she ever found out the real reason behind the hastily arranged ceremony she would be devastated...

It was too late to think like that, too late to turn back the clock. He was committed to a path and nothing could stop the wheels of fate turning.

CHAPTER SEVEN

MIRANDA'S throat was so tight she could hardly answer Agalia's questions. It was early morning, and she was dressing for her wedding. Sunlight was streaming in through the windows of her bedroom at the taverna, lighting the rugs hanging on the whitewashed walls.

The colourful hangings provided the perfect backdrop for her gown—a dress so beautiful she defied any of the top fashion houses in Paris to produce anything lovelier. Layer upon layer of silk chiffon billowed at her slightest movement, and the dress was cunningly cut so that when she stood perfectly still it clung to her like a sheath. The dressmaker had interpreted her wishes faultlessly: nothing fancy, no long and cumbersome trains, and no ornate trimmings. It was a dream of a dress, with a pure and simple line.

It was only the colour over which she was agonising now.

Right from the start Theo had tried to put her at her ease, joking that if a man waited for a virgin he would wait for ever. He thought her concerns about their wedding night were all wrapped up in whether she was a virgin or not, and had insisted that the past was the past, and all he cared about was their future together.

He made it all sound so simple, but it wasn't simple. She

wasn't a virgin, but she wasn't experienced either. And though her body wanted Theo, her memories told her that she hated sex. And the dress was snowy white, which she found both symbolic and alarming.

She wished she knew more, and could be more confident about the role Theo would expect her to play in the bedroom. She felt such a fool, knowing that she had forged a career, was even reasonably attractive, and yet was so ignorant about sex—something everyone else seemed to take for granted...

Agalia had finished lacing the gown. '*Kalo!* Good. We are ready,' she declared with satisfaction.

'Thank you.' Miranda's voice wobbled.

'Tears, Miranda? But this should be the happiest day of your life.'

And maybe it might have been, if she hadn't been beset by doubts. She could never be the sophisticated lover a man like Theo deserved. He was highly charged, sexually in the prime of his life. He would expect an explosion of passion on their wedding night, and all he was likely to get was a damp squib. And his moods worried her too. Try as he might, Theo could not hide the fact that something was on his mind. Was he having second thoughts?

'I know,' Agalia said, clapping her hands and reclaiming Miranda's attention. 'They are tears of happiness.'

'That's right, Agalia,' Miranda agreed, grateful for the let-out. 'Can I hear music?' She seized eagerly on the distraction. 'Is that the wedding party?'

Unlike her charge, Agalia was beside herself with excitement as she ran to the window. 'Yes, they're here! They're here!'

Joining Agalia at the window, even Miranda smiled as she leaned out and waved to the boisterous villagers streaming down the beach. It looked as if everyone in the village had turned out for her wedding. Far from it being a hole-and-corner affair, as she had feared, the whole population of Kalmos seemed to be on the march. Her spirits lifted. Sharing the day with all the people who had made her so welcome would make it special for her.

Two elderly musicians were leading the procession, one of them playing a fiddle and the other an ancient instrument Miranda recognised as an aoud. She frowned as they continued on past the taverna. 'Are they going without me?'

'No, of course not,' Agalia reassured her. 'They are on their way to collect Theo from his yacht in the harbour, and when they have done that they will come back here for you.'

'How long will that take?'

Agalia laughed. 'You make it sound as if you are dreading Theo's arrival!'

Agalia had no idea how close to the truth she had come, Miranda realised as she dipped her head and allowed the Greek woman to place a simple headdress of fresh flowers on her hair. She was going into this marriage blindfold, and dragging decent people like Agalia and Spiros along with her. 'I'm not dreading his arrival...'

'Then what?' Agalia pressed gently.

'I'm concerned that we have only known each other a short time.'

'Now, you listen to me.' Agalia spoke sternly as she drew Miranda round to face her. 'Theo is a good man, Miranda. I've known him all his life, and you are the woman for him. Do you think Theo is such a fool that he has made the decision to marry you lightly? Or that he would bring the wedding forward unless he had a very good reason for doing so? And I think we both know what that reason is...' Her eyes began to twinkle, but then she turned serious again. 'Theo rescued the Savakis shipping line and turned it into a world-class company. Do you think that was by chance? No. Theo wouldn't be marrying you unless he had the very best reason for doing so. And his reason is that he loves you, Miranda.'

'I hope you're right.'

'Of course I'm right. I'm standing in the place of your mother today, and if she were here she would say what I am saying—that all brides are nervous on their wedding day. But you have no need to worry because you are marrying a wonderful man who will take care of you and cherish you for the rest of your life.'

Miranda couldn't bear for Agalia to see all the doubt in her eyes. She turned away. 'Is is time to put on my veil?'

'Yes, it's time. Sandals?' Agalia reminded her when the veil was fixed, taking them out of the protective tissue paper and placing them on the floor for Miranda to step into.

As she slipped her feet into the dainty beaded mules Miranda caught sight of her reflection in the mirror. Agalia had polished her hair with silk, so that it shone blue-black in the light, and she was wearing it down so that it fell almost to her waist. With the white dress and the crown of flowers the transformation was marked. She looked so young—serene and docile, like a sacrifice.

'Miranda, come. We must hurry.'

Miranda started as Agalia's voice called her back from her trance. She had to snap out of it. She was being melodramatic—and if you looked hard enough for trouble you would always find some.

'I can hear them!' Agalia exclaimed.

Raising her chin, Miranda went up to Agalia and embraced her. 'Thank you for everything you've done for me. I'm going to have a wonderful wedding day thanks to you.'

'These are for you, Miranda.'

She was shaking, Miranda realised. She had to take a long,

steadying breath before she could lift her head and smile into Theo's eyes.

'Take the flowers,' he prompted.

Everyone was silent as they waited for her to do so.

'Theo…' His name rang between them. There was such intensity in his gaze, and Miranda was thankful for the gossamer veil masking her own turbulent emotions.

'Are you ready?' He smiled encouragement.

People were jostling for position in an effort to see her. Everyone was dressed casually, in a way that perfectly suited the sunny climate and picturesque setting. Even Theo was wearing traditional clothes rather than a formal wedding suit. Miranda was surprised, but thought the white linen shirt he wore loose over trousers made from the same fabric reinforced his raw masculinity. The black waistcoat, heavily embroidered with gold, complemented his fierce glamour, and his strong, tanned feet in the simple thonged sandals gave her such a sexual charge she had to look away.

'Miranda?'

Theo was growing impatient, and soon the crowd would be too. She waved as she stepped forward, and was touched when everyone cheered. The wave of enthusiasm bolstered her up as she walked into the brilliant sunlight and took her place at Theo's side.

The simple wedding ceremony touched Miranda deeply. And she could hardly wait to share her happiness with their wedding guests. But at the taverna she discovered that Theo's business had no respect for a bride on her wedding day. He had already been called away to take a phone call.

She took her place without him at the top table, and for a while chatted animatedly with the guests on either side. But as time went on she grew increasingly disappointed, and eventually angry. Surely Theo could put his wedding before his business commitments? After all, it was only one day..

She could see him still talking rapidly inside the taverna, receiver clenched tightly in his hand. It had to be a crisis or he would have explained that the call was interrupting his wedding feast. She must be patient, and ready to support him if there was trouble. Hadn't she felt that same level of commitment in her own career?

But the light was fading and people were hungry. Gathering round the barbecue, they were casting surreptitious glances at the top table—specifically at the empty place at her side. And Agalia had gone to so much trouble—it would be dreadful if the food began to spoil…

Miranda's attention was drawn to the heavy gold wedding band she was unconsciously twirling around her finger. Unmistakably Hellenic in design, it was intricately etched and studded with diamonds. When she had commented on its age and beauty, Theo had asked her what she expected when she was marrying into a family who could trace their origins back to Mount Olympus. At the time they had both laughed, but right now she didn't find it so funny. Was this what it meant to be married into a family like Theo's? Did he think she could be put on hold whenever it suited him, like some latter-day Penelope? If there was a crisis, why didn't he share it with her? If there was no crisis, why couldn't he ask the caller to ring back after their wedding feast?

Guests had started expressing their concern more openly, and there was a distinct rumble of unease as they stared at her. She couldn't just sit in her place as if nothing was wrong. Rising from her seat, she lifted up her skirts and made her apologies.

She found Theo still talking on the telephone. 'Theo—'

He put up his hand to silence her. 'I'll only be a few minutes. Would you mind waiting for me outside?'

His tone astounded her. She was his wife now—not some minion to be ordered out of the room. 'Yes, I would mind.' Miranda kept her voice low and closed the door carefully behind her. 'Our guests are waiting. We can't just abandon them.'

He gave her a savage look, but then, quite suddenly, and to her relief, the cloud hanging over him seemed to lift.

'You're right, and I apologise,' he said, covering the mouthpiece. 'This call has taken a lot longer than I anticipated. Please forgive me, *thespinis mou*, I will be with you in a moment.'

'I'll wait here until you finish.'

With a brief nod he turned away, and fired off a few more words in Greek before cutting the line.

'Was it so important?' Miranda reined in her anger, seeing the tension lines on Theo's face. 'Do you have a problem? Can I help you with anything?'

Coming up to her, Theo traced the line of her face with his finger. 'You are so gentle and so good, and you have already helped me just by being here.'

'Can't you tell me?'

Theo silenced her question with a kiss.

'Should I be worried?' she said, when he let her go.

Capturing a strand of her silky hair, he wound it around his finger. 'No, *pethi mou*, there's nothing for you to worry about. It was only a business call, Miranda. I hope you know that I wouldn't leave you alone for a moment unless I had to—'

'*Had* to? And yet you dismiss the call as *only* business?'

He dropped the coil of hair and pulled away. 'Don't quiz me, Miranda.'

'Then please don't behave so badly towards our guests!'

'Agalia and Spiros are taking care of everyone for us...'

Following his glance, she saw Theo was right. 'That still doesn't excuse our absence, Theo.'

She recoiled as he snapped, 'You should remember that you're my wife now! You must learn to fit in.'

'To whatever small space you can find for me in your diary? I don't think so, Theo. I think you should remember that right now our marriage is nothing more than a piece of paper, and I can still walk away from it!'

Briefly, he looked stunned, and then, catching hold of her upper arms, he brought her back to him. 'I've never seen you in a temper before, Miranda…and I think I like it.'

As Theo stared down into her face his lips drew her gaze. She fought him off for a second, but he was too strong for her, and when he deepened the kiss she responded hungrily.

'Damn this wedding feast,' he husked fiercely against her neck when he let her go. 'Damn all interruptions! If you want me to make this marriage something more than a piece of paper I'm happy to oblige right now—'

'Then why wait?'

Silence hung between them as they both took in what she had said. Theo couldn't have been more surprised by her blatant suggestion, Miranda realised. But here in the shadows she felt little would be expected of her and maybe it would be all right. It was the set-piece drama of her wedding night on Theo's yacht that she was dreading.

'Are you asking me to kiss you again?' His voice hinted that he was open to suggestions.

'Yes, I'd like that…to begin with.' She met his gaze steadily.

'But not here?' He frowned.

His wife was a mass of contradictions. Inexperienced, even nervous, but then suddenly she was easing her shoulders back to reveal the deep valley between her breasts, making his senses roar.

'We can't stay here.' Even as he said the words he could

feel the tightening in his groin. Miranda's eagerness for intimacy was a revelation to him. 'Have you forgotten our guests?'

'They're busy eating now, and soon they will be dancing…'

Glancing out of the window, he saw she was right. No one would care if they were absent for a little while longer. He pulled the blind.

A single ray of light still managed to escape. It was enough for him to see everything she was offering him beneath the filmy chiffon of her gown: the curve of her thighs, the rosy swell of engorged nipples, the provocative line of her belly. He wanted nothing more than to pleasure her, to savour her responses…

Cupping her face tenderly in his hands, he brushed her lips with his mouth and drank in her sigh. She was pliant and relaxed, her limbs like liquid gold, and she was his. It was like drinking at the deepest well of the coolest water in the hottest part of the day…

But was this what he wanted? Was he going to make love to his bride for the first time in the back room of a taverna?

'No, Miranda. This isn't right.' Very gently he unlocked her hands from behind his neck and brought them to his lips to kiss them in turn.

'Don't you want me?'

He smiled against her mouth as he whispered, 'Of course I want you. But when I make love to you for the first time I want it to be something we remember for ever…'

'So why can't it be here?'

'Because there are better places to make love than on a table in a taverna. If you have a little patience, I will show you.'

Maybe some women would have been happy as they waited for a night of passion with their lover, but for Miranda it was the most refined torture Theo could have devised for her.

'And now it really is time to join our wedding guests,' Theo said, dropping a kiss on her brow.

But he still hadn't given her an explanation for his lengthy call, Miranda realised as he slipped his arm around her waist and steered her towards the door.

CHAPTER EIGHT

THE wedding party came to an end when Miranda was least expecting it. Theo swept her into his arms in the middle of a dance. Weaving his way across the crowded dance floor, he carried her down the steps of the taverna and onto the beach. The two musicians who had led the procession earlier spotted them and, seizing their instruments, drew the wedding guests after them like Pied Pipers.

Theo strode on, with everyone singing and dancing in his wake. The moon was like a beacon in the sky, and the sky was a star-studded canopy over their heads. But the vigour had gone out of their guests, Miranda noticed when she glanced behind. Or maybe Theo was simply outpacing everyone. Certainly his vigour was undiminished.

The distance between the taverna and the harbour melted away quickly, and soon the monstrous shadow of Theo's yacht loomed ahead of them. She could feel her heart thundering, and was sure Theo must feel it too. This was everything she had hoped for—the beginning of her new life with the man she loved. But she was frightened she was going to lose him on their first night together as man and wife. And, much as she hated herself for still doubting him, it wasn't just the sex she was dreading. She couldn't rid herself of the feeling that nothing was ever as good as it seemed. And this was so good…

Striding up the gangplank, Theo drew to a halt and lowered her gently to the deck as if she was precious porcelain. Or his best investment yet.

Miranda brushed the rogue thought aside. Her imagination was running away with her.

The remaining guests had caught up with them. Putting his arm around her waist, Theo drew her close. Everyone was clustered around the foot of the gangplank, waving, and when Miranda waved back they all cheered.

At this cue, Theo took a velvet pouch from one of his crew and handed it to her.

'What do I do with this?' She smiled, forgetting her doubts. They seemed ridiculous now.

'It's another of our traditions,' Theo said, 'and one I think you'll like.'

Peering inside the pouch, Miranda saw that it was full of sugared almonds. 'To eat?'

He laughed, 'Not unless you want a riot. Throw them—like this…' He showered the waiting crowd, and then took charge of a second pouch as everyone applauded.

'But you've got gold coins!'

'So that everyone can share in our good fortune.'

Miranda felt another frisson of superstitious alarm, but, remembering her vow to keep her imagination in check, quickly followed Theo's lead.

When the pouches were empty, and everyone had drifted away after calling their good wishes, Theo escorted her onto the aft deck.

'You think of everything.' Miranda gazed around, hardly able to believe that all this had been prepared for their pleasure.

'I have an excellent crew.' Drawing her arm through his,

Theo brought her to an alcove where an unbleached linen canopy had been erected to protect them from the breeze. So many candles had been lit that even the night was held at bay, and a small group of musicians was playing to one side of a buffet table.

They sat at an intimate table laid for two, then danced to the sinuous rhythms of South America beneath a sky thick with stars. As the pulse of the music thrummed Miranda felt all her worries melting away. She was safe in Theo's arms, safe and confident. She had been wrong to look for trouble, wrong to be so angry when he had wanted to bring the wedding forward. Instead of challenging Theo she should be rejoicing because she had found a man who loved her so much.

As if sensing the turn her thoughts were taking, he dropped a chaste kiss on her brow. But its very innocence was provocative, particularly when the touch of his hands held so much promise. She wondered if Theo knew the effect he was having on her with just the smallest adjustment of his grip. Relaxing into him, she dared the doubts to assail her now.

'Are you hungry?' he murmured.

The expression in his eyes made a quiver of arousal run right through her. 'I'm starving…'

'Then shall we?'

Miranda wasn't surprised when Theo led her straight past the buffet table and on towards the companionway that led to his sumptuous quarters on board the yacht. And by the time he carried her over the threshold of his stateroom she was shivering with anticipation rather than fear.

The room had been subtly lit, and was lightly fragranced with sandalwood. There was a deep fur rug on the polished wooden floor, and the sheets on the huge circular bed were black satin. It was like a set from a film, Miranda mused dreamily as Theo softly closed the door behind them.

Leaning back against it, he stared down at her. 'Welcome to my world, Miranda.'

There was such a mix of emotion on his face. Tenderness, desire, and even something close to triumph. She felt it like a cloud briefly covering the sun, and realised that she would have to remind him that she would always be her own person: two in one, not one and a bit. But there was all the time in the world for that...

And when he kissed her his lips were so cherishing, so loving, she forgot. It was as if Theo, recognising her inexperience, wanted to reassure her, and in the end it was she who showed him what she wanted with the touch of her hands and the press of her body.

Drawing back, he studied her face in silence for a moment, and then kissed her again, deeply, in a way that touched her soul. His palms were warm and firm as they moved down her arms, but even then she wasn't prepared for him taking hold of her damaged hand and raising it so he could study it more closely.

She pulled back in alarm and even shame as he broke the mood. Did Theo find the ugly scars as repulsive as she did? Was this his way of showing her that he couldn't face taking her to bed? She had never examined the damage as closely as he was doing. She had never been able to bring herself to the point where she could accept the full horror of her fate. She held her breath until he had finished his examination.

'The next couple of weeks are going to be very busy for me, Miranda. But when things quieten down I want you to agree to come with me and see another doctor.'

When she tried to explain that it would do no good, he laid a finger on her lips.

'You think a cure is impossible. You think no one can help you. I don't accept *impossible*, Miranda. I never have.'

Theo's voice was low, but fierce, and she could see how his business adversaries might shrink from it. 'You'd be wasting your time.' She held his stare.

Without breaking eye contact, he raised her hand to his lips. 'Don't tell me this isn't worth fighting for.'

She had to look away. It was the one battle she had always been frightened to face.

'I'm sorry if I've upset you, but—' Dipping his head, he looked her in the eyes. 'You may not know it, but your happiness is tied up in the damage to your hand. I'm going to make sure that you are set free to find happiness again.'

That same certainty and confidence fed Theo's success, Miranda realised. She could only hope it never turned into something harsher and more restrictive where she was concerned. If he tried to manipulate her it was the one thing that would split them apart.

'Why are you shivering? You need never be frightened again, Miranda, you are a Savakis now.'

Again the pride. Again the absolute certainty. But when he started unlacing her gown she couldn't hold on to the worries niggling at her—not with her senses under siege like this.

'Do you want me, Miranda?' he asked softly.

'You know I do…'

Yes, and she trusted him completely, Miranda realised, as Theo slipped the wedding gown from her shoulders. As it pooled on the ground she stepped out of it, naked now except for the shimmering silk chemise and tiny briefs she wore beneath.

Holding his gaze, she reached up and started unfastening the buttons on his traditional shirt. Her hands were trembling, and she had little dexterity at the best of times, but instead of growing impatient and trying to help her when he saw she was struggling Theo didn't interfere.

Her breath left her lungs in a rush as she pushed the soft

fabric aside. Theo was so beautiful she wanted to touch every part of him. His warm scent was an aphrodisiac that made her want to melt into him and lose herself.

She gasped when his hands moved to slip the dainty straps on her silk chemise from her shoulders, and when he eased the delicate garment over her breasts her arousal was evident to both of them. Her breasts seemed fuller, and were flushed pink around nipples that stood erect for his attention. She moaned softly at his first delicate touch, wondering if she would survive the sensation of firm thumb pads teasing her.

'Don't torture me...'

'I'll stop if you don't like it.'

'No...' Her nipples were straining towards him, growing taut and increasingly sensitive beneath each feathering touch, and then he moved to circling, before tugging gently with his thumb and forefinger.

'More?' he demanded softly, disposing of the chemise.

'Yes...oh, yes...'

Cupping her heavy breasts, he weighed them apprecia- tively while his thumbs worked steadily on her nipples. Rivers of sensation were streaming through her, and when he stopped she cried out with disappointment.

'Tell me what you want, Miranda.'

She couldn't believe Theo was asking her to become the architect of her own pleasure. She had never dreamed that a man might be capable of treading such an erotic path.

'You have to tell me exactly what you want me to do, Miranda, or I'll have to stop...'

'Touch me, Theo...stroke me...'

'Like this?'

She cried out with pleasure as he increased the pressure on her breasts.

'Or like this?'

Her mouth fell open as his searching hand found the source of her pleasure.

'Are you ready for me yet?'

He stroked and stroked again, delicately and persuasively, and all the time he watched her with dark, knowing eyes so full of promises. 'Yes…' She stared up at him, mutely begging him for release.

She hadn't expected him to drop to his knees, or to ease the flimsy briefs from her hips and bury his face between her thighs. She hadn't dreamed such extremes of sensation existed, and she sobbed with relief when after a brief kiss of homage she felt the rough scratch of his stubble on her thighs.

Theo's tongue was so bold, so demanding, and her legs were too weak to hold her now. She might have slipped to the floor without his strong arms supporting her.

Gasping for breath, she planted her hands on his shoulders and, rolling her head back, begged, 'Take me to bed, Theo… Take me now.'

For the first time in her life she felt the power of her sex, and as Theo carried her across the room and lowered her down onto the satin sheets she was ready for him.

She was like a flower whose petals were opening beneath him, Theo thought. She was everything he had hoped for and more. Dimitri was wrong. Life had no meaning, no purpose, without emotion, without someone to care for, someone to love. What a dynasty they would found together. Miranda would teach him how to care, and he would protect her with his life.

Allowing his clothes to drop to the floor, he heard her gasp. Half turning, he made sure he was angled away from her. The last thing he wanted to do now was frighten her. The urge to shield Miranda from harm was growing stronger by the moment. Whatever life held in store for both of them, he would do everything in his power to make her happy.

Slipping into bed beside her, he covered himself with the satin sheet and, smoothing a wayward strand of hair from her brow, demanded, 'Do you trust me now, Miranda?'

'I trust you completely…'

That was all he needed to hear. He relaxed and stretched out beside her. Her breathing was rapid and her eyes were almost black, with just a fine ring of jade to remind him of their colour. Pulling the sheet back, he relished every tiny change that marked the blossoming of her arousal: her swollen lips, her almost painfully erect nipples, and, most of all, the subtle undulation of her hips that called his attention to the source of her need.

Trailing his fingers lightly, so they barely touched her quivering frame, he brought them down from the hollow at the base of her neck, on between her breasts and then over the swell of her belly. But as her eyes widened with anticipation he brought his hand up again, and began idly toying with her breasts.

'Stop teasing me, Theo.'

'I thought you liked it?' He pretended surprise, but he saw how she squirmed with pleasure each time he cupped her firmly and chafed her puckered nipples with his thumb pads. 'More?' He knew how it turned her on to ask.

'Take me in your mouth…'

She angled her breast and spoke so softly it was almost a sigh. Then, reaching for him, she drew him down to suckle. She writhed beneath him while he pleasured her, but he made her wait until she begged, 'Theo, please! Don't make me wait any longer…'

Moving over her, he nudged her thighs apart, and was pleased when she opened herself even more for him. He caressed her intimately to be sure, and then was forced to take her mouth and hold on to his control, plunging his tongue deep instead of all the other things he wanted to do to her. Tasting her sweetness was a sharp reminder of how inexperienced she was...but then she arced towards him, forcing their bodies together, and he knew he was lost.

Holding her firmly, he made a single pass, feathering over her. She delivered the answer he had hoped for, drawing up her thighs even more as she choked out a single word. 'Yes...'

He made a second pass, and this time allowed the tip to catch inside her. She exhaled raggedly and held his gaze with half-shut sleepy eyes.

'Yes,' she breathed again, moving her hips in an attempt to take him deeper.

He resisted the temptation to follow her instructions. He would set the pace. He would choose the moment. And then she closed her eyes, relaxing completely in his arms in an attitude of complete trust, with one arm resting languidly above her head on the satin pillows.

But still he withdrew and made her wait. She was tender and innocent, and she was his...

He had underestimated his wife. Wrapping her hand around him, she made him gasp. The sensation was like nothing he had ever known before, and now Miranda was guiding him back, bringing him to where her hips were lifting from the bed.

He kissed her deeply, groaning as she tightened her hold on him. She made an insistent raw sound as he eased inside her, and then clung to him as if terrified he might change his mind. When he moved from side to side, settling himself inside her, she rose against him, closing her muscles round him to draw him deeper still.

His bride was perfect. Miranda was perfect. Nothing on earth could come between them now.

* * *

As Theo thrust inside her, Miranda wondered if she would survive the waves of pleasure washing over her. She had never dreamed there could be such extremes of sensation, and in that moment she lost all her inhibitions. Crying out, she allowed him to guide her with his strong hands, moulding her buttocks as she worked her hips in unison with his. Their lovemaking gathered pace until they were both lost, until she felt the breath gathering in her chest, the cry collecting in her throat...

Holding her in his arms, Theo urged her fiercely in his own tongue until her lips parted in a long, silent wail. She thrashed her head about, fighting off the moment, but as her throbbing muscles gripped him she screamed his name and they tumbled together over the edge of the abyss.

She came to in a state of complete relaxation. Her body felt as if it might float away. She turned her head to stare at Theo. He had collapsed on the pillows at her side and rolled away. Maybe he was asleep? She had no strength to find out. Her eyelids were so heavy...

'Theo?'

Waking slowly, Miranda realised it was morning and she was alone in the vast bed. Swinging her legs over the side, she searched for him, but their suite of rooms was empty. She checked the balcony too, and the bathroom, but there was no sign of her husband.

And they were at sea. But hadn't Theo said they would be spending their honeymoon on Kalmos?

After she'd showered, she slipped on one of the towelling robes hanging in the bathroom. Her wedding dress was still on the floor by the bed, where they had discarded it along with Theo's clothes.

Caressing it, she scooped everything up and laid the clothes straight, smiling as the events of the night came back to her.

Who would have guessed she had such an appetite? Theo had awoken a whirlwind. And who would have guessed he possessed the power to hold her nightmares at bay? Tension poured out of her in a sigh.

She found some slippers to match the robe on a shelf beside the bed, and was so impatient to see him again she didn't wait to dry her hair.

She found him seated at the table where they had been supposed to eat supper the previous evening. All signs of romance had been removed: the candles, the linen windbreakers. Now an awning cast shade across the table and he sat with a coffee cup in one hand and what looked like a report in the other. He was surrounded by documents and had his satellite phone within reach, Miranda noticed, grimacing.

He was too preoccupied to notice her padding up to him. 'Good morning,' she said brightly, resting her hands on his shoulders as she planted a kiss on his neck. 'Why didn't you wake me?'

He lifted his hand to silence her. 'Forgive me, I must read this…'

Miranda's smile died and she pulled her hands away from Theo's stiff, unyielding shoulders. She felt a chill, a premonition.

'Have some breakfast?' he suggested, flashing her the briefest smile.

Perhaps he was being discreet for the sake of the crew and she was overreacting? She glanced around, but they were alone.

'Don't you want any breakfast?' he pressed, without lifting his head from the papers he was studying.

'Yes, thank you. That would be nice.' She felt hurt and angry. There wasn't a word of endearment from him, not even a look.

'I had a place laid for you in case you woke up…' He

shrugged apologetically as he glanced round at all his business paraphernalia.

Her place at the table was as far away from him as possible. Maybe he was like this in the morning? How would she know? She didn't know him…and Theo clearly didn't know her either.

She made no fuss; just moved a stack of folders aside to make room for a place-setting closer to him, and when a steward appeared with a jug of orange juice she asked him, 'Would you mind bringing that chair over here for me?'

'Certainly, madam.'

'I'm sorry to be dressed like this,' she tried as an icebreaker once she had sat down. 'I don't have any clothes with me, as you know. If you'd warned me I would have packed a case. Goodness knows, it wouldn't have taken long…'

No response from Theo.

'I didn't realise we were going to sea. I thought you said our honeymoon was to be in Kalmos.'

Nothing.

She waited until the steward had disappeared down the companionway. 'Theo, is something wrong?'

'No, of course not. But I must read this.'

'On the morning after our wedding night?'

'This can't wait. I'm sorry.'

'I'm afraid it's going to have to wait.' Taking the document from his hands, she laid it aside. 'I haven't got any clothes with me; I don't know where we're going or what's going on. The least you can do is spare me a few minutes to explain.'

'You have to understand that you haven't married the boy next door, Miranda. I run a very complicated business, and I have to check each day to see which way the wind is blowing—'

'Well, I can tell you which way the wind is blowing in your

marriage, Theo!' She stood up. 'If you don't make space for me there's no point in our being married—'

'Don't talk like that!'

She had his full attention now. 'If you think I'm going to sit around waiting for you to fit me in between meetings, you're wrong. You promised me time. You said there would be all the time in the world for us to get to know each other. How can that be right, Theo, when you can't even find time for me today?'

As he reached for her she took a step back. 'Think about what I've said, Theo—think about it good and long. You have to decide if you want me, or if you want your wretched business more. Because if this is how it's going to be, I'm warning you now—you can't have both.'

CHAPTER NINE

MIRANDA was still shaking ten minutes later, in their stateroom. She had expected—hoped—that Theo would come after her, to apologise and to reassure her. But there was no sign of him.

So was the fairytale over? It seemed so. She hugged herself, wondering about the practicalities of leaving her husband in the middle of the ocean. It wasn't like stalking out of an apartment—she could hardly paddle back to shore. Theo's helicopter was squatting like a big black bird on the helipad on the top deck, but she didn't imagine he would lend it to her so she could leave him.

And where could she go without clothes, without money, without even a satellite phone at her disposal to call for help? There really was no alternative. She had to go back on deck and sort this out with him.

'Kyrios Savakis is taking calls inside his office,' the steward informed her when she found Theo had left the breakfast table.

'I see.' So that was how much she meant to him! Thanking the steward, Miranda headed off.

When she found the right door she belted her robe a little more securely, knocked once, and walked straight in.

'Do come in, Miranda.'

Ignoring the sarcasm, she shut the door. 'I'd like five minutes of your time.'

He was seated behind a vast expanse of desk—which as far as Miranda was concerned was a welcome barrier between them. The blinds were drawn and his face was in shadow, as if he needed a blank canvas in which to think.

'Won't you sit down?' As he spoke, he switched on a desk lamp.

'I prefer to stand. Shall I draw the blinds?'

'As you wish.'

She did more than that; she opened the window, allowing the sea breeze to bring a refreshing draught inside the room. 'I asked you to make a decision about our marriage, Theo, and so far you haven't had the courtesy to let me know what you have decided.'

'Maybe I haven't decided how best to achieve a suitable balance in my life.'

'Indecision?' Her voice was sceptical. 'Not you, Theo.'

'What do I have to say to convince you that I love you, but that I run a very large and very complex business—a business that refuses to remain in suspension while I take a honeymoon with my bride?'

'You might have warned me that it would be like this!'

'So it's *you* who is having second thoughts, Miranda?'

'That's a low blow, Theo. Don't try and turn this around on me.'

She loved him so much that it hurt—but could she give up her free will, as well as all her own hopes for the future, to provide comfort in bed for a busy plutocrat? Was she to walk obediently at Theo's side and provide him with children as and when required? Was this what she had intended when she set out to rebuild her life? Was she destined to be a handy vessel, waiting for the blessing of his seed?

'I don't know what you had in mind when you married me, but I won't be your whore, Theo—'

He started as if she had slapped him. 'Don't use that language!'

'Why, Theo? Because it's a little too close to the truth? Do you get a kick out of inexperienced women who have everything to learn at your hands?'

'What women?' Theo was equally angry now. He leapt up and came angrily round the desk, grasping her shoulders. 'Don't sully what we have by even thinking such travesties about me!'

'Let me go,' she warned.

'No.'

She stood stiffly in his arms, averting her face when he spoke again. 'There is bound to be a period of readjustment—'

'Readjustment?' she said furiously, shaking him off. 'I'll say there is. You can't expect to make love to me all night and then ignore me in the morning because of business—because of *anything*. It's time to get your priorities straight, Theo, and think about the things that matter!'

And that was exactly what he had been doing; that was why he had woken up so early and why she had found him in a sombre mood. He had neglected Miranda for the best of reasons—because she had made him see what was important in life. He loved her, really loved her, and he hadn't thought himself capable of the emotion.

'Miranda, please. I love you—'

'And that makes everything better? I need *time* with you, Theo.'

'This isn't a normal time for me.' He battled with all the things he wanted to tell her but knew he couldn't. 'Please believe me when I say that if circumstances had been different I wouldn't have left you alone for a moment.'

'Then share your problems with me! Let me understand. I
want to help you, Theo, but you have to let me in...'

How could he find the words to explain that Dimitri was fading, and that after a lifetime of indifference between them he
wanted to go like a peacemaker and show the old man his bride.
And not because it would guarantee him control of the Savakis
shipping line, but because he was so proud of Miranda—because
he wanted his grandfather to share in his happiness at the end.

Never having experienced love before, he hadn't known
how it would affect him. It was as if everything that had been
suppressed in him had suddenly come to the fore. But he
couldn't risk it. Dimitri might say something, and Miranda's
courage wasn't inexhaustible. Her belief that her life could be
rebuilt had been the catalyst that had set him thinking, but did
he want to destroy that belief and show her what their marriage looked like through Dimitri's eyes?

The truth was, he was locked into a deceit from which there
was no escape. He hated himself for it, and that was why he
had shut himself away. How could he look Miranda in the face
when she had given herself to him so fully, so honestly? How
could he look at her now without the spectre of the golden
shares standing between them? She meant everything to him,
but if she ever found out about the contract he had signed she
would never trust him again. Was that the foundation upon
which he hoped to found a dynasty?

'So you've nothing to say to me?'

She sounded so sad, and, drawing herself up, she shook her
head in disappointment. 'If you can't share your life with me,
Theo, I've got no place to be. Can't you see that? If silence
is your answer you have to let me go—'

'No!'

'You have to. Or is your pride such that you can't bear to
admit that you've made a mistake?'

'I haven't made a mistake.'

'Then why can't you confide in me?'

He hesitated. 'Because it's confidential.'

'Confidential?' As she stared at him he felt more pain than triumph as understanding coloured her gaze. 'Then why on earth didn't you say so?'

His throat was so tight he could only manage a noncommittal sound to go with his shrug.

'Oh, Theo…' She touched his face. 'We're both novices at this. Forgive me?'

Seizing her hand, he pressed it to his lips. 'So you've changed your mind about leaving me?'

'What do you think?'

'Now it's my turn to ask you to forgive me. I've been alone too long. I can't see any further than the problems in the business. They blinded me to how you might be feeling.'

'Then leave all this—' she gestured round his office '—and be with me now. Otherwise you had better set me ashore with some clothes, and I'll be a castaway.'

Her humour made him feel worse than ever, and as she pressed her lips together in a rueful smile he knew he had to come up with a better strategy. 'All this can wait,' he told her, pushing the documents on his desk aside. 'You're more important to me than any business deal.'

'Just be sure you mean it, Theo.' She turned serious. 'I don't want to make another mistake, and I don't want to be pushed around by anyone—not even you. I know the consequences that can have. If I'd hadn't let myself be pressured into getting in that car when I should have waited for my taxi, this might never have happened.'

His mouth dried when she raised her damaged arm to make the point, but he followed through with the lighter mood she had set before. 'I'm not calling for a taxi, so you're stuck with me. You're everything I want, Miranda.'

But as he heard the words he was saying and looked into her eyes he wondered if it were possible to despise himself more. Deceiving Miranda about his motives for marrying her would keep their marriage alive for now—but at what cost?

Perhaps this was his punishment for breaking every one of Dimitri's rules. Miranda was artistic, and perhaps fleetingly he had been guilty of seeing her as a worthy cause—someone who might be grateful for his attention—but he was over that. She had taught him more than he could ever repay her for.

'Come on.' Walking to the door before she could see the emotion in his eyes, he held it open. 'Let's have that talk.'

They exchanged reassurances over coffee, and talked on through lunch when an easy mood was restored.

'You'd better find me some clothes to wear,' she reminded him. 'Or did you imagine you were going to keep me in bed for the whole trip?'

He kissed her brow and was relieved to hear her laugh. 'There's a whole wardrobe of clothes waiting for you in your dressing room.' He gestured down the deck towards their stateroom. 'I wanted to surprise you.'

'Theo, you're full of surprises,' she mocked him gently.

'Should I have them moved to another stateroom, or are we still married?' He slanted a glance at her; outwardly smiling, inwardly tense.

'Still married.'

He made a sound of deep contentment.

Their reunion was explosive. Having stripped away her fear of sex, Theo had awakened a hunger in Miranda she had no idea how to control. Fortunately Theo was tireless and inventive, and had plenty of ideas when it came to channelling her energies

What was happening to her? Miranda wondered as she got dressed again. Adrenaline was still pumping through her veins; she couldn't get enough of him. She had always shied away from involvement and hadn't been looking for love when love had found her.

It must be some really bad flaw in her character that always made her question anything that seemed to be too good to be true. For once she should just lie back and accept that her marriage to Theo was that good.

Emily had always been the more confident twin—the twin who took the lead, led her class, seized opportunities. Ten minutes might be nothing in the scheme of things, but when it came to which twin was born first it had made all the difference. Even at the music *conservatoire* Miranda had been content to stay in the background until winning a major competition had made that impossible.

And then had come the accident and a whole new set of rules. They had all been special at college, all hothouse flowers, and it had bred a complacency that hadn't prepared her for life after the crash. If she wasn't a world-class musician, then what was she?

Theo had answered that question. She was a woman who had survived a devastating trauma and was ready to move forward to the next stage of her life. Take the violin away and she was still out there fighting; take her self-belief away and she was nothing.

Trusting Theo had brought her life into sharper focus. Their chance meeting had changed her life. She mustn't let her fears sabotage her future.

Tilting her chin, she adjusted the collar on a beautifully tailored shirt she had discovered in her dressing room after his prompt. Their marriage was safe, their love like a white light blazing steadily between them. It was more than she could have hoped for when she agreed to be his wife. Theo was the air she breathed, the force that had given her life meaning again. He was everything to her now.

'What's that?' Miranda stared at the documents Theo had laid out in front of him on the desk in his office.

'I've drawn up a contract—I'm afraid it's longhand, but I thought it would be something that might reassure you...'

'I don't need anything else to reassure me.'

'You may do—you never know. One day when you're feeling down—for no reason,' he added hastily, adding a smile. 'Why don't you sign? It would make me feel better if you do.'

It was hard to refuse him anything, but if she had learned one thing during her short career it was: Don't sign anything until you've checked it over thoroughly. And she shouldn't close her mind to Theo's moods. Okay, he was in a stressful business, but they had a long way to go yet.

Miranda chewed down on her lip, hesitating. Theo's eyes were half closed as he sat watching her. He wore a similar expression when they were making love. But was good sex enough to hold a marriage together?

Theo had answered that question with a contract. A man thing, Miranda realised, smiling inwardly. As far as men were concerned anything and everything could be put to bed with a contract. 'I'd like to read it before I sign.'

'Of course.' He pushed it across the desk.

She studied it. 'What's this lump sum?' Pointing to the relevant paragraph, she pushed it back to him.

Scanning the item briefly, he looked up. 'That's not a lump sum; it's your monthly allowance. *Calendar* month,' he stressed, as if that were a limitation she must consider.

'Why, that's...' She had been about to say *ridiculous*, be-

:ause the sum was extraordinary, but remembering the world
Theo came from, she amended it to, '…reasonable.'

'I'm glad you think so. So, will you sign?' Uncapping a
ountain pen, he held it out to her.

'I haven't quite finished reading it yet.' Her mind was rac-
ng with possibilities for the future, and various ways she
night use the money.

This was a surprise to Theo. He had expected hesitation,
iad expected she would be a little bit daunted, but instead
Miranda appeared to be coolly accepting the fact that her
nonthly allowance would be roughly equivalent to most peo-
ile's annual salary. He had to admit he admired her style.

'I don't like this.'

Instinctively he bridled as she pointed to a passage. 'I beg
our pardon?' No one found fault with a contract *he* had approved, let alone one he had drawn up himself.

'I can't be called upon at your whim, Theo.' She passed the
heet back to him. 'We will *both* keep diaries, and then we
:an consult *each other* regarding our availability.'

'Very well.' He could feel a muscle working in his jaw.

'And I'd like you to fax the contract to my sister Emily, for
ier to take a look at.'

'Your sister?'

'She's a barrister, civil law, and though she married a prince
he is still in practice. This kind of thing is right up her street.'

This kind of thing? Was she referring to their marriage
contract? As their looks clashed and held, Theo found him-
elf on the back foot. He wasn't happy with the notion of out-
iders intruding on his most private business, even if that
utsider was Miranda's twin.

'And there's one more thing I'd like written into this.'

'What?' He cut across her abruptly, and then reined back,
urprised at the surge of emotion he felt at her challenge.

'What's missing?' He managed to lower his voice, but found himself shaking his head as if denying the possibility that he might have overlooked so much as a comma.

'*I* decide what I do with my monthly allowance.'

He relaxed. 'Of course.' Shopping was a harmless occupation. And it would give her something to do when he was busy.

'Good. I'm glad we've got that straight, Theo, because I'm going to be using the money to set up scholarships for promising music students who couldn't otherwise afford the best tuition. I will also do some teaching myself, and of course I will sit on the committee that auditions prospective candidates.'

Theo sat back, feeling a mixture of emotions. He was surprised, of course, and a little put out that being his wife wasn't enough for Miranda, but above all he was exhilarated to see her so recovered emotionally—to the point where she was making plans for the future. And why was he surprised? That was Miranda, always bouncing back, always with an original take on life.

But he had to pull her up on one point. 'So you won't be partial?'

'What do you mean, partial?'

She was defensive, and he guessed she had expected him to say categorically no. 'I mean you can hardly cherry-pick the best students and then award them the scholarships. You must remain impartial if you want other teachers to subscribe to your scheme—or did you intend to teach all these gifted students by yourself? How about setting up a trust, with a board of trustees to administer the programme?'

'That's a great idea,' Miranda admitted, thrilled that Theo was getting on board. Music was her forte, but business just wasn't her thing. 'Okay, perhaps you could help me?'

'Me?'

'Why not you?' She stared at him. Necessity was the

mother of invention, and she was going to need some professional help to bring her ideas to fruition. Theo was the best, and he was cheap too, under the principle 'keep it in the family and he'll work for nothing'—which in turn left more money for the students. 'Well?' she pressed.

'I'd have to think about it. I'm a very busy man, Miranda.'

The shadow of Theo's business passed over them once again, showing that she was right not to weaken. Their marriage would have to be an equal partnership or it wouldn't survive. 'Too busy to work with me, Theo?'

'I said I'll think about it.'

'Then put the cap back on your pen and think about it while I take this contract away to read through it quietly. When I've finished I'll let you know, and then we can fax it to my sister Emily in Ferara.'

Rising politely from his seat, Theo granted her a faintly mocking bow.

The reply came through from Emily almost immediately. Fortunately she had been in her office at the palace when the fax arrived.

As Theo handed Miranda the reply, she pictured the scene in Ferara. Emily would have been tearing her hair out after scanning the document and realising it was a post-nuptial agreement rather than a pre-nuptial one. She would have erupted before she got down to studying it closely. This supposition was borne out by the fact that Emily had penned a swift response by hand, not even bothering to type it out first. Written in her twin's uncompromising script, the words positively vibrated with frustration.

> *Why the hell didn't you ask me to look at this BEFORE you married him?*
> *Em.*

There weren't even any kisses by her name, though Emily had underlined the abbreviation—as if there could be any mistake, Miranda thought, biting back her smile.

'And here's another one,' Theo informed her with a heavy sigh, leaning back on his chair to retrieve a second fax. 'Also from Ferara.'

Miranda shot him a warning glance. His irony only made him more attractive, and she wanted to keep a clear head. Taking the fax from him, she turned her back to concentrate.

And don't expect me to read this contract in a hurry. I don't sit around waiting for you to do something silly, you know. I do work. And how are you, by the way? Are you all right? For goodness' sake, let me know.

'May I?' She turned around again and glanced at the pen tray on his desk.

He dipped his head. 'Be my guest.'

Choosing a corner away from him, she wrote:

I'm fine. Please don't worry about me. Marriage to Theo is rather more complicated than I had expected, that's all. Tell me what you think when you come to the blessing!

And then, as an afterthought she added:

Sorry for all this! M xxx

'Will you send it for me?' she asked, turning to Theo. He held out his hand.

She waited until it was safely dispatched and then turned to go.

'You'd better take these with you. I've no wish to intrude.'
He gave her the faxed copies.

'I'll shred them.'

'So?' Theo said at last, when the shredder fell silent.

'So?' Miranda repeated.

'Are you going to give me a clue? Did Emily give you her first impression?'

Oh, yes, she had! And who could blame Em for feeling the way she did, when Theo's handwritten contract had arrived on her desk within a few short days of her learning that her twin was about to be married to a stranger? Shock, horror, incredulity—those wouldn't even begin to cover Emily's reaction. And that was before she got round to indignation and hysterical laughter, Miranda guessed.

'She said she would read it through and let me have her thoughts at the blessing,' she said carefully.

'I want an answer now. Or at least by close of business today.'

Theo kept his voice low, but he might as well have thumped the desk. Miranda bristled. She wasn't another of his business assets, to be quickly dealt with and filed away. 'Close of business?'

'Yes.'

'Well, you can't have it. My sister's very busy.'

'And I'm not?'

Theo controlled his impatience with difficulty. The contract had to be signed. The documents he had been poring over the morning after their wedding had come from Dimitri's lawyers. They reminded him that, according to the instructions in his grandfather's will, he must remain married to Miranda for at least thirty days for the share transfer to take place. The contract he had drawn up bound Miranda to their marriage for double that time. Naturally the true purpose of the agreement would never come out, and in the unlikely event that she balked at sixty days he had sugared the pill with a huge cash incentive and every safeguard he could put in place for her. No one in their right mind would refuse to sign.

It was another step on the road to his goal, and helped to salve his conscience as well. He had thought the contract would give her something to mull over, something to get excited about—something to keep her busy while he took the helicopter and made his peace with Dimitri. This last gesture meant a lot to him, and he owed his change of heart to Miranda. But he would go alone. He couldn't risk any last-minute complications...

'Why are you in such a hurry for my answer, Theo?'

'Such a hurry?' Repeating Miranda's words with a garnish of incredulity, he adopted an affronted expression. 'I am making over a king's ransom to you, and yet you are reluctant to sign?'

She turned her face away, as if she needed a moment to put her thoughts into words. 'That's very generous of you, but this is our honeymoon. Must it always come down to business for you, Theo?'

She was right, and he wished at that moment that it wasn't so, but money, business, they were the only things he truly understood. 'I'm sorry. I thought the contract would be like a wedding gift—a reassurance for you...' He sighed as if he were the one who was hurt. However bad it made him feel, on this occasion he had to manipulate the situation.

'It is very generous. Perhaps too generous, Theo. But I can't push Emily into reading it for me right away.'

Why not? He curbed his impatience, knowing it wouldn't help his case. 'Perhaps you could send her a fax expressing your impatience, and mention that project you have in mind?' She hesitated, but he could see he had hit the right spot.

'That seems reasonable…'

Handing her a pen, he stood over her while she quickly wrote a note.

'Well, that's done,' she said, after he had faxed it to Ferara. 'Now all we can do is wait.'

'I disagree,' he said, drawing her into his arms.

CHAPTER TEN

MAKING love was all-consuming for both of them, Theo reflected as he kicked the door of the stateroom shut behind them. Would they make it to the bed this time? It seemed unlikely. They were already wrapped around each other as if every inch of their bodies must be in contact for them to survive. Clothes were discarded with indecent haste. Miranda was insatiable, and he…he just wanted to forget.

Gathering her into his arms, he locked her legs around his waist and carried her the few steps to the long console table that ran against the wall. Sweeping some papers aside, he lowered her down.

She yelped as her naked flesh came into contact with the frigid marble, but when he moved in for a kiss, murmuring endearments, trying to take it slow, she curled her fingers around his neck and dragged him down to her. As their tongues clashed in a prelude to the greater intimacy they were about to share he slid his hands up her thighs, and when she moaned encouragement he drew his tongue along the full swell of her bottom lip, keeping their mouths touching so that he could feel as well as hear the little cry she always made when he entered her.

She gasped, and, reaching for him, clutched his buttocks

to force him on, but he drew back, making her wait. 'Don't be so impatient.'

'Oh, please, Theo…'

It was tempting to follow her desperate command, but so much better for both of them if he directed the pace. 'Not yet,' he husked against her lips.

'I can't wait,' she wailed, stabbing her fingers into him.

He was so engorged he thought he might hurt her, and proceeded slowly, easing himself into her little by little. Throwing back her head in triumph, she worked her hips urgently to draw him deeper.

'Theo, please…'

He moved more firmly, keeping the rhythm slow. He loved to give her pleasure, loved to see her flushed and quivering with excitement. It made him want to give her more. He upped the pace. It made him want to give her everything…

He waited until the first climax had subsided, and then, lifting her into his arms he carried her over to the bed. He was still deep inside her, and she was still begging him for more. 'Soon,' he promised. 'The moment we get there…'

'Theo,' she sighed, as he settled her down on the satin sheets.

'What do you want, baby?' Her eyes were half closed, and her breathing through damp, parted lips was soft and rapid.

'Kiss me…'

'How could he resist? Dipping his head, he kissed her tenderly on the lips.

'Kiss me properly.'

He smiled, and tried again.

'Mmm, that's better,' she said at last when he let her go.

He loved to see the effect of his restraint. It was always the same. She responded so eagerly. Her nipples were almost painfully erect, and her breasts were like two perfect globes, all of which demanded his attention. Cupping her breasts, he made her gasp, and that gasp soon turned to a whimper as he began to chafe each perfect bud with his thumb pad.

'I want you now. I don't want to wait...'

Her voice was soft and insistent as her eyes implored him. She was exquisite, sweetly scented, and warm beneath his lips. And as he suckled and tugged and heard her sob with pleasure he knew that all he wanted was Miranda, and that he had to make this marriage work.

She had been foolish to doubt him. Theo had taken every one of her doubts and obliterated them with a kiss. She loved him so deeply there were no words to describe how she felt. It was already impossible to imagine what her life had been without him...without *this*, she knew, as he thrust into her again. Would she ever get enough of him? It didn't seem possible.

When Theo left her to tie up some loose ends Miranda took a long bath to consider her thoughts about the scholarship scheme. She was in a ferment of new ideas, and Theo had promised to discuss them with her over dinner.

After drying her hair, she dressed with particular care, making full use of the beautiful selection of clothes and accessories she had found in her dressing room. Leaving her hair loose, she had applied the minimum of make-up and just a spritz of scent. When she had boosted her student income by working as a cabaret singer, mask-like make-up had been *de rigueur*—to the point where she'd felt naked without it; she hated it now.

She wanted to make the extra effort because they had never been closer. She wanted to show Theo how happy he made her, and how she wanted to play a full role in his life as he would in hers. For the first time since their hasty wedding she felt like his wife.

And now she was ready, Miranda decided, as she examined her reflection in the mirror. Goodness knew what Theo saw in her, when he could have anyone, but she would stand by him now through anything—everything.

Remembering his caution that the Savakis equivalent to a lottery win would be delivered to her door every calendar month, rather than every four weeks, she smiled. Didn't he know how that sounded to someone who had been prepared to work for the minimum wage? Twelve payments each year instead of thirteen, when each of those payments was in the stratosphere? Were people really so rich, so distanced from reality?

But she was one of those people now, Miranda remembered, and with wealth such as the Savakis family possessed came a scale of responsibility she had never encountered before. It made her all the more determined to make good use of the money. She would remember her roots too, and how luck had played such a huge part in her life. Without her brother-in-law's gift of a priceless violin she would never have been able to enjoy her short-lived career, and now she was in a position to extend that same opportunity to someone else. Money couldn't buy happiness, but it could open doors and enhance the prospects of the type of student she had in mind. Theo's monthly allowance was an unexpected gift, but she would grab it with both hands—even if one of those hands was pretty useless.

With a wry grin Miranda realised she hadn't felt this good since before the accident—or maybe ever. Without even knowing it Theo had restored something vital in her life; she had a cause to champion, as well as the chance to give something back.

She found him leaning on the rail, staring out across to sea. Climbing the last few steps of the companionway, she felt a new tension building as he turned and they stared at each other. The connection between them was powerful and unique.

They stared at each other in silence for a few moments, and she knew that he appreciated the trouble she had taken with her appearance. Theo didn't stare as some men might, as if she were a product they were evaluating and comparing with the rest. When Theo looked at her he made her feel like the only woman in the world. And he had taken the same amount of trouble, as if he had guessed she would choose a formal outfit from the selection in her wardrobe.

The gown was a simple fall of blue-grey silk, and she had draped a beautiful beaded shawl around her shoulders—but only to protect her against the unpredictable breeze that could spring up on the sea at night. Thanks to Theo, she was no longer so self-conscious about her injuries.

'Are you hungry?'

It was an innocent question, but Miranda still had to smother the smile tugging at her lips. The last time Theo had asked her that same question the food his chef had prepared for them had gone to waste. 'I need to eat,' she agreed cautiously.

'I need to eat too,' he assured her. 'I need to build up my strength.'

'Do you?' She feigned alarm.

With a wicked grin, he linked her arm through his and strolled with her to the table that had been set for them beneath the stars.

Miranda couldn't help reflecting that Theo was a very sensual man, which was a world apart from being a sexual athlete. But it was impossible to be in his company without at least considering how long it would be before he took her back to bed…

'We can't disappoint my chef a second time,' he murmured,

as if her thoughts were an open book to him. Briefly locking glances, they sat down. 'Though you do make it hard for me,' he added, 'because you look particularly beautiful tonight.' Raising her damaged hand to his lips, he kissed it in a way that made every part of her feel beautiful.

The table was laid with glittering crystal and a wealth of silverware on top of a fine white damask cloth. A dozen candles flickered in an exquisite Art Deco candelabrum, and Miranda thought the indolent pose of the figure gracing the stem the most erotic example of the silversmith's art she had ever seen.

'Exquisite, isn't she?' Theo murmured, noticing her interest.

'You're very lucky to have such things.'

He held her gaze, and suddenly Miranda was wondering if she was the most recent addition to his collection. Miranda Weston, off-the-shelf-bride, with her short-lived, if glorious musical career—something of a curiosity. It irritated her to discover that the insecurity was always lurking ready to pounce, but she couldn't hold back now. 'Why did you remain unmarried and then settle on me a matters of hours after we met, Theo?'

'Have you never heard of love at first sight?'

Miranda smiled, and Theo saw that she had relaxed, but her question had given him a jolt. Her bluntness was extraordinary, but of course that was one of the things he liked most about her. Would he tell the truth? No. How could he, when the truth was that he had needed a bride, and Miranda Weston, attractive and vulnerable, had happened along at the right moment? She would find the truth, that he had indeed fallen in love with her, just a little later, impossible to believe if he revealed the facts behind their hasty marriage.

'Ah—vichyssoise. My favourite chilled soup.' He straightened up with relief as the steward served them. 'Please thank the chef for me, will you, Marco?'

'Certainly, sir.'

'Champagne?' he suggested, turning to Miranda.

'That would be lovely.'

As she smiled into his eyes he wished he could tell her that the helicopter was fuelled, the flight plan filed, and that he would be taking off for the Savakis stronghold to see Dimitri as soon as they finished dinner. But he couldn't bring himself to break the mood, and there was too much at stake to risk upsetting Miranda and throwing yet another difficulty into the mix.

Miranda was glad Theo didn't ply her with wine. He didn't drink at all, she noticed, preferring to keep a clear head. But he did insist on feeding her morsels of food—food she couldn't resist any more than she could resist the expression in his eyes. The touch of his fingertips each time they accidentally brushed against her mouth was electrifying, and she almost rubbed her lips away with the linen napkin in an attempt to reduce their sensitivity.

'What's this?' she said, when the steward brought a low burner to the table and lit the flame. How many courses must they sit through before they could retire to their stateroom? Wicked thoughts, but she couldn't help herself. 'I thought we'd finished the meal?'

'Not until we've tasted my chef's *pièce de résistance*. Why? Are you in a hurry to get somewhere?'

She confined her answer to a look.

'I must do all the work now,' Theo informed her coolly, shrugging off his jacket.

'Dirty work?' she teased. A flick of each wrist was all it took to ditch his cufflinks, and he rolled back his sleeves.

And then a fresh fruit platter arrived: strawberries, mango, pear, pineapple and crunchy juicy apple slices, all of them ready to dip into warm chocolate sauce.

'Oh…' Miranda groaned. This was going to be very dirty

work indeed. And how was she supposed to behave in front of the crew when chocolate was dripping down her chin and Theo was catching it on his finger and sucking it clean?

The chocolate fondue had been a masterstroke. He was glad it had worked, relieved to see her so relaxed. This was their honeymoon, after all, and she deserved some fun. If the latest communication from Dimitri's doctor was to be believed, the fun was all but over for both of them. He didn't speak, because he didn't want to encourage questions. He was content to sit and wait for his co-pilot's signal.

As they sipped coffee Miranda wished the night could last for ever. It was so peaceful out on the ocean, with only the stars to keep them company and the sound of water breaking beneath the bow. She felt so close to Theo without the need for words. But when the steward returned with fresh coffee, she reached out with her damaged hand and clumsily knocked her cup over.

'Don't worry.' Theo waved the steward away. 'Here—let me pour you another cup. It's not important,' he insisted when she tried to mop up the mess. 'How did your injury happen, anyway? You never told me the whole story.'

She was unprepared for his directness, and her heart lurched at his mention of the accident. The feeling was as unpleasantly familiar as her nightmares.

She had locked the door in her mind on some horrible secrets, but as Theo continued to hold her gaze Miranda knew he wouldn't be fobbed off with any flimsy excuse. 'It happened after a concert, when I was still buoyed up on adrenaline and champagne. Unfortunately, the man who gave me a lift was in the same state. If only I'd been thinking clearly, I'd have taken account of the fact that he was drunk…I must have thought I was invincible.'

'People frequently do think that after a drink.'

'I should have waited for a taxi, I know.' She grimaced. 'It sounds so lame now, so obvious.'

'The lead-up to an accident always does. Otherwise we'd all know how to avoid them, wouldn't we?'

'Don't make allowances for me, Theo.' Her face tensed. 'Someone died. The driver was killed because of me.'

'But how could that be your fault? You said he was drunk.'

'Yes, he was. But—' She stopped, biting her lip. 'I distracted him.'

'How? Who was he?'

'He was my professor at the music *conservatoire*.' She sighed. 'There were two men, my teacher and my manager, and after the accident it became clear that both of them had been using me for their own reasons. My teacher had wanted to keep me to himself, lock me away like the heroine in *Phantom of the Opera*. He was a control freak.'

'And your manager?'

She smiled bitterly. 'After the accident, when I was no longer a meal ticket for him as a classical violinist, he tried to sell my "tragic story" to the tabloids.'

'I imagine you loved that?'

'I hated it.' She said the words fiercely under her breath, her mind a million miles from him.

'And your teacher died? That must have been devastating.' There was something wrong here, he knew it. He sensed she was hiding something, and was suddenly filled with an irrational fear. What was it? What was keeping her apart from him?

Coming to, she focused on his face. 'The whole experience was devastating. I was grateful to both of them for building my career, but I didn't want to be owned by them or manipulated by them. And then one died because of me, and the other betrayed me.'

She seemed so frank, yet something was still niggling at the back of his mind. 'How did your family take the news of the accident?'

'My family?' Miranda hesitated. She hadn't told them everything. How could she? 'They…' She could never tell lies to her family.

'They do know?' Theo pressed.

'Of course they know.'

'Everything? The full implication of what has happened to you? The fact that you will never play the violin on a concert platform again?'

'Of course. Theo, please.' She saw him looking at her as if he knew how raw her wounds were—but he couldn't know. 'Oh, the steward's here!' Leaning forward, she distracted Theo, welcoming the interruption.

'Excuse me, sir, but this fax has arrived for Kyria Savakis.'

'The royal crest of Ferara!' Miranda exclaimed as the steward passed it to her. 'Yes, it's from Emily,' she said after checking it. 'Do you mind?' Clutching the fax, she left the table.

Theo waited tensely, his dark gaze locked onto Miranda's back as she stopped a few feet away from him. He might have known Emily would drop everything the instant she'd received the handwritten contract. That was what was missing in *his* life—family members to rely on. There was an invisible bond between Miranda and her twin that even Miranda's absence had been unable to break. Emily probably had Alessandro's troops on standby right now, ready to fly out and execute a rescue mission.

He envied his wife's deep bond with her family. It was something he could never buy. After his parents had been killed in their light aircraft he had been raised in Dimitri's household, where a succession of highly paid professionals had overseen his upbringing and education. Dimitri had remained a sinister, shadowy figure, his only virtue in the eyes of a boy growing up the beautiful women he wore on his arm like so many bangles…

No, family was something he didn't know a great deal about. Before Miranda business had been his only passion; it responded to his control and grew ever stronger beneath his direction. It was the one unwavering point in his life—without it, what would he be?

Glancing up at Miranda, Theo felt another stab of envy. She had half turned towards him as she double-checked the fax again, and her pent-up excitement told him she was back, at least symbolically, in the bosom of the family to which she belonged. That closeness contrasted starkly with his own life to date.

But if he was nothing without his business, what did his future hold without Miranda?

CHAPTER ELEVEN

EMILY'S fax was like a comfort blanket after Theo's insistence that she tell him about the accident. He had been right to attempt to draw it out of her. It was the proverbial pus from a wound—the tragic death, the devastating consequences brought on by her own foolishness and two men's determination to manipulate another human being. But that didn't make it any easier to relive.

Wanting to share the news from Emily, she turned to go back to him. But the same steward had returned and appeared to be confiding an urgent message.

Miranda's heart thumped ominously when Theo shot up from the table. Meeting her gaze, he excused himself with the briefest nod.

His face was so bleak it frightened her. She stood motionless, watching him disappear in the direction of his office, still with Emily's fax clutched to her chest. She told herself to relax. Whatever had happened, Theo would deal with it. She would return to the table and wait for him.

The steward brought fresh coffee, and even some warm towels for her to refresh her hands after the messy pudding. But there was only so long she could sit counting stars. She had to go and see if she could do anything to help. She had just pushed her chair back from the table when he returned.

'You must forgive me, Miranda…'

She could tell he didn't want to sit down. He was tense and distracted, his face a grim mask. She stood up and tried to take his hand. 'Theo, what's happened?'

'My grandfather has passed away.'

'Oh, Theo, I'm so sorry—'

'I must return to the Savakis compound immediately.'

The Savakis compound? That didn't sound very inviting. 'Of course.' She could see he was sparking with impatience. 'I'll do anything I can to help you.' An image of her parents' small, cosy home flashed into Miranda's mind. She couldn't let him go alone. 'I'm coming with you.'

'Of course you'll come with me.'

Theo's voice was fierce, but she made allowances. Family was something she understood. He was devastated, but she would be there for him.

'Can you be ready quickly?'

'Of course.' Her mind raced. 'If you have a small suitcase I can borrow?'

'Borrow?' He stared at her as if she were a stranger. 'I'm sure the steward will find something for you. Look, there isn't time for a long-winded discussion, Miranda. Go to the stateroom and make a start.'

'If it's easier for you to go without me—'

'Without you?' He stared at her as if she was mad. 'Out of the question!'

Theo's face was pale beneath his tan—pale and tense. She had only wanted to reassure him, not add to his anguish.

'The helicopter will be ready to fly in fifteen minutes,' he said.

'The helicopter? Theo…' But he had already turned to go.

'There should be a black suit in your dressing room. Make sure you bring it,' he tossed over his shoulder.

She was already shaking, already quivering with the deep

and irrational fear of flying that had never eased, no matter how many times she took to the air. And now Theo was asking her to sit in a Plexiglas bubble and be held in the air by whirling cricket bats?

She had to do this…for him. 'How long will we be away?' she called after him, trying to focus her mind on what to pack.

'As long as it takes. Now, go!'

His commanding gesture took her by surprise, but she had to remember that this was a family bereavement—and it was also the first time she had been called upon to stand at his side. She had to put her fears aside, and, however brusque Theo's manner, she understood. She was his wife, and it was her duty to support him. He had obviously been very close to his grandfather, and must be feeling guilty for being away on his honeymoon at such a time. Sometimes life could be very cruel.

The helicopter ride was everything Miranda had dreaded. To make it worse, although Theo chose not to fly the aircraft himself, he sat next to the pilot—so she didn't even have his reassuring strength to cling on to. She sat as close as she could to him in the seat behind, trying not to vomit as the wretched machine sucked her stomach up with it into inky nothingness.

Theo must have given the pilot instructions to break all air speed records, Miranda gathered as they bounced through some bone-shaking turbulence. She was sure her face was white as her stomach turned over, but even then she sensed Theo was willing the aircraft to go faster if it could.

'Will it take long for us to get to your grandfather's home?' She had to ask. She had to know how long it would take. But Theo couldn't hear with his headphones on, so she had to lean forward and touch his neck.

'What do you want?' He frowned as he turned to look at her.

'Will it be much longer?' She hoped he didn't hear he voice quiver.

'I'm sorry.' His face softened, and, reaching out, he stroke her hair. 'This is an ordeal for you. Forgive me. I have so muc on my mind—'

'Please, don't apologise.' She cut him off, hoping she ha succeeded in masking her terror. 'I understand, Theo. Yo don't have to say anything.'

'Unless the weather closes in we should be there in unde the hour.' With a smile of reassurance, he turned away.

Of course he was preoccupied; apart from missing hi grandfather's last hours, he had a funeral to arrange and rel atives to console. She had never considered Theo's relative before, Miranda realised, her tension easing fractionally a her mind turned to practical matters. She had no idea if th Savakis clan was as large and loving as Spiros and Agalia' extended family, or a small, close unit like her own. But however many people arrived to celebrate Dimitri's life she was ready to help. She was free from any emotional en tanglement and therefore could attend to practical matters like food and who would sleep where, while Theo spen time with people who would undoubtedly be as distresse as he was.

It was a woman thing, Miranda realised. Theo wa wounded, and her natural instinct was to care for him. And on top of that they had a strong relationship. When one o them was down, the other pulled them up.

Taking Emily's fax out of her pocket, she curled her fin gers round it like a talisman. She couldn't wait to share th contents with Theo, but it would have to keep until a more ap propriate time. She didn't need to read it again to remembe the words Emily had written.

They say lightning doesn't strike twice in the same place.
I think it just did! Where did you find him? Love Em xxx

The moment they climbed out of the helicopter Theo was surrounded by men in dark suits who barely acknowledged Miranda's presence. Theo was dressed formally too, as she was, but he looked different somehow—different and forbidding.

Her legs were still shaking so badly it took her a moment to regroup and chase after him. She was relieved when he stopped and, holding up his hands to silence everyone, turned back to look for her.

'Miranda…' He held out his hand.

But only as a signal that she should stop dawdling, Miranda discovered, when she hurried towards him and he started off again.

The huge building they were approaching looked like something out of a Gothic horror movie. Every window was shuttered and not a glimmer of light escaped, as if Dimitri Savakis had wanted to shut out the world. She couldn't help imagining the transformation that might occur if lights were blazing and there were people buzzing back and forth behind the shuttered panes…

No, money couldn't buy everything, and here was the proof. The Savakis ancestral home might be grand, but it was soulless, and even an energetic imagination like her own couldn't stretch far enough to picture a family living there.

By the time they reached the entrance Miranda was feeling a deep and irrational sense of dread. She put it down to the fact that beyond the house she had spotted a wire fence, and even lookout posts. From the warning signs she gathered the fence was electrified. If this was what the super-rich called home, the appeal was lost on her.

As vast arched doors swung open, the men striding in

front of her stopped abruptly and she almost bumped into them. Theo was waiting politely to one side, allowing her to cross the threshold in front of him. Tipping her chin, she walked in.

Her first footsteps sent an echo spinning round a vast marble hallway, and in her peripheral vision she was aware that liveried servants were bowing low. Beyond that, there was silence. Irrationally, she longed for a hug, or a sound—any sound. But her introduction to the Savakis compound was about as cosy as walking into an airport terminal building…though this one had mammoth chandeliers, and what might have been antique French furnishings. At the far end there was a grand sweeping staircase, and lined up in front of it a motionless group of about thirty men and women, all wearing the same unrelieved black.

Miranda's stomach did a fast loop. None of them was looking at her, she realised; they were all staring at Theo, as if he had brought with him the very air they had to breathe.

'The relatives,' he explained, dipping forward to murmur in her ear, and then, placing a hand beneath her arm, he steered her forward.

It was a receiving line of black crows. Not a nice way to feel about your husband's family, Miranda reflected as she moved down the line, but it was an apt description for this group. Keeping her own face schooled to neutrality, she murmured a few words to each, searching for a single pair of eyes holding sorrow or sympathy, anything other than shrewd calculation. There wasn't a single pair. Instead she detected the barely suppressed excitement that sometimes—horribly—accompanied a death, when people started to fathom what it might mean to them in terms of financial gain.

How terrible it must have been for Theo to grow up in such a place and with such people—and to be amongst them now, when he had just lost his grandfather. She couldn't wait for this to end, so they could be alone and she could reassure him.

'I regret I must leave you for a short while, Miranda.'

'What?' She gazed up at him distractedly as he drew her aside, her stomach contracting as she imagined making small talk with his relatives. But then she saw the look in Theo's eyes. Far from grief, his expression held all the watchfulness and urgency she had sensed around her. 'Is something wrong?'

His lips pressed down, and he breathed as if to speak, then thought better of it. She laid a hand on the sleeve of his jacket, knowing she had to help him somehow. 'I understand, Theo. Don't worry about me. I'll be fine. You must have a lot to sort out—'

'It's rather more than that,' he said, watching the ebb and flow of relatives now they had broken into small groups.

'Politics?' Miranda guessed, murmuring discreetly, 'It's the same in every family.'

He hummed cynically. 'While we're on the subject of families, Miranda, what did your sister think about the contract? We haven't had a minute to talk, and it's unlikely to get any better for quite some time.'

Miranda's faced softened into a smile as she answered him. 'I think she approved.'

'Then will you sign?' Reaching into his breast pocket, Theo pulled out the original copy. 'I want to make sure that, whatever happens, your future is secure.'

'Now?'

'Better had…with so much going on it's bound to get overlooked. And I want to protect your interests.' He stared her straight in the eyes and smiled. Then, uncapping his fountain pen, he held it out to her.

Moving to a side table, Miranda signed the paper. Anything to make life easier for him—and she had Emily's backing.

As she handed the contract back to him Theo exchange
glances with a group of men.

'Do you have to leave me right away?'

'Unfortunately I have a meeting to attend.'

'A meeting? Oh, no, Theo, that's not fair—'

'Don't look so worried. The staff will take care of you
They'll make sure you have everything you need.'

'I wasn't thinking of myself…' But he didn't seem to be
listening. She tried again. 'Why must you be made to sit in a
meeting so late at night when you are just coming to term
with the death of your grandfather? Don't these people un
derstand anything?'

'It isn't like that, I can assure you.'

'Really?' She threw a fierce gaze around the room, encom
passing all of them. 'You need time to mourn, Theo. It's an
important stage in the grieving process. You should be plan
ning the funeral, not attending a meeting—'

'I don't have time for this, Miranda. I'll find someone who
will show you where to go.'

'But the formalities following a death are the foundation
upon which we build the rest of our lives—'

'You have to understand that my circumstances are quite
different from your own,' he said impatiently. 'Unless this
family is properly managed—'

'Managed?' She stared up at him, feeling a chill run
through her. Was that Theo's idea of the perfect family…one
that was 'properly managed'?

'Yes, managed,' he confirmed. 'There's an awful lot of
money at stake, Miranda. It changes things.'

'Does it? Can't you still have a family that cares for each
other?'

As Theo sighed, Miranda could see how far apart they
were on this.

'Miranda, you're a hopeless romantic.'

'Maybe so, but—'

'Understand one thing, Miranda. This isn't about grieving, or love. It's about money and power.'

When she saw how hard Theo's expression had become, Miranda felt her heart go out to him. 'Then I'm very sorry for you, Theo…for all of you.'

Before he could draw away again she put her hands around his waist and laid her head against his chest. He didn't know what to do at first, and remained stiff and unyielding. But he could hardly thrust her away in front of everyone. When she turned her head to drop a kiss on his chest, he laid his hands on her back, hoping that satisfied her requirements whilst maintaining the decorum he felt it was necessary to adopt in public.

'Oh, Theo…' Miranda smiled sadly as she lifted her face to look at him. 'Has no one given you a hug before?'

'Miranda, you're being ridiculous.' But he spoke softly, and was gentle with her as he disentangled himself. 'And now you must let me go.' He looked around until his gaze finally settled. 'Not perfect—but she'll do.'

'What are you talking about?' Miranda sighed with frustration as Theo walked away. He wasn't making it easy for her, but she wouldn't stop trying to offer him support—or behaving with the utmost self-control, she realised, when she identified the woman he was shepherding out of the shadows. 'Lexis.'

'Miranda,' Lexis said, with equal enthusiasm. 'Or should I call you Kyria Savakis now, and bow?'

'I think we both know that's not necessary.' Offering her hand, Miranda made it impossible for Lexis to refuse. 'Welcome to the Savakis—'

'Compound? Yes, I know.' Lexis cut across her, gazing around. 'And you're welcome to it.'

'Yes, well,' Theo said. 'I'll leave you two ladies to it, if you don't mind.'

'And if we do?'

He stopped. 'Sorry, Lexis, but in your case you'll just have to grit your teeth and stir your cauldron. Miranda…' Coming back to her, he cupped her face. 'I won't leave you alone a moment longer than I have to.'

Reassured, Miranda smiled as she watched Theo ushering the other men into one of the rooms off the hall.

'Touching.'

She turned at the cynical remark. 'Lexis, we are where we are, and neither of us can change a thing. But we're here for a funeral, so do you think we could call a truce?'

Lexis studied her face, and, finding her unflinching, shrugged. 'That's fine by me. So…' She looked Miranda up and down. 'You're one of them now.'

'One of them?' As Miranda followed Lexis's glance around what she had already gleaned was a materialistic gathering, she firmed her jaw. 'I can assure you, Lexis, that there is not the smallest similarity between these people and me. I'm here as Theo's wife, to support him and to offer whatever comfort I can.'

And to stand in his place as host if I have to, she added grimly to herself, following the women who were starting to file into one of the rooms off the hall. 'Will you join me, Lexis?'

'This is the small salon,' Lexis murmured discreetly, evidently mellowing enough to accompany her.

As they entered the brilliantly lit room Miranda guessed her entire family home would fit easily into the 'small' salon. 'It's very nice…'

'Nice?' Lexis raised a brow. 'And I'm sure you can't have failed to notice how friendly everyone is?'

Lexis's irony was well founded. As much as she tried to

atch anyone's attention, Miranda couldn't. It seemed every-
ne preferred either to sit rigidly, sipping tea, or to stand
tiffly in silence, lost in thought. 'What's wrong with every-
ne?' she whispered to Lexis.

'This is a tense time for them.'

'What do you mean?'

'Look around the room and tell me what you see.'

'Theo's grieving relatives?' Miranda found it hard to sound
onvinced.

'Even *you* don't believe that,' Lexis commented cynically.

'Then explain,' Miranda pressed.

'This is a room full of women who depend for the very air
hey breathe on the men they married. They're all sitting here
vaiting for the outcome of their husbands' meeting with Theo.
They want to be sure that things will remain the same now
hat Dimitri's dead. He always paid out to keep the relatives
ff his back.'

'But that's so cold-hearted of them!'

'Yes, isn't it? The only thing these women care about is that
heir allowances won't be hit. There's not a single person
ere, except for you and me, who has an interest outside the
ome that isn't vetted first by their husband.'

'Really? What are your interests?'

'Well, I don't sit around spending my allowance. As it
appens, I run a small animal charity.'

Miranda found herself smiling at this unsuspected side to
Lexis. Theo might think her a tearaway, but Lexis had more
lepth than he thought. 'It's not up to us to judge them, Lexis.
We've been out in the world—maybe they've never had that
pportunity.'

'You're too soft,' Lexis insisted. Taking Miranda's arm, she
teered her towards a door that led outside. 'There is such a
hing as free will, you know.'

Miranda had been wrong about Lexis, and it was a relie
to find an ally in such an unexpected quarter. 'Thank good
ness it will never be like that with Theo and me. I'm alway
going to work—'

'And he's agreed to that?'

'He can't refuse me. Music is my life—*was* my life befor
we met.'

'But you can't continue as a top-flight musician,' Lexis sai
bluntly, nodding to the attendant who was waiting to ope
doors for them.

'No, you're right.' Miranda was surprised to learn that i
didn't hurt so much to admit it now that she had somethin
else she felt a passion for. 'But I can carry on teaching—pass
ing on the knowledge and experience I have gained.'

Lexis made an approving sound as they walked outside
'Times change,' she conceded. 'At one time men like The
were expected to marry virgins and make a dynastic match
And a dynastic match is still expected in families like ours
Take me, for instance.' Linking arms with Miranda, Lexi
drew her further into the garden. 'My father wanted me t
marry Theo.'

'And did you want to?'

'That's not the point, Miranda. Whether I wanted to or no
I was sent over to Kalmos for Theo's inspection like a priz
heifer.'

'But that's outrageous!'

'No, Miranda, that's business. Fortunately Theo didn't bu
into the idea, and had enough sense to ship me home.'

'But why did you go along with it?'

'I love my father…'

A look of understanding passed between them.

'At least if Theo lets you work you'll always retain you
independence.'

'There's no if about it.' Miranda smiled at Lexis. 'I have no intention of ever becoming completely dependent on a man. I almost went down that route once—emotionally, at least—believing my confidence to perform was based solely on the approval of my teacher or my manager, when in actual fact it was up to me to put in the work and make sure I was good enough to stand before an audience. I think it's important never to lose sight of your own identity, however much you love someone.'

'You really mean that, don't you?'

Instead of sharing her mood of optimism, Lexis's face had clouded over. 'Yes, of course I do,' Miranda said, wondering why Lexis had suddenly grown so quiet. 'Were you in love with Theo?' she asked gently.

'What if I was? He never wanted me. It was just a cold-blooded business deal cooked up by my father and Dimitri Savakis to merge two great shipping lines. I could have told my father that a man like Theo would never go along with it, but he wouldn't listen.'

'I'm really sorry.'

'Don't be. I can look after myself.'

As Lexis tipped her chin, Miranda smiled. 'Well, if you ever need a friend…'

'I appreciate that. And I'm sorry too, because I thought you were like all the rest, looking for a meal ticket, and now I know you're not.'

Miranda wondered why Lexis seemed so uneasy. 'Is there something else? Something you're not telling me?'

Lexis looked at her, and then her gaze faltered, as if she was trying to find the words to voice some unpalatable truth.

'Come on—tell me what's worrying you,' Miranda pressed. 'Surely we can trust each other now?'

Lexis sighed and firmed her lips.

'Is it about Theo? If you think he will make it difficult fo
me to be independent now we're married, you're wrong, Lexis
I'm going to create scholarships for promising music students
and Theo has agreed to help me with the administration—'

'You really don't have any idea why Theo married you
do you?'

'He loves me…' Miranda's brave statement tailed away a
she saw the expression in Lexis's eyes. 'Lexis?' she prompted

'I'm so sorry. You don't deserve this.'

Miranda steeled herself. 'Go on.'

'Theo had to marry because Dimitri made it a condition o
his will.'

'Dimitri's will? What are you talking about? No.' Miranda
shook her head. She was definite on this point. 'Theo mar
ried me because he loves me and because of all this—' She
gestured back towards the room where all Theo's dependent:
were waiting with their stony faces. 'Theo wants a loving fam
ily, and I can give him that.'

Lexis made a sound of frustration. 'Theo hasn't got a ro
mantic bone in his body. I don't know what he told you, bu
this was never some idyllic "love at first sight" nonsense fo
him. Theo planned this marriage cold-bloodedly for no bet
ter reason than to gain power and control over the Savaki:
shipping line.'

'Power and control?' Miranda gave an incredulous laugh
'I can put your mind at rest there. My family has no influence
in the circles in which Theo moves—even if my twin dic
marry a prince.' Her conviction was growing stronger—Lexi
had made a terrible mistake.

'You still don't get it, do you?'

'I think you'd better tell me everything you know,' Miranda
pressed. She had done enough running away to know that un
pleasantness only followed you around. This time she wa:

going to face up to whatever Lexis had to say, and then decide what to do.

'All right,' Lexis began hesitantly. 'Dimitri made it a condition of his will that Theo must be married if he was to inherit the controlling interest in the Savakis shipping company—otherwise he'd lose the lot. Dimitri wanted to be sure that the dynastic line would continue.'

Miranda said nothing for a while, and then, raising her head, she stared Lexis in the eyes. 'So I'm the prize heifer?'

'I'm really sorry, Miranda, but I'm betting no one else would have told you.'

The meeting had ended, and the goal he had aimed for had been reached. Now it was on to the next challenge, Theo reflected, smiling to himself as he gathered up all the papers in front of him.

His mind was uncharacteristically packed with romantic thoughts. Miranda touched him in a way no one had before. The sound of her voice was enough to fill him with love. She was so tender, so devoted, and though he had tried to harden his heart and concentrate solely on business, on this day of all days, she had brought his whole life into clear focus with something as simple as a hug, had shown him what really mattered.

He'd spent his life pushing people away, knowing most had been paid to make a fuss of him. It had bred a coldness in him. He hadn't known how to be affectionate until Miranda. But she had shown him how to love without restraint, without boundaries, proving just as she'd done before the meeting that a simple touch or a tender glance was worth more than all the power and money in the world.

He was greedy for more, and he wanted to show her the same devotion. He wanted to prove how special she was and forge a future for them both, a future his grandfather had been denied. It might be too late to make his peace with the old man, but with Miranda at his side he could found the dy nasty that had meant so much to Dimitri.

It hadn't been easy for her since they met, and circum stances had turned their honeymoon on its head, but still she was taking everything in her stride. He would make it up to her. He could concentrate on being a good husband now that the contract was signed and his position as chairman of the board had been confirmed.

'No, thank you, gentlemen,' he said as someone offered him a second glass of champagne. 'If you will excuse me, I'm going to celebrate with my wife.'

CHAPTER TWELVE

MIRANDA. At last! I didn't think I was ever going to get away. Thank goodness someone showed you to our room. Is it all right for you? We can move if you don't like it…'

Even as he hunkered down beside the sofa to take her hand Theo realised something vital had changed between them. 'Miranda?' Ice sluiced through his veins as she turned to stare at him.

'Is it true, Theo?'

'Is what true?' He couldn't pretend he didn't know. Miranda's face was like an open book to him, and right now all the pages were twisted with hurt and disbelief.

'Did you marry me in order to secure your grasp on the Savakis shipping line?'

'Who told you that?'

'It doesn't matter who told me. Is it true?'

'Miranda… Come and sit with me for a moment. Let me explain—'

'*Explain?*'

He blenched and turned away. With that single word she had managed to express all the disillusionment he had heaped upon her.

'How can you explain that I was just part of your business strategy, Theo? And why can't you look at me if it isn' true?'

He had been so buoyed up as he raced to their room, so ex hilarated by the plans spinning round his head. What coul(he possibly say to reassure her now that it wasn't a lie?

He couldn't lie to her.

'Everything you say is true, Miranda. I didn't start out o this with the best of motives—'

'*This?*' She interrupted him. 'This marriage, do you mean?

'Don't make this any harder than it has to be.'

'How much harder does it get, Theo?'

Her voice was breaking, and it cut right through him. Bu what frightened him most was the way she was looking at hin with such furious disdain.

'You said you would never hurt me. You said we wer(marrying quickly because you couldn't wait to make me you bride. You said you wanted to share Kalmos, your favourite place on earth with me—remember that, Theo?'

'Miranda, please…'

'Get off me, Theo!' she warned him in a furious cold voice 'You manipulated me. You made me sign a contract when didn't realise what it entailed. You deceived me, and yo deceived my sister—'

'I put every safeguard on earth in place for you—'

'You bought me like a whore!'

'Don't say that!'

'You bought me with tarnished coin—'

'I gave you money to make you feel secure!'

'Do you really think you can buy anything, Theo? Eve a wife?'

'That's not what I intended.'

'Well, goodness knows what you *did* intend!'

'Your happiness and security mean everything to me—'

'My happiness? My security? You said you loved me, Theo, and I believed you. In the light of what I know now, your love doesn't count for anything.'

'Nevertheless, I do love you,' he said simply.

With a contemptuous exclamation Miranda sprang to her feet. 'Well, if this is your idea of love, you can keep it! And you can keep this, too.' Tugging off her wedding ring, she flung it at him. It rolled across the marble floor and skittered to a halt at his feet.

'What can I say to make you believe me?'

'Nothing.'

'I left the meeting to be with you. You're all that matters to me. You're the most important thing in the world to me—'

'Is that right?'

'When did you become so cold, Miranda?'

She gave a short, humourless laugh. 'Strangely enough, not when I learned that you had married me to acquire the controlling interest in the Savakis shipping line, but later— when I had read this.' She slapped her hand onto a document on the table. 'Dimitri's will. That was when I realised that you had only tied me into our marriage for sixty days because Dimitri's will stipulated that we must remain together for thirty days before the share transfer could take place. You really wanted to make sure of me, didn't you, Theo?'

He tensed. 'How did you get a copy of Dimitri's will?'

'It's surprising how accommodating people become when you bear the Savakis name. I have discovered that I only have to ask and I receive.'

'What are you talking about?'

'I went into the hub of Dimitri's world—his office,' she clarified, when Theo looked puzzled. 'Wasn't it you who said that the business meant everything to your grandfather? So I really wasn't surprised to discover that he kept a full secretarial service here, or that they were working overtime tonight. It was a small matter to say that you had sent me for a copy of your grandfather's will,' she continued mercilessly. 'They were hardly going to refuse me—hardly going to express surprise that you had sent me, a mere woman, to run an errand for you.'

'Miranda…' Theo wiped a hand across his face as if he couldn't bear to see what she had discovered reflected in her eyes.

'No wonder you faxed only that handwritten contract to my sister. If you had sent Emily a copy of your grandfather's will I suspect her response would have been very different.'

'And you've read the will?'

'Of course. There's no need for me to spell it out for you, is there, Theo?'

Dipping down, he picked up her wedding ring and, balancing it on the flat of his hand, held it out to her. 'I'd like to tell you that you're mistaken, Miranda, but I can't. Our marriage has to last for thirty days before the share transfer can be completed. Tonight I was voted unanimously onto the Savakis board as chairman, but that means nothing in practical terms without a controlling interest in the business. It would make me the puppet of greedy, unscrupulous men and I would have to resign. If I had done this…' he closed his hand around her wedding ring '…for my sake alone, then, yes, I would be as guilty as you paint me. But the future of too many people is hanging in the balance, and I have to think of them.'

'And for this you were prepared to sacrifice not only your own happiness but that of whichever woman was unfortunate enough to come along at the right moment?'

'Yes,' he admitted bluntly.

Touching her hand to her head, Miranda made a sound of incredulity. Closing her eyes, she shut him out.

'I realise that this has been a less than perfect start to our marriage—'

'*What?*' She cut across him with disbelief. 'This isn't the start of anything, Theo. There is no marriage.'

'Please put this on again, Miranda.'

'You are joking?' She stared at the ring he was holding out to her.

'No, I'm perfectly serious. Like I said, too many people are depending on me to get this right for it to stop now.'

'And what about me, Theo?'

The resolve in his face only intensified. 'Stop thinking about yourself, and help me help them.'

'I'm not frightened of sacrifice, Theo, but I do like to know what's expected of me from the start.'

'I've never asked you to do anything you don't want to do—have I, Miranda?'

'Do you know what you're asking?'

'For you to act as if everything's all right—for you to support me for the next thirty days. I'm asking for your help, Miranda.'

She was in turmoil. Before she had opened her eyes and seen the truth behind their marriage she would have laid down her life for him. 'But I love you…and you lied to me.'

'I loved you from the first moment we met.'

'You swore at me and called me an idiot!'

'We Greeks are a passionate people,' he murmured. However I felt at the precise moment we met, I love you here and now. We've here for the funeral of my grandfather Dimitri,' he continued, reining in his passion. 'Is it too much to expect my wife to stand at my side?'

'The same wife who played such a crucial if unwitting role in your victory at the board meeting today, Theo?'

'It's late.' He ignored her jibe as he glanced at his wristwatch. 'And I still have many people to see. You can stay here in the room, and I will arrange for the helicopter to take you back to the yacht, where you can collect your things and return home, or you can come downstairs with me and play your part. It's up to you, Miranda.'

'Can't these people wait until tomorrow?'

Theo gave her a look that suggested she had a lot to learn about her new relatives. 'Most of them will leave the moment the funeral is over. I imagine those who have already spoken to me and received their cheques will be packing now.'

Miranda exhaled slowly, trying to comprehend the new world in which she found herself. 'And what about the people who worked for your grandfather?'

'What about them?'

'I thought we had come here to offer comfort?'

'Comfort?' He lost patience with her. 'I'm here to write cheques.'

'But surely *some* of the staff must have cared for your grandfather?'

'Cared for him?' Walking across to pick up a decanter, he poured himself a drink. 'Do you mean like that group of vultures waiting downstairs?'

'No, Theo, I'm thinking of Dimitri's valet, his butler... I don't know.' The number of staff who might work in a house as large as this one was beyond her ken. 'There must be people in this house who have been affected by your grandfather's death. Don't you think we should find out who they are and try to help them?'

'We?' He swallowed his drink in a single gulp and swung around.

'People must be worried about their jobs, Theo. They need reassurance.'

She was right, he realised, but what was she saying? '

thought, like the rest of them, you couldn't wait to get away from me?' He made an impatient gesture. 'Well, here's your chance, Miranda. I'll deal with them.'

'We'll deal with them together,' she said coolly.

He still had her wedding ring clenched tight in his fist. She had made no move to take it back, and that riled him. But did he want to be married to some compliant milksop? 'Haven't you forgotten something?'

'Have I?'

Holding out the ring, he held her stare.

She didn't move. 'And your grandfather's staff?'

'All right! I'll call for Dimitri's major-domo and see if he can help us.'

They had worked their way steadily through the queue of relatives, and Theo was forced to concede that it would have been a lot harder without Miranda at his side. She was good at finding the right words—while he wrote the cheques.

He had issued a warning to all the idlers. They would have to fund their extravagant lifestyles themselves from now on, or draw in their horns—because he had something better to spend his money on. He had taken pleasure in outlining Miranda's plans to them, pretending not to see how her cheeks flushed red at every mention of it.

'We can't stop now,' she said, the moment he put his pen away.

He stood and stretched. 'It's getting late.'

'Nevertheless, we still have people to see…'

As he turned and met her gaze he felt a spear of longing and regret. He heard an echo from the past, the voice of his own mother, who had fought a losing battle against the idleness and excesses of his father. Was he in danger of turning into Acteon Savakis? The thought appalled him. But the thought that Miranda might have the same steel in her back bone as his mother had the opposite effect.

They sat up late, meeting every member of the household staff as Miranda had insisted. Theo explained that, in the Savakis way, Dimitri's funeral would be held the following morning. Everyone had their own lives to get back to, he said. And he was right about his relatives: the moment they had pocketed their cheques all their talk was of travel plans.

They were drinking coffee when Theo told her that their wedding blessing would have to be postponed.

'We have a few things to iron out before we talk about blessings.' Miranda stared at him steadily. Theo held her gaze as if measuring her resolve.

'Well, I'm tired,' he said, 'and we'll only have a few hours' sleep as it is. So we'll talk about it after breakfast—'

'No, Theo.' She tensed inside. He made it all sound so cosy and predictable, so neatly ordered to suit his will. 'I can't just forget everything that's happened.'

She saw his face change and knew that he had imagined she was over her tantrum. For in Theo's eyes that was all it was. Her manner had been calm and relaxed as they had talked to people, and that had reassured him. He seemed to think he could brush everything under the table and start again.

'I'd like to eat breakfast privately—just you and me,' she said. 'It will give us a chance to discuss where we go from here—'

'Where we go from here?' He cut across her. 'I would have thought that was obvious—back to the yacht. And as for dining alone? Like so many of your ideas, Miranda, romantic, but impracticable. We must breakfast with everyone else. It is important that I provide strong leadership. The Savakis clan must be one unified force. I can't afford to have the family splitting into factions because they think I'm ruled by my wife.'

'Don't try and simplify everything, Theo, by blithely tell-

ng me that we're going back to your yacht. You know what
'm talking about. What's happened between us is far too se-
ious to dismiss. And as for being ruled by your wife—surely
you are ruled by your loss, and by your wish to receive com-
ort from your wife?'

'So you have comfort to spare for me?' He gazed at her
cynically.

'Yes, Theo. In spite of the fact that you have treated me
shabbily, I do know what a strain this must have been for you.'

A strain? His lips curved in an ironic line. This was the
norm for him—this battle to remain at the top of a greasy pole.
As far as his feelings for Dimitri were concerned, it was too
late for him to pretend there had been any real connection between them other than blood and business. He regretted that
now. He regretted the fact that they had both let pride get in
the way of what might have been.

'I don't want to be unreasonable,' Miranda said, reclaiming his attention, 'or make things harder for you. So I suggest
we have breakfast with your relatives, attend the service and
host the wake, and then meet afterwards in private.'

'You're calling a meeting?' He wanted to smile, but wisely
suppressed the urge.

'Yes—unless you're too busy to see me?'

He ignored the sarcasm. 'That's not an unreasonable request.'

His business skills had always outstripped his people skills,
and he wondered about the strain on Miranda. She had been
involved in an accident that had stolen so much from her—
not just her career, but a family who adored her. And now
his... He should reassure her. Hell, he wanted her back.

'When we have the blessing—'

'*If*, Theo.'

He pressed on. 'I want you to tell your family everything
you've told me about the accident. I want you to tell them

about the prognosis on your hand, and the fact that we're going to try again with another doctor, and I want you to tell them about your idea for the scholarship scheme. I want you to tell them everything, Miranda, and I want you to promise me now that you will.'

Her eyes filled with tears. 'So many promises, Theo. How many of them do we keep?'

She was drawn tight like a bowstring, and the last thing he wanted now was to provoke another outburst of emotion. They were both exhausted, and if anything was to be salvaged from their relationship they needed peace above everything else.

'You're tired. It's been a long night.'

'I'll tell my family in my own time,' she said firmly.

She was more resilient than he'd ever given her credit for, but that same strength could take her away from him. He couldn't let that happen yet—for the sake of the business as well as for himself. But she meant so much to him that once the conditions of Dimitri's will were met if only leaving him would make her happy, then he would let her go.

But if she did go, then he had to be sure the rift with her family was properly healed. 'By keeping the details of the accident to yourself you have turned your face from people who love you, people who want to help and support you—'

'People like you, do you mean?'

'I was thinking of your family.'

'I have never wanted to be a burden to them.'

'A burden? Don't they love you?'

'Of course they do—'

'And yet you deny them the right to show their love for you?'

'How I handle things is up to me, Theo. At least I have experienced a warm and loving family.'

He frowned at her use of the past tense. 'Meaning what?'

'Meaning that for all your money and power, and your proud boast of a Savakis clan, at present all you head is a collection of dysfunctional money-grubbing wasters.'

He almost laughed out loud as he stood up. Did she think he didn't know that? But somehow it thrilled him to hear her say it—to know she'd got the measure of them so quickly. 'I'll see you at breakfast, Miranda. I'm sure you'll be relieved to hear that I've had my things moved to an adjoining suite of rooms for our remaining time here.'

Miranda wasn't relieved. In fact she had never felt so lonely, so cold, or so uncertain about the future. She had vowed to seize control of her life, and now it was running away with her again.

She supposed she should be grateful she had been spared the nightmare. Instead of thrashing about in the grip of some dreadful dream, she had spent the night staring at the ornate cobwebby drapes hanging in her room, wondering what wildlife they might harbour. The high bed had a lumpy mattress, and the only good thing was that dawn came quickly. She noticed the first pale strands of light while she was raining blows down on the pillows.

The early part of the day passed in a blur of duty, with the sticking plaster of formality to hold it all together. Once the funeral was over there was a mad scramble to see who could be first to leave the Savakis stronghold.

She found Theo waiting for her in the hall with his overnight bag at his side.

'What about our meeting?'

'Nothing's changed.'

'But you're ready to leave,' she said, puzzled.

'Ah, here's your case now.'

Miranda turned to see one of the servants carrying it down

the stairs. 'What? You promised me that we'd have a meeting today once everything had quietened down—'

'And so we will—but on the yacht.'

'That's not what I agreed.'

'You didn't specify a venue,' he pointed out.

'Very clever, Theo.'

'It's time to leave—unless you want to stay here?'

How stealthily he had manipulated the situation—patiently, confidently baiting the trap. Theo was a consummate predator, Miranda realised. There were no fanfares, no crass displays of strength—no wonder he was so successful in business. He moved in like a black panther, his looks and easy manner distracting from his main purpose which was always the same: to win, to defeat, to prevail.

'You know I don't want to stay here,' she said tensely.

'Then shall we go?'

'Do we have to keep the electric fences?' Miranda murmured as Theo's helicopter soared high above the compound. She was thinking aloud, weighing the grain of an idea against a whole silo full of reasons why she should leave him.

'My grandfather had many enemies. I am not so controversial a figure.'

'So are you saying they don't have to stay?'

'Why are you asking?'

'Oh, no reason. I just can't imagine what you will do with such a place. You surely don't intend to live there?'

'No, I hope to renovate my late parents' home on Kalmos. This island is more convenient for the mainland and the airport, thanks to the bridge, but I don't think anyone could make a home out of the Savakis compound, do you?'

As Theo turned to look at her Miranda knew she had to

make a decision. 'A home, no. But it would make an impressive music *conservatoire*.'

Theo's expression was hidden from her behind a sweep of black lashes, but her gaze was drawn to his mouth and to the faint smile playing around his lips.

'We'll discuss it another time,' he said, turning away from her to gaze out of the cockpit.

Their arrival back on the yacht was so smooth, so effortless, that within a few short hours they had slipped back into shipboard life as if they had never been away.

But Miranda started packing immediately. She drew the line at sharing a bed with Theo. He took everything for granted. He was so certain he had everything under his control. But she couldn't forget that he had lied to her. He had tricked her into marrying him quite simply to ensure his grip on the Savakis shipping line, and he hadn't made any attempt to explain or apologise. Instead he thought he could buy her compliance, with his promise to support her scholarship proposal.

She still wanted him. She had seen a dream and had believed it could come true. But how could she ever forgive what he had done? Theo was acting as if nothing unusual had happened between them. His clothes and possessions were still in their stateroom, a clear signal that he thought she would be happy to forgive and forget now they were safely back on his territory.

He didn't knock before coming in. Of course he didn't knock, Miranda realised tensely, turning to see Theo standing behind her.

'I thought we might take a walk on deck?'

He looked past her towards the bed, where her suitcase lay open, as he spoke, and instinctively she moved in front of it, shielding it from his gaze.

'What are you doing?'

His voice was soft, but it chilled her. 'What does it look like?' She held his gaze, determined he wouldn't change her mind.

'Don't be facetious with me, Miranda. I asked you a question. Why are you packing your suitcase?'

'Because when we dock I'm leaving you, Theo.'

'Leaving me? You can't do that.'

'I think you'll find that I can.' *And I will*, she vowed silently. She had weighed her dream against a future of compliance and found it lacking in every essential. Without freedom, without spirit, without self-determination, she would have nothing to offer her students.

Theo moved so fast he had hold of her arms before she realised he had crossed the room. 'I won't let you do this! Are you listening to me, Miranda?' he demanded when she turned her face.

'No!' With an angry jerk she broke free. 'I've finished with listening to you, Theo. I've done my duty as you asked. I stood by your side at Dimitri's funeral, and supported you in every way I can—'

'Except when it comes to breaking the contract you signed?'

'Is that all you can think about?' Feelings welled in her throat when he didn't answer. 'Unlike you, Theo, I do have some finer feelings, and though I don't want to be used by you, I don't want to cause distress to your co-workers either. I'll stay married to you for thirty days, so that you can benefit from the share transfer, but there's nothing in the contract to say I have to live with you during that time.'

'I thought we were going to discuss this first?'

'Is this your idea of a discussion?' She opened her arms wide and he took a step back.

'You called the meeting, so talk.'

'A meeting which you chose to reschedule without consulting me. Good grief, Theo! Just listen to us! Call this a marriage? You wouldn't know how to conduct a personal relationship with a puppy, let alone with a wife.' Picking up a dress she started folding it, needing something, anything, to keep her from breaking down.

'Perhaps it's not too late for me to learn…'

She didn't soften. 'The first thing you have to learn is not to use all those subtle, scheming manipulative tactics you use in business, Theo. Surprisingly, people you are trying to engage in a relationship don't take too well to being duped.'

'There's only one person I'm interested in engaging in a relationship with—'

'You lied to me, Theo. You lied and tricked me into marriage.' Miranda allowed the clothes she was folding to drop from her hands. 'And you've said nothing to reassure me since we returned. And what was it all for, Theo? More money, more power, and a hideous mausoleum?'

'You agreed to marry me. I didn't force you.' Theo took another step back, feeling an inferno rising inside him. Miranda provoked feelings that went so deep and were so fundamental it frightened him. He felt as if he was about to embark on the fight of his life. 'And I suppose you have nothing to gain from this marriage? Have you forgotten your music students so easily?

'I had hoped to gain a husband who was a man of his word!'

'Are you calling me a liar, Miranda?' His pride would take many blows, but not that one. 'And where do you think you will go when you leave me?' he pressed, when she dug her hands into the suitcase and carried on packing. 'Back home for some more humiliation? To spend the rest of your life wallowing in self-pity?'

'How dare you say that?'

Her voice was like a whiplash and her eyes were emerald ice. Her face was ashen, except for two red blotches on her cheeks, and every part of her was tense. Her lips were white and her poor damaged hand was balled into a fist by her side. But at least he had provoked a reaction. He pushed some more. 'Are you going to keep running all your life, Miranda? Or just this once are you going to find the guts to stay and fight?'

The cruel words hurt him a lot more than they hurt her— and they hurt her a lot. He waited tensely, watching her expression change from shock, to anger, and then again to the awakening of another possibility—that just this one time he might be right.

'What if I've no fight left in me?'

It was as if she was asking herself the question.

'I don't believe that for a moment.'

'You won't change my mind, Theo.' Refocusing, she gazed at him. 'I've made my decision. I'm going home to my parents.'

'So, you *are* running away?'

'No...' Slamming the case shut, she rounded on him. 'I've stopped running. I thought that would have been obvious since I'm going back, not running away.'

'Back home, where you think life will be easier?'

'I don't expect anything to be easy.'

'Well, that's something—because take it from an expert life is never easy, and if you turn your back on problems they just grow.'

'I'm only turning my back on you, Theo. Nothing else.'

'Well, that makes a change.'

She stared at him. 'What did you say?'

'Are you going to see another doctor about your hand?'

'Yes! No... Well, not right away.'

He cocked his head and viewed her sceptically. 'So nothing changes?'

'I didn't say that.'

'You didn't have to. I think you're just scared, Miranda. Scared of facing up to what the future might hold. Instead of exploring every avenue, you prefer to hide your head in the sand and pretend the accident never happened.'

'And if I stay with you all that will change?'

Her voice was strained, verging on hysteria. It frightened him. It told him that whatever she was hiding was so bad it could take her from him. 'Yes,' he said fiercely. 'If you stay with me I will make you face the truth. There have been too many secrets between us already, and if we're to make a success of this marriage we have to be completely open with each other…and honest to ourselves.'

'You *dare* to lecture me on the benefits of truth?'

'I dare to change. Do you, Miranda?'

'You talk as if I can just put all this behind me and start again. You talk about our marriage as if it had been built on sound foundations and a little more mortar is all that is needed to put it to rights—'

'Is there a sounder foundation than love?'

'Love built on lies?'

'You can't leave me. I won't let you,' he said flatly.

'I think you'll find that the law in my country allows a woman to change her mind if she discovers that her marriage was a mistake.'

'And is that what our marriage has become, Miranda— a mistake?'

'It always was a mistake, only I didn't realise it. I loved you, Theo, loved you completely. And, yes, love was blind. I walked into this with my eyes wide open, but I didn't see a thing. And now I'm walking out again.'

'Don't forget you signed a contract—'

'The terms of which, as I have already told you, I have no intention of breaking.'

'What if I refuse to let you go?' He moved menacingly, one step towards the door.

'I don't think you'd want to keep me here against my will, Theo.'

'Try me.'

As Theo stared at her, Miranda was surprised to feel her breathing quicken. The curve of his lips, the set of his jaw, the look in his eyes… She was being bombarded by so many conflicting messages, each of them guaranteed to set her heart-rate soaring. Heated emotions between a man and woman could lead to dangerous consequences. Anyone knew that. And now there was danger all around her, and she was causing most of it.

CHAPTER THIRTEEN

How could Theo do this to her? How could he make her want him so badly when all this was happening—and with nothing more than a look?

Reason had no part to play. There was a dragging sensation all the way from the pulse beating hectically in her neck to the apex of her thighs…

'Miranda?'

Swallowing hard, she muttered something indistinct.

'Shouldn't you be packing?'

There was too much innuendo in his voice. Arousal was surging through her so that when she tried to nod her head she shook it instead.

'Well, then?'

Theo's firm tone, the unyielding stance, everything that had drawn her to him in the first place…

She didn't want this—this oblivion, this chance to escape. She wanted to run as far and as fast as she could from him, to try and forget what she felt for him, as well as what she had lost. But given a choice to rail at Theo and have his cold face turned against her, or to lose herself in a world where the only reality was sensation—

'Have you decided what you want yet, Miranda?'

As Theo eased onto one hip and stared at her with his dark, lazy gaze, she knew he was utterly confident of her response. He knew he had awakened an undreamed-of hunger in her, and that now that hunger was demanding to be fed.

'Or do you need me to tell you what to do this time?'

Beneath the prim white shirt her heart was thundering. Theo had made no attempt to come any closer, but it was as if there was an invisible rope, drawing her in. She resisted it, physically holding herself back.

He moved away from the door, as if to show her that she could go if she wanted to. She exhaled a ragged sigh of relief—of regret. But then, turning swiftly, he locked the door and went to lean back against the wall.

'You know you want to,' he murmured.

One last time? She did—and so very badly. Taking her time, she walked across the room and stood in front of him.

'It might be easier if you slip off your briefs first.'

'You mean here—against the wall?' It was so cold-blooded, as though Theo was performing an exercise in self-control.

Miranda searched for some strength to resist him, but found herself staring at his lips instead, and then on into a gaze full of irony and self-assurance. She started as he traced the outline of her body with his fingertips. Was it possible anyone could deny they wanted this? And then her thoughts shattered into infinite shards of lust as he turned her and pressed her back against the wall.

'Are you going to take them off, or shall I?' he murmured, freeing the buttons on his fly.

As his fingers slipped beneath the waistband of her briefs, Miranda's gaze was drawn to the jutting erection so clearly defined beneath his casual chinos.

'Quickly,' he murmured, and he only had to brush his lips

against her neck to make her gasp. 'Good girl. Now, spread your legs and bend your knees…a little more…perfect.'

He couldn't allow her to leave him. In business when every door had been slammed in his face he'd always found a window. He never gave up. He had a dream, and Miranda had given him that dream; he wasn't about to let her take it back.

Testing her readiness, he took her firmly, without delay, driving home to the hilt. 'Is this what you want, Miranda? Is this what you need?' He heard her whimper of agreement, felt her trembling as he withdrew to thrust again. And this time he supported her, cupping her buttocks to lift her off the ground. 'Do you want more, Miranda? Yes? Then let me hear you say it…'

She gasped out her answer, and for a few moments he obliged, but then, releasing his grip carefully, making sure she didn't sink to the floor, he withdrew completely.

'Theo?' she managed at last, panting.

'So will you stay with me?'

'You—'

'Fiend?' He supplied confidently.

'You'll stop at nothing, will you?'

'That's right.' And there were more pleasurable ways of achieving his goal than she would ever know. Unless she stayed. 'So should I stop now?'

'Don't you dare.'

Dragging her into his arms, he kissed her deeply, and as she moulded against him he swept her up and carried her to the bed. Stripping off the rest of her clothes, he took off his own with her help, and then, taking her into his arms he gave her everything, bringing her beneath him and plunging deep.

Holding her firmly, he brought her maximum pleasure, maximum excitement, with every stroke driving the message home. She needed him every bit as much as he needed her.

For different reasons, maybe, but there was no escape for either of them. When the lines of destiny crossed, as theirs had done, there could be no turning back.

The abandoned suitcase was a potent symbol. It gave him a rush just to see it lying there, Theo realised as he walked back into the stateroom from the bathroom, where he had been showering. The maids would hang up her things again.

Swinging a towel around his neck, to catch the drips from his hair, he gazed at his wife's sleeping form. Miranda's limbs were spread across three-quarters of the mattress in a pose that was both innocent and provocative.

It was generally accepted that a woman's primary drive was the desire to build a nest and have a family, while a man was driven by the need to mate. But in his marriage that hypothesis had been turned on its head. The events of the past few days had crystallised his thoughts and proved to him that what he wanted more than anything in the world was not the power and wealth Miranda seemed to think he craved, but a family. Simply that… Except nothing was ever that simple. He had to win her trust again. It wasn't enough to hold her with sex; he wanted more, a lot more, from the mother of his children.

'Miranda? Miranda, wake up.' He needed to see her face, to look into her eyes, see what they might hold for him. Snatching up his robe from the chair where he had discarded it, he tugged it on, belting it firmly.

'Theo, what is it?'

She reached out to him sleepily, her eyes still closed, her voice soft and beguiling. He wanted nothing more than to go back to bed and make love to her. 'Wake up, *agape mou*. I have to talk to you.'

'Our meeting?' she breathed, stretching provocatively. 'Can't that wait, Theo?'

It was too much temptation, but he resisted. 'No, this can't wait, Miranda. I need to speak to you now.'

Hearing the change in his voice, she sat up, brushing her hair from her face. 'Theo, what is it? What's wrong?'

'I want you to get up so that we can talk. It's important. Shower, dress, and I'll call for some food. We'll eat here, on the veranda outside.'

'I'd like that.' She rubbed her eyes.

He didn't think she sounded so certain—and who could blame her? Lovemaking was uppermost in his mind too. He ached to be deep inside her again, but they could spend their whole life having sex and nothing would change.

She came back quickly, dressed in a towelling robe with her hair still wet and hanging down her back in a sleek inky curtain.

'You're dripping,' he murmured, lifting the towel from her shoulders to mop her face.

'Then dry me,' she suggested, letting the robe fall open.

'Later,' he promised, retrieving the belt and securing it.

Drawing her out onto the balcony, he sat next to her on the sofa and drew her close. Then, taking her hand, he removed the wedding band.

'What are you doing?' she said, stiffening.

'It's good between us, Miranda…in bed.'

What was he going to say next, this man who had taught her to trust again and then betrayed her? The man she loved more than life itself…the man she knew, for all her bravado, she couldn't bear to lose.

Seeing her wedding band glittering on Theo's open palm made Miranda feel as if Theo had reached into her chest, taken hold of her heart and twisted it.

He was right: it *was* good between them in bed. Theo had taken her to the extremes of sexual love and brought her back again safely in a way she had thought would never be possible. Was he saying that was all there could ever be between them? And should she want any more when she was tied to this marriage by a contract she had been tricked into signing?

'I want more than sex in my marriage.'

He sounded detached, but utterly determined. It made a shiver course down her spine. Was this the end? And, if it was, shouldn't she be relieved that his betrayal had reached its inevitable conclusion?

'I want love.' Theo spoke softly, almost as if voicing her thoughts, and then, chewing down on his lip, he slipped her a wry smile. 'You see, Miranda, sex isn't enough for me.'

Love? He wanted love?

His wry humour didn't surprise her. Theo used humour as a shield in the same way she used anger about the accident to fuel her fear of coming under anyone's influence again. But could she lay aside her insecurities? Staring at him, she found she couldn't look away. Did she need love so badly she was prepared to give their marriage another try?

'It's been a tortuous process getting this far,' he admitted, 'and I guess we could both walk away—'

'Is that what you want, Theo?'

'You have to trust me before we can move on.'

'How can I do that? You don't know how far I've come in how short a time. And that was all because of you, because I trusted you. But now…now I don't know what to think.'

'I'm sorry I hurt you. I did what I had to do—'

'Regardless of the consequences?'

'The consequence is that we are married. The question now is do we stay married?'

'You talk so sensibly, so unemotionally, Theo, I could almost believe you when you say you want more from a marriage than sex. But love? You talk of love when I don't think you have the remotest idea what it means to love someone.'

'So you would walk away on the basis that I don't express myself as well as you do?'

'I'd stay if I thought I could trust you never to betray me again.'

'Must I prove myself to you over and over again, Miranda? When will it stop? When will you be satisfied?' He looked wounded. 'I've explained my reasons, and I'm a proud man— I'm tired of playing games. You have rights in this marriage, with or without a contract, but please remember that I have rights too.'

'You forfeited your rights with your pride, Theo, and your blind acceptance of the Savakis family rulebook that allows for no mercy, no understanding, no flexibility. You have lived your life by those rules, and they have brought you great success in the world of business, but because of them you talk of love as if it can be written into a contract like anything else. Well, it can't. And I don't recognise your rulebook.'

'And you accuse *me* of pride? Listen to yourself, Miranda.'

Lifting her hands, she let them drop back to her sides. 'If only *you* would listen to me, Theo, perhaps then you'd understand that for everything that's been missing in your life I had love to plug the gap. But you took that love and, not recognising it for what it was, you squandered it. If only you'd been honest with me from the start—'

'You would have accepted my proposal?' he asked dryly. It was the first flicker of doubt he'd seen in her eyes. 'No, I didn't think so.'

Silence fell between them.

'So is fate the enemy?' he said at last.

'What do you mean?'

'Well, by your own admission we should never have met,

and we should certainly never have married, and yet here we are. I'd call that fate, wouldn't you?'

'We're here because you needed a wife and because, foolishly, I allowed myself to fall in love with you.'

'I don't think we have any control over love. I don't think we can decide not to fall in love with someone. I think we just do—as I fell in love with you. Not because it was convenient, or because I felt sorry for you, but because I couldn't help myself.'

'What are you saying?' Miranda stared at him. Theo was speaking in the considered manner he always adopted when he had something important to say, but the words and the expression in his eyes told her that this time it was different.

'I'm saying that I love you. I'm saying that I want to spend a lot longer than sixty days with you. I'm saying that I want to spend the rest of my life with you. I'm asking you if you will wear my ring.' As he spoke, he slipped down onto one knee on the ground in front of her. 'Will you be my wife, Miranda?'

'Will you be my husband?'

She asked him in a way that left him in no doubt as to what his priorities would have to be if he wanted to keep her. 'I will,' he vowed.

They never got round to eating breakfast. Miranda barely waited until the steward had left them before getting up to lock the door. The diamonds in the wedding band Theo had replaced on her finger glittered in the sunlight as she returned to the veranda, but before she could join him Theo got up from the sofa and, pausing in the entrance, held her gaze.

Taking hold of the lapels of his robe, she drew him close. Lacing her fingers into his hair, she pulled him down to her and kissed him deeply. Capturing her face in his hands, Theo deepened the kiss until she moved against him, wanting more.

'You've learned no patience,' he chastised her softly.

'You've taught me none.'

"Then I must remedy the situation…' Resting his hands on her shoulders, he traced the curve of her lower lip with his tongue.

'Theo…'

'It's no good warning me not to tease you when I'm already addicted.' The hands that had settled just above her waist slipped lower, to cup her buttocks, and, lifting her gently, he rolled her against him so she could feel the power of his erection.

'You're so unfair…'

'Are you complaining?' Slipping the robe from her shoulders, he swung her into his arms and carried her to the bed. 'And, look, we're making progress.'

'Progress?'

'We made it to the bed…'

'Theo!'

'Miranda! I'm here. I'm not going anywhere…'

Theo was at her side in a moment, cradling her in his arms like a baby as she woke from the nightmare, and Miranda held him tightly, as if the closeness they had recaptured could all disappear as quickly as her dream. 'You didn't leave me?'

'Leave you?' He stared into her eyes. 'Of course not. You were having a nightmare, that's all. Can you remember what it was about?'

She couldn't believe it had happened again—not now, with Theo lying beside her. Worse still, she had woken from the dream still calling out.

'Did I say anything you could understand?' Acting unconcerned, she forced a bright note into her voice.

He answered carefully. 'Why do you ask?'

She sighed dismissively, staring directly at him, as if she

wanted to reassure him. 'I must have been dreaming about the accident again.'

'The details will fade in time.'

She couldn't hide the flicker of doubt, of pain, and this time Theo refused to let her slip away.

'No more secrets, Miranda,' he reminded her, still holding her gaze. 'What happened that you haven't told me about?'

She blenched, started to say something, then stalled. Her voice barely made it above a whisper, but he held back from pushing her, sensing that it would achieve nothing. To his relief she drew a deep ragged breath and tried again.

'He encouraged me to call him Papa.'

'Who did? Your teacher?'

'That's right.' She met his gaze again. 'And I did call him Papa, because I grew to think of him as a second father. I trusted him…completely.'

'And what happened to break that trust?'

As she grimaced it turned her face ugly, and her pain ran through him like a knife.

'That night…while we were driving…he reached for me.'

He went still. She surprised him with her calmness, and even more with the way she was still able to hold his gaze. But he felt that if he turned away now it would destroy her.

'We were driving down a busy road,' she continued, 'when suddenly he reached out his hand, laid it on my thigh, and then started to slip it higher, beneath my skirt. I was so shocked I lashed out… It was my fault the accident happened, Theo. A man was killed because of me.'

'No,' he said fiercely. Cupping her chin, he made her look at him. 'Your teacher was the only one at fault. The accident happened because of his greed and his inappropriate feelings towards you. He wanted too much of you, Miranda. He wanted all of you. He abused the trust placed in him by the college, by your family, and by you—'

'But if that's true then why do I feel so guilty? Maybe I led him on. I don't know—'

'But *I* know.' He fixed her with his stare, willing his certainty into her, knowing he had listened to her since the day they had met but he hadn't heard a word she was saying. He hadn't seen the injuries that cut far deeper than the damage to her arm. 'You did nothing wrong.' He spoke slowly and deliberately. 'You are the victim, Miranda, not the one at fault.' He held her gaze until she relaxed. But he made no move to touch her, to reassure her, because that belief had to come from inside her, not from him.

'It taught me something, Theo.'

'What?'

'Desire doesn't equal love.'

He smiled sadly, because she spoke so seriously about a truth that anyone who hadn't fallen beneath the shadow of a sexual predator would already know. 'I know that,' he said gently.

'So if the sex between us wasn't so good, you'd still love me?' She stared at him with concern.

'But it is good…' He wasn't sure how best to console her, or what to say, but he did know that what she'd confided in him was key to her happiness, her wellbeing, and to everything that made her whole as a person.

And if he had to pull back from the physical side of their life to give her time to heal, then he would.

'Did you mean it when you said you would take me to Athens to see another specialist?'

He thought his heart would explode with happiness. 'Of course.'

'What if it doesn't work?'

'Then we'll have tried.'

'You make it sound so straightforward.'

'Because it is straightforward. You have to try, unless you want to spend the rest of your life asking yourself *What if*?'

'All right,' she said hesitantly.

'Where is your violin now, by the way?'

'It's with Alessandro and Emily in Ferara. I asked them to keep it for me…until I was ready to play it again. It's in safe-keeping,' she added, brightening, 'and that's all that matters.'

That was *not* all that mattered, Theo reflected tensely. However valuable and precious the violin might be, it was still an object that could be replaced; Miranda, his wife, his heart, his love, could never be replaced.

When the yacht slipped into its berth on Kalmos, Theo dispatched his staff to help Agalia and Spiros with the preparations for the blessing.

Since she had told him the truth about the accident Miranda felt their relationship had shifted into another gear. Theo had changed towards her. He had become focused on the operation he believed would repair her arm, and had spent hours on the telephone to Athens. When he was with her he was gentle, and considerate—as he might be with a sickly relative—which was not what she wanted from him.

Was he repulsed by her complicity in her teacher's death? He had seemed so genuine when they'd talked about it—but maybe he'd had time to think things through since then? Maybe he had come to believe that she had played some part in the sexual game? It was all such a tangle in her mind. There was too much emotion involved. Too much had happened, and so quickly…

To add fuel to her concerns, Theo had backed away from her sexually. Maybe it was because of her secret, maybe he just felt sorry for her, but either way he was keeping her at a distance. He was treating her like a patient, not a person, acting as if she might break, or as if pity—either that or disgust—had replaced passion in his mind.

She couldn't rid herself of the feeling that she was unworthy to be his wife, that she had let him down, and, to add to her sense of isolation, within minutes of approaching harbour he said he had a business appointment arranged for when they docked. She knew then that she had to get away. She needed time to think, time alone...time to get used to being alone.

It was a simple matter to slip down the bustling gangplank unnoticed. She walked swiftly, head down, towards the town, crossing the paved esplanade that skirted the beach and walking on to where she could see the small apartment block, blindingly white in the midday sun.

Theo was right. She had floated with the current long enough. There was a public telephone booth just inside the swing doors where she would settle her mind and then make a call to Ferara.

When his meeting drew to a successful conclusion Theo was buoyed up with plans and eager to make a start. The jet was already fuelled and waiting for them on the tarmac. The appointment with the specialist had been made. Having talked to the surgeon who had obtained Miranda's medical records, he was hopeful.

He had to be hopeful; he was an optimist by nature. That was the character trait upon which he had built an empire. If the operation on her arm and hand went wrong, if the doctors really couldn't help her, then that same optimism would show him how to blunt her disappointment and help her through it.

The optimism vanished when he went back on board the yacht.

'What do you mean, my wife isn't here?' Theo felt the blood drain from his face.

'No one has seen Kyria Savakis since we docked.'

Theo stared at the member of crew unlucky enough to deliver this piece of news. 'Then search again!'

'Yes, sir.'

He had given instructions that Miranda's every wish should be accommodated, so what had gone wrong?

He marched into his office and stared at the envelope on the desk. His name was written on it in Miranda's unmistakable script. Ripping it open, he scanned the page.

> *I just need a bit of time. I have to find myself, Theo, and I need help. I can't ask you to do that for me...*

How could she still doubt him? Did she think he was incapable of love? He had thought that once…but now he had to go after her. Tightening his fist around the paper, he tossed it in the bin.

Calls to Ferara from a small island in the Greek archipelago were anything but straightforward, Miranda discovered. She had only just got her head round the complex dialling system when she spotted Theo coming towards her across the sand. Replacing the receiver, she stood back in the shadows. Her stomach clenched and unclenched. She felt as if she was balanced precariously on a knife's edge and her entire hope of happiness rested on that blade. He must have called at the taverna first, and now he was homing in on the only other place on the island to which logic had told him she would return.

Pushing through the doors, she stood waiting for him.

'*Theos*, Miranda! What are you doing here?'

'I wanted to speak to Emily—'

'Emily?' He stared at her, his expression a taut mix of anger and confusion. 'You leave me a note saying you have to find yourself, and that I can't do that for you, and then you come here to call your sister? Do you think Emily can succeed where I have so obviously failed?'

'Theo, please. It isn't like that.'

'Then what is it like, Miranda? Explain to me, please. Because I don't understand.'

'You've done so much for me already—'

'Don't talk to me as if I'm a casual acquaintance whose cup of kindness is running out. I'm your husband, Miranda, and I love you. Don't shut me out. Don't turn to your twin first. Emily has her own life to lead, and we have ours—'

'Do we? *Do we*, Theo? You've hardly spoken to me since I told you the truth about the accident. And you haven't touched me since!'

'I haven't touched you because I respect you too much—'

'That sounds like a cop-out, Theo—as if you couldn't bear to touch me once you knew the truth.'

'What do you want of me, Miranda? If I give you space, you think I'm ignoring you; if I try to help you, you push me away…'

As Theo raked his hair in a familiar gesture Miranda shook her head. 'I just thought if I spoke to Emily…' Her voice sailed away.

As he held her gaze she could see the truth reflected in his eyes, and her reasons seemed so thin suddenly, like a chimera brought on by insecurities left over from another life; a chimera as insubstantial as the morning mist that burned away so swiftly in the face of the sun.

'You couldn't call your sister from the yacht? Have you any idea how worried I've been?'

'I didn't want to disturb you. You were busy…'

'So you turned to your sister, when *I* am here for you?'

Miranda stared at him and realised he was right. Why had she blanked him out? Was she so afraid of risking her heart?

'Do you know how many people I've got looking for you? Couldn't you have told someone you meant to leave the yacht? Couldn't you have spoken to me first?'

Reaching up, she stopped him, caressing his face. For a few seconds neither of them spoke, and then, capturing her hand, Theo brought it to his lips.

'I know I've been preoccupied, but I never meant to ignore you,' he said. 'And it wasn't just the accident that made me draw back. When I'm on the trail of something I don't know how to let go. Truth is, I've been trying to organise a surprise for you.'

'A surprise?'

'I know I've been clumsy…will you forgive me?' His lips tugged up ruefully, but then he frowned. 'You may not like your surprise.'

'Try me.'

'It's not very romantic.'

'Theo! What is it?'

'A visit to a consultant in Athens. I warned you it wasn't very romantic.' He waited tensely to see what she would say.

Miranda shook her head, beginning to smile. 'You've got an original take on just about everything, Theo.'

'So I'm a romantic now?' His tongue was firmly planted in his cheek.

'You're something,' she said, turning her face up for his kiss.

CHAPTER FOURTEEN

THE prognosis was better than Miranda had dared to hope. The Athens surgeon felt confident she would regain most of the flexibility she had lost in her fingers, and that her arm would straighten if she underwent the appropriate physiotherapy once her elbow was reset. She would never play the violin professionally again, but she could teach—and that was all that mattered if her plans were to come to fruition.

She was sitting across from Theo in a capacious and very comfortable leather armchair on board his jet on their return journey to Kalmos, wishing she knew what he was thinking. The hospital visit had turned him serious again. He was all purpose and practicality, setting dates for the operation and for the follow-up treatment, and now he was making notes in his diary.

'You're not turning me into a business, are you?'

His gaze flicked up and he gave her a slow smile. 'Not turning…you *are* my business.'

As another judder set everything rattling Miranda braced her feet against the floor, as if by sheer force of will she could hold the giant aircraft in the air. What she needed was a distraction, and the attendants *had* been told not to disturb them. Peering out of the window, she decided they must be at least a mile high. 'Theo…?'

'Miranda? Is there something I can do for you?'

'Maybe…'

'Only maybe?' Theo cocked his head to slant a glance at her

She decided to go for the direct approach, but the plane chose that moment to buck, and so she yelped instead, and pressed back in her seat.

'Why are you shaking?'

'You know I hate flying.'

'Then I shall have to see what I can do to change that Chess?' Theo suggested, reaching into a pocket by the seat.

'No. Theo.'

He shrugged. 'Then do you have any other ideas?'

'Do *you* have any idea how annoying you can be?'

'I have some idea.' Standing up, he held out his hand to her

Miranda shrank into her seat. 'Is it safe to be walking around while there's turbulence like this?'

'No, you're right.' He frowned, and appeared to consider her suggestion. 'You'll be much safer lying down…'

The bed in Theo's jet was firm and wide, and the journey back from Athens taught Miranda more than most people ever got the chance to learn about turbulence. It removed her anxiety about the appointment, and gave her something else to concentrate on other than the physics of flight—which remained, as always, a mystery to her.

'Do you feel better now?' Theo held her close as the jet made its final descent.

'Are you ticking off my hang-ups one by one?' Miranda demanded, and then whimpered as his searching fingers found her again.

'I'm sorry—I have to punish you for finding me out.'

'Don't apologise,' she gasped.

'Look at me, Miranda,' he ordered. 'There isn't much time We're coming in to land…just keep looking at me.'

'Are these doors soundproof?' Miranda asked, when she had calmed down enough to speak.

'Totally,' Theo promised.

'That's a relief.'

'And now we really do have to get out of bed—unless, of course, you'd like to stay here overnight?'

'Tempting as that is…'

'So what do you think about flying now?'

'I think I'm a convert.'

Theo made sure that Miranda's reunion with her family on the deck of his yacht was a very special occasion. She had never felt so alive, she realised, as she watched him talking easily to her sister's husband, Prince Alessandro.

'They have a lot in common,' Emily observed shrewdly, following her sister's gaze.

'Probably friends in common,' Miranda agreed. 'After all, they move in similar circles.'

'I was thinking more of their wives…'

'Us?' Miranda grinned into jade-green eyes that mirrored her own. 'Of course. Poor them.'

'It can't be easy for them. No wonder they feel the need to compare notes.'

'But you're happy, aren't you, Emily?'

'What do you think?' Emily traced the contours of her expanding waistline. 'I love my new country, my husband, and his adorable father. And with an heir and a spare, and now another baby on the way, I'm not the only one who's happy. There's Alessandro's father… Doesn't that smile speak volumes?'

They both smiled and waved at the distinguished older man who was presently talking to their mother.

'Family life is perfect. Alessandro is happy, I'm happy, his father's happy, and the dynasty is assured.'

'And you don't mind the dynastic element? The restrictions imposed by such a high-profile life?'

'Should I?'

'No, it's just that—'

'I'm a career woman? I have a thriving practice? I have never given up the law. It's a balancing act, Miranda; you'll get the hang of it.'

'Do you really think so?'

'I'm sure of it. What did we always say to each other? The most important thing is for a woman to retain her independence in here...' She tapped her head. 'That doesn't stop you loving someone, or having a family. And, with men like Alessandro and Theo, how could you resist doing either?'

'Only with the greatest difficulty,' Miranda agreed, beginning to laugh.

'You know, there was a time when I wondered if I would ever see you laugh again. He's good for you, Miranda.'

'You knew, didn't you? About my arm?'

'When I visited you in the hospital I could see the prognosis in your eyes before the doctors said a word to us.'

Miranda ground her jaw. 'I'm such a fool, Em. You all knew...the doctors told you. I should have known.'

'Yes...but you didn't want to talk about it, and we respected that. We wanted to give you space. Tell me we did the right thing?'

'Don't you start feeling guilty. I should have said something. I should have come straight to you—or Mum and Dad.'

'I'd say your behaviour was completely understandable. It was a terrible shock.'

'Maybe, but I shouldn't have run away to Greece—'

'But aren't you glad you did?' Emily slanted a mischievous smile at her twin as she gazed across at the two striking men,

alking together at the bow rail. 'Just as I'm glad I had to take
our place on stage the night I met Alessandro.'

The sisters barely had time to exchange a smile before
heir mother bore down on them.

'Darlings, we must move to the aft deck…'

Mrs Weston was in her element, complete with large-
rimmed hat topped off with a flurry of violet feathers.

'Calm down, Mother,' Miranda said, smiling. 'It's not like
his is the first wedding you've ever attended.'

'No, but it's my first blessing on board a billionaire's
acht.'

'Your mother's right in this instance, Miranda…'

'All right. I give in, Dad.' She wasn't going to escape,
Miranda realised happily as her father took her arm.

There was quite a crowd gathering on the aft deck. She
could see Agalia and Spiros being ushered forward to a place
of honour alongside Lexis and Alessandro's father. 'What's
going on?'

'This is my wedding present to you,' Theo said, stepping
orward.

Miranda's face broke into a smile. 'What is it? What's
happening?' she said excitedly, staring up at him as her parents relinquished their hold on her.

'Wait and see,' he said mysteriously, as a pathway cleared
or them.

And then she saw the young Chinese girl standing on an
mprovised stage in front of all their wedding guests. Wearing
a simple sky-blue dress, the slender girl was barely in her
eens. 'I don't understand—'

Putting his finger over his lips, Theo led her towards the
wo chairs at the centre of the front row. 'You will in a minute. I promise,' he whispered with a smile.

As soon as they were settled, Alessandro, Prince of Ferara,

Emily's husband, stepped forward with some ceremony. He was carrying her violin. Bowing low, he presented it to her.

'Li Chin is waiting to play her audition piece for you, Miranda.'

'Oh, Theo...'

The beautiful old instrument seemed to come alive in Miranda's hands without a string being touched. It was a powerful symbol of how far they'd both come.

'This is for you,' he said quietly.

'This is for both of us,' she corrected him. 'How can I ever tell you what this means to me, or how much I love you?'

'You can make a start the moment Li Chin has finished her recital,' Theo promised dryly.

'Have we found our first exciting talent?' he asked, the moment Li Chin had finished playing.

'Yes. Li Chin has a remarkable talent. I don't remember hearing anyone quite like her before.'

'No?' Theo demanded softly. 'I do...'

Miranda smiled, and then stood with their guests to applaud the gifted girl.

'I think this scholarship programme's going to run and run,' Theo confided above the cheers.

'For ever?' Miranda demanded, holding his gaze.

'Oh, I should imagine a lot longer than that...'